BELVEDOR AND THE DESERT OF SECRETS

THE BELVEDOR SAGA | VOL 3

BELVEDOR
AND
THE
DESERT
OF

SECRETS

ASHLEIGH BELLO

Nothing stays buried
forever under a shifting sea of sand.

Other publications by Ashleigh Bello in the Olleb-Yelfra Universe:
Belvedor and the Four Corners
Belvedor and the King's Curse
Belvedor and the Trail of Fire
Belvedor and the Golden Rule
A Myrmaid's Kiss

For more information, visit: www.ashleighbello.com

ISBN-13: 978-0-9987974-6-5
ISBN-10: 0-9987974-6-4

10 9 8 7 6 5 4 3 2 1

For Maddison and Gabriel,
Welcome to the world! It's full of wonderful, magical things.
You're the living, breathing proof.

—With lots of love, from Auntie Ashleigh

For Lisa,
Fine, you were right.
What's a fantasy series without mermaids?
You win this one, amiga! Carry on.

CONTENTS

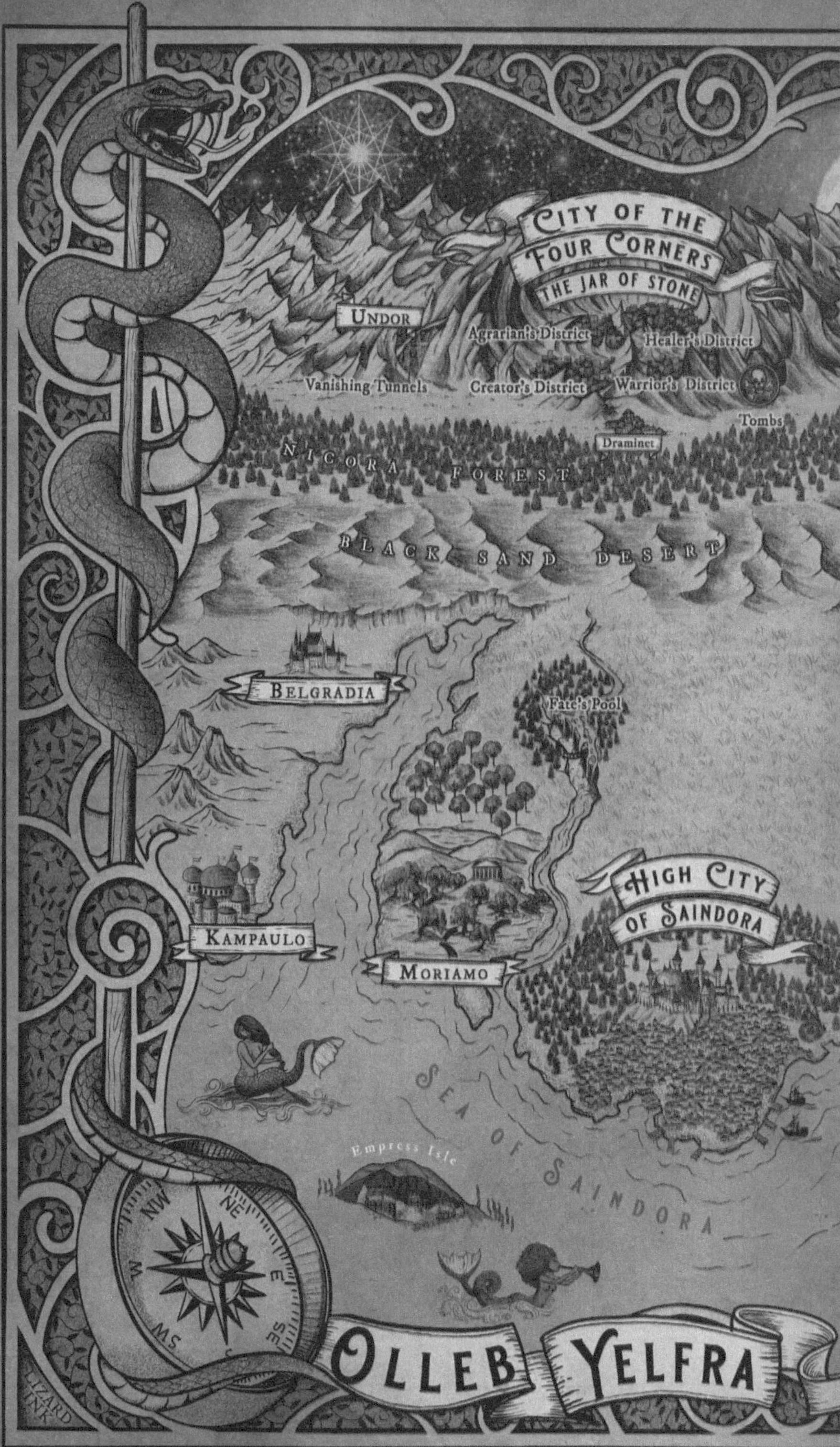

City of the Four Corners
The Jar of Stone
Undor
Agrarian's District
Healer's District
Vanishing Tunnels
Creator's District
Warrior's District
Tombs
Draminet
Nigora Forest
Black Sand Desert
Belgradia
Fate's Pool
High City of Saindora
Kampaulo
Moriamo
Sea of Saindora
Empress Isle
NW
NE
W
E
SW
SE
Olleb Yelfra
Lizard Ink

BLANCOREN MOUNTAINS
NORTH LUOSE
SOUTH LUOSE
ZAMBIENTH
The Greenhouse
LANZATARÉ
Island of Idris
IMPENETRABLE FOREST
The Treehouse
Starr Caverns
GUANAMARA

"The world outside of the Four Corners is sometimes more vicious and unforgiving than even the Jar. But at least there is something and flowers grow there."

–Liam Black, *Warrior's District*

PART ONE

I

DIE TO DREAM

IT HAD BEEN THREE DAYS trekking across the Black Sand Desert. Or maybe the count was at four? Time was lost to Arianna, but Eli had assured them they were still on track. The compass steered steady toward the south.

There were still a few hours until the sun would begin its daily descent beneath the earth, and her friends slept on, gathering their strength for another night dedicated to travel. Arianna, on the other hand, lay wide awake, waiting for the others to stir so that they could renew their journey toward the City of Zambienth; she just couldn't get used to dreaming when the sun was out, though her tired mind begged for sleep.

Even with the shade of the carriage, the blistering heat was unlike anything she'd ever experienced. And her clothes clung to her like they had a will to become one with her skin.

Solza, the snow leopard orphan turned faithful avatar companion, curled at her feet, making her warmer still. And Sano, the little white monkey who had connected to Lessa as her avatar ever since the Jar, jumped from lap to lap.

Though the carriage was spacious enough for the five travelers and two avatars, there was an uncomfortable closeness with the heat joining them and sand wedged into the most inconvenient of places. Each time the sun rose, they stopped to camp. And each time, Arianna found herself wishing for the cold desert nights to return quickly.

As the hours crept by, the welcome chills of an approaching nightfall settled in. Arianna slipped out of the carriage, afraid to wake everyone with her tossing and turning. Looking toward the darkening sky, she saw thousands of stars begin to pop up all around like small candles slowly set aflame behind a thick haze of dazzling indigo. The stars eagerly waited to show off their full light with the coming of night, and the bitter evening winds were kept at bay by the sun's final rays.

This fleeting moment of harmony, created between the shifting weights of the sun and the moon, represented the very same balance that the world needed so desperately restored. Like the short spring transition between long winters and summers, the feeling of this peaceful desert hour—neither too hot nor too cold, neither too dark nor too light—was absent from Olleb-Yelfra.

Never forget.

Arianna breathed a deep sigh as she let the expanse of the desert and sky overtake her; there was still a while yet to wait, but her friends should wake soon and the heat was starting to die down. In the meantime, she attempted to enjoy this brief period of a desert day where the natural elements didn't add to her worries.

As she busied herself with cleaning up their campsite, something moved in the distance, whizzing across the sands; it appeared as if one of the hiding stars had jumped down from the sky and come to life.

She couldn't help but become entranced as the light danced

around her with a warm, soothing hum. Its colors swished in and out of a sunny yellow to a brilliant blue and then back again. It continuously teased her, inching so close at times, only to zip away at the last moment.

Arianna stopped what she was doing, drawn to it; it grew closer and closer yet stayed *just* out of reach. But, eventually, the starlight decided not to return.

It edged farther away until almost out of view.

Arianna had to follow, compelled to know its source. Wishing to hold the warmth in the palm of her hands, to grasp the strange energy, she felt pulled in its direction. She took a step forward, unblinking—nothing else mattered.

Nothing at all.

WATER IS LAPPING AT MY TOES, calm and coaxing. But the waves are warm, too warm; I back away from the endless sea.

Small pebbles ball beneath my toes awkwardly. There's no way to find a comfortable balance here, and the heat from the sun worsens by the second. I strip off my cloak, letting it fall to the white, rocky ground, and begin to run alongside the black waters.

I was happy at first… I think. But then, as everything shifts, suddenly all I feel is fear. I'm no longer running because I want to—I'm running because I must.

If I stop, the thing I fear most will certainly catch me. And I don't know if this time I can resist.

A wind encircles me now, my hair flinging all about and whipping at my face. Working against me with every breeze, it makes it harder and harder to run. Each time I push through a gust, it bursts all around me in an explosion of dark shades, as if I'm breaking through a wall of liquid dye.

The colors of this painted wind circle me—ensnare me—but I still fight my way forward. I'm getting so tired, though, nearly willing to give in.

I look to the right, to the dark waters, and they're no longer calm. The waves have begun hurling themselves toward the shore, roaring in anticipation and delight. They seem ready for what comes next. There's no stopping it now.

I'm not sure I even care anymore to try, but I do push onward. The last burst of wind is resilient; it hits like a wall. Fighting is futile—it slams me to the ground.

I'm bleeding now. I'm always bleeding, and the blood is always red, making a scarlet image on the bleached-white land.

I look up and the wind has again changed its form. As it solidifies, I see what appears to be the figure of a man swathed in black standing before me. He's holding out his hand, as if I might be obliged to take it. But all I can see is this hand. And as I look closer, there's nothing more to indicate he's even a man at all.

The fear settles in again, numbing me from head to toe.

This man, this monster, seems to yearn for my trust and acceptance; I don't want to, but it would be so simple… to go with him willingly, to just grasp his hand and end this tireless chase. It's just easier not to fight him anymore.

Without a second thought, I extend my own hand and feel the bony, barely-there skin wrap around my palm. I stand, and he lifts his hood from his eyes. I can see him clearly now.

I want to scream, but I can't. I want to run, but I'm frozen.

First, the man's face was only a shadow, black where there should've been skin. Then it shifts, and I see the face of Solomon Bell—his beautiful smile turned wicked.

The shadow continues to morph through all the monsters of my past and present—General Ivo, Sir Dean Westing, Grinda Risso, Godfrey, Ophelia, Sir Vladamor, and even beautiful Apprentice Aridyn leer back at me. Lastly, I see King Devlindor with the stolen crown atop his head.

And here I am, grasping his hand voluntarily...

I feel as if my fingers might break.

As the face of King Devlindor sinks back into the shadows, the ultimate shift was not a man, nor a monster, nor an enemy at all; I tear my hand away and reach for my swords as I stare into a crystal-clear reflection of me.

It's always been me. And if I'm being honest, I've known that for a while.

My worst fear is what I've been holding inside—what might I become if I let this evil grip tight? No matter who I focus my anger on or hide behind like a shield, I can't fight the truth of something more lingering in the shadows of my soul. I can't fight the truth of who I truly am; I grasp the handles of my weapons and prepare to cut that darkness out.

Alas, I can hardly win such a fight in this state. Before I even raise my swords in her direction, my dark reflection shoves me in the chest with all her might.

As if defying gravity, I'm lifted from my feet with the aid of the treacherous wind and fall slowly toward the roaring, black sea. And as the water engulfs my body, clinging to me as if a thousand watery arms had emerged to hold me down, my swords swept away to the mercy of the waves, I know this is as far as I go...

The light at the surface of the water gets smaller and smaller, until there's only a blackness all around. And as I continue falling through that darkness, my eyes glued to the last, waning light, I can't shake the disturbing feeling that I've been here before. Though this time, I'm certainly not swimming in the right direction—I'm being sucked deeper down through the deafening dark.

I fear that the light will be lost to me now forever.

JUST SURVIVE

ARIANNA WOKE TO SWEAT soaking her skin, the sun beating down with such a heaviness that she had trouble adjusting her eyes to see properly. Disoriented, she pulled her hood up around her face to block the harsh rays and find focus, peering out at the sea of sand stretching around her from every angle. Endless dunes carved across the desert, shifting with each gust of warm wind.

The black grains sparkled beautifully in this light, like twinkling jewels sewn to the earth. But she found it extremely hard to appreciate the scenery now with her friends nowhere in sight…

She reached for her swords, but they weren't there. And they would've done her little good here anyhow.

Stark white bones of those long gone protruded out from the ground, swelling atop the land as if in attempt to free themselves from their hasty burials and sandy prisons.

Arianna sat upon a grave—but the skeletons of the unnamed

dead weren't her only company. Many colossal structures, possibly statues or headstones, stuck out from the sand. They took on the shape of crosses and were as white as the bones surrounding her. Stringy designs decorated each one; from the tops to the bottoms, a web of silver veins created intricate carvings across the stones.

This abandoned gravesite clearly marked the remnants of a great battle—a final resting place for the broken and battered, a maze of cracked stones and shattered bodies forgotten with time. *Probably another one of the many 'great' battles attributed to the King.*

But Arianna couldn't recall a single desert combat from her studies in the Learning Center; she could only assume that if this history had disappeared from the books, she was going to have a heck of a time finding her friends—she must be well off course to have stumbled across such findings.

Everything about this environment unsettled her, and as she took it all in, she noticed that several of the skeletons seemed unusually large. The bones were scattered about so haphazardly that Arianna could hardly piece them together to make one whole. Not that she was any expert, but she'd seen her fair share of bones and bodies. And though it was hard to trust her disconcerted mind at the moment, these were definitely much larger than anything she'd ever known.

Some kind of animal… maybe?

She ran to the top of a high dune, clambering up the loose sand. Cupping her hands around her mouth, she called out for Lessa, Jeom, and Demetrius. She even yelled for Eli and Solza, hoping that her voice might be carried across the winds. But when she finally stopped her screaming, there was only silence in return—save for the hiss and rattle of an unfriendly snake slithering through the eye socket of a giant skull at her feet.

"Okay, don't panic," she whispered to herself as she tiptoed in the opposite direction to the maroon serpent, recalling the poisonous venom from their appearance at her Free Falls. "You can figure this out."

Heading back to the spot where she had awakened, Arianna looked all over for anything to help her out of this mess—a clue or a signal for the way back. The tip of what looked to be a buried parchment poking up from the sand, stuck underneath a large rock, caught her eye. She carefully dug it out. As she unfurled the paper, she found it to be blank but well-kept, thanks to a sturdy seal she didn't recognize.

A blank scroll could always come in handy, she mused.

Perhaps a goodbye letter?

She stuffed it inside her robes with a cynical laugh that quickly turned into a shriek as several brown, long-legged spiders, the size of her head, poured out of the hole she'd plucked the parchment from.

Bounding in the opposite direction and itching all over from just the sight of such horrid creatures, she glued her eyes to the ground, fearful of what other terrors might be lurking underneath the sand.

She spotted her own footprints, and to her relief, an idea surfaced—she could follow them out, literally retrace her steps, as she had once done to locate Lessa in the districts.

Alas, her hopes were soon dashed after trailing them for just a few minutes. Any trace of her tracks disappeared with the next breeze, wiped away as if they'd never even existed.

"Are you serious?" she shouted at the top of her lungs, turning in circles with her arms flung out wide.

She had no idea where to go next, though she knew she couldn't have gotten *too* far from their campsite on foot. Taking deep breaths, she gathered her wits to think of her next plan of action.

My friends should wake any minute now. That was her only comfort as the sun began lowering in the sky.

They had to realize she was gone soon, right? Maybe they already even did, because Arianna hadn't the slightest clue how long she'd been missing. And she didn't even let her mind wander over the 'how.'

Trying to remain calm, she toyed with her options. *Either stay put and wait for someone to find me, or start walking…*

There was no way she could just sit around in a desert and hope for someone to rescue her. The chances of no one finding her were incredibly high. She looked up and identified the South Star already in the sky, fighting the sun for its turn.

It was a natural compass and could hopefully lead her back to the same path as her friends if she didn't stray from its light. She'd follow the star, as Eli had taught them over the last few days, and pray that they might meet again before her body gave out from lack of food, water, or worse.

One foot in front of the other and eyes steady on the South Star, Arianna began the longest journey of her life; this was the first journey that simply had no end in sight, and the loneliness of it was even more suffocating than that thought.

The Black Sand Desert stretched onward with an incredible uncertainty about it. She could walk for hours—or just minutes—and still seem stuck in the same place.

Arianna never felt any closer to the end, but somehow she found the energy to keep going as the maze of monuments faded into the distance and the eerie display of bones disappeared. Occasionally, she'd spot a strange-looking cactus or a withering bush, and it would give her a tiny shimmer of hope that she at least wasn't walking in circles. As each step became more difficult with time, she shoved her fears to the side and focused on only one thing.

Just survive—a mantra that never seemed to lose its luster in this world.

Her thoughts shrouded her now, and the only sound other than her breathing, her heartbeat, and the howls of the wind was the voices in her head. She hadn't spent much time alone with herself since she'd embraced and lost Aridyn, and now her mind shouted at her to listen.

Aridyn. Just the memory of that stranger made Arianna shiver under the hot sun. She'd let herself down by trying to ignore the most important parts of her soul to make room for the apprentice highlife. And she had to face that now, had to face the nightmare that was her reality.

Liam and Keeper Kassime were dead, Solomon was a monster, the other guardians had been compromised, left to clean up their mess, and now she was lost in more ways than one. The voice of her subconscious screamed rather loudly, not to be silenced.

How did I get here? Was any of it even worth it, given this mess my life has become? Would death be easier?

Every turn she'd made since the day she left the Warrior's District had led her to this very spot—alone in a desert and left for dead. If she died here, if she joined the sandy graves beneath her, what a waste that would prove to be of her second chance at life.

She couldn't blame Aridyn for everything, though. *Aridyn was never even real.*

It was Arianna who had naively thought that the highlife costume had conveniently solved all her problems. Keeper Kassime had warned them of the soul-eating side effects that inevitably came paired with long-term identity shifts, and he had been right. Her problems had never really disappeared. They were just lurking in the background behind a well-crafted and finely groomed mask all the while.

The disguise had merely been external, never eradicating what would always be on the inside.

"But it isn't my fault… it isn't," she said, unabashedly talking to herself out loud to cope with the lonely walk. "You know what the real problem is? The *real* problem is a king suppressing magic with necromancers on his side. And he's slowly killing everyone I care about just to find *me*."

Arianna's voice was lost to the wind.

"Until that's not a problem anymore, everything else always will be. He must be stopped."

Just survive and never forget.

ARIANNA DRIFTED ACROSS THE DESERT, the sun showing off the last of its embers as it disappeared behind a mound of black. It was as if a fire burned miles away, a crown of golden yellow striped across a rich, navy sky; she watched as the final sliver of sunlight hovered over the horizon in a breathtaking, vermillion display. Large birds flew overhead and steered far clear of this wasteland, as if they aimed to melt into the warmth of the sun before it vanished for good.

It was then that she understood Lessa's wish to fly and be one with that sky—such a life seemed so much safer than this derelict desert. *I wish for the very same.*

Stars began to sprinkle the evening, and Arianna kept her eyes raised as she walked in the direction of the South Star now glowing brighter against the darkening world. And she furiously ignored the cold settling all around, the warmth being sucked from the air with the rise of the moon.

How stupid of you to yearn for such a thing as the cold!

She moved slower, her legs heavy with every footfall. Aching for water, her tongue completely dry, she wished for the salvation of a drop of rain. *Anything* to quench her thirst. But the more she let herself dwell on the aches and pains of continuing forward, the harder it was to keep going. She stared up at the wispy clouds—they seemed to mock her, not a hope that they might grant her wish for the release of water.

To think, all my new experience with magic just goes to waste out here. It's not fair! What's the point of any of it?

Arianna had grown quite accustomed to calling on magic for help by now, but she'd been too afraid to face the penalties this time.

With all of Eli's instructions, she knew enough about survival in a desert—energy must be protected at all costs. And without food and water, and with no way of knowing how long she might be lost, hers was depleting by the second.

In her year of training as a guardian under Keeper Kassime, she'd learned all about the crucial lesson of magic's unpredictable drain on energy levels. Surely, even the tiniest of spells would spill every drop from her body now, and she wasn't exactly in a hurry to die if she could avoid it. Instead, she fumed inwardly at knowing magic could probably solve all her problems… if she had better control of her abilities.

A distant sound that she prayed wasn't credited to her imagination drew her attention; she froze, willing it to come again.

"Arianna! Where are you?" A voice drifted to her across the wind.

"Here," she said, answering the call. Her throat was so dry that her voice barely came out. "I'm here!"

She heard the whine of a horse and the rush of hooves on the ground. From over a hill, she saw Eli speeding across the desert on the back of Phantom. He looked like a dark spirit swathed in black cloaks as the sparkling sand kicked up behind him in a dust-like cloud.

"Whoa, now," he said, pulling back on the reins and stopping right in front of her.

In that instant, Arianna's entire body gave out; the relief of someone there at her rescue allowed her mind to feel its true exhaustion, and it came in an overwhelming wave.

Eli leaped off Phantom and caught her in his arms before her knees could touch the sand. He offered her his water canteen and she drank greedily.

"Thanks," she said after a long while, catching her breath.

"What happened to you?" he asked. "It was so careless of you to run off like that!" He refrained from screaming, but she could tell he wanted to by the way his lips tightened after each word.

But all Arianna could do in this moment was drink, so he gently brushed the hair from her face as he continued to hold the canteen steady—she had never wanted anything so badly in her life. Her focus was completely trained on the water revitalizing her body and the beautiful tattoos stretching across the arm that fed it to her.

She reflected on how hard her body had worked to survive under the pressure of thirst. It was unlike any battle with swords or forcing her legs onward when being chased. Survival had been a mind game this time, and the only thing that had kept her going was *her*—sheer self-determination not to lie down and die.

That's what she needed to master in her dreams.

A shiver rolled across her skin as the many-faced shadow of her nightmare flickered across her mind. Still, any longer without water and even pure willpower wouldn't have been enough to save her life.

"I didn't run off," she finally replied to Eli, feeling the burn of judgmental eyes as he awaited an explanation. "I just, I couldn't sleep well with the sun so hot. And then, I saw this… well, I don't know exactly. It was some sort of light. I followed it to see what it was, and—"

She pressed her hand to her pounding head, trying to think, trying to remember how she'd gotten in this mess in the first place. But of course, the answer was anything but clear.

"I really don't know what happened next… I just woke up, and I was all alone. But the sun is only setting now. I couldn't have been gone for *too* long." She looked up at him with pleading eyes. "Maybe I was sleepwalking? Sometimes my dreams can get the best of me," she mumbled, slowly sitting up.

As the water settled in her stomach, she was starting to see a bit clearer.

"Arianna," said Eli, his forehead wrinkling as he stared down at her. "You realize you've been gone for hours, right? It's the middle of the night now, nearly tomorrow. We've been looking for you everywhere since sundown *yesterday*. I almost gave up searching. I don't know how you kept up under these conditions with no cover but a cloak for more than a day. I thought you were..." He looked her over, pure surprise and relief in his expression.

"The middle of the night?" she said, shaking her head. "No, that's not possible. The sun has only just set."

Eli gave her a worried look as he pulled her to her feet. "Let's just get you back, okay? You're cold as ice. This desert isn't very kind to travelers, but at least you're safe now." He helped her steady herself, brushing the sand from her clothes. "I'm utterly shocked at how far you've managed to wander on foot, but I promised I'd find you. No one else knew how to ride or navigate confidently enough, and we needed to bring you back fast. They're all worried sick."

"How far did I..." She cleared her throat. "How long is the ride back to camp?"

"A few hours at best to retrace our path," he said.

Arianna looked around. Like being slapped awake, her eyes adjusted to the dark and to the terrifying reality of it all—it was as if she'd been dreaming all this time, in a trance from the moment she'd set eyes on that beautiful, dancing light.

There was no sun in the sky, not even a flash of fire to suggest it was just setting. Instead, a giant moon smirked down at her, a dollop of bright orange paint in the sky, and the night was as strong as ever.

She turned her eyes to the ground and had to stifle a scream as she brought a shaking hand to cover her mouth—the pile of unearthed bones and maze of monuments she thought she'd left long ago surrounded her still, and she was sitting at its center.

She shook her head in disbelief, trembling at the realization. "I don't understand."

I haven't traveled anywhere at all…

"Come on," he said. "If we hurry, we can make it back before sunrise. Hopefully your friends are still waiting for us, but I fear they'll think the worst if we take much longer. We need to get through this desert. It's starting to play tricks on us, and we have to heed its warnings." He tensed as he took in their setting, stepping around the skeletons with care. "I wonder what happened here?"

"I have no idea, but I'm ready to go!" said Arianna, rushing toward Phantom. "Who knows what ghosts still linger here."

She decided not to speak of her fantasy journey through the desert just yet, wanting to leave as fast as possible lest he fall victim to such trickery too.

Eli chuckled. "There's no such thing as ghosts," he said, matter-of-factly, jumping back up onto Phantom.

Arianna flashed him a shaky smile and took his hand as he helped her get seated behind him.

"Thank you, Eli," she said. "I would've died if you hadn't—"

"Really, there's no need. That's the duty of a desert guide," he said, turning to face her. "Besides, I owed you one."

For a moment, Arianna saw that alluring smile return to his face, a flicker of the man he used to be. Then, with a flick of the reins, that man disappeared again.

But it was good to know he was still in there… somewhere.

"Let's go!" he called out.

Phantom happily obliged and sped off, racing to leave the forgotten boneyard behind.

ATONEMENT

GALLOPING OFF INTO THE NIGHT, Arianna felt as if they ran forever in place, trying to catch up with the stars. And here she was, chasing after the stars with none other than Elijah Neve, a man she thought to be long departed from this world up until just a couple of weeks ago.

Her mind whirled across their violently short history and the shocking surprises life had thrown their way. She was bouncing across the desert with another returned from the dead, on the back of the lucky horse who had inadvertently brought them together.

Alas, before she and Eli could even make it clear of the vast region covered with the broken statues and skeletons, Arianna looked up to see another obstacle headed straight for them.

"What's that over there?" she called, pointing ahead. "Is this the deceitful *mirage* you warned us of before?"

The sky seemed to wave in and out, the stars shimmering

along with it. But Arianna didn't yet trust her mind to see the truth of things.

"That's no mirage," said Eli, pulling back on the reins so fast that Phantom kicked his front legs into the air; Arianna screeched, clinging to his waist to keep from falling. "We need to take cover fast!"

He steered Phantom around in the other direction, leading them back into the midst of the graveyard at full speed.

"What do you mean? You're going the wrong way!" said Arianna, her cheek pressed against his back as she hung on for dear life.

"Faster, Phantom!" The horse kicked up sand behind them, slowing only at Eli's command after a short, jolting ride. "That's a sandstorm, and it's rolling in quick. We have only minutes to find cover if we're going to survive."

"A sandstorm? *Survive?*" said Arianna, looking again toward the rolling clouds. Only now she saw this phenomenon with a much clearer understanding.

It was not the sky that bowled toward them in waves—it was the desert. The black sand came thick as a thunderous cloud with its own glittering dust rivaling the stars, guided by fierce gusts of freezing wind and lightning carving its ruthless path toward them.

Arianna's heart dropped to her stomach. "Even the elements are against us," she breathed. She shouted toward the wind, not caring what Eli thought. "What more can we prove?"

Her sense of shame or embarrassment had been pounded away with each false step she'd taken trying to escape this very spot—the desert graveyard still had a hold on her.

"There isn't time," said Eli, grasping for her hand to drag her off the horse.

"It seems as if the earth wants me rooted to this place forever, buried beneath the sand to lie with the bones at our feet," she said, planting her boots on the ground. "Well, if the gods wish it so!" She shook her fist at the sky.

"Do *not* taunt those who control our fates," shouted Eli, whipping around to face her and taking her strongly by the shoulders. "Now is hardly the time to make such a statement."

His fierceness took her aback, the fear in his eyes more apparent than ever. And it must have echoed in her own because he softened.

"We'll be all right, but please keep your faith," he said. "I know you hold an abundance to have made it this far from your chains. I need you to be strong for the both of us right now, because I'm still very weak. And... I fear, more than *anything*, to go back to the darkness again."

Arianna pressed her lips together and nodded, watching him attempt to prepare for whatever new troubles a sandstorm might bring their way; his words resonated with her, his candor with his feelings shocking her back to sanity as the roaring sand inched closer, the wind picking up faster.

Eli instructed her to sit at the base of two giant crosses that had collapsed into each other, creating a tent of solid white stone. She pulled her hood up over her head and sat inside, watching as he guided Phantom to safety as well; he coaxed him to lie down on the ground in front of her.

"What are you doing?" she called as he removed his cloak and covered Phantom's head. "You'll freeze to death without your robes! The temperature gets colder by the second."

She wrapped her arms around herself, trying to lock in the warmth.

"I'll be fine," he said, already shivering. "He won't stay calm otherwise. And if he runs off and dies, we won't need to worry about a sandstorm killing us. The desert will surely win if all we have is our feet to carry us back to your friends. It's almost on top of us now. Get ready."

He sat down next to her, and they waited in silence for only moments before the storm had them fully surrounded.

The sand swirled around their hiding spot, as if trying to sniff out their whereabouts, but this stone shelter made the perfect cover from its search for blood. Unfortunately, though, there was nothing to protect them from the biting cold that came paired with such fierce night winds.

Arianna couldn't see anything but curtains of sparkling sand on all sides, as if they were sitting in the center of a black tornado ornamented in crystals and endowed with the breath of a blizzard. She could feel Eli trembling next to her and thought he might turn into a statue of ice and break into pieces if it got any colder; he tried to act strong, but she knew he suffered greatly. Even with her heavy cloaks and hood pulled tight over her head, she wasn't sure she would survive herself until the storm was over.

"Here," she said, scooting closer to him so that he could share her robes. "It'd be foolish of us to suffer this alone."

"Thank you," he said through chattering teeth. As their arms touched beneath her cloak, she instantly felt the heat from her skin warm his own. "That's so much better."

He let out a deep breath and Arianna saw a frozen cloud come with it.

"How long do you think it will last?" she asked. "If the storm doesn't kill us, this cold surely will."

"There's no way to be sure until it's over," he said. "We can only wait."

"Do you think the others will be okay?"

Her voice quivered.

"I'm sure of it. They have the shelter of the carriage to protect them," he said. "And Demetrius will know how to care well for the other horses. They'll be fine to go on, if…"

She didn't need him to finish his sentence to know the bitter end of it. *If we don't return.*

"Good," she said, sucking in a deep breath.

She couldn't help herself as a heaviness overcame her. Her

head lolled to the side to rest on Eli's shoulder, so weak and exhausted from enduring all these unexpected battles. In a way, she almost welcomed this isolation from the world with another who had been so brutally beaten down by it. In this moment, the idea of a future, of life, was out of their hands entirely—and Arianna couldn't help but feel a sort of liberation by being released from the burden of survival.

This time, it really wasn't up to her.

Would the storm stop before they starved? *Froze* to death? Would the broken, brittle stones of their shelter withstand these tortuous winds?

Destiny would decide the next direction, and for once, Arianna saw no way to sway her verdict.

After a while, she felt Eli relax too. His arm draped around her until they were so close together that she couldn't quite feel the cold anymore, and he no longer shivered. Even if it was just a numbness settling in, at least it offered some comfort. There was a mutual goal shared between them tonight, and that goal was to live.

"Arianna," said Eli, rousing her from her thoughts. "You shouldn't sleep. You might not wake again."

Was I sleeping?

He squeezed her closer to him, rubbing at her skin until her blood warmed back up a little. She mumbled her thanks and sat up straighter to try to wake her dozing mind, not knowing how much time had passed as the vortex of sand engulfed them stronger still.

She lifted her head off his shoulder, turning to look at him for the first time in a while. His piercing green eyes were so absorbing in such proximity, and she couldn't help as her own traced the mesmerizing tattoos slinking across his skin to hide beneath his shirt.

As she did, something of contemplation, of struggle crossed Eli's face. The next thing she knew, his lips were pressed against hers with such a fierceness she thought they may never part, his hands holding her head in place.

Jolted awake from her stupor as the storm raged on, like a bewitching symphony to emphasize this stolen moment, Arianna lingered there in the warmth and unexpected pleasure of it all—then she pulled away.

"I'm so sorry," he stuttered, dropping his hands from her face. He bowed his head. "I shouldn't have done that without your permission. But all this time..." He found the courage to look her in the eyes. "All this time, I thought *you* were dead too. I couldn't miss my chance again, should death come for us for real this time."

Arianna froze, realizing that they must have shared the same sentiments over their abrupt separation, each of them assuming the other dead and gone from this world without even a chance for a goodbye. But Eli had rotted in the dungeons with only his thoughts for comfort—how much of that time had Arianna's fate been the center of his wandering mind? She had never once considered that he'd had much more time to spend lamenting over her death than she'd ever spent on him.

But a kiss?

She wouldn't have thought Eli capable of such compassionate feelings with all he'd been through. Not to mention that they really hadn't known each other for very long beforehand. Certainly not long enough to warrant such feelings.

She shook her head, looking away—she wasn't sure she could reciprocate... not now.

Everyone she let herself care for ended up either in danger or dead. And any feelings she might've spared for him, or any man for that matter, were certainly buried underneath a deep layer of constant pain, suffering, and, ultimately, distrust.

Such terrible timing.

As she considered Eli now, withstanding a sandstorm by her side, she couldn't help but note that each time she laid eyes on him marked the beginnings of drastic change in her life—in the forest with Solza before waking up in South Luose, in the tavern before meeting Keeper Kassime, in the palace dungeons on the day she learned of Solomon's betrayal… on the day of Liam's death. And now *this*.

There was no ignoring the fact that they kept falling into each other's paths at the most paramount of moments, both good and bad.

Some might say that Fate keeps bringing us together.

Arianna remained quiet, no words seeming right to say with her mind so foggy; Eli appeared to grow more ashamed of himself with the enduring silence, the cold settling back in around them both.

Then her thoughts took a different, lighter turn, the warmth from his kiss still lingering on her lips.

For the first time in weeks, something had made her feel good, a twinge of light escaping the darkness trapped inside her. She couldn't explain this sudden shift of mindset—maybe the storm forcing them together, the enchanting vortex encasing them, the powerful hum of the wind, or the sand ceaselessly singing in her ears—but she didn't quite care…

She didn't care if this was *real*, or right, or lasting. She didn't care if they were both damaged beyond repair or if her heart had been broken too many times to mend. All she knew for certain was that a kiss was a sign of hope, love, and of true feeling. Eli had let her feel something good again, and she didn't want to let it go.

She *needed* to feel right now, before the numbness took her over completely.

She needed to feel anything but the certainty of a cold, dark death knocking at her door over and over—and just the thought of his kiss warmed her heart even more.

"Won't you say something?" urged Eli, his face etched with worry.

She touched his cheek as all these thoughts flooded her mind at once.

"I fear the darkness too," she finally said in a whisper. "At least, this night, we don't have to face it alone."

Arianna pulled him toward her and kissed him back with all the energy left to her—this time, the moment seemed to last much longer, thawing her from the inside out. He wrapped his arm gently around her neck to bring her closer, and she felt as if she might melt into him.

For once, it didn't matter what the future held, just the here and now. In each other's eyes, they had both risen from the dead, so tonight, they would turn their backs again on darkness together.

NOT LONG AFTER THEIR LIPS finally parted, the sand seemed to settle as well. The winds subsided and the air cleared once again.

"We're still quite alive," said Arianna, her head lying across his chest.

"I'd say that's an understatement," said Eli, his arms still wrapped tightly around her. She could feel his heart thumping within his chest, so full of joy like her own.

"I think we better be going now before we're assumed dead," she said, finally separating herself from him. She got to her feet. "Looks as if everything's back to normal."

With the end of the storm, the desert landscape had entirely changed, but they still had to cross it. The time for such vulnerability was over.

"I wouldn't be that bold," he said, a sort of daze in his expression as he watched her shake the sand from her clothes.

She offered a soft smile in return, holding out her hand for him to take. "That was… quite nice, but please, let's not speak of this when we're back at camp, all right? My friends have enough to worry about without them thinking my priorities have shifted—" her eyes narrowed "—which I assure you, they haven't."

Eli chuckled, jumping to his feet and leaning in close to her so that she could feel the warmth of his breath on her skin once more. "My lips are sealed," he whispered with a wink. "For now."

Arianna couldn't help the laughter that escaped her—they shared in it together, for a moment, before readying to leave.

She felt so rejuvenated, motivated by the sheer fact that she had come out of another challenge stronger than she'd entered it. And she was overjoyed that Eli seemed to have regained some missing piece of himself. It was becoming easier now for her to see again that cheeky man who had once wooed them all.

Eli helped Phantom to stand, hopped on, and then pulled her up to join him in the saddle.

After a short time riding across the desert, Arianna realized there was still so much she wanted to know about Eli, especially after giving him her first kiss. She took this opportunity to bring up a burning question she had long wished to ask, one she had given up on the minute she thought she'd watched his life taken by the whip of a city regulator.

"Eli, can I ask you something?" He met her with silence, only the sound of hooves on sand and the panting horse to be heard. "When you tried to warn us about the ambush in Mya's tavern, you called out my name… *Arianna,* you said."

With her body pinned against his and her hands wrapped around his waist, she didn't miss it as all his muscles tensed.

"That's not a question," he replied.

She took a deep breath, trying to recall her memories of those final moments before their abrupt parting.

"I know it was you in the Nicora Forest," she said. "It was you who saved me from Solza's mother, wasn't it?"

She paused for his reaction.

When he didn't say anything still, all her nerves ignited, just as they'd done when he'd yelled out for her to run from the regulators—she was about to finally receive answers to the questions lingering in the back of her mind, but now she wondered if knowing the truth would prove a good thing. Especially after they'd shared such an intimate moment together.

"Why did you lie back in South Luose if you knew who I was all along?" she pushed, not letting herself stall any longer. "You knew I was the 'wanted' slave, and you could've turned me in. Why didn't you? What aren't you telling me?"

She squeezed her arms tighter around his waist, her face pressed against his back, afraid of the answers.

It was too long a moment before he spoke, his focus staying straight ahead.

"I was in the Village of Draminet when you fled the districts," he said with a heaviness, slowing Phantom to a trot. "I had taken a job as an escort for a trainer in South Luose who was traveling to the Four Corners for a new placement, and so I stayed in Draminet a few nights before the journey home. Just in time to witness our newest citizens to the Olleb."

The dark of the night seemed to grow thicker with his words, the stars glaring endlessly on ahead of them.

"I noticed you there with your friends, seeming so out of place, ahead of schedule and without any guide. That village is so small… I'd be having a drink at the tavern or walking back to my room and just catch snippets of your conversation, without even meaning to. So when the district regulators arrived with news of escapees from the Jar, I knew it must be you all on the run." He took a deep breath. "Arianna, you must remember that I'm a warrior, too. I won my freedom during the 282nd Free Falls. We were peers once, though you were probably a bit too young to recall."

Arianna felt as if the wind had been knocked out of her.

I'm a warrior, too.

Of course he would have known her face. By her calculations, she had already been a thirteenth year by the time he had earned his citizenship, which made it very likely they had crossed paths in the district.

Could he have even trained with me once?

What did he remember of her? What moments had they shared in that cold chapter of her life in the Jar?

"How didn't I think of this before?" she mumbled to herself, her mind spinning as she tried to recall a sliver of him from before South Luose.

But she had only been a young girl, with goals of freedom absorbing her focus. As she dug now through her past, it seemed her vulnerable mind wished to falsely implant his face in her every memory—in the Dining Hall, in the Square, in the Dueling Arena—passing her on the way to her quarters or leading a group training of her and her peers. Suddenly, Eli's face was everywhere, distorting the truth.

She shook her head, trying to think straight as he continued with his explanation.

"When you left the tavern in such a hurry, I felt it in my gut that it was you," he said. "Those drunken fools in Draminet wouldn't have noticed if you danced in front of them holding up your own 'Wanted' poster, but I knew who you were right away. I remembered your face."

Arianna tried to picture her last night in the village, to see a face that resembled Eli in her mind, but she couldn't recall ever laying eyes on him before South Luose. "But if you knew who I was, then—"

Eli cracked the whip and startled her out of talking as Phantom again picked up the pace.

"I tracked you to the forest, Arianna," he said, curtly. "I *was* tracking you. Your friends had started a campfire, so the smoke led me straight to the clearing. I waited there for you to return, to try and catch you alone, but Phantom got spooked and ran off.

I had to go after him. To my fortune, he led me straight to you. Got yourself in a whole mess of trouble, though, by the time I'd caught up."

"So you *weren't* trying to save me?" she said, her heart drumming faster, fueled by a storm of emotions she couldn't even make sense of right now.

He shook his head.

"No," he whispered. "I was trying to capture you… for the King." His voice cracked on the last word. "For the highlife reward. That meant first killing the beast if I were to bring you in alive. You see, I didn't want your blood on my hands."

He cleared his throat.

"But your friends came soon after, and I knew I'd be out-numbered then. So I went back home to the city and decided to let you go, to forget it ever even happened. You were in such a state when I left you, at the time, I didn't even think you would make it out of the forest alive."

"Let me get this straight… you're telling me that when I was fighting for my life, you gave yourself the options of leave me for dead or turn me in for the highlife reward? Is that right?" She could hardly wrap her head around this nasty picture Eli painted of the person he truly was.

She had always speculated about that man in the forest swathed in regulator cloaks—had he been hunting or rescuing her? And when she put the pieces of the puzzle together that had revealed that man as Eli, it was an even harder question to ponder. Yet, she had kept hope that someone who seemed to be so good and kind wouldn't have voluntarily tried to cause her, or anyone, harm. She hoped that he had acted as honorably in her moment of need in the forest as he had been on the day he'd tried to warn her to run.

Now the mystery had finally been solved in this heady moment with the desert stars as sure witnesses—Elijah Neve was *not* a true friend. There were only a few she could trust in this world, and despite what they'd shared on this night, he wasn't one of them.

"Please, know that I'm utterly remorseful for my actions on that night," he said. "I thought you might ask me sooner or later, but I had hoped that—"

"That *what?*" she snapped. "Hoped that I wouldn't have asked at all? I understand your disappointment perfectly, because I had hoped, for a very long time, that my gut instincts were wrong about you. But I've come to realize that they hardly ever are."

"Arianna, I'm sorry! I don't know what more to say," he said, clearly searching for the right words to mend the situation—there weren't any that could. "That's the truth of it. I wish I had been a better man."

She leaned away from him as her disbelief grew even more.

"You think the King would've let me live had you been successful?" She barked in mock laughter. "I hate to break it to you, Eli, but that's just the same as blood on your hands. How spineless of you! You, who pretends to be so strong."

She felt her defenses rise back up instantly, thinking of all the ways she could win the battle against him if it came down to a fight. All this time, she'd thought him a friend. And not an hour earlier he was much more than that. For a year, she had mourned someone not worth the trouble, and now she had even given that coward an intimate piece of her—a thought that now made her blood boil.

"And how do I know you weren't even part of the setup with Godfrey and Mya?" she said, fully releasing her grip around his waist now. She wobbled dangerously on the horse with no support.

With one hand still holding the reins, Eli reached back for her hand, forcing her closer to him again; she could feel every muscle on his body. He held on tight, not willing to let her go.

"Don't you dare with that accusation," he said, firmly. "I

knew who you were from the minute you walked through the tavern door. If I had wanted to turn you in still, I could've done so easily. Godfrey only guessed as much and used his control over Mya to plot against you. I was *drugged*, just like you, passed out on the bar table and woke to regulators storming the place."

He whipped the reins again, still securing her with one strong arm.

"Mya was the coward, not me," he said. "Godfrey was using her, and she let him out of fear. I killed her for her betrayal that morning, for *you*. And I would've gone to kill Godfrey too had the regulators not gotten to me first."

He shook his head.

"I don't know what it is about you, but I've been under your spell since the moment you walked into the tavern."

Arianna scoffed. "You know nothing of spells," she said under her breath.

She felt the piercing guilt left by Mya's death diminish greatly—and if she'd understood her part in their capture at the time, truly understood, she thought she probably would've killed her herself if given the chance.

But without the emotions from that day taking the lead, Arianna somehow found empathy for the sweet girl who was struggling to run her partner's business under the weight of constant coercion by Godfrey. Doing anything other than the option least likely to get her killed or jailed would've been extremely brave for any citizen of Olleb-Yelfra. And bravery was an exceptional trait to have in such a world.

Mya hadn't been exceptional nor brave enough to stand up for the morally right thing at the risk of her own life, but that didn't make her a coward—it just made her human in a ruthless place. This was a 'kill or be killed' world, and if everyone acted brave for the sake of morals, the Four Corners wouldn't even exist at all.

Braveness was a rarity in Olleb-Yelfra, and the 'exceptional' minority were continuously purged by the Crown.

Never forget.

"I just didn't want to be that kind of person anymore, scavenging," said Eli after a while.

He began to ramble as Arianna was still trying to work through her thoughts.

"And for the King's own benefit, no less! I could've let that animal kill you and dragged your body back to Saindora to claim the reward, but I didn't. And I'm forever glad for that." He shrugged. "Then I got to know you a little bit, and I envied your strength and your courage. I realized that you were the lucky ones, and anyone who escapes the Four Corners deserves honor, not a life on the run. If it wasn't for that Godfrey—"

"Godfrey is dead," she said, refusing to acknowledge his excuses. "He won't be anyone's problem ever again."

Eli turned his head to try to meet her eyes, and she wanted him to see the fire that burned there.

"Can you forgive me for that weakness, Arianna?" he pleaded, shrinking under her gaze. "Can you trust my change of heart? I've bared it to you fully this night. You can't deny that truth either."

One hand still grasped hers, holding on firmly as if he were willing her to forgive him; Arianna thought hard for the answer. No one had ever asked for her forgiveness before…

Eli had hunted her, purposefully pursued her and her friends with the intention of handing them over to the King.

But then, he let us go.

She thought back to the boy in the tavern she'd first laid eyes upon, singing that chilling melody to his guitar. He *had* recognized her when they'd locked eyes, faltered with his chords, but then he'd just played on. *He let us go.*

She couldn't help it as the anger evaporated from her body, remembering the horrible price he'd already paid for his actions to try to help them.

"I can forgive you," she finally said, having no room left on her list of enemies or problems. "I know that you've suffered enough, and I don't want to add to it. We've all had our share of mistakes and punishments, and what's done is done. But now that I know, I'll never forget."

"Thank you," he said, breathing a sigh of relief.

"I won't speak of this to my friends," she said, her tone sharp, "but I might never trust you now. And if you betray us in any way again, you'll meet the same fate as Godfrey. That is the only warning you get. I won't risk my friends, my *family*, any more than I already have, no matter what has passed between us."

She felt the warmth of his grasp vanish as he dropped his hand from hers. But she still held on to him, replaying their first encounter over and over in her mind, knowing it wasn't the same one he remembered as their 'first.'

"Then I'm forever in your debt," he said in a whisper. "It's you who saved *me* this time."

"After today, that just makes us even," she replied.

Her voice came a bit softer now as she wanted to put the past back where it belonged.

"Eli, there's something else that's been gnawing on my mind, another question."

"Go on," he said, wary.

"Well, I just wondered… what *was* it like in the dungeons?" She knew it'd be a touchy subject, but it was nothing short of a miracle that he had survived such trauma, and she wanted to know if there was any secret behind it. "I saw you at the Altar. They whipped you over twenty times. How could you have survived something like that?"

Eli took a deep breath, turning his attention back to the desert.

"I didn't," he said.

Arianna said nothing more—it wasn't a stretch for her to understand such haunting words. She felt herself slipping away with every tough decision, every betrayal, and every loss. She was surviving by a thread, and with one more cut to it, she thought she might be lost to herself forever.

But that wasn't going to be today. Not yet.

Just survive.

She kept her hands clasped around his waist, the wind making her feel more alive than ever as Phantom sped on toward the rising sun. She turned back for one last look at the mysterious desert graveyard. As it grew smaller and smaller in the distance, she swore she saw again a colorful starlight, dancing across the scattered bones—or maybe even eyes. And if she listened closely, voices whispered for her to return.

4

TRUST FALLS

"YOU COULD'VE DIED!" screamed Lessa, racing toward them from their camp, livid to the point of tears. Arianna got down from the horse as Lessa shouted at her to explain, Jeom and Demetrius exiting the carriage too.

It pained her that she'd caused her friend such distress after all they'd already suffered—Arianna had never heard Lessa lose herself like this before. She seemed broken now, a ghost of the girl she'd discovered in the Vanishing Tunnels.

"This isn't a joke. This is our *lives*," she said. "We don't have any more time for this! What's wrong with you?"

"Don't be so harsh," said Eli, coming to stand between them. "It's this land. I tried to warn you all. Many men have disappeared here, vanished from their camps to the lure of the desert's song."

Lessa shoved him out of the way with a warrior's skill, and he fell to the ground.

He looked after her in disbelief as Demetrius helped him up.

Then Eli took a step forward, ready to restrain her, but Jeom's expression made him pause; he was, clearly, just as upset as Lessa.

Jeom towered over Eli as they stood face-to-face, both unblinking, staying the other's challenge. Arianna couldn't help but wonder who might win in that fight—the warrior turned regulator or the creator turned guardian?

"I know that I worried you," she said, inching back as Lessa came toward her, fists balled at her sides. "It wasn't my intention, I swear."

She thought Lessa might lunge for her throat any second, and it reminded her of a hotheaded, emotion-driven, younger version of herself. They were alike in so many ways, yet it was their differences that kept them close. And one of their biggest differences of all was temperament.

Lessa had always been the calm, rational one, considering all the options before agreeing to one of their many chancy decisions; and Arianna would run straight into battle without thinking it over twice.

Their friendship had brought a much-needed balance to each other's lives. Though, on this day, Lessa had finally let herself lose a little bit of that control.

"There were these colorful lights, calling to me from somewhere out there," said Arianna, trying to explain. "I know it sounds crazy, but, one minute, I'm standing right here, preparing for our trip… and the next, I'm waking up alone in the middle of some desert graveyard. And I had another dre—"

"If you say 'dream' *one* more time!" hissed Lessa, pulling at her hair. Long, blond locks pooled in her hands as she restrained herself from acting on her rage.

"Please, just listen to me," said Arianna, holding up her hands. "I didn't do this on purpose."

She leaned in to whisper to her so that Eli couldn't hear.

"I believe there was something more at play. I think it was

some sort of magic… or ghosts, maybe?" She shot a cautious glance at Eli. "I don't know, but he's right. Something's happening in this desert, and it isn't natural. But I *am* sorry, okay? I didn't mean for any of this to happen."

Lessa shook her head over and over, as if to shake Arianna's words away.

"Yes, you're sorry," she breathed through her teeth. "You're *always* sorry, but did you ever stop to think what might've happened if Eli hadn't found you in time? If I hadn't pulled you from that bath before you drowned? If Master Tayshin hadn't dragged you from the burning palace?" She threw her hands up. "Or any of the other *countless* situations where you've put your life at risk… do you ever stop to think, *hmm*?"

Arianna just stared at her, mouth running dry with shame and guilt.

"You'd be dead! That's what would happen," said Lessa. "You're not immortal, Ara. None of us are, and yet you keep chasing after your death as if it might not find you in time." She pointed an accusatory finger. "And do you know what would happen to *us* if you died? Do you even care at all?"

She pressed her lips into a thin line and shook her head. Then she spun on her heels to walk away.

Arianna caught her by the wrist. "Les, please—"

"No, don't! Just leave me alone," she said, pushing her off.

Arianna lost her balance and tumbled to the sand. Demetrius and Eli both rushed to stop the impending fight, but Jeom blocked their way again, clearly taking sides.

Lessa stared down at her, holding back tears.

"We need you to live so that we can live," she said through quivering lips. "We're supposed to be a *family*, and one you started, no less! If you can't see this through to the end, how can you expect any of the rest of us to survive? We will only get through this together. Don't you get that?"

"I do now… yes," stuttered Arianna, searching for the right

words. "I won't leave you again. I promise."

"Calm down, everyone," said Demetrius, ducking out of Jeom's hold. He ran to help Arianna up, and she took his hand, brushing the sand from her clothes. "We're all just tired and famished. Let's not waste our energy on this anger. Of course she didn't get lost on purpose. I'm sure there's some sort of logical explan—"

Lessa let out a howl of frustration, shoving past him. "I just can't take this anymore," she said, stomping away to the confines of the carriage.

Arianna could hardly fathom how damaged their lives had become, when it seemed only yesterday their days had been lined in gold and silk.

Even Lessa—the forgiving, kind-hearted, faithful-to-a-fault Lessa—had lost herself to whatever inner demons haunted her now.

"She's spot on, you know," said Jeom to Arianna, shoulders slumped. "Haven't we been through this enough?"

He didn't even wait for her to respond, joining Lessa in the carriage and slamming the door behind him.

"Don't worry about them," said Demetrius, leading her and Eli back to the campsite. "They're just exhausted. We all are." He prepared them each a skimpy plate of food from their earlier spread. "But it's *such* a relief you made it back in one piece, Ara, really. You too, Eli. You both had us quite frightened there for a moment. I can't imagine what we would've done if you hadn't returned."

"Thank you," said Arianna, graciously taking the food—only now did she notice her absolute hunger. "I wasn't sure if I would find…" She cleared her throat. "Thanks, Demetrius."

He gave her a knowing smile. Then he sat down on a broken, dried-out tree trunk and buried his head in his hands while she and Eli scarfed down their rations.

Arianna saw the campsite in ruins from the storm, many of

their belongings scattered haphazardly and covered in sand.

"Solza? Sano?" she said with a jolt of worry, the food helping to mend her foggy mind.

"They're both fine," said Demetrius, his voice muffled by his hands. "Still sleeping, I think, in the carriage."

Arianna let out a sigh of relief.

"We've lost another full night now," said Eli, following her gaze. He set his plate aside to tend to Phantom after the long ride. "And the desert is already having a go at us."

"What do you suppose we do?" said Demetrius, eyes cast down, long hair falling over his face—even he seemed to be losing his luster.

"I think we should get moving as soon as possible. Walk through the rest of the day," said Eli.

He used his hand to shield his eyes from the sun as he peered out across the sand.

"We're almost there. We might be able to make it by nightfall if we hurry, and we have enough water left to drink a little more greedily if it's just one more stretch. Should keep us going through the day. We'll just have to be sure to stay covered from the sun's rays as much as possible."

"Are we that close?" said Arianna, hearing the hopefulness in her voice.

Eli nodded. "I think so."

"Then we have to try," she said. "I think we've overstayed our welcome here, and I don't want to leave anything else up to chance."

She dreaded even another hour of sleep for fear she might wander off for good this time.

"Agreed," said Demetrius, starting to comb the area for their scattered belongings. "Let's get the heck out of here."

"I'll get the horses ready," said Eli. "They need to be watered first." He glanced to Arianna. "And you and I both need to get some rest."

She nodded her agreement but averted her eyes quickly. He walked to the front of the carriage to tend to the other horses, and Arianna lay back on the log to rest for a moment.

A LITTLE WHILE LATER, Lessa burst from the carriage with Jeom at her heels and Sano wrapped around her shoulders. Her eyes were rimmed red, but they both looked eager to share something—whatever it was trumped their anger at Arianna because Lessa could hardly hold in her excitement.

"I think I know what happened to you," she said, though there was a bite to her tone. "It wasn't ghosts at all. You were right. I think it could've been magic. Fairies, if you'll believe!"

"*Fairies?*" A small laugh escaped her lips. "That's—"

"Absurd? Add it to the list," said Jeom. He rolled his eyes, crossing his arms at his chest. "Just hear her out. Obviously, she's right. She's always right."

"I've read about them before in the attic library," said Lessa. "They're even mentioned in *Olleb-Yelfra the Fallen*. Do you remember?"

Arianna faintly recalled a mention but wasn't quite sure. Nevertheless, her interest was piqued at this new tidbit from the Golden Age. "I can't really recall anything about fairies... but go on. I'm listening."

Lessa sat across from her on the log, and Demetrius came to join them, standing beside his brother.

"Well, you said something about seeing colorful lights, and it jogged my memory," she said. "Fairies were supposedly powerful, magical creatures. Before Devlindor's time, there used to be millions of them all over the Olleb! I can't believe it, but I guess they're not extinct after all..."

"But how do you know that's what she encountered?" asked Demetrius, scratching his head. "What are they, exactly?"

"From what I recall from my studies, the light they give off isn't *really* a light at all," said Lessa, her voice pitching with enthusiasm. "It's a magical dust, and it can be used as a sort of hypnosis, only affecting humans."

Jeom wiggled his fingers in the air. "Fairy dust!"

Demetrius' mouth fell open, alongside Arianna's.

"And I read that if you stare too long after the light… or dust, or whatever you want to call it, the fairy can gain access to your mind, making you see things that aren't truly there." She scooted closer to Arianna, as if searching for some proof of this magic on her skin. "They'll lure you away with their light and their whispers, and they can trick you with illusions."

Arianna didn't have trouble picturing this type of magic. In fact, she vividly recalled her lonesome journey through the desert—the one that had only happened in her mind as she wasted away for hours in a boneyard.

"They're small as can be but dangerous little things," said Lessa, nodding to herself. "That is, if they feel threatened."

"I suppose a power like that could prove pretty deadly should the hypnosis never be released, or even if the illusions themselves aren't particularly pleasant," mused Demetrius, peering out across the sand.

"Certainly," whispered Arianna, a shiver rolling up her spine.

Lessa twirled a strand of hair around her finger as she thought. "From what I remember reading, though, they're actually supposed to be quite docile."

"Then why would they feel threatened by *me?*" said Arianna as Solza emerged from the carriage, coming to lie by her side in the shadiest spot she could find.

Her presence instantly rejuvenated Arianna, filling her to the brim with an inexplicable energy and joy; she felt as if she could walk for hours more with nothing to aid her except for her avatar.

Though, as she stroked Solza's fur, she could sense her agitation over their separation.

Nothing to worry over, girl. I'm here now.

She knew their minds would connect, that Solza understood her reassurance. And in this moment, their bond grew tighter, as if Solza had declared in response that it would take a force much stronger than supposed fairy magic to separate them again.

"Why do you think?" Jeom blurted out, breaking Arianna's connection with Solza.

"Huh?" she said, shaking off her daze.

"Why do you think a magical creature of the Golden Age would be threatened by you?" Jeom raised an eyebrow. "Need I remind you of the tomb that is the City of Undor."

"I see," said Arianna, her eyes drifting shut with the heaviness of this continuous burden. "King Devlindor. He would've wanted them gone."

"And it seems he sure gave it his best effort," said Jeom. "At least he didn't succeed… this time."

There was a moment of silence, each surely remembering the devastation they'd uncovered in the dwarf realm beneath the Blancoren Mountains.

"Fairies were known to reside in forests or heavily wooded areas," said Lessa. "And I'm sure the King waged a war against them just the same. I wouldn't be surprised if they viewed all humans as threats now, because of what he did. Of course, we can't know the reason for certain. I'm just speculating at this point."

"Yes, we can," said Jeom, firmly. "I've no doubt in my mind about that."

Arianna nodded her agreement; if Jeom didn't have a shred of doubt, then surely no one else did either.

"Some must've escaped him then," said Demetrius. "And if they have any animalistic instincts at all, they would've established a new home in an environment where they would never encounter such threats. It's the most basic law of nature. Flee or fight." He swished his foot back and forth in the sand as they all contemplated this lost history. "I'd bet anything that the remaining fairies established new territory here, abandoning their home in the Nicora Forest after the King's attacks."

"Survival of the fittest," said Jeom, a distant look on his face. "King Devlindor's favorite game."

"So, basically, you're saying that these fairies were threatened by me because of what the King did?" said Arianna, piecing their theory together. "Saw me on my own and pounced at the chance… because I'm human?"

Lessa met her eyes, and she felt the warmth returning between them. "That's *exactly* what I'm saying."

A heaviness settled in the air as they all locked stares, and Arianna wondered if in that moment they each thought the same thing… a thought that had been dancing around her head for days and one she had yet to voice to the others.

We must kill the King.

She looked down to Solza who crouched at her feet—she knew, at least, that her avatar shared the same mind.

"What in the *King's* name are you talking about? Have you all gone mad?" said Eli, ripping open their bubble of secrets about the demise of the Golden Age. He gawked at them, a mix of horror and dread paling his face. "What are you playing at here?"

Arianna jumped to her feet with a gasp. "How long have you been standing there?"

"Long enough," he said, his voice barely audible, hands shaking—he appeared wholly disturbed and looked as if he might also choose to 'flee or fight' at any minute.

Lessa threw her hand over her mouth to silence herself, but it was far too late. They'd already divulged too much. In all the excitement, they'd all but forgotten he was there—a non-believer in their midst.

"Eli, maybe you should sit down," said Demetrius, standing up slowly to offer him his seat. "We were just—"

"I'm quite all right here, thanks," he said, taking a step back.

He gripped Phantom's saddle, as if it were the only thing grounding him in this moment.

"I think it's time to talk about what's happened these past few weeks," said Jeom, brusquely. "Let's not sugarcoat it anymore. He can either saddle up or get out."

"*Jeom!*" snapped Lessa. "You forget yourself. Show a little empathy, please."

He puffed out his cheeks. "We don't have time for that."

Lessa looked daggers at him.

"You're one to talk! When we told you, you all but ran in the other direction." She turned to Eli, addressing him as gently as possible. "There's a lot of things you don't understand yet. Don't listen to Jeom. Please, let us explain."

Eli looked to Arianna with a pleading expression, and she knew the last thing he wanted her to do was say anything else that might shatter his fragile reality. She questioned if his mind could even take the truth at this stage, but now they didn't have a choice. He'd already heard too much, and they needed to all be clued in if they were going to make it through to the other side together. He had to understand their pasts *and* the future they truly ran toward, if he wanted to continue running alongside them.

Without giving him time to object further, Arianna started at the beginning. She told of her initial chance encounter with Lessa Thur, the ghost girl of the Healer's District, and how they came to be together in the Warrior's District with the help of Solomon and Talis. She explained about the day she died and of magic's hand in offering her a second chance at life. And the others chimed in to tell their own personal stories related to the remnants of the Golden Age, avatars and all.

After the storytelling and reminiscing wound to an end, Arianna sensed much of her own stress dissipate, and she knew her friends shared the same feelings—they had been reminded of the purpose that led them to this desert in the first place, and of all the good and justice they might do if they survived. It was such a relief to let everything spill out, to let one little stress slide over so that the rest had room to breathe.

For Eli, though, that didn't seem to be the case.

Arianna saw plainly that the weight of this knowledge was far too great for him to bear, just as she'd feared; his attention stayed glued to the South Star, unblinking and unhearing. She worried that in relieving some of her own stress she'd only added to his.

Emotions had run high between them during their journey back to camp, both good and bad. And with this added, magical layer, she wasn't sure how much more he could withstand before breaking.

Too late now.

"And that's only the beginning," said Lessa, breathless. "Wait until we tell you about our time with Keeper Kassime."

Bags hung underneath her eyes, and she looked tired, as if she'd aged another year since they'd fled the palace. But her hope was still there, shining bright nonetheless.

"I know it's a lot to take in," added Demetrius, smiling with encouragement. "I'm still trying to wrap my head around a lot of it myself, but it's true. All of it is!"

Arianna braced herself for Eli's reaction, gritting her teeth.

"Say something, please," she said, ready to handle anything.

After all, she had prepared for so long on how to tell Liam.

It occurred to her now that this might be her only chance to put that practice to use; and if Eli could accept their truths, then maybe Liam's death wouldn't feel like such a terrible waste.

"Let's just go," he finally said, backing away from them and jumping onto Phantom's saddle. He looked toward the dying sun. "We're losing light. We have to go now if we're to make it out of here before nightfall… and we *need* to get out and clear our heads."

He spoke more to himself now, far away in his own mind as

he held out his hand for Arianna to join him.

She gave a solemn sigh and stood. "First, I need to get my swords."

When they'd all readied to leave, she joined Eli again in Phantom's saddle; Arianna had been just beginning to grow comfortable with this closeness, but now something felt colder between them.

"Solza, get in the carriage with the others. I won't be far off this time," she called down to her eager avatar. Gesturing for the others to follow, she mouthed, "Don't worry."

Demetrius hopped up to guide the now two-horse carriage with Lessa, Jeom, and the avatars inside. Then they were off again, Eli and Arianna leading the way across the desert, toward the falling sun.

THE KING'S SHADOW

A LONG WHILE LATER, as the night settled in and the cold settled with it, a huge crater stretched out before them. Arianna walked to the edge and saw hundreds of red, orange, and yellow translucent stones jutting up from somewhere deep down.

"What is this place?" called Jeom, hopping out of the carriage. His voice seemed to bounce back and forth off the stones until it got lost at the far-away bottom.

Arianna stepped back, pulling Jeom to a safe distance—the Warrior's District Pit came to mind.

Though this would be a much more beautiful place to die.

"Must be the site of the last meteorite," said Eli, the first words he'd spoken in an excruciatingly awkward while.

He gazed down into the colossal hole and whistled. "That's a far drop."

"Meteorite?" Lessa came to join them.

Eli nodded, pacing the perimeter of it as they all looked

down. The glistening stones added their own light to the night, jutting out from the sides of the crater.

Demetrius crouched low, stretching his hand out to touch one within reach. "It's… so warm. When did it land?"

"That's odd," said Eli, tapping his chin as he stared off into space. "I'm sure this thing landed over a year ago now."

"What exactly is a meteorite?" said Arianna.

She was transfixed by Sano as he darted expertly between the long stones, seeming to fly about them as he bent the wind to his will, much more the master of air after a year of practice under the guide of Lessa and Keeper Kassime.

"It's the name for when a piece of the sky falls to the earth," said Demetrius. "It's one of nature's longest unsolved mysteries." He lifted his hands up to the stars, as if to welcome them nearer. "There's no explanation as to how or why it happens, but some-times a star just simply falls right out of the sky to join us. Pretty spectacular, huh?"

"Quite," said Eli, nodding. "It's a rare sight to see in anyone's lifetime, and they speculate that none has made such a dent in the earth before as this one. I heard that it was possibly *the* largest meteorite to be seen falling in ages."

He leaned forward, and Arianna thought he might topple downward to his death.

"But its true size has been a guess. No one ever found the site to lay claim." His voice echoed in the vastness. "Not before now… I bet those stones would be worth a fortune in the cities." He wobbled at the edge, and Arianna resisted the urge to yank him back to safety. "I was working with Mya and Gabriel at the tavern on the night it fell. I'll never forget that. It was right before the last Gathering Ball I attended."

Arianna could almost taste the snowfall of a far-gone memory. Then it clicked.

"We saw this, *too*," she whispered to Lessa; Eli's words had awakened something in her that made all her hair stand on edge, in the best of ways.

"Saw what?" Lessa's attention strayed to Sano, her eyes gleaming with the reflection of the crater crystals.

"Les, we saw this happen!" said Arianna, shaking her by the shoulders. "Don't you remember?" She laughed, overjoyed at finding a connection to such a momentous time in the middle of nowhere. "It was the first night you came to stay in the Warrior's District with me. The start of everything."

"What's the big fuss?" said Eli, brows raised. "Anyone even close to the north saw this happen. It lit up the entire region."

"I didn't see it," mumbled Jeom, crossing his arms.

Demetrius snickered. "I'm utterly unsurprised."

Lessa's hands flew over her mouth as she stared at the crater. "By the gods, how mysterious you are!" She turned to Arianna. "I could never forget it. It fell over the mountains and must've landed here, I suppose." She shook her head, gaping all the while. "That's just remarkable. So much time has passed since. I never would've imagined…"

There just weren't any suitable words to describe this miraculous coincidence, so they hugged instead, both giddy with excitement.

"Eli, please," said Arianna, rejuvenated by this beautiful, uncorrupted piece of Olleb-Yelfra and anxious for his acceptance of it. "This is what I'm speaking of." She pointed to the crater. "*This* is proof of magic!" He just had to see, as Solomon had once forced her to see. "Can't you try to understand? Please, let us show you. Let us prove it now."

"Prove what—"

Arianna ran to Lessa and whispered something; they beckoned Sano and Solza and clasped hands. Not allowing Eli even a moment to protest, in chant-like voices, the girls began to speak in rhythm, calling to their magic.

"This land is dark, let us see," they sang. "The land so cold, let us breathe."

"Come now, stop that. There's no time for this foolishness," said Eli.

He moved to touch Arianna's shoulder but froze—she knew he saw it then, their eyes glowing silver just as bright as the stars above. And with their avatars also joining for a frighteningly beautiful display of tangible magic, how could he deny them again?

Demetrius put a finger to his lips, gesturing for Eli to stand back. "Everything's okay, mate. *Just* wait. Wait to see what happens next."

"What… what is this?" whispered Eli, stumbling backward into him.

They all looked up.

It appeared as if the stars in the sky had begun to tumble to the earth all around them in slow, shining streaks, just as the meteorite had done long ago. As they got closer to the earth, they transformed into small droplets of liquid dancing all around them—water.

The enchanted rain held a golden light that Arianna knew, without a doubt, to be a literal reflection of magic itself. And it was warm to the touch as it rolled off her skin, a relief in this cold desert evening. It fell in gentle, drawn-out movements, as if time had slowed; the Black Sand Desert seemed to be readying for a fantastic party, thousands of golden droplets decorating the sky.

Arianna looked toward them, letting the water warm her face and satisfy her overwhelming thirst. "You never know what you're going to get," she mumbled, pondering the miracle of magic as Lessa started spinning around, her arms out wide, beside her.

Their magic had certainly grown since their training under Keeper Kassime. That much was certain. Arianna barely even felt a drain of energy now, with their avatars lending their own charms to the mix.

"I don't believe this," said Eli.

His breath came heavy, eyes glued to the sky. But the expression on his face held anything but excitement.

He fell to his knees in the sand, still staring up as the enchanted rain soaked him from head to toe.

Arianna thought his heart might give out from shock.

But... he surely cannot deny our claims now. He just needs time to let it sink in.

"Neither do I sometimes," she said, smiling as the rain washed away every worry she felt weighing on her heart.

After all she'd learned of magic, she now fully understood and respected that it had a mind of its own; it was somehow alive. Though one could expect or pray for a certain outcome, it was impossible to predict what might truly come to be from any spell. Thus, practice would *never* make perfect. It just heightened the chances of a favorable result.

She would forever heed Kassime's wisdom in that. '*Magic can be just as dangerous as it is fascinating,*' he had once said.

And as she glanced again at Eli, his warning rang true; although this magic had been wonderfully pleasing for her, the man Arianna saw before her now could prove to be the *dangerous* result of their spell.

Her smile faded, the fear palpitating off him wiping away anything good she'd felt before.

There was no room for him to understand the beauty in this yet, something so profound. The space for it in his mind was probably filled with whatever unimaginable horrors he had endured in the Luose Dungeon and the stress of leading a near-fatal trek across an unforgiving desert.

He covered his eyes with his hands, rocking back and forth. "This isn't happening," he muttered to himself over and over. "I'm not here anymore. I'm not here anymore!"

"It's okay," said Lessa, laying a hand on his shoulder. "We can stop—"

"No!" he shouted. "I'm *not* here anymore."

She pulled back her hand.

"He's unraveling," said Jeom as they all huddled a little distance away.

"I think he's talking about the dungeons," said Lessa, her lips twisted with guilt. "This was too much. We should've waited."

"Well, I think it's a bit too late for that now," said Demetrius, shifting his hands in his pockets. "Unless you know a spell to turn back time."

Jeom huffed. "*Good* going, girls. You broke our guide."

"Oh, please. He's not… broken," said Arianna.

They all glanced back to Eli—he looked so much the definition of broken that it was a wonder he'd even led them this far in the first place, so close to losing his mind.

"Let me see if I can try and calm him down," Arianna said.

Her friends agreed.

She took a deep breath, trying to gather what words could possibly pull him back. When nothing came, she faced him anyway, hoping whatever she said would be strong enough.

"Eli…" she said in a gentle voice. "It takes time to fully understand this. But we can teach you. We can show you all that we know, explain everything. You don't have to be so scared. You can… you can trust us."

She swallowed the lump in her throat, thinking they were quite square now in this nasty game of secrets.

Arianna moved closer, reaching out her hand. Eli flinched, crawling away from her, sand flying in every direction.

"No! You stay away from me, you *monster*," he roared. "Just stay where you are. I should've done away with you when I had the chance."

Arianna stopped cold.

Eli pointed at her with a condemning finger, his face so red with fear she thought he might burst into flames.

"I'm not here anymore!" His voice broke into a cry, and he shook all over.

"Please, calm down," said Demetrius, coming to intervene—Arianna could only stare down at Eli, her lips pressed into a thin line as his words settled around her.

I should've done away with you when I had the chance.

Her swords began to burn at her back, wanting to be held. Still, she resisted.

Now Demetrius was the one offering him a reassuring hand. But this time Eli didn't run nor scream… he attacked, twisting Demetrius away from him with a regulator's reflex; Demetrius shrieked, and Arianna's fingers grasped the hilts of her swords.

"*Reveliantom!*" Jeom was already running to his brother's aid. He slipped the metal tube from his belt and tossed it into the air; the Axe of Crissy instantly took shape, Jeom plucking it from the cloud of magic now glowing around it.

"Believe us now?" he snapped, brandishing the gleaming axe at Eli—it still dripped with magic. "Get your hands off my brother!"

His words were sharp and remorseless as he positioned himself in front of Demetrius, in front of the others, splintering Eli off from his friends; Arianna could practically see Jeom itching to use his weapon on the boy who had yet to prove he belonged… and now she could not blame him.

Something final shattered within Eli in this moment. Arianna could see it in his eyes. A light went out, as if he'd slipped off the edge he'd been standing on all this time, falling back into darkness.

Since the day they had rescued him, he'd been dealing with much more than they could have possibly imagined, rivaling even their pains. The Luose Dungeon had erased the Eli they had once known, that he *himself* had once known, and Arianna saw clearly now that he wasn't coming back—not anytime soon. And not ever, if he forced her hand to kill him.

"None of you deserve your freedom! None of you," he

screamed. "No wonder you lot are being hunted. You're monsters!"

"Eli," said Arianna, a warning in her voice; she kept one hand on a hilt. "You *don't* have to fear us. That's what the King wants. Just let us explain. We can talk about this, calmly—"

She took another step forward, about to release her grip.

"Stay back!" Eli scooped up a broken shard of crystal from the ground, surely lethal if any of them should find it in their necks. And he was so unhinged, Arianna thought he might actually lunge at someone.

She withdrew a sword, holding it down by her side as Jeom let her have front and center; she could feel it coming, feel him inching nearer to the same path that those she labeled 'enemies' had disappeared down. Her grip tightened on her blade, ready for the ultimate and unfortunate moment when Eli would step over the line she'd laid out for him.

A frightening calm seem to wash over Eli. His eyes came back into focus and they found Arianna's, seeming to search straight into her soul.

"Do *not* come any closer," he said. "You're a curse, Arianna Belvedor. Since the moment I laid eyes on you, darkness has swallowed me." She felt it swirling inside her too—could he see? "I meant what I said. I should have slain you when I had the chance. I had so many chances to rid the world of someone so disgraceful. I wish I had done it."

Each word felt like a stone stacking atop her body, pressing the air out of her lungs. Only hours ago they were kissing amidst a raging sandstorm. And now...

I warned you.

She felt the active magic in her ebb, and the enchanted rain ceased to exist.

She lifted her sword.

"Arianna, don't!" said Demetrius, distracting her just long enough for Eli to make a move.

He put two fingers in his mouth and whistled loudly; Phantom raced to his rescue. He jumped into the saddle and rode off into the night.

Lessa ran forward. "Eli, wait! Don't leave us here," she screamed. "Come back!"

"He's not going to return," said Arianna, anger filling the place where joy and hope had been only minutes before. "He's abandoned us."

"If I hadn't been so careless before about the fairies," said Lessa, staring after him. "It was too much for him to handle after such a trauma."

"It's not your fault, Les," said Demetrius.

"Yeah, I had a bad feeling about bringing him along from the start," growled Jeom, returning the axe to its shielded form. "He knows *too* much now. He could lead our pursuers right to us! Assuming we can even find our way out now that we've lost our guide." He kicked the sand, glittering specks flying to the wind.

"So much for his promises of loyalty," mumbled Demetrius, rubbing at his bruised wrist. "Do you really think he'd say anything?"

"If he does, no one will believe him," said Lessa, coddling Sano in her arms. "It'll be fine… no one would ever believe him, right? *He* didn't even believe it himself."

She looked up, the doubt plain in her expression.

"The King would," said Arianna—the darkness weighed heavier.

The world needed to learn of magic, yes, but at the right time and from the mouths of those who didn't fear it. It would only help King Devlindor's cause if magic was exposed in a negative light. Moreover, Eli's knowledge could reveal the names and faces of many honorable guardians, put targets on the heads of their friends.

There was nothing left to wonder—Eli had proven himself a threat to the guardians now, a serious threat that would need to be dealt with. His loyalties were malleable at best; he'd already proven that in more ways than one.

"What do we do about him?" said Demetrius.

Arianna gazed at Solza, who looked ready to race after him, echoing her own sadness and anger; Keeper Kassime would have done *anything* it took to protect the knowledge of the Golden Age and the Guardians of Gold, and so would she.

"You already know," she whispered.

If they couldn't learn to wipe memories as Keeper Kassime had mastered, Elijah Neve would have to endure the more severe consequences of his choices. If it meant taking the life of one person to have a better chance at ensuring the life of the world, they had all already vowed to choose the Olleb and proven their loyalty to that oath ten times over. Eli would have to die—that was, *if* they ever saw him again.

"Damn him!" said Jeom, pacing back and forth. "How are we going to get out of this gods-forsaken place now?"

"We're better off on our own." Arianna forced the words through her teeth. "We did a kindness by bringing him along, and he's made his decision. One day, he'll pay for it as well."

She was so disappointed in herself for trusting him at all after what he'd confessed to her. Now he'd betrayed her and her friends again, abandoned them to their probable deaths in the desert and taken with him the biggest secret in history. She couldn't help but feel pure hatred over the thought that her Liam had died just so someone like Eli could survive.

A real coward.

"Oh, I think we'll be all right," said Demetrius, pointing off into the distance, pulling Arianna from her darkening thoughts. "Look! That *has* to be Zambienth, like Eli said. We must be closer than we thought."

They all peered across the crater, and sure enough, they saw what looked to be the shadows of giant pyramids standing tall in the distance. Small flames wound up and down the structures, presumably lanterns, more and more cropping up as the night grew thicker.

"That's a few hours' walk at most," said Jeom with a dumbstruck look on his face. "We can definitely reach it before the sun rises again."

He seemed giddy with curiosity as he studied every detail of the structure illuminated before them, craning his neck to see better.

"Let's just have a rest for a bit, shall we?" said Demetrius, already unpacking the last of their food. "We'll need our energy if we're going to start causing more trouble in a new city."

He laughed, and Arianna relaxed, thinking that at least their spirits hadn't been broken to the point of no return—not just yet.

Not like Eli… just survive.

WHILE THEY TOOK AN HOUR to gather their strength for whatever surprises the City of Zambienth might throw at them, Arianna decided to get a better look at the mystical crater. Carefully, she climbed to the bottom, using the giant stones as a makeshift ladder.

"Nothing but a bunch of rock down here," she called to her friends—they kept eyes on her from far above.

"I see you're finally starting to grow fond of climbing," sang Lessa, her voice echoing down after her. "I'll join you in a minute."

"Don't remind me," mumbled Arianna, registering how far down she'd gone… and how high she'd have to climb to get back up. She began to explore the large hole, kicking at the white pebbles beneath her feet; something sparkled in the upturned dirt, so she bent down to retrieve it.

There, beneath the fallen earth, lay a beautiful, blue stone unlike anything she'd ever seen before. It was surging with sparkles and so small it could've been prepared for jewelry.

She examined it, and it seemed to pulsate with a sort of life, as if glittering waves of energy roared within its tiny shell. She stuffed it into the inner pocket of her robes for safekeeping. As she did, she heard it tinkle against something else.

After digging out the cause of the noise, she held it in the palm of her hand—the aura and ora stones were just as striking in Keeper Kassime's ring as they had been surrounding her in the Vanishing Tunnels. In all the disorder since the Gathering, she'd forgotten that she even still had it.

"Thank the gods this wasn't lost," she said, squeezing it tight in a gesture of tribute to their fallen teacher.

"Ara, you better come back up here, quick!" said Demetrius—something in his tone made her heart beat faster. "We've got a bit of a problem."

"Coming!" she called back, unsure of what to expect. What further problems could they possibly have at this point?

She placed the ring back in her pocket, alongside the little blue stone, and started the lengthy climb up the side of the crater. When she reached the top, she immediately wished she could've just lived out the rest of her days in the safety of that hole.

Arianna drew her swords, beckoning Solza close to her side. She squeezed the hilts tight, trying to shake off the numbness of fear wrapping all around her.

"Arianna Belvedor," said a chilling voice. "I've been looking *everywhere* for you."

Standing there before them was none other than Sir Vladamor—a necromancer born of dark magic, and the King's very own shadow—sitting atop a brawny, gray stallion.

His hood draped low over his masked face, and he bore no weapons. But Arianna supposed the army of the walking dead behind him would fare just fine in a fight.

6

FACING DEATH

FROM WHERE THEY STOOD, the four had an aerial view of the impending battle, Sir Vladamor at the epicenter. The land sloped upward toward the crater, so they were trapped upon a hill now surrounded by enemies, sand dunes flowing down beneath them in sheets of gleaming black. Behind the necromancer was an army—though not an army of Olleb regulators or palace soldiers.

They weren't people at all.

No, this was an army of the dead, raised from their desert graves by some of the most unnatural and dark magic that Arianna had ever witnessed. The moon shone down on the gathering, lighting the way for what would surely be an epic slaughter. *How can we survive? We must.*

"How did you find us?" Arianna's voice was a whisper, though she knew the necromancer would hear.

His grip tightened around the reins of his horse, gold-threaded gloves shimmering brilliantly in the night. And a thick, gilded mask obscured his face but for the eyes; he dripped splendor, hiding behind the King's riches. But Arianna knew there was nothing but a grotesque monster underneath it all.

The necromancer tilted his head as his horse pawed at the ground—it was saddled with trimmings fit for a king, and Arianna wondered what type of opulence the true monarch might display… should she survive this night and ever come to meet him.

The army at Sir Vladamor's back was silent yet overwhelming in their masses. There had to be hundreds, spreading out in a fan at the base of the hill. Their bones shimmered a silvery white, as if a school of fish had washed upon land to die, leaving only their shining skeletons behind. And from what Arianna could tell, most of this afterlife army was devoid of any flesh, though their rot must've stayed with them in their graves—an overwhelming stench filled the air.

As the cool night breeze whipped around them, all she could smell was death.

"The King demands your head," Vladamor finally called back. "It's my duty to deliver that trophy. The '*how*' is wholly irrelevant. You have only moments to live."

"Why can't you just let us alone!" screamed Jeom, summoning the Axe of Crissy to again reveal itself.

The necromancer flinched, his eyes narrowing, but it was enough to give Arianna the courage she needed to stand her ground. *He wasn't expecting magic.*

She pushed aside her panic, strengthened as her friends prepared for battle, Solza right by her side.

Lessa wrapped Sano safely across her shoulders, stowed their most valuable possessions in the pack at her back, and nocked an arrow, others at the ready in the sand; Demetrius, too, gathered his things. He tied his hair up and readied his staff. With a squeeze of his brother's hand, he took a strong fighting stance.

'Never let your emotions control you. They have no place in

a duel, unless you intend it to be your last.'

Solomon would've encouraged Arianna with such words before. *Before.*

She wished she could travel to the past and choose a different path, head in a direction that would take her anywhere but here. This might be the final cut to her thread of life, the last stab to send her hurtling toward the darkness forever, giving up as Solomon and Eli had done.

"It's quite simple, really," said Vladamor. He guided his horse closer, staring them down atop the shifting hill. "*Free* for the slaves who earn their citizenship. *Falls* for the ones who die." The air seemed to grow colder, bumps rising on Arianna's skin. "You have earned nothing but a quick and painful departure from this world."

"Why do you fight for him?" said Lessa, desperation in her voice—it was obvious to anyone with ears that she'd calculated they stood no chance of survival. Still, Arianna kept her chin high.

"We know the secrets the King hides," she cried. "We know them well now! And we know who you are and what you've done. Why fight for someone who's wiped out your entire kin, your entire *history* from this world? You're an elf of Nicora!"

"I am a *necromancer* and your High King's right hand!" His voice shook the sands. "Your young minds couldn't possibly fathom all that we've done to build a world fit for such power. And despite what you might think, you haven't even made a dent in our rule. Others have tried with far more effort, and failed far more gloriously, than you'll ever know." Arianna could sense the smile, hidden behind the mask. "But you will know what pain is… as I remove the souls from your bodies!"

His voice exploded clear across the quiet night, and the wind seemed to pound stronger with it. Arianna could practically feel his dark magic radiating off him. But his army didn't move an inch; it was as if they slept standing up, their skeletal limbs not giving way to the brewing storm.

"He's no king of mine," spat Arianna, brandishing her swords. "We'll no longer bow to a man whose rule is built on murderous lies and insatiable greed. We won't let you win!"

At this, Sir Vladamor lifted his mask to sit atop his head like a crown, sniffing at the air with snakelike nostrils; Arianna recoiled, his sunken face blending right in with the dead army around him. He let out a deep sigh, as if relishing the sweet scent of her rage.

"A strange child, you are. This is quite unexpected." He closed his eyes, still sucking at the air in his grotesque manner. "I can sense the darkness within you, Arianna *Belvedor*." He whispered her name like he delighted in the way it rolled off his tongue, laced with an accusation that frightened her beyond reason.

She froze, wondering if her heart had literally stopped in her chest. His eyes flashed open, and she became lost in their pools of black, entranced by the dark—just the same as when the fairies had enthralled her with their light.

"You've walked a similar path as me, have you not? Taken many lives and caused much death?" He nodded. "I can smell it *dripping* off you. You don't have a true noble bone in your body, if I had to guess. Maybe you even hope I win this fight and rid you of your guilt."

As if he planted them there in her mind, names filling her with guilt circled her thoughts—*Pippa. Liam. Lily. Kassime.*

Even the ones who had darker souls still made her cringe, their blood stained on her hands forever—*Grinda Risso. General Ivo. Sir Dean Westing. Godfrey. Mya.*

The nameless faces of regulators and palace protectors.

All dead, because of me.

He spoke softer now, his glare so intense. "I think you *want* to die, don't you, Arianna? Rather than pretend you're anything but black in your soul."

"You're wrong." Her words came out in a stutter. "No, you're wrong!" She took a step forward, pointing a blade in his direction—Solza roared her agreement.

His lips curled up in a smile, and he let out a sickening sound that must've been the remnants of a laughter he could no longer properly conjure up from his past elven life.

She could sense her friends were confused, shifting on their feet as they glanced back and forth between them—they didn't understand what was going on… what he insinuated.

But she did. Arianna couldn't even bring herself to explain, couldn't utter the words.

"*Yes*," he said with a cackle. "I know death when I see it. It's mine to control. You've made this much too easy for me, I'm afraid." He tilted his head, puckering up his lips to form something resembling pity on his face. "And I was hoping we'd have a little fun first."

"Don't listen to him, Ara," said Lessa, panic streaking her face as they locked eyes—Arianna knew she'd caught up now.

Sir Vladamor coiled his fingers into a fist, and Arianna felt her chest contract, as if he were trying to tug her soul straight from her body… just as promised.

She dropped her swords to the sand, one hand grasping at her heart.

"You've walked the fine line between this world and the beyond, just like me." An insidious smile grew on his face. "You're *just* like me!" He shook his fist in the air. "I don't know how you died or who brought you back, but you've wasted your power, girl. Let it slip right through your fingers! And now, I'll make sure you'll never be revived again. Such a nuisance you proved to be."

An excruciating burn ripped across her chest, coursing through her body; she screamed, tearing at her shirt.

"It's not true!" Her knees buckled and she hit the ground. "Lies. All lies."

But she'd always known the truth, ever since she'd learned

the history of the necromancer's creation. Now, she could no longer ignore her dark reflection—in this agonizing instant, all her nightmares, her assumptions were validated.

"Actually…" He cocked his head to the side, something staying his hand. "Why don't we see if we can try this again? Really do it right this time."

He clenched his fist tighter, and Arianna felt the air leave her body; she struggled to reel it back in. She rolled onto her back, crying out for help, but her friends were unable to do anything to relieve her pain.

"Please, stop this!" His features blurred, but Demetrius was there, hovering over her. "Ara, you're going to be all right."

"*Solza ven immito!*" The sound of an arrow doused in magical flame sliced through the air, Lessa taking her place to confront the necromancer.

From the corner of her eye, Arianna saw when Sir Vladamor stopped it with only the wave of his hand. And with another, he sent Lessa flying off her feet—she landed on her back beside Arianna, Sano tumbling across the sand.

"Lessa! Are you hurt?" Jeom ran to her aid.

"I'm fine," she said, scooping Sano back up. "But… Ara."

They both looked to Demetrius.

"Brother, what can we do?" said Jeom, clinging to his axe.

"I don't know," he said, wrapping his arms around Arianna. "I don't know. I think… I think she's dying."

"One with the strength enough to cheat death at all would be much more valuable to our cause alive," said Vladamor. "If you can survive a second time and discover your darkness within, the King may let you keep your miserable life after all. That kind of power belongs with the Shadow Resistance." He shrugged. "And if you don't, then I'd still count that in my favor. What say you?"

His magical grip clung tighter to her heart, her soul.

Arianna felt so near death now as her heartbeat slowed that she could barely focus on his words. Each time her heart pounded, she thought it might be the last.

Sir Vladamor began moaning a string of words—a spell that Arianna had heard once in her past but couldn't quite place in this agonizing moment.

His voice was like the scrape of nails against stone. Then a familiar warmth began growing inside her body, manifesting as a blue ball of light. It glowed brightly beneath her skin, winding all around her insides.

My next breath will surely be the last.

Her head lolled to the side, finding comfort against her arm as she still struggled to pull air into her lungs.

"Ara, what's happening?" said Lessa, crawling to her side with helpless tears in her voice. "What's he doing to you?"

The blue light beneath Arianna's skin turned a bright red, then almost black, shifting back and forth between dark shades of color; it no longer held any warmth.

"I can't be like him," was all she choked out before the air left her lips and did not return.

Her soul was too tired to keep fighting.

"Arianna, stay awake! Please, get up." Lessa pulled her body into her arms.

"*Onasyuda!*" finished Vladamor—he lowered his hand back to his side.

With that, the bulbs of light engulfing Arianna's skin dropped like dazzling sparks all around her, fizzling away into nothing.

"Just let the darkness take over now," he said, his voice searching for Arianna in the engrossing black that her mind was now drowning in. "Make it easy on yourself. Your soul will be safe with me."

Lying on the sand and staring up at the blurring stars and distorted faces of her friends, Arianna felt herself plummet to the will of her mind.

Then, the desert vanished.

"What have you done to me?" she called to him—words she knew her friends could not hear, for they couldn't join her in this dark place.

"I killed you, as promised." His laugh echoed around her, rippling the strange liquid that now entrapped her from all sides. "In death, you have a great opportunity, a second chance to seize power instead of weakness. If you come back this time, you can be one of us. You can *truly* live. No one rejects the dark twice. I leave it for you to decide."

As his voice drifted away so did the remaining light.

Arianna was left now with the agonizing truth that her nightmare had not been a dream at all but a foretelling of this tragedy to come. She was all alone again, struggling under the heavy weight and seduction of the blackness, and she feared no amount of searching would ever bring her light again.

She had a choice to make. *Die or live.*

CHOICES

ARIANNA WAS LYING BACK in the Square, Grinda Risso leering down at her with a sword in hand, her sword. And a stadium of her warrior-slave peers cheered at the prospect of her imminent death. Time seemed to fast forward and again she sensed the presence of the *Onasyuda* spell, its magic working to heal her from the inside out.

It all felt so real, but there was one thing off from the truth of this memory—Arianna now knew of magic.

She knew it well, knew how it ticked, and this had its stink all over it.

You cannot fool me.

The necromancer had forced her into an unthinkable position. This magic did not work alone; she would have to choose to accept its gifts, *or* its curses, just as it had chosen to help her in that fortunate moment long ago.

It hadn't been an easy choice to make then, and it certainly wouldn't be now, not with Sir Vladamor pulling the strings of her fate this time.

A fog of darkness seemed to hover over her, beckoning her into its arms. At the same time, Arianna could hear Talis speaking her very first lesson of magic, as if only a veil separated her from the past.

'*… here you are because you chose to follow a light that came to you in the shadows. You chose this path, Arianna. It led you here… In my experience with life and death, it's much simpler to be consumed by the unrelenting darkness. It's always easier to just let go. The real struggle is holding on to what little light has been left to us.*'

The shroud of darkness seemed to close in tighter, tempting her to step into it willingly, to accept the heavy burden on her shoulders rather than try to push it back and spot the hope. It was a strong temptation too, a taste of a life void of so much complication and endless pain—and she was starting to get so tired of the fight.

But within the darkness, Arianna couldn't deny that a light did still join her. Like the fairy in the desert—faint though it was and far out of reach—it floated there like a beacon, bouncing with just enough flare to remind her that she would need to stand up and earn the catch.

But was it worth chasing? *Is it worth the struggle?*

She needed to decide quickly, before her opportunity vanished forever.

"Ara." A voice called to her—it was an airy, heady, warm sound that seemed to envelop the dark air around her in a wonderfully welcome sensation. "Ara, don't you dare give up! You hear me? You're stronger than this, and you're never alone. *Never.* Fight for your freedom, like we did all those years together! I won't see your life stolen in this way."

She caught her breath as she recognized who the voice belonged to.

"Liam, is that you?" She turned in circles, trying to get a glimpse of the man she knew in her heart was with her somehow, speaking to her.

But all she saw was that tiny light getting closer and closer. Or could *she* be moving toward it?

There was no way to tell.

The golden light grew brighter, and she knew his spirit was there with her then. She didn't even need a reply to know it was him. Even in death, he would always fight in her corner.

"Oh, Liam!" she breathed, the darkness melting away as his ghost materialized from that light before her eyes.

He was just as handsome as he'd always been, but in this ghostly state, he was nothing short of stunning. The scars from his short, brutal life had been erased entirely and replaced by a glowing sheen of what she could only hope was happiness. And the sparkle in his hazel eyes let her know that wherever his spirit rested, he was at peace.

"Liam, I'm so, *so* sorry," she choked out, fighting the urge to run to him. "I thought keeping you in the dark was the right thing. I thought I was protecting you and my friends by waiting until you were ready. But now I know… the dark is not where anyone belongs! I'm so sorry, Liam. I did this to you."

Her words poured out in desperation, wanting to convey so many feelings in an instant.

"Please, forgive me for not saving you. I wanted to save you from this life more than anything. You were my best friend, and—"

"Hush." Liam glided toward her.

He lifted his hand, as if to wipe the tears from her cheek, but all she could feel was a tickle of electricity… she wasn't even sure if she had a physical body in this place.

"What happened to me was not your fault," he said. "And you did save me, Ara. I didn't know it then, but I had been searching for magic my entire life, and I found it in you. For that,

I'm forever grateful." He stared at her with a longing in his eyes. "There's only one person to blame for my death."

"*Solomon.*" The darkness surged. "I'll kill him for what he did to you," she said. "I swear it!"

"Solomon is not the enemy I speak of," said Liam. "You must listen to me now, Arianna." His expression hardened. "It was Kyrone Devlindor who stole my life. Nobody is at fault but the King. Do you understand? You must *never* forget that, for as long as you live."

"I know," she forced out through gritted teeth. "How could I ever forget? Every horror in my life is owed to him."

She understood his plea, for her to focus on the puppet master. But Solomon had ultimately ended Liam's life, and that wouldn't go without punishment if she had any choices left to her.

Arianna grew nervous as the next question passed her lips. "But will I… *live?*"

"As Vladamor says, that is entirely up to you." Hope twinkled in Liam's eyes.

"I don't know if I want to anymore," she whispered, knowing the dark drank up her words with delight. "It's so hard sometimes. This world… is it even worth the fight?"

"Don't let your feelings cloud your judgment," said Liam. "Not when you're so close. The world outside the Four Corners is sometimes more vicious and unforgiving than even the Jar. But at least there is something and flowers grow there."

He smiled, drawing a smile from her too; that was something he'd always been good at, and something she greatly missed.

The darkness rolled around them, impatient and hungry— Arianna sensed it meant to push Liam back to whatever afterlife he'd come from.

"You must kill the King," he said, firmly. "He's the reason for all of this. Hear me now, for there isn't much time. The Olleb needs you, Ara." He began to back away. "She *chose* you. I know that now. I've seen it."

"Please, don't go!" she cried out, reaching toward him.

His light dimmed and his figure lost focus, morphing back into the luminous ball.

"Don't give up," she heard Liam whisper. The light disappeared in a wisp of smoke, melting into the cloud-like fog with only a flickering, golden glow remaining in his absence. "You can do this. Just follow the light."

"I will," said Arianna. "I'll try my very best. I promise."

It was then that she felt Liam's love wrap all around her, as if he'd shouted out the words in her ears. She didn't need to hear them now to know his love lingered like a shield of protection, guiding her always. And she grasped onto that light, that love, with every bit of strength she had to pull herself out from the dark.

AS IF THE LIFE FORCE had been pounded back into her body, Arianna's eyes flew open and she inhaled with a gasp, sitting up and choking on the crisp air.

"Oh, Arianna!" cried Lessa with a start. She was still holding her in her arms as tears fell down her cheeks in streams.

"We thought you were dead," said Jeom.

He tried to contain his emotions, but Arianna saw the sheen in his eyes too.

"I think… I was," she stammered, placing her hand across her chest, feeling her heartbeat there.

Lessa stood back by Jeom's side to give her room, Sano safely curled around her shoulders.

"Are you okay? How do you feel?" asked Demetrius.

Arianna saw that he had one eye on Solza—she looked to be

awakening as well.

"What happened to her?" she gasped, crawling through the sand to check on her avatar.

"I don't know," he said, his voice stricken with panic as he went to stand with the others. "After you passed out, Solza collapsed next to you. I couldn't find a heartbeat."

"Thank the gods you both woke up," said Lessa, hovering.

Arianna gently stroked Solza's head as she came to. *We're all right. We're alive.*

As they made contact, the energy of their bond gripped Arianna with a fierceness unlike anything she'd felt before. Every nerve in her body awakened—somehow she could sense that Solza had followed her into death.

She remembered the words from the scroll Jeom had found in the attic library.

'The connection between man and avatar is such that if death should come to the master, the avatar's soul would soon follow to the afterlife. Conversely, should the avatar die, the master would experience a second chance at the world of the living.'

A chill swept over Arianna then, but it didn't come from the wind; her battle with death wasn't over yet.

She tore herself away from Solza's electric gaze and looked up to find another—the villain version of herself stood among her friends like the pure predator she was, another ghostly presence added to the night.

It outstretched her arm toward Arianna, offering her hand to take. And what a temptress she proved to be.

Her lure radiated off her, a seductiveness that called to corrupt the most selfish parts of Arianna's humanity—and she wanted so badly to grasp her hand.

"So, you live!" said Vladamor. "I'm rather impressed, I must say. That's not an easy task to accomplish. Now, go on." The excitement in his voice was palpable. "Join us. The Shadow Resistance will enjoy having another necromancer on our side.

Think of the power we could wield together. You are *so* very close."

"What's he talking about?" said Lessa.

Jeom shook his head, frantically looking back and forth between the pair.

They couldn't see what was right in front of them; only the dead could see the dead, and that's *exactly* what this monster embodied—death and darkness.

"Don't listen to him," whispered Demetrius. "Stay with us. Snap out of it!" Arianna knew he couldn't see it either, but his intuition was alarmingly spot on; he followed her line of sight to stare straight into the eyes of the wickedness, even if he didn't know it.

She couldn't just snap out of it though. The time had finally come that would force her to decide her life's path. Every disturbing dream she'd endured and the many nights agonizing over their meanings, the paranoia of the last year, was to be put to rest today.

She *had* to face it, whatever the outcome may be.

Stepping closer, the dark reflection of herself smiled, eagerly waiting with her extended hand hanging limp in the air and looking more dangerously beautiful than she could have ever imagined. If she took it, the pain Arianna felt would end and be replaced by an unbridled power. She could practically see that black future pulsing in her reflection's electric, silver stare—the power of darkness, of a necromancer, just waiting there as a gift for the taking. *A curse.*

Everything would be so simple if she stopped resisting and let the darkness swallow her whole.

Sir Vladamor stood below, pressing her forward.

"I could train you, take you under my wing," he said with fervor. "Ah, what a pair we'd be. You cannot resist her twice. Think of what you could do, of the life you could live. *Choose!*"

His voice pierced her sanity, as if cruel magic stitched to his very words, conjured solely to sway her to his side.

Arianna tilted her head to the now murky sky and away from her reflection's deadened stare. She glimpsed the South Star's brilliant light breaking through the brooding clouds, nothing to keep it from shining.

I choose light.

The thought seemed distant, but as she looked again upon her demon, it became the only thing she could fully understand. "I choose the light!"

As the words escaped her lips, the hovering shadows seemed to implode all around her, the dark reflection of her soul caught in the resulting flames with a deafening scream. She watched her burn away with the smoke and knew that the girl in the mirror would never return, the nightmares vanquished forever.

More surprising still, having endured the *Onasyuda* spell for yet a second time, Arianna realized that she had never truly been threatened by darkness at all; it had been a fear of her own conjuring, incited by outside pressures with her own magic aiding its way.

Long ago, before she'd known anything of magic, good *or* bad, she had chosen to follow the light when presented with a choice. And thanks to Sir Vladamor, she was reminded of that choice and would never again question what had been true in her heart all along.

I am good.

"You're weak, girl," he said, shaking his head. "Nothing like me at all! You've lost your most powerful weapon. The dark is no longer on your side."

"I don't need such cruel power to be strong," she shouted back. "A crutch. You're the weak one! You gave up the pieces of your soul that really matter. True strength is turning down the dark."

Whatever he had done, or tried to do, had failed—and that made her feel all the more powerful.

"We'll see about that," said Vladamor, a look of deadly calm washing over him. He slid the golden mask back over his face and held his fist in the air.

Arianna sensed the tug of his magic on her soul once more as he tried to send her back to the dark for good. But this time, she actively blocked his magic.

A necromancer had no control over her now. 'Death' was his most powerful weapon, and Arianna had already proven she could escape it. Thanks to him, she felt more alive than ever, whether or not she'd already died twice before.

"We're Guardians of Gold. You're just someone's shadow, a puppet," she said. "What we stand for *is* noble, and we'll fight you at any cost. Even if that means that I must die again tonight."

She plucked her swords from the sand and stood to challenge him; Solza followed her lead, and her friends flanked her sides.

"Guardians," he spat. "You lot are like rats, always breeding and just as soon falling dead in waves. You know nothing of the truth in this world or the Golden Age, and you never will."

He smiled and raised his fist high in the air again, an eerie glow illuminating his golden-gloved hand this time. His army jolted to life, the centers of their ribcages filling with blue flame and the pits of their eye sockets glowing where eyeballs should have been.

The night grew bright, and colder still.

"The time for words is done now," he said. "This will be over quickly."

SIR VLADAMOR'S CONTROL over the dead shocked Arianna's optimism away—or rather, it shocked her into better sense. She stared upon the skeletons with their rusty armor and old swords lifted and couldn't readily see how she might win.

The thought of any more of her friends dying for the sake of the King's wrath made her take pause. She was a survivor—but no matter her lucky experiences with death, she couldn't deny their looming fates in this desert.

Someone else's life could end here, permanently.

"Wait!" she called down to him over the silent hum of the impending war. "I'll come quietly, if you let my friends go."

The words had just spilled out; but realistically, she saw no way to beat an army of the dead and a necromancer with centuries more experience than they had, and she couldn't bear to let her friends suffer alongside her too.

If something wasn't done, tonight they would all surely perish, or suffer irreversible loss.

This is my fight, not theirs.

Sir Vladamor lowered his fist, the flames of his necromancy instantly snuffed out of the skeletons so that all was dark again.

He pondered her offer, head tilted to the side, his mask starkly gold against the sea of black engulfing him.

"Do we have a deal?" she said, trying to make her words sound firm.

He nodded. "I think we do."

"Good," said Arianna, walking forward.

"What are you talking about?" said Lessa, clutching a fistful of Arianna's robes. "You can't do this!"

"If you go, he'll kill you, Arianna," said Demetrius, pointing his staff at her. "That's it. *Dead.* And surely you won't be coming back this time. We can think of something else. We can make a new plan."

Arianna took a deep breath, hardly able to look them in the eyes. "If I don't go, then he'll kill us all," she said, softly. "This is the only way. You know it is. Tell me now if you have a better option."

She looked at them somberly, their silence solidifying her decision. There was no certainty of escaping Sir Vladamor, and she couldn't leave their lives to chance if she had an opportunity to spare them.

"But we're a family," muttered Jeom, head bowed low.

She smiled at him, holding back her tears.

"That's right. We're family," she said, lifting her chin high. "And I must go, so that you can live. *My* family."

Lessa just kept shaking her head back and forth.

Arianna met her gaze, not waiting for her blessing. "Here, Lessa. Kassime would've wanted you to have this."

She let out a sob as Arianna pushed his ring into her hands.

"No!" she said, clutching it in her fist and glaring back at her in defiance. "No, you're not going to sacrifice yourself to that monster. You're not going anywhere. We will fight like we always do."

"We're guardians now," said Arianna, focusing on the weight of her swords in her hands, "and we made a vow to protect our knowledge."

She stepped back, taking them all in.

"The King only wants my head, but you can still live. You have a chance to keep going and finish what we started, so you must let me do this." A single tear escaped her control. "You know it in your heart that I'm right. I'm sorry."

Before her friends could think of anything else to say to try to stop her, Arianna swiftly crossed her swords at her chest and spoke a barrier spell. "*Ni passe!*"

"No! You promised," screamed Lessa.

She ran forward and collided with the enchanted wall.

It was too late—her friends couldn't move from the place where they stood. It was just like the invisible partition that they'd encountered in the City of Undor, and it would last as long as she willed it to… or until she died.

Arianna could hear their fists pounding against the magical

force, and she knew that to them she'd disappeared altogether. By the time the wall dissipated, she hoped she would be truly gone and that Sir Vladamor would have fled with the news to his king.

"Please forgive me," she whispered to the wind.

She turned now to Solza, who had yet to leave her side through these terrors.

"Solza, I'm sorry it has to be like this," she said, choking on the words. "But we have to do what's right for this world." She understood that her death would result in her avatar's as well, but she had no other options. "Protect them for as long as you can, and I hope to see you again in the next life, my dearest friend."

She kissed Solza's head and commanded her to stay, feeling in her heart that her avatar understood the hard decision they faced together.

"Bravery at its finest, saying goodbye to your pet," said Vladamor, adding slow claps to her torment. "How touching."

"It's not bravery, it's sacrifice," snapped Arianna.

She took a deep breath and marched toward him, heart racing. She felt anything but brave in this moment, but 'The Song of the Brave' pounded fiercely in her head like a wild drumbeat, her supportive shepherd to the end.

Don't be brave, little slave. Be a warrior!

As she got closer, the mass gathering of the dead appearing to grow larger, Arianna pondered if the desert fairies had made some kind of death deal with the necromancer—he so conveniently had an army's worth of skeletons on hand.

Sir Vladamor swung down off his horse, his boots heavy on the sand. He towered over her.

Never in a lifetime would she have thought she might stand this close to the King's Shadow, nor a necromancer. He tilted his mask up and lifted down his hood, leaning over her to get a better look at his prey.

Arianna couldn't help her intake of breath, frozen under his scrutiny. This near, she could see all the veins pulsating underneath his pale, paper-like skin, and his eyes bulged from a sallow, sunken skull—and slithering out from beneath his robes, up his neck, wrapping around to the top of his bald head, was the tattoo of a golden snake, mouth wide open and fangs ready to sink in.

Arianna was horrified and enthralled all at once.

She thought of her own radiant markings—silver scars from the magical bond with an avatar and the golden dragon embedded on her palm from the touch of a guardian—a testimony that her life had meant something good and worthy to this world, the *true* Olleb-Yelfra buried beneath the lies.

A peace settled over her with this awareness, a certainty about her decision.

I am Arianna Belvedor, and I'm a Guardian of Gold. That is my legacy.

She sheathed her swords at her back, fully surrendering.

"Do your worst," she said, never looking away.

GHOSTS OF THE PAST

WITHOUT ANOTHER WORD, Sir Vladamor grabbed her by the neck, his fingers wrapping around her skin so tightly that she could hardly breathe.

This is it. This is how I finally die.

Her life didn't flash before her eyes in any grand way as she'd half expected to happen in her true final moments. She just stared ahead, memorizing every detail of the monster who would take credit for her demise. It was, after all, her third time facing death—and she doubted magic would waste any more of its power saving her if she should truly slip away.

Arianna clutched at the necromancer's strong grip, his hands ice cold like stone shackles; her body convulsed, fighting against her final choices, begging for air.

Just when she thought she might black out, he threw her to the ground, pinning her there. She managed to suck in a deep breath as he toyed with her, like an animal relishing its kill. She didn't fight him, though, knowing it would only be worse for her if she did.

My family is safe.

This thought was placating enough to numb her senses, the ones shouting at her to try to escape.

She closed her eyes, ready for the final blow.

"No, don't," he said, his breath enveloping her face in a way that made all the hairs on her body stand up. "I want you to see this."

See what? She didn't want to look.

Her eyes flew open just as Sir Vladamor raised one glowing fist into the air—his phantom army began to spark into life all around her again.

This time, though, they didn't stay put; as if shoved by the wind at their backs, the skeletons rushed past them. They headed up the large sandbank toward her friends who stood open for the taking, left vulnerable behind her wall of magic near the crater.

They'd have no time to do anything but die once Sir Vladamor killed her—her magic would follow her to the grave, leaving them exposed and defenseless.

"We had a deal!" screamed Arianna. She reached for the hilt of one of her swords, but Sir Vladamor was quicker.

Still straddling her, he placed both hands back around her neck to finish what he'd started; she tried to roll him off, but he was so heavy, heavier than a living ghost should be.

"I'm not known to be a man of my word," he said, smiling blackened teeth at her as he laughed the sound from her nightmares. "I absolutely *despise* martyrs, and I wanted to be sure you knew that your friends wouldn't be far behind you in the journey to the afterlife—that your death means absolutely nothing."

"You can't," she sputtered, struggling to stay conscious. "We had… a deal." Solomon had taught her that warriors were always beholden to their honor—this monster hadn't a lick of honor left in him.

He squeezed harder.

"Goodbye, Arianna Belvedor," he said. "You'll not be mourned by this world."

This agonizing moment dragged on as she kicked her legs from under his weight. The fight for air, the vision of death all around her, the necromancer's sickening voice, the peril her friends faced—all of it made her wild inside to find a piece of control.

But she couldn't.

Her body was no longer in her possession.

The necromancer leaned in closer, breathing her in; he was literally sucking the last of her life from her with his dark magic. She felt a thick tug in her chest every time he inhaled—her hold on herself slipping and his hold on her strengthening.

She faintly wondered what might happen to her soul if he managed to get his hands on it before she died.

A red aura danced all around him as she resisted.

I can't go now. I won't!

Not if her friends needed her to fight. Sir Vladamor had betrayed her offer, and so that offer no longer stood.

It was then that she took back control, thinking of her friends' survival. She felt her magic fill her anew, just as hot and fiery as she felt; the necromancer jumped back in surprise, and Arianna knew he'd seen the magic burning in her eyes.

She crawled away from him through the sand, gasping for air. Without thinking, she found herself connected with Solza, who was still at the top of the hill.

This time, though, the connection was much different.

Arianna felt as if she were the powerful snow leopard herself, a hunter, an alpha predator. And predators didn't just lie down and die. They fought for their territory, their family, and their lives at any cost.

Somehow, Arianna could even *see* through Solza's eyes—the skeletons were closing in on Jeom, Lessa, and Demetrius, and they had no idea that they were about to be attacked.

Arianna cleared her mind and called to her magic, the enchanted wall tumbling down at her command.

Her friends fell forward through the barrier, and she watched through her avatar's sight as they scrambled for their weapons, no time to worry about Arianna or anything else. Then the army collided with them.

Arianna feared they only had moments.

The sounds of a bloody battle resounded across the land as her friends struggled to keep the skeletons at bay. But each time one was struck down, it was only seconds before they inevitably stood back up again, impossible to kill.

Solza, I need you to fight!

Like the igniting of a flame, Arianna fully connected with her avatar—mind, body, and soul—and an incredible power flowed through her, power unlike anything she'd ever tasted before. She was completely engulfed by the magic.

The sand shifted as Arianna got to her feet, reacting to her every footfall. It was the essence of the earth; she knew it in her soul. She could feel everything for miles, as if the lands of the Olleb possessed her body to do their own bidding.

Revitalized by this new energy flowing through her veins, she thought she could live a thousand years with such a life force. Whatever its source, she knew this was *real* power, and Sir Vladamor was about to know it too.

Arianna glanced over her shoulder just in time to see the necromancer pounce at her—with only the flick of her hand, the earth lunged, like a mighty fist of sand, knocking him to the ground.

He shouted curses at her, the deadliest kinds, but they were no match for this power; the earth seemed to respond to Arianna's very breath.

She had absolute control over the element.

With just the twist of her finger, Sir Vladamor sank up to his waist, as if quicksand had instantly swallowed him.

Solza's deafening roar came next as the avatar battled alongside her friends, strengthened as well by the will of the land. The strong vibrations of her voice sent waves of tremors across the sand, the skeletal army slowing as they tried to regain their balance in their quest to mutilate them all.

That's my girl. Solza had bought them more time.

"*Levantis bora!*"

Lessa's voice echoed down to her from the top of the hill, magic exploding all around her as the skeletons in the vicinity were thrown into the air, left to fall back to the ground in pieces. And her arrows took them out in pairs, lit with an enchanted pink flame as they blazed through the night sky.

Jeom's mighty axe put many down for good, its protective personality proving to be a worthy opponent for a necromancer's dark magic. And Demetrius sent skeletons flying backward down the dune, a master with his staff—her friends all fought side by side.

"What sorcery is this?" shouted Vladamor as the ground shook beneath him, breaking apart at the seams. He struggled against the quicksand, his powers weak in the face of such strong, elemental magic.

Arianna faced him. "I call it the power of friendship," she said, coolly. "What's the matter? Your dark magic isn't enough? I thought you were *all-powerful.*"

She couldn't help but toy with him now. She wanted him to pay—she released her hold, and he wobbled to his feet.

"Ara, snap out of it!" she heard someone say; it took everything she had to focus on the voice. "It's too much."

She glanced back toward the hill and saw Demetrius trying to get her attention, waving his arms in warning.

The earth's spirit pulsed within her veins. She could feel it trembling with only her thoughts, the ground shaking with her every emotion; the power just felt too good burning through her, so she chose to ignore his call of caution.

Though—somewhere deep, deep down—she knew she shouldn't have.

"You have the help of avatars," said Sir Vladamor, cautiously pacing at her front. "I don't believe this. And you've mastered an element!"

He gaped up at Solza, and Sano had now joined in on the fight. Flying back and forth on the wind, the little monkey used his big power over the air to protect the others with gusts of sand acting as shields.

"I don't care what you believe," she snapped, the earth cracking with her words.

Arianna lifted both hands out in front of her, feeling the balance of power between the two. And as she did, she sensed the energy of allies join her—Lessa and Sano had also managed to tap into new avatar powers; together, they took full control over the wind from atop the sandbank.

With the manipulation of two elements now on their side, the sand began swirling in a tornado-like fashion, engulfing Sir Vladamor in a dark, glittering vortex. He cried out, nothing to shield him from the force of such nature.

But as the vortex grew, so did the whipping motion of the sand and the strength behind it—Arianna was yanked out of her dangerous trance.

Her magic lost its blaze, and she felt the connection with Solza fade, her energy drained almost completely.

The ground still shook beneath her from all the disturbance, except now she felt a victim of its will. Even the tornado she and Lessa had conjured from the dust continued to naturally grow, consuming everything in its path.

Arianna darted in the opposite direction, shielding her eyes as her hair whipped about wildly. Racing to the aid of her friends, she drew her swords to fight her way back to them, savoring the familiar weight of metal in each hand.

She was so tired, though, barely any energy left to keep running… let alone battle an army of the undead.

"We have to get out of here," called Jeom, hardly able to hold the skeletons back anymore. "The ground is caving in!"

A burst of power seemed to push off from his axe, clearing the area around her friends, buying them all a little more time.

Lessa was aiming arrows Arianna's way, targeting the skeletons at her back; she still had control of Sano's wind magic too, so they swept her path clear.

With just one look at Lessa, still full of fight, Arianna knew their avatar experience had not been nearly the same.

What happened to us, Solza?

Silence, only silence. They had both been weakened.

"Hurry," screamed Lessa. "You must run!"

"You're not going anywhere," sneered Vladamor—with Arianna no longer in control, he had managed to escape his sandy prison.

At his command, the bony, sharp hands of skeletons grasped onto her limbs. They shot up from the earth and cornered her at every angle, stopping her in her tracks.

"Let me go!" This time she fought back.

Her swords sent skulls flying, but their limbs lingered, still holding her down. She looked helplessly up to her friends as the sea of skeletons threatened to bury them too—they couldn't help her, and there was nothing she could do for them. They were all on their own.

"I said, let me go," she shrieked again, squeezing her eyes shut—her magic surged once more.

This time, she felt the power come from within.

When she opened her eyes, the night was almost too bright to look at. Ghosts, hundreds of them, had appeared right before her, as if she had conjured them from the afterlife herself. She assumed them from the phantom army, dotting the land in vibrant versions of their former selves.

What's more, they appeared just as surprised at their arrival as her... and Sir Vladamor.

She had somehow released them from whatever necromancy he had used to suppress and control their spirits in the first place—they immediately glided to her aid.

Some gathered around the necromancer, distracting him, and others appeared to reclaim their own skeletons, collapsing to the ground to play dead again as natural; it was a frightening scene, hundreds of shining white bones and rusting swords falling from the sky to litter the black sand sea.

She gasped. "What in the gods' names... I don't understand."

"You speak of the gods as if they're not here now," said the ghost of a man with silver and gold chains dangling around his neck. "You must possess great magic to free us from such a strong hold. What is your name, little witch?"

"Arianna Belvedor," she said, her voice trembling. "Who are you?"

He bowed low.

"We're at your service then, Arianna Belvedor."

It was apparent this man was the leader of whoever these ghosts were. Though, as she looked closer, she wasn't sure he'd ever been a man at all.

"We are the Elves of Nicora," he said, holding his arms out wide.

Arianna gazed past him—all ghostly eyes were on her as a chilling silence settled in the air, replacing the last sounds of battle.

"Master Lethander?" breathed Vladamor, falling to his knees before him. "No, it cannot be! Your body lies in Saindora."

The great elf responded with such a passion that Arianna had trouble believing he wasn't physically present.

"Vladamor, you traitorous soul!" he bellowed, swiftly floating toward him.

Arianna stepped out of his way, sheathing her swords and listening closely.

"My body lies here, where your *king* unceremoniously dropped me after you helped him slaughter our entire clan. You'll pay in this life and all that come after for the wrong that you've done."

There were angry murmurs of agreement in the crowd as Sir Vladamor tried to crawl backward, a look of terror on his face; if he wasn't already the palest thing walking the land, Arianna thought all the color might rush from his skin—he placed his golden mask back on, hiding away his shame.

The ghost turned again to Arianna, speaking only to her as Sir Vladamor scurried away in haste, muttering in a language she didn't understand.

"Listen, child, we've lingered on this earth, tethered to the small space between our fallen home in the forest and this desert, for a very long time." He looked back at his brethren. "And we shall stay until we know our Olleb-Yelfra is once again returned to her former glory. There was a great war long ago, the Golden Wars, and another is on the horizon. We lost many—"

He shot an angry glance toward Sir Vladamor, who still seemed to shudder with shock as he prepared a getaway. Then she followed his line of sight as he gazed toward the dune where her friends stood waiting.

"—But not all. The time has come. Go and ready your armies, for there is another battle to be fought. It's the will of the world, the Golden Rule. And you, my dear, seem to have been given a *very* significant role to play in this fight. Do not fail us."

The Golden Rule, the prophecy, was burned into Arianna's brain by now, the guardians' entire existence shaped around such a hope that the Olleb would one day right its balance.

'Light is light and dark is dark, but never shall they live apart...'

"You must tell me more," said Arianna, desperately wishing

for him to impart the answers before the ground gave way beneath her feet. "What army do you speak of? Who will help me?
The King is too strong! And I'm just... I'm just one person."

Master Lethander smiled, and she saw the other ghosts inch
nearer to hear, all trying to get a look at the little witch who rescued them from a necromancer's dark magic.

"Arianna Belvedor, whoever you are, something tells me
you're a born leader." He leaned down to whisper so that only
she could hear. "And from one leader to the next, there's always
a great many willing to fight for a noble cause. You need only
find them and show them what's worth fighting for."

His eyes again flicked to the top of the hill—her friends were
waving frantically at her to run.

"From the looks of it, you're already off to a wonderful start."

The ground shook again, and Arianna nearly lost her balance.
"But I don't—"

"You must go now," he urged. "It's no longer safe here for
you. Good luck, young one. May the gods keep you in their favor,
until the end."

With that, Master Lethander and the ghosts of his family
flung themselves toward the necromancer in a wave of shimmering white.

Sir Vladamor screamed, cowering where he stood as the
ghosts of his past surrounded him in a torturous wave. Crying
out again, he pointed a condemning finger at Arianna.

"You're an animancer," he stuttered. "What have I done? It
isn't possible..."

He struggled to make it toward his horse, the ghosts hinder-
ing him.

"This isn't over. The King will not rest until you *and* your
friends are dead, and neither will I!"

He jumped on his horse and seemed to fly away across the
desert. Arianna swore she even saw him disappear in a puff of
smoke before he was out of sight. The King would know of their

secrets soon enough—the desert had revealed them all and more this night.

But she would have to ponder later just what Sir Vladamor meant by accusing her of being an 'animancer.' And with her mentors dead in more ways than one, she had the feeling that the answer to this new riddle wouldn't be very easy to come by.

"Many thanks!" she called back to the elven ghosts of Nicora. "We won't let you down."

"Only time can ensure such a promise," replied Master Lethander. He bowed low. "But you have our hopes, regardless. We'll be watching to find out what becomes of you. Go well, child."

They all stared after her with shining, hopeful eyes, the ghosts of a lost tribe swaying eerily on the wind, adding their light to the blackness of the desert. Then, with a '*pop*,' like extinguishing flames, they vanished.

ARIANNA RAN UP THE HILL, the ground still shaking as it opened up below her, skeletons falling through the cracks. Her magic had caused a huge disturbance that seemed to have a terrible, uncontrollable ripple effect.

She grabbed Solza, briefly hugging her before facing the next problem.

"Any more bright ideas?" said Lessa, hands on her hips.

"What do we do now?" said Demetrius as the earth consumed another pile of skeletons.

"Can't you stop it, Ara? We'll never make it out of here," said Jeom; he called for the Axe of Crissy to conceal itself again and fastened it safely to his waist.

The others secured all their belongings. Then they clambered up to the highest point of the dune, watching in horror as their carriage was swallowed whole, poor horses and all.

Demetrius' hand flew over his heart, tears streaking his dirtied face.

Arianna looked all around for a way out, but there was no running or hiding from the disaster she'd created. For miles in every direction, it seemed as if the desert was falling into itself.

Ahead, just beyond the crater, the pyramids of the City of Zambienth twinkled in the night, taunting her.

We were so close.

"I can't," she finally said with a sigh. "I can't control that kind of power at will. It just… *came* to me in a moment of need when I connected with Solza. It felt like borrowed time. I'm no master yet."

"It was godlike," said Demetrius, considering her with a twisted expression. "You don't know what it was like watching you."

"Well, if we survive this, you can tell her all about it!" barked Jeom. "Now, what's the plan?"

Arianna mulled over their options, feeling the burn of eyes on her; she only saw two.

They could either take their chances outrunning the twister and unstable earth, or they could dive into the depths of the crater—sharp stones jutting out from every angle—and hope to last out the night until things stabilized.

"I know that look," said Lessa as she followed her gaze downward. "It's *too* deep. We'll never make it to the bottom safely in time. And the sand could bury us alive down there. And if we fall…" She gulped. "We wouldn't survive."

Demetrius glanced down, too, sucking in a breath between his teeth with a hiss. "It'll never work. We'll die for certain."

"If we go back the way we came, we'll die too," said Arianna. "We'll be swept away by the sand. This is our best shot. Our only option is to move forward."

She felt energized by her meeting with the elves, invincible in the face of yet another challenge—and she trusted her gut instincts now more than ever.

"We can hide down there until this quake is over," she implored. "Where's your faith? We need it now!"

Arianna shot a nervous smile at Lessa, knowing her agreement would seal the deal.

Lessa shook her head, stroking Sano. "I still don't—"

The ground rattled again, this time nearly knocking them to their knees as the lands screeched and roared.

"There's no more time to argue," said Arianna. "Either you follow or you don't." She went numb with fear as she glanced down the dune; the sand was pouring into itself like a black waterfall. "Go, now!"

With the avatars in the lead, the four friends started climbing down the wide, jagged stones, as quickly as possible. Not moments later, the earth made a truly terrible sound, as if screaming out from the pain of such catastrophe with its last dying breath.

The Olleb shook even more violently all around them, and Arianna felt her grasp slip from the glassy stones, as if the land wished to purge her from this life for good. The others screamed by her side, but she had nothing left to offer as she watched the sky move farther away—the South Star was the only thing left she could see that remained steady.

She felt so vulnerable now, so helpless as she tumbled to the depths of the crater with the sand chasing after them in a thick curtain. The sharp stones scratched at her skin as she bounced between them, her friends plummeting down alongside her.

It seemed like they fell forever through the air as the earth swallowed them whole, the desert collapsing into itself as it roared defiantly. Arianna thought it strange, though, how they just kept falling—waiting for the ground to come.

9

THE AWAKENING

WHEN SHE OPENED HER EYES, she knew she was gone. Dead for sure, but death didn't seem so bad.

Why had I been so afraid before?

The air felt warm here, swathing her like a cozy blanket. And she heard the serene splashing of water somewhere nearby.

There was grass too—smooth and fresh against her skin—the first time she'd ever experienced such a sensation. Arianna would lie there forever, if she could.

And that's exactly what she thought she might do.

It was, after all, her death.

"GET UP!" SAID LESSA, shaking her violently and breaking her daze. "Something's happened."

Arianna jumped to her feet, considering Lessa with her eyebrow raised.

A conjuring of my imagination?

"You're definitely not supposed to be here."

"And where is *here*, exactly?"

Arianna looked to her right and found Jeom, rubbing at a rather large lump growing on his forehead. A battered and bruised Demetrius, Sano, and Solza were also all coming to.

"None of you. No, you're not supposed to be here," she said, scratching her head.

"We should be dead after that jump!" said Demetrius, groaning as he inspected his many injuries—his leg was covered in blood. "We should be dead, period."

"Aren't we?" said Arianna with a satisfied sigh.

She lay back down in the grass, gazing toward the moon. A soft breeze enveloped her, and she felt drunk with a happiness that surged from somewhere deep within.

"That, or this is the best dream I've ever had."

"This isn't a *dream*, and it's not some family gathering in the afterlife," said Lessa, giving her a sharp pinch on her arm.

"Ouch!" Arianna screeched, slapping her hand away. "What was that for?"

"This is life," she said, sternly. She looked around, a panicked expression taking over her calm. "And we better figure out what's going on if we're going to continue living in it."

She popped a tiny mirror into Arianna's hand for her to look upon her own face.

Arianna couldn't help her sharp intake of breath as she understood what she must look like to the others, skin badly bruised and bloodied—by the light of the moon, her neck glowed red with the reminder of where Sir Vladamor had attempted to crush her throat.

As she assessed her injuries further, the adrenaline from the battle began to wear off and the uncomfortable truth became more apparent with the aching of her sore muscles and the throbbing of wounds across her body.

Lessa had already begun tending to the others, giving their injuries priority above her own.

"*Helthra saludis emencia*," she hummed while spreading an ointment over Jeom's arm where a skeleton had struck him quite deeply.

"Thanks," he said, sucking the air in between his teeth.

"Don't worry, it just missed your creator's brand," said Lessa with a wink. "You should be back to normal in no time."

He chuckled, watching as the magic-laced gel quickly stitched his skin back together.

"Sano, do you have anything left in you?" she asked, gently scratching the avatar behind the ear; he'd found his perch on her shoulder. "I know you're tired, but I could use a hand."

The little monkey hopped down without protest and went to Demetrius' side.

"Thanks, pal," said Demetrius as Sano laid his paws across his leg—his wound was soon replaced with a thin scar of silver. "They got me pretty bad out there."

"You were incredible," said Arianna, humbled by the strength and courage her friends had shown. "You all were."

Looking them over, she felt nothing but overwhelming joy that they all still lived after enduring so much struggle. They had suffered greatly, scarred from a more than trying battle. But she thanked the gods that they had survived this terror at all and would live to see another day.

"As were you," said Demetrius, glancing her way. "I could've never imagined you were capable of so much magic, Ara. Where was that hiding all this time?"

Lessa busied over her injuries now, whispering words of healing without acknowledging the conversation whatsoever. Arianna flinched under her touch—not at the sting of the ointments but at the cold, unfeeling way Lessa applied them. It couldn't be clearer that she was still angry with her, no matter their victory to be celebrated this day.

"Yeah, so go on. What on earth happened to you out there?" asked Jeom, poking at his fresh scar.

"I don't really know," she said, picking at the grass. "Something in me just… snapped when I saw his army racing toward you all, defenseless. He said he would let you live."

Lessa scoffed. "This coming mere moments after he nearly killed you," she said. "How trustworthy did you think he'd be, a slave to the dark?"

Arianna gave a small whimper of pain as Lessa made sure her last bit of aid stung the worst before she walked away to tend to her own ailments.

"He was trying to *turn* me with the *Onasyuda* spell," retorted Arianna. "Didn't you recognize it?"

"I didn't have any room to think about what he was doing," she snapped back as she dabbed a green gel over a cut at her knee. "You stopped breathing, and you wouldn't wake up." She paused, looking her square in the eyes. "I didn't think you'd wake up, so *apologies* if my focus was swayed."

Arianna softened, seeing Lessa's pain quite clearly. The shock of the earlier events, of the close calls, still hadn't worn off—everyone would deal with this in their own time and in their own ways.

What's more, she knew they hadn't seen what she saw during those life-changing moments; they didn't witness Liam guiding her back from the dead, and they hadn't understood her internal battle with destroying the darkness that she'd carried with her for far too long.

They would probably never fully understand, but Arianna could, at least, empathize with them. They had struggled in many ways too.

Feeling helpless to aid a friend in their moment of need was no easy burden to bear while also battling to live—the loss of Solomon and Keeper Kassime had taught her that firsthand.

"I'm sorry I put you through all that," said Arianna. "But I resisted Vladamor's necromancy, and I'm confident in saying that I'll never fall for the tricks of the darkness again."

"You don't have a dark bone in your body," said Demetrius with a laugh. "I could've told you that."

Not anymore, she thought, offering him a soft smile.

"Really though…" he said, "what you pulled out there, it was incredible to witness! Your eyes were glowing like stars, nothing like they've ever done before. Normally, it's just a flicker of magic, but this was much different."

"And Solza too," said Jeom, patting the avatar on the head as she nuzzled his hand. "She looked mighty fierce out there. Saved my butt a fair few times."

"We connected somehow," said Arianna, looking fondly toward Solza. "I've always been so in sync with her, but this time it was like we became one. I felt nearly possessed by the bond, if that makes any sense at all."

"It does," said Lessa, who couldn't help but listen keenly now.

"I could even *see* through Solza's eyes," she said, closing her own to try to recapture the moment. "I could see you all, clear as day, atop the hill through her sight."

"I can't really wrap my mind around that," said Jeom, shaking his head. "And what about the desert, Ara? How did you bend it to your will like that?"

"I don't… quite know." She felt her cheeks redden at the attention. "But it definitely had to do with our link. I was connected with the earth, as if it were an extension of me. I just knew what to do without even thinking about it, really. The feeling was so… overwhelming. I don't know how I found the strength to let go."

"Well, you sure had Vladamor running scared by the end!" said Demetrius.

"Not without some serious help." Arianna nodded toward Lessa, and everyone turned their attention to her.

"I can't say that Sano and I had quite as strong a connection as what I saw out there with you," she said, biting her lip as she thought. "But something new did happen to us too." She began to repack the remaining remedies. "His mind linked with mine, like it had done before once when I accidentally healed myself in the attic. But, this time, I felt as if my magic could lasso the wind if I so chose. It was the most power I've ever controlled in my life." She lifted Sano into her arms. "Who knew such a little healer could hold so much magic?"

"Well, I won't complain about their timing to show off their true colors," said Jeom. "That's for sure."

"Here, here," said Arianna, drinking out of a canteen of water before passing it around. "You boys were really something to watch too, you know." She looked at Jeom. "The power you can wield with your axe was incredible to watch. I wonder what other magic it holds? And, Demetrius, your skill with your staff had me dizzied by the end. I thought you might turn those skeletons inside out!"

"Speaking of '*end*,'" said Jeom. "How did it?"

"What do you mean?" said Arianna with an incredulous smile, pulling back her hair to rub at the healing bruises on her neck. "You were there, weren't you?"

He rolled his eyes.

"I *mean*, what had Vladamor so scared that he ran from you like that? I saw he had ahold of you, but then he just let you go and seemed to be fleeing for his life."

The others nodded at his statement, waiting for an explanation.

"Oh, *that*," she said with a nervous laugh. "I always seem to forget that you can't see them as well... but the necromancer could."

"See what?" asked Demetrius, cocking his head to the side.

"Ghosts," breathed Arianna. "Somehow they appeared in the desert. They said I freed them from Vladamor's magic, and they scared him away. He was *absolutely* terrified of them." She shrugged her shoulders. "I don't know what I did to earn that credit, but they introduced themselves as the elves from the Nicora clan. I spoke to the elf lord himself, Master Lethander."

"Don't kid me!" said Lessa, gawking.

"Elf ghosts or otherwise," said Jeom, shuddering from head to toe, "not my cup of tea."

"Of all we've just been through, and you're still afraid of ghosts? *Benevolent* ghosts at that… which you can't even see!" Demetrius slapped his hand to his forehead. "How are we brothers?"

"Beats me," said Jeom with a playful shove.

"Well, go on then. What did they say?" said Lessa, holding her breath.

"They said that war was coming… again," said Arianna, the seriousness weighing on her as she thought back to that surreal moment. "And that we needed to ready an army to have any chance to survive and win back the Olleb."

"An army?" said Demetrius, his eyebrows furrowed.

"They didn't hand you another prophecy, did they?" said Jeom, his shoulders slumped.

"No!" said Arianna, unable to help her snort of laughter. "Thankfully, no. There's only the one that I know of. But… Master Lethander *did* happen to mention the Golden Rule."

Everyone grew quiet.

"He said that they wouldn't rest until the Olleb was safe again, so I fear that this prophecy is racing us to the finish." She sighed. "We can either get ahead of it or be trampled by the chaos it's leaving in its trail."

"Maybe we shouldn't avoid it anymore, then," said Jeom, turning quite serious himself. "Maybe next time, we bring the fight to them." He fingered the tube at his side concealing the

Axe of Crissy. "At this point, who cares if the prophecy truly has anything to do with us or not? In fact, this *isn't* about us. But we're so tangled up in this mess now that we can't keep playing both sides. Either we own this fight, this *war*, or we run from it as best we can."

It was one of the wisest statements Arianna had ever heard come out of his mouth. A stillness followed his words, and she realized they all *must* be thinking the same thing—if even Jeom could draw such a conclusion.

She knew what path her heart was leading her down, and she was ready to face it now. No longer conflicted between the ghost of a life she had once dreamed of as a child and this reality that King Devlindor forced upon her—she thought to the future, putting her grief and anger to the side to make room for the bigger picture.

In truth, her life as a warrior-slave, as a South Luose highlife, *and* as a guardian on the run were one and the same once she stripped them down bare. They were lives all driven by a tyrant king, his decisions and her reactions ultimately forcing her to this present. Arianna understood destiny then, understood better what Jacob and Damon had tried to show her in the Vanishing Tunnels long ago.

There's no changing course. It's what we make of it by the end that matters.

She felt it in her bones that with every move King Devlindor made and every result that followed, one day their paths would collide. But now, after being shoved this far by fate, Arianna decided she'd make sure that nothing was left again to chance, if she could avoid it. *Down with the King.*

"Before we started our journey, I watched Solza give life back to the Olleb," she said with vigor. "Her magic helped a piece of the forest return back to its former glory. It was… magnificent, really. I wanted to tell you about it sooner, but I couldn't with Eli around."

She glanced to the avatars snuggled together, seeing them in a new light.

"There's no doubt that Sano has healing magic of his own, and now Solza too… I know there's an opportunity here for us to rise against our oppressors with such restorative powers on our side, especially after what Lessa and I experienced during the battle with Vladamor."

Demetrius whistled. "That's incredible, Ara. She truly brought life back to that dried-up desert? I don't think I could've even done that with a thousand years in front of me."

Arianna nodded.

"Kassime had said that Solza might be most in tune with the earth, and Sano the air, by nature of their physical forms," said Lessa, remembering their lessons. "Elemental magic. I know Sano can heal, but now Solza too… I guess I never realized how powerful they really are."

"*You* really are," said Demetrius. "Without the both of you, they wouldn't even be here at all, remember? They can only exist alongside a rightful avatar master. They chose you, and now you're one and the same."

"Fair point," said Jeom, crinkling his eyes as he studied Sano and Solza with new consideration.

"There's more," said Arianna, clasping her hands at her front. "Vladamor called me an animancer just before he fled. He said that I had *mastered* an element." She shook her head. "Though I have no clue what he meant by the first, I know what he meant by the latter." She turned to Lessa. "The bond that we share with our avatars is truer than we can probably fathom, and their magic is growing fast."

"With that kind of power on our side," said Demetrius, "we could heal the land. Do so much good."

"*And* we could have an opportunity to kill the King," said Arianna, firmly, touching eyes with them all.

The statement seemed so heavy and so strange to speak out

loud, such words never uttered before by any of them.

For a moment, nobody immediately replied; Arianna could see her friends wrestling with the strange reality that was their shared existence. Somehow they had each found themselves at the beginning of what might become a literal war for peace, power, and justice for all. Four children of the Olleb could rise against a mighty tyrant in the hope that the world would be better for it.

It seemed so unthinkable, yet it was their truth—if they cared to accept it.

"The King will come after us with more might than ever before once he knows of our secrets," said Lessa, taking a deep breath. "When that day comes, I fear that one way or another, this prophecy will pass. Kassime said that we set it into motion, so if we can help to see it through, I wouldn't protest. I just hope we come out on the right side of this, for all our sakes." She hugged Sano to her chest.

"We will," said Demetrius, giving her a squeeze around the shoulders. "Something tells me we'll fare just fine."

"So that's it, then?" asked Jeom, resting on his arms—Arianna thought him much too comfortable with the idea floating about. "We're going to murder our High King?"

"Not *murder*," said Lessa, cringing. "You can be so glum sometimes, truly, Jeom."

"Call it what you will," he said, waving her off. "If we're keeping positive, the goal is that he'll lose his head before we lose ours. Tell me I'm wrong."

Lessa scoffed but said nothing.

"Unfortunately, you're quite right," said Arianna, resigned to his lack of eloquence. "We have to try. Our lives are at his mercy either way, so rather than waiting for him to keep chasing us down, we need to prepare for what's coming, ready ourselves. We're Guardians of Gold with the help of avatars on our side, and I believe our duty is to do more than just sit back on a heap of knowledge." Her hand lay atop Solza's back, the hum of her purr sending a calm throughout her body as she thought again of Master Lethander. "We're supposed to fight. That's *our* role in this."

Arianna gazed at her hand, the brilliant mark of the dragon giving her inspiration and hope—and she knew her friends felt the same.

In this moment, no matter their emotions, their fears, or their differences, the resounding bond of their oath as guardians and their passion to protect their makeshift family took hold fiercely.

Arianna cleared her throat, taking a deep breath.

"So… are you all with me, then?" She balled her fist and placed it over her chest.

"Couldn't be rid of us if you tried," said Jeom, making a fist just the same; Lessa and Demetrius raised their own in agreement without hesitation.

"Hail to the World! Hail to Olleb-Yelfra," they rang out, the avatars singing alongside them with their hearts.

"NOW THAT WE'VE GOT THAT SETTLED," said Jeom, puffing out his chest as he tried to shake off the show of emotion, "where do you suppose we can get an army up here?"

Demetrius stood, limping a few paces forward; his mouth fell open.

"I think we've got a few more mysteries to solve before we can tackle that one, brother," he said. "But at least we got that talk out of the way. Now maybe we should talk about this…"

Arianna went to his side and realized that they were perched on top of a tall, grassy hill. Peering down, she witnessed a land so beautiful it shouldn't have been real to their world in any lifetime, even covered in shadows.

This high up, there was a full view of the most extraordinary backdrop she had ever dared to dream of; a lush rainforest—edged by an endless body of water, with dark waves lapping at its shores and the reflection of stars twinkling in its depths—wound down all around them. It reminded her so much of the little wonderland Solza had created from the ashes of the forest, though on a much grander scale.

Maybe this is a glimpse of the new world... should we achieve our goal.

Rivers of water jutted out in every direction, a maze twisting across green lands and all leading to the same pool of ocean. And tall trees sprung up from the ground, ornamented with courageously colorful flowers.

"I think it's an island," said Demetrius as everyone craned their necks for the best view.

It was hard to see everything clearly without the sun to guide them. But, most importantly, there was no necromancer, no skeleton army, and no foreboding desert to be found—Arianna saw only gorgeous green life.

She'd heard of such a thing as an island, but there were only a few noted in the Olleb that she knew of; and none of them had ever been depicted to be such a treasure as this. Most were nearly destroyed by their inhabitants.

"An island?" said Jeom, his lips scrunched with bewilderment. "All right, can someone now *please* explain what in the King's name just happened here?"

A sudden wave of shock seemed to pass over him; his finesse from their earlier conversation was quickly replaced with something more familiar.

"How do you explain jumping into a meteorite crater in the middle of a desert and landing on a beachfront?" He put his hands to his head as if to squeeze out the answer. "Just... no. Impossible."

"Did you say a spell, maybe?" said Arianna, turning to Lessa.

"This has to be our magic. Did you feel anything?"

"Nothing at all," she replied with a bite to her tone—it was evident Lessa was still a little mad. "I was too busy falling to my death to think of anything worth saying."

"I didn't either. My mind was completely blank when we jumped."

Arianna paced back and forth, trying to think of something sensible. Nothing surfaced.

"I haven't the slightest clue as to what just happened," she said, laying a hand across her chest to feel the death-defying drum, "but what I do know is that our hearts are still beating." She smiled. "We are, in fact, alive."

"For now," said Jeom. "Until the next monster shows its teeth."

"Then we'll destroy that one too," she said with a nod in his direction.

He returned it, a seriousness in his eyes.

"Let's get some rest," suggested Demetrius. "A lot happened today, and wherever we are, I'm sure it's the safest place we could hope to be after the night we've had."

Lessa relaxed back on the grass, gazing up at the sky. "Up high, where no one can see us," she whispered.

As the four lay together, basking in the stars, it wasn't long before exhaustion overcame them. And when no threat showed its face, they each gave into a pending trust with this island—it seemed that they'd at least be safe for one night, the universe gifting them a break from the constant dangers that came hand in hand with stolen freedom.

"This is the last time I'm saying it," said Lessa, fighting sleep. "Never leave us like that again, or you'll have a lot more to worry about than what a necromancer or evil king can do to you."

Arianna didn't respond—she couldn't make any more promises like that. Not with the future they'd decided on.

"*And,* ladies and gentlemen, the adventure continues." Jeom sighed, rolling over and almost instantly falling into a fit of snores.

"She'll come 'round," said Demetrius. "You did what you had to. But we're not ready to let you go just yet."

"We're alive," Arianna said toward the sky. "That's all that matters now."

Just survive.

For at least this one night, she had no more wants or wishes, no more fears or doubts.

There was only a peaceful present that she had fought with every fiber in her body to earn—and though she had no idea where exactly 'here' was, there wasn't any other place in the world she'd rather be in this moment.

PART TWO

IO

THE OASIS

THE SUN BEAT DOWN, hot and heavy, forcing Arianna from her corpse-like sleep the next morning. Her body ached with every movement, and her skin felt too warm as she dared to open her eyes to another day.

She sat up and her breath caught in her throat as a bright blue sky and a deep orange sun smiled down at her. She had half expected to wake once more surrounded by black sand on all sides, half expected she'd dreamed yesterday's happenings. But with the mesmerizing sound of waves pounding at a shore somewhere nearby and the beating of warm wind against her face, she knew this was no dream—no death at all.

This was indeed *life*, as sweet and as welcoming as it had ever been. And she didn't want to waste one more second of it lying down.

She stood, jammed her robes inside her pack and rolled her pants up to her knees so that her legs could breathe; she noticed her skin had slightly darkened around her ankles, lines identifying who she had been yesterday and the defiant difference between then and now.

She slipped on her boots and jiggled Solza awake; Jeom and Lessa were still fast asleep, but Demetrius was already up and exploring. He sat with his legs dangling over the edge of the cliff. Arianna joined him, leaving Jeom and Lessa to have the pleasure of rising naturally to the sun.

"I can't believe this is our life sometimes." Demetrius didn't take his eyes off the backdrop as she sat down. "It's been a difficult road, but I regret nothing."

She smiled at him and then turned to fully see what he saw—without the haze of a battle wearing off or the weight of exhaustion distorting her view, her heart opened wide to really witness where she was. She reflected on every hardship, every fight that had led to such a spectacular vision; it had all been worth even just this single second in time.

"I regret nothing at all," Demetrius mumbled again, laying his hand atop hers.

Arianna didn't reply, struck silent in the face of sheer, natural beauty.

She had learned in a very short time that Olleb-Yelfra held tight to many secrets. And to constantly uncover them was not without its consequences. But every experience, good or bad, had allowed them to grow and mature, ultimately paving the way for dazzling moments and memories such as this.

It's all been worth it, hasn't it?

"There are many things I regret… but this is not one of them," said Arianna after a while.

A new world stretched out before her under this sundrenched setting, a luscious landscape complete with twisting trees and vines of flowers covering every sheet of rock within sight. The sun was closer than it had ever been—a hot, bright, golden yellow. It made visible what looked to be miles of untouched land.

The waters were so blue that they looked to be made of dye. And Arianna even spotted a waterfall thundering down alongside their cliff, warm sprays caressing her skin as white, puffy clouds of water rose high into the air from a bottom she couldn't see.

Lessa snuck up behind them, another witness to this magical morning. There was a long silence before she finally spoke.

"Ready?" she asked, a sharpness lingering in her voice.

Arianna flinched, drawn out from her blissful daze to the reality that Lessa had yet to fully forgive her, even after a good night's rest.

There were hard discussions to be had, choices to be made, and new paths to be forged out of what life had handed them. But she hoped that, perhaps, they would become stronger for it, that these hardships that strained their relationships now wouldn't have any true lasting effects.

"We're ready," said Demetrius, getting to his feet with a helping hand from his brother; Jeom gave Arianna a grunt of recognition and followed at Lessa's heels as she took the first steps down toward another unknown destiny.

AS THEY BEGAN TO DESCEND the steep, grassy cliff, Arianna remembered the last descent, not long ago, that had sent this adventure into full motion. Her mind lingered on the enchanted glass tunnel leading out of the City of Undor and to their final escape from the Jar, spiraling their lives away from the bitter mountains.

Her mind raced onward now to this strange present they had somehow landed in. At the very least, she was thankful for their current situation, to be free of the consuming desert and Sir

Vladamor's sure wrath. But there was truly no sensible explanation as to why—none except that magic must've played a part, regardless of if it had been intended.

They walked in silence for over two hours pondering the 'how,' carefully placing their feet and hands as they climbed down the large hill and through a vast tunnel of trees.

Absorbed in her thoughts, Arianna lingered for a moment on Eli. *Had he escaped the desert? Could he have survived the earth-shattering tremor I caused?*

Would she ever see him again, the man who had saved her life more than once, yet had also stolen the biggest secret of the world from her… along with a kiss?

Her heart grew heavier still, her mind darkened from far more terrifying realities.

Liam was dead. The man she had loved for such a short time and the friend she had loved for always—*dead.* The boy who had given her courage and friendship as a child-slave was now just a memory, though a fresh and painful one that encouraged her still.

And to what end? *Solomon Bell.*

When her mind wasn't reeling with questions about her master fallen from grace, it was plotting its revenge on the Wolf of the East, the General of the Warrior's District.

In her present, Solomon didn't exist anymore, not with Liam gone. He only existed in her past, and she would see to it that he stayed there—she'd avenge the loss of both the men she had loved.

If securing the Guardians of Gold means striking down Master Bell in the process, should he stand against us again, then so be it.

There were obstacles in their path, Solomon and Sir Vladamor proof that they wouldn't be simple to conquer. But this journey had uncovered powerful truths that wouldn't be easily buried again.

The Olleb was on their side, fighting to be heard, and that

alone gave Arianna the motivation she needed to keep going. However, it was hard to ignore the looming outcome of such a war—she and her friends would one day either be named victors or be declared dead. This was a fact that couldn't be refuted, and both possibilities made her uneasy… she never asked for any of this.

I just want my freedom.

Alas, no matter what they did to try to reach it, they would always be playing at the King's game.

Win or die.

She had faced Death many times now, and it no longer frightened her in the way it obviously did the King. He had been running all his life from the day when his heart might stop beating, taken every precaution to save himself from going cold. And in doing so, he had ensured that his life would one day come to a brutal and bitter end.

Arianna just hoped, with all her beating heart, that whatever afterlife awaited him, it would be just as forgiving and kind as he had been to his precious Olleb—*and* she hoped she had a part to play in putting him there.

IN NO TIME AT ALL, they reached the bottom of the winding cliff and followed one of the many rivers through a muggy forest filled with plant life she didn't have names for. Blossoms of every shade sprouted from the trees, and large, spiky, green leaves provided them cover from the sun.

When the river dissipated along with the jungle, they found themselves wading through a patch of tall, wild grass licking at their sweat-drenched skin and sticking to their clothes. Breaking through to the other side, their feet planted on a beautiful beach decorated with multicolored stones—Arianna thought they were stones anyway, but as she bent down for a closer look, she found they were more like thick, smooth crystals, heavy and rich in color.

She could see straight through them, like the glass window-panes from their enchanted attic, an assortment of twinkling hues. As the shore grew closer to the water, the stones dissolved into a stretch of sparkling, white sand.

The glass-stone beach then met the bluest water Arianna had ever laid eyes upon. Up close, it was as if a painting of a sea had come to life right before her eyes, with strokes of every azure shade one could imagine. Water lapped at the sand, glittering as it took on the weight of some of the straggling, shimmery crystal pebbles.

Arianna sucked at the warm, salty air. It revitalized and awakened her, bringing her back to the present and out of her mind's dangerous desires for justice and revenge.

She watched the waves, hypnotized by their calming motion, never having before witnessed such a magnificent body of water as the sea. She had seen paintings, of course, and dreamed of such beauty, and even at times imagined the Black Sand Desert as a sea in its own right—but this was real.

An ocean of water as large as the land of the Olleb herself, she thought.

"We're just at the edge of the trees now," said Demetrius, gazing back at the jungle. "I don't see any paths on this side. It's completely overgrown."

There had been nothing on their journey across the island to suggest any human had ever set foot there. It was completely raw with nature—enthralling, enticing, and frightening just the same.

Jeom sighed in annoyance.

"I imagine we'll have to go back there to find food," he said, pulling strands of grass from his clothes. "Surely, there must be something."

His stomach roared, and only then did Arianna realize her own hunger.

"Don't forget to count the sea," said Demetrius. "Anyone ever learn how to fish before?"

"And where do you suppose we would've learned that?" said Arianna, hands on her hips.

"I might give it a shot." Lessa patted the bow at her back— its blue and silver designs glimmered as it caught the sun.

Jeom raised an eyebrow at her. "We'll at least need to craft some kind of net," he said. "Unless you want to spend quite some time fashioning new arrows."

Lessa kicked off her shoes and stepped into the shallow edge of the water. Swinging her elegant bow around to her front, she nocked an arrow, pulled back and let it fly.

"I'm in need of some new arrows," she mumbled, gaze glued to the water. "Be my guest, creator."

She was clearly still frustrated, consumed by her own anger or fear. But with the release of that arrow, it seemed she was able to, at least, let *some* of her stress go.

Little by little.

Arianna hoped they'd all find their way back to normal before something else terrible happened.

"I don't think we'll be going anywhere anytime soon," said Demetrius, nudging Jeom in the side. "You'll have plenty of time to work on that craft."

There was a moment of silence as they all let that realization sink in—they were on an island, surrounded from all sides by water, and Arianna hadn't noticed any other landmarks from their aerial view earlier in the day.

It seemed as if life would never stop handing them puzzles of the extraordinary sort, for as it stood, they were very much stranded in what appeared to be uncharted territory.

Lessa pulled the arrow out of the water where its end stuck out from the shallows. A large, bronze fish flopped at the end of it for several moments before it finally died.

"Here, let me," said Demetrius as he took the fish and laid it down over a clean pile of stones.

Jeom hovered over the fresh kill, wrinkling up his nose as he scratched at the stubble on his chin. "I could make you some new arrows," he said to Lessa, "but first, I need wood. And we'll need some for a fire too, if we're going to make a proper meal out of your earnings, Miss Thur."

He flashed her a grin, and Lessa blushed a bright pink, her foul mood slipping away with each minute she stood among friends under the soothing sun.

Keep that up, Jeom.

"So why don't you boys see if you can find the wood?" suggested Arianna. "And anything else that might do good for eating. Lessa and I could stay here to catch more fish and scope out the area."

She glanced down the beach, trying to get a sense of how big this place might be.

"I suppose we'll need to make some sort of campsite here… until we figure out what's going on."

"Whatever you say," snapped Lessa, her smile vanishing just as quickly as it had come.

She turned her back to her as she fastened another arrow to her bow and let it fly, more fish for the taking.

"Here on the edge of the grass will make for a good camp," said Jeom, musing over their options. "Out in the open, where we can see everything, but still reaching the shade of the trees so we don't burn." He looked back to the jungle. "I just don't trust something about this place… I want to be able to see from all sides."

"Fine by me," said Arianna. "Easier access to the ocean rather than having to trek through the trees."

"Good idea," added Demetrius. "And I think I saw some fruit that would be safe for eating. Come on, let's hurry! I'm starving."

He pulled Jeom back through the tall grass with a jolt in his step.

As the boys made their way across the outskirts of the jungle, Arianna and Solza wandered down the beach to leave Lessa in peace with her thoughts.

It quickly became apparent that the island they now inhabited was quite small; she thought that if she didn't have to turn back, she could make it around the entire beach before the sun even started to set. It would take her several hours at best, but she had a funny feeling that there wouldn't be much more to find than they'd already discovered.

She noted a few new things here and there, the scuffling of small, yellow crabs that Solza had no hope of catching and strange, stringy plants washed up from the sea. But other than the glistening water and its inhabitants, and the addition of the vibrant jungle, there didn't seem to be anything else *alive*. Not another soul was present here—not even the *suggestion* that anyone had ever stepped foot on this island before.

Arianna pondered this, nerves stirring in her gut.

If no soul has ever discovered this piece of land, how can we have any hope of leaving it?

Trying to keep her mind positive for once, she forced herself to dismiss thoughts of Sir Vladamor, of her strange and destructive avatar-state, of finding more guardians, of killing a king… and, *now*, of escaping an island.

She skipped a glass stone on the welcoming waves, the waters gently greeting her at the edge; it bounced only a couple of times, adding its own ripple effect to the surface until it ultimately disappeared, sinking to the bottom of the sea.

Arianna turned away from the beach to gaze upon the sloping hills they had descended earlier that morning. They were covered in moss, littered with trees and vines, and dotted with vibrant flowers. But the lack of birds, of other creatures like Sano and Solza, or even the small critters that normally crept across every corner of the earth gave her an eerie feeling in the back of her mind.

Something's not right here, Solza.

Her eyes again found one of the crabs scurrying back to hide beneath the waves; only creatures of the sea showed any proof of existence. And with the rivers snaking the island, the powerful waterfall at its center—it all suggested one thing.

This land is ruled by the sea.

She had never thought such a thing possible, that a piece of the earth could be ruled by anything other than humans, anyone other than the King. But she supposed the desert had governed itself. No man or woman had yet to find control over such a wild, heartless thing.

Arianna couldn't help the prickle crawling up her neck as she lingered on that thought.

Will this island prove heartless as well? Will the sea turn on us if there's no one to control it?

Before heading back to Lessa, she walked toward one of the streams they had noticed on their journey downhill and decided it wise to collect some fresh water in her canteen. She filled it to the brim while Solza drank her fill and then made her way back down the beach, not letting her eyes linger too long on the waves.

The boys found their way back as well, bringing plenty of wood and a mound of fresh fruits to add. Jeom quickly threw together a makeshift table from broken logs, and everyone gathered around to help set up the campsite.

After everything was almost ready, Lessa plopped down on a stone and jammed one of the apples from the fruit pile onto her arrowhead, eating around it in haste.

"This is the *most* delicious thing I've ever tasted," she said with her mouth full.

Jeom greedily snuck a bite as Sano vied for her attention.

"Get your own!" she said, swatting him away.

"Be careful, Jeom, or you'll lose a finger," said Demetrius

with a chuckle, laying everything out.

"Worth the risk." Jeom smacked his lips. "Shall we get this party started then?" He nodded to the firepit they'd arranged.

"Very well," said Lessa, scowling after him. She called for fire. "*Solza ven immito.*"

Pinkish flames licked around the wood, adding an uncomfortable heat to the already very warm day.

"*Yeesh*, warn me next time!" howled Jeom, jumping back from the pile as the fire consumed it.

"That's what you get," she said, finishing off her apple with a satisfied smirk.

Demetrius mumbled directions to himself as he prepared the catch of the day with the addition of herbs he'd plucked from the jungle, always in his own little world when there was nature around. And Arianna and Lessa worked diligently to arrange their belongings for a comfy night's sleep, clearing the area of anything unwanted to make it as cozy as possible—they even wielded their magic to make cups and plates from the glass stones, though misshapen they were.

Finally, when everything seemed in place, they all sat down to enjoy their hard-earned meal. After everyone was served, the four began to discuss their findings under the setting sun.

"Did you happen to see anything of interest in the jungle?" asked Arianna as she arranged food for the avatars.

Solza turned her nose up at most of the food, not taking too kindly to the fish, but Sano was in heaven with all the trees and vegetation around.

You'll get used to it, girl. Don't worry, we won't be here for long. Arianna urged Solza to eat and replenish her strength as they linked minds.

"A whole lot of nothing!" said Jeom, throwing his arms up. "No animals, no birds. Just the trees for company. We couldn't hunt properly here if we wanted to."

"It's quite strange, really," said Demetrius. "Where there are trees or plants, there is always some kind of animal, something to call it home."

"Hiding, maybe," said Lessa, gazing back to the trees.

"*Maybe*," said Demetrius, but he didn't seem convinced. He took another bite of his food. "At least there are fish!"

Arianna kept one eye on the avatars as they explored the edge of the jungle—Sano soaring through the limbs of the trees and Solza pawing at the bark, trying to catch him. Though they expressed themselves quite differently, she swore they could speak to each other; they always seemed to be in sync when they were together.

She glanced to Lessa. *Just like us.*

She recalled the desert battle and the moment she felt her mind truly connect with Solza's as one. The avatars were such mysteries still, their powers all the time growing, and she desperately wanted to discuss this with Lessa... once her mood lightened.

"Oh! I know *just* what will lift our spirits," said Arianna as she rummaged in her pack.

She refused to let Lessa go on ignoring her, holding so tightly to her anger. There wasn't time for it.

Liam is dead.

"Is that what I think it is?" said Lessa, softening a bit as Arianna pulled out a large canteen.

"I added it to my getaway pack the first night we were made highlifes," she said with a giggle. "There was just such a big supply, and I figured we'd need it at some point."

"Well, I don't know if we *need* it," said Jeom, clapping his hands. "But we more than deserve a toast."

Arianna nodded and passed it around, each replacing water with wine in their colorful cups.

"I know that we're all dealing with our own... thoughts right now," she said, softly, "and I know that we're pretty much stuck on an island. But we did something incredible yesterday, so let's at least cheers to that win."

"Not to mention, thanks to Lessa, we're not all bleeding to death on the hill up there," said Jeom, showing off his healed creator's brand.

"That's enough cause for celebration for me!" said Demetrius, examining the silver scar on his leg.

They all lifted their cups, smiles flickering across their faces and denting some of the darkness that had latched onto them from their time spent surrounded by black sand. Arianna sipped her wine, letting it calm her anxieties from the inside out and not taking for granted another night free of danger.

We just need some time to heal.

She knew well by now that Time proved the greatest master of all at curing the deepest of wounds—both body and soul. And as today had demonstrated, time would pass quite quickly here in this mysterious oasis. Arianna just hoped that it could heal them all back to normal before their time here was up.

II

MIND MAGIC

ARIANNA WAS BEGINNING TO LOSE track of the days, forgetting to count each moment the sun set and rose… forgetting to care. The weeks ticked on, uninterrupted and blissful. Talk of necromancers or dead friends, betrayals or phantom armies, and even of legacies to be fulfilled became less and less imperative. Existence was *here*, and bringing such stories to what they now deemed a sacred land seemed taboo at best. For the first time since the Gathering Ball, she felt her hope return and she was in no hurry to chase it away again.

There was no rain to dampen their spirits, no one pursuing them so that they need hide, and nowhere to go so that they need journey. She found that even Lessa and Jeom let her back into their good graces as the days wore on, slowly but surely allowing the conversations to develop as they each dealt with their feelings in their own time. Each worry and dark memory was pushed aside with the aid of the gentle sun and relaxing waves—and, for once, they could enjoy each other's company not as witches and warriors but as friends.

The girls splashed in the waters, swimming all around the shore as fancy fish swam alongside them. The water was fresh and revitalizing, and Arianna moved through it easily—as she had learned to do so many years ago in her secret cavern.

"To think that the district regulators rationed our water for bathing!" sang Lessa as she splashed playfully in the foamy sprays. "How greedy this world can be when there's plenty to go around."

Lessa had proven quite the natural, too, when she had given swimming a try; in no time at all she rivaled Arianna with her agile form.

It was as if she were one with the water, truly absorbed by the sea when she swam. In fact, Arianna thought that Lessa never looked so at ease in her normal life as she did when underwater. It was fascinating the way she had found such comfort in something so new and unknown.

Of course she would best me at yet another talent. Arianna laughed to herself.

They spent hours wading in those waters—day after day—and Arianna felt herself grow stronger, the mighty currents proving a worthy challenge. The weakness that had settled around her after fleeing South Luose was long gone after weeks on this island. Her mind was so rested that she no longer shied away from planning her next escape but delighted in the fact that she didn't yet have to.

With so much time to reflect on all that had happened and all that was sure to come, Arianna found confidence and assurance in the new strengths she'd developed as a guardian. And though she wasn't quite ready to let go of this freedom, she knew that when the right moment came, she wouldn't hesitate. She was no longer afraid of the future.

Let it come!

Arianna glanced toward the shoreline as Demetrius and Jeom battled as brothers—axe versus staff and perfectly matched. Jeom was classically strong, his muscles bulging with every swing. But Demetrius had a nimble step, manipulating Jeom's strength against him in delicate movements he'd learned after much training from both her and Keeper Kassime.

She thought back to Master Tayshin and her first days as his apprentice. Her cockiness had done nothing but embarrass them both; she'd thought she was already some great warrior to be respected. *What a fool I was.*

Arianna had quickly found her humility then. And with that maturity, she acknowledged there was still much to learn.

To think, a year ago I couldn't have even bested Demetrius' skill today.

Her heart glowed with excitement at such a realization—they had all come so far, yet there was still so much to discover; she wondered what the next lesson might teach them.

"I'm absolutely *dead*," said Lessa, floating on her back as she stared up at the fluffy clouds. "Hungry?"

"Naturally," said Arianna, wading toward the shore; Solza ran to greet her.

"Better run," said Arianna, playfully chasing her avatar around the beach, using her magic to twist small strings of water after her.

Solza dodged her with skill, running so fast that Arianna could hardly keep up.

"You win!" called Arianna, hands on her knees as she tried to catch her breath; Solza was nearly out of sight. "I'll get you next time though. Just wait."

Solza returned a roar that sounded something like a laugh, circling back toward the campsite.

The sun grew hotter, so everyone began to wind down for the day—the girls dried off and made themselves comfortable on the makeshift benches Jeom had fixed up during their first stranded days, and the boys ended their duel.

Arianna closed her eyes a moment, soaking in the sun. "And the winner is?" she asked.

"Me, of course!"

Jeom was strutting toward her, wiping the sweat from his brow, muscles gleaming.

"This time," she said, looking him up and down with a smirk. "But what about the last five matches? Don't they count for anything?"

Arianna winked at Demetrius, who tied up his long hair and pulled on a shirt. His skin had tanned significantly after so many battles under the sun; she thought he appeared more her brother now than Jeom's.

"Nope," said Jeom, setting his axe to the side; the sun bounced off its metals in such a way that it appeared to be wielding the rays as a weapon. "We started the count over. So far, I'm winning."

He threw his head back and cackled.

"Let's see if I can't knock that count back a bit tomorrow, shall we?" Arianna grinned, swinging her feet off the bench.

She was itching to get a good practice in with her swords.

"Sure," said Lessa, waving Jeom over. "You both just keep talking, and stand *right* here while you're doing it."

She maneuvered him directly into the path of the sun so that he was blocking it from her view.

She let out a satisfied sigh. "Perfect!"

Jeom didn't move a muscle, and Demetrius and Arianna suppressed their giggles—no one wanted to face her wrath again after she'd nearly put an arrow in Jeom's backside for poking fun at her sunburn; her skin clearly struggled to keep from turning bright red day in and day out.

If Lessa weren't a healer with a constant supply of remedial magic, Arianna thought she would be hiding in the trees for the rest of her time here… however long that might be.

"You know you're bleeding, right?" Lessa squinted up at Jeom, shielding her eyes as he shifted on his feet.

"Am I?"

"On your knee," she said, examining the wound.

Both Jeom and Demetrius had resorted to ripped pants and no shirts to keep from overheating during the long days, so their skin was quite exposed to the elements.

"Hmm... didn't even notice." His knee was gushing a good amount of blood. "Must've scraped it during the duel."

"Nice work," said Arianna with a poke at it. He hissed. "Looks like you're getting soft, Jeom."

"Please!" he said, banging on his chiseled chest. "Scars only make us stronger."

"Here, let me have a closer look," said Lessa, hopping to her feet. "I have something in my bag that can clean that right up, or Sano can work his magic. Which do you prefer?"

"The traditional way! Magic doesn't have to fix everything," said Jeom, marching to the water. He let the waves rush all the way up to his knees, squirming as the salt sank into his flesh. "There, all better. No more blood."

"Fine, suit yourself," said Lessa, rolling her eyes. "But don't come crying to me if you get an infection and a little scrape on your knee turns out to be the death of you."

He laughed. "I can't cry if I'm dead!"

He ran back toward the bench and swept Lessa into his arms, swinging her around the beach.

"Stop!" she squealed in delight, trying without much effort to wriggle away.

"Why don't you make me?" he teased. Arianna and Demetrius met eyes, both with smirks on their lips.

Though they had all grown as close as friends could possibly be given the unusual circumstances, Jeom and Lessa seemed to have developed a fondness for each other that surely ran deeper than just friendship; Arianna couldn't help the blush that rose to her cheeks as she watched the two in perfect harmony. She wondered if something bigger wasn't growing there.

In fact, if she thought back over time, she was sure that there was, and she made a mental note to prod Lessa for more details later.

Jeom must've noticed the audience. He set Lessa on her feet, scratching the back of his head with a giddy expression on his face.

"Come on, let's eat. I know you're both starving, as usual."

He glanced at Arianna, and she pretended to be absorbed with a strand of her hair. Internally, though, she was excited at the thought of two of her friends finding such companionship—that kind of connection, happiness, seemed so far out of reach when they were being hunted at every turn. Love matches weren't much of a priority in Olleb-Yelfra, so for their misfortunate group, it seemed nearly impossible.

"Sure, I'm starving!" said Arianna, too emphatically.

She and Demetrius began preparing their meals. But her mind was elsewhere now, lingering on someone who had shown her similar affections once.

Soon they were seated for dinner, each with enormous appetites after another afternoon in paradise. They rested around a roaring fire, munching the endless fruit collection and drinking down the day's supply of fresh water.

Their tasks were delegated fairly evenly now, so they each did their part to ensure a comfortable existence in this new dreamland life they'd adopted; the girls had caught numerous fish for their dinner, using a net Jeom had whipped up to keep Lessa from losing her arrows. And Demetrius took on the role of nightly cook.

With such collaboration, they enjoyed a hefty meal this evening—just as they had every day since their arrival.

Arianna took a bite of a giant yellow fruit they didn't know what to call, and her thoughts were yanked to the delicious present, relishing the sweet taste; nothing of the sort had ever been available to her in her cold climate homes of South Luose or the Jar.

It was almost as if they'd found themselves as highlifes again, living in luxury and wanting for nothing—well, all except freedom from being trapped on an island. But they were used to chasing different forms of freedom, and that desire was easily suppressed in this present, the peace and quiet not to be taken for granted.

Though time passed them by quickly in this haven, Arianna couldn't help but ponder how much longer they might have left to enjoy it. Her mind was always racing to the future, no matter how much she tried to slow it down. And while her disturbing nightmares may have died back in the desert, they had been promptly replaced with dreams of the face of someone she knew to be quite alive—King Devlindor.

He was waiting somewhere in the world for them to come out of hiding, and she was sure he would find them again... one day.

"Ara, what's this here in your robes?" said Lessa.

Arianna shook out of her daze. "What's what where?"

"I was just looking for the last of the prillyberry juice in your pack and this fell out."

"Oh! I had all but forgotten that was there," she said, noticing the paper in Lessa's hand. "It's just a piece of old parchment I found back in the desert. This was the only thing that apparently *wasn't* an illusion, I guess." She chewed on her lip. "It was the day Eli found me and brought me back to camp. I saw it half-buried in the sand and just picked it up."

"Why did you keep it?" asked Lessa, looking it over. "It's blank."

Arianna shrugged. "I just needed something to hold on to at the time." She averted her eyes, not enjoying the reminder of such suffering. "Toss it if you like. It's nothing but waste and a bad memory."

Again, her mind traveled to Eli and their stolen kiss in the desert storm; it was frustrating how much she actually thought about whether or not he survived after leaving them, her feelings always tossing back and forth between anger, sadness, and hope.

Lessa balled it up and threw it straight into the fire.

As soon as the paper landed in the flames, the fire seemed to spark with a sort of life, a frenzy, spewing out flickers of bright, burning colors in every direction.

Lessa screeched, and everyone jumped back, gaping.

The flames grew unnaturally high until a bubble of glimmering smoke rose from its center to float above them.

"What's going on?" said Demetrius, teetering on his feet, gaze traveling up with the sparkling smoke.

Arianna couldn't find the words to speak, her focus sucked deep into the display.

"No idea," said Lessa, stunned. "But it seems like some kind of magic. Has to be!"

She drew nearer to Jeom as they all watched and waited to see what this magical, mysterious smoke might do next.

It expanded evermore, and as it did, their oasis was wiped away in a rolling sensation and replaced with the desert of their recent past—right before their eyes, as if a veil had been lifted over them, or taken away, they were surrounded by black, sparkling sand on all sides.

A haze hovered over the land, and Arianna mused if this was what ghosts felt like when they saw the world through their eyes; she felt like an observer of a place that didn't belong to them, stuck right in the middle of something that wasn't quite real but must've been at some point in time.

"Where *are* we?" Jeom's words wobbled out in a hush. "Are we back?"

The sands glowed black, just the same as the ones they'd battled over with Sir Vladamor. But the army that stood to face them now was not a skeletal swarm controlled by a necromancer—

these people were alive… and they were massive.

Staring back at them, pain contorting their faces, were what could only be described as *giants*.

They appeared to have the same features as normal men and women, but their bodies were five times the size in height alone of any human Arianna had ever laid eyes upon. They were walking mounds, and their weapons were as big as small trees—long swords made of elaborately crafted stone.

The giants charged into battle without even sending the four a glance.

"It can't be." The scene was inconceivable. She couldn't look away.

One of the giant women raised her sword high into the air—Arianna knew then that she had seen the makings of such a brilliant weapon before; it was crafted of stark white stone and carved with designs that looked like strings knotted from the top to the bottom.

She remembered such craftmanship quite vividly, sticking out from the sands in the desert graveyard.

"No… this is from the past."

Arianna swiveled her head to find the giants' adversaries—an army of darkness, led by King Devlindor himself, raced forward. She could not see his face, but she recognized his crown; he commanded men and women dressed in all black, metal chains dangling from their necks and the King's Crest at their backs. And most bore no weapons, only incredible power flowing from their hands.

Unmistakably, and not surprisingly, the necromancer of Arianna's desert nightmares was also there, though a much smaller and younger version of himself.

He headed up the King's Guard.

Disgust twisted at her insides as Sir Vladamor, along with the greatest warriors of Olleb-Yelfra, knowingly slaughtered creatures of an ancient, enchanted world. Arianna wondered then if those in the King's Guard at present had similar insight into the Golden Age—the guard Solomon Bell would eventually join to be honored with a name such as 'Wolf of the East.'

Was there ever a time that he was truly one of us? Arianna used to tell herself yes. But seeing the King's Guard now, using such destructive magic… she couldn't be so sure.

It was hard to get a good look at the King, so she glared instead toward Sir Vladamor galloping around the area and shouting orders to his army. His golden mask was pulled to the top of his head.

Arianna was shocked at what saw when she looked upon his face—gone were the skeletal features, the shadows that dented his skin. This Vladamor had a fiendish yet handsome look about him, silvery-blond hair spilling down around his face, chiseled features, and a sharp stare that cut like glass.

"That's not like the monster we saw before," said Demetrius, gasping. "What happened to him?"

"Time," said Lessa. "I'm sure such dark magic would take its toll."

"This had to have been decades ago then," said Jeom.

The sheer number of followers the King had who wielded magic was baffling.

"This must be the start of the Shadow Resistance he spoke of," said Arianna, remembering the necromancer's threats. "It could only have grown by now…"

The sounds of enemies clashing filled the void.

"And the start of the Golden Wars," whispered Lessa. "Giants were some of the first to go, the most vulnerable of the magical creatures and the most outwardly defiant of the King."

"How do you know that?" said Demetrius, focus glued on the terrifying magic and the sure destruction of a species unfolding before them.

"Giants were supposedly kind, caring creatures of the Olleb," said Lessa. "I read that there weren't many of them to begin with, and they inhabited lands like the deserts or mountains where they could be sure not to disturb the smaller of Olleb's creatures, like humans. They couldn't blend in and didn't understand the threat the King posed, so he picked them off when they didn't bend to his rule."

"They look all but defenseless with only weapons! Why don't they use magic?" said Jeom, looking wild as a male giant fell to his knees in front of them.

The tip of his sword slammed into the ground, and he leaned all his weight against it—it was then that Arianna understood just exactly how the desert graveyard with the stone statues came to be. They weren't statues at all.

They're the swords of fallen giants!

"These must be the faces of the skulls I saw in the area where the fairies brought me," said Arianna, whipping around to face the others. "Why would they lead me to that spot? It can't have been coincidental."

"Maybe they were trying to show you this…" said Demetrius, shaking his head. "Maybe the magical world is on our side more than we think."

"Maybe," she whispered, turning back to face the slaughter. "I guess it doesn't really matter."

It was torture to have to stand to the side and watch these monsters wreak havoc on innocent people of Olleb-Yelfra. Arianna longed to join the battle as giant after giant died on their knees, shaking the ground with every fall. But they'd been dead a long time now, and there was nothing she could do about their sealed fates.

Instead of shedding tears this time for the fallen, Arianna felt her chest grow heavy with anger over such wasted life. She could see the gentleness in the giants' eyes, not wanting to swing their swords and take human life. They hadn't been prepared for a war such as this.

Though she knew surely that no giant here had survived this

slaughter, Arianna prayed that somewhere in the world another tribe could be hiding, waiting until the day the Olleb was made safe again, just like the desert fairies must be doing.

The battle seemed to collide with them then in a sparkling wave of chaos—the four ducked out of instinct as it struck them in the middle. It felt as if they were bystanders to someone else's memory or to a buried piece of the past. And as the battle raged on, swords clashing and giants falling to the ground, it was made excruciatingly clear who the victor had been.

Arianna lost her breath as King Devlindor galloped toward her, the first she'd ever seen of him. She looked him straight in his beady, black eyes as he raised his glittering sword high above his head, his horse kicking its feet into the air.

He looked too young, though, probably as young as she was now; she couldn't believe that someone barely a man could bring such devastation to the world. *How could one become that corrupted at such a young age?*

The thought of her dark reflection and the destructive powers she'd wielded before crossed her mind, and she supposed it wasn't that odd of a reality after all.

Thank the gods for guiding me down a different path.

But to see the King in the flesh was nothing short of an agonizing wake-up call for her.

"We have to get off this island!" screamed Arianna, clenching her fists as the King gave the final stab to a fallen victim, a smile of triumph curling over his lips.

She knew this was an old memory of a very young king, maybe even still just a little lord while the rightful King Damas was on his deathbed, but something about seeing him now in this way made her feel evenly matched. She had power, just as he had, and she'd beaten his right hand, his loyal necromancer, at his own game.

Unable to stop herself from drawing these comparisons that gave her confidence, Arianna refused to acknowledge that the one she'd named as her future opponent was no longer a boy. He was a man, a *monster*, the High King of her land, and he'd had centuries to learn the tricks of his trade.

She glowered his way, unblinking for fear she'd miss some detail of him she desperately wanted to memorize.

I'm coming for you.

His head snapped up, and Arianna thought for a moment that he had heard her threat; it seemed as if he stared right at her with the purpose of accepting her challenge. But then he spoke, and his voice surrounded her like a thorny rope.

"Raja, finish this filth," he commanded as the captured giants were forced to their knees by the dark magic of his followers.

An elegant black jaguar ran through their invisible bubble to stand at his side; the King's eyes glowed a terrifying silver, as did the animal's. Then Arianna and her friends witnessed what was possibly the last of the giant species being wiped away—with the force of the jaguar's mighty roar and the wave of the sand that buried them.

Arianna covered her ears to dull the painful sound that emerged from the animal. But just as suddenly as the last giant died, the desert vanished in a sparkling '*swoosh*.' Their bubbly haze popped and they landed right back in the present.

"King Devlindor has… an avatar," whispered Arianna, trying to steady her dizzied mind.

"No, I don't believe that." Demetrius' whole body shuddered, as if to rid himself of such a thought.

"He's had years to master all of the elements, *centuries!*" cried Lessa, turning to Sano. "What's not to say that—"

"That what?" Worry wrinkled Jeom's expression.

Her whole body slumped. "Well, you heard what Kassime said. What if the King controls a… a *dragon?* We could never stop him."

"That's absurd!" howled Jeom. "How could one possibly hide a dragon from the world? I hate to say it isn't possible, but a cat shifting into a dragon…" He shook his head. "Nope."

"Do you have to see everything first to believe it?" said Ari-anna, shaking him by the arms—she was losing her control. "Open your mind, would you. We just witnessed part of the Golden Wars! *Anything* is possible."

She started pacing back and forth.

"But even if Kassime was wrong about our avatars actually shifting into something else, whatever that even means, an avatar with that much experience on the side of the King…" She tossed her head back, staring at the stars that had now begun to poke out above the horizon. "He's not just a scared little boy anymore. And it seems that magic doesn't discriminate between good and evil in the slightest. He's extremely powerful, and so are his fol-lowers."

She spoke more to herself, realizing cockiness and confidence would do them no good in this battle for freedom. They needed more practice and a fool-proof plan to have the best chance at achieving their goals.

"How did we just see that?" said Demetrius, still quite shaken. "I don't understand."

"I think it's mind magic," said Lessa. "The flames on the pa-per must've triggered the memories to be released. Kassime was the master of similar enchantments."

"I remember," said Demetrius, beginning to calm down. "He told me once that the mind was so fragile that many sorcerers didn't even attempt such magic for fear they'd go mad or drive others to the same fate. But this was much different than what I've seen him do…"

"Well, mind magic is the giant race's specialty," said Jeom, matter-of-factly.

"What are you talking about?" said Lessa, skepticism written all over her face.

"That's right! I've learned a few tricks from you. You're not the only one who knows things," he said, cocking his head with his hands on his hips. "I read about them in the library when I was trying to learn more about the dwarves. They came up in the scrolls once or twice as comparisons. Dwarves were obviously small creatures, but their elemental magic and creative abilities made up for that in a *very* big way."

He patted the Axe of Crissy.

"Giants, on the other hand, were massive and strong. And their magic proved quite weak, all except for their mind magic. They were revered in the Olleb for their ability to transmit their memories from one mind to the next, should they so please."

"I suppose it makes sense... that they could preserve their memories too," said Lessa as everyone soaked in this new bit of information.

With the stir such magic had caused for them this day, Arianna saw a new light return to the group. She was sure they were all of the same mind, ready to renew their adventure as Guardians of Gold.

"But how could giant magical creatures just vanish without people finding them?" asked Demetrius, looking very flustered. "How can such history just... just *disappear* and nobody remember?"

"Because that history was buried in the Black Sand Desert by a king with too much power for his own good," said Arianna. "The desert is the perfect place to hide a secret as big as the bones of giants. But we know a lot of the King's secrets now, so we'll be the ones to uncover them for the world."

She looked to the dying fire as the ashes of the magical parchment blew away on the wind.

"Nothing can stay buried forever. We're proof of that."

MOONLIT MONSTER

IT WAS NEARLY NIGHTFALL, the water calmer than ever as the moon gently rose to replace the sun in the sky. Everyone had settled in for the night, preparing to sleep; Solza snuggled close to Arianna, as she always did, stretching her long body out on the grass. Sano nestled near Lessa's head, protectively, while she curled in a ball.

Jeom was sprawled out wide, taking up an obnoxious amount of space. And Demetrius lay neatly nearby.

As the fire died down, they all soaked in another spectacular starry night, eyes on the moon with full stomachs coaxing them to sleep; Arianna was finally beginning to wind down from the day's surprising trip to the Golden Age past.

Just before she had slipped into dreams, she was shaken awake by a loud splash in the water.

"What was that?" she said, pushing up on her elbows.

Solza lifted her head as well, bright eyes following her own toward the shore. It was dark, though, and all Arianna could see were the foamy, white edges of the water and a sparkling beach under the moonlight.

The others barely stirred, not nearly as interested.

"Probably just a fish too close to the shoreline. Shall I catch it so that you can rest peacefully, princess?" Jeom snickered, and Arianna scoffed at him.

"Calm down, it was nothing," he assured her, rolling back over. "There's never anything here."

Arianna lingered on his words… haunted by them.

He was absolutely right—there was truly nothing to fear in this place. It was almost dull in comparison to the last year, except for the inexplicable magic tricks like burning parchments tossing them into someone else's memories, of course.

This can't last forever.

They had spent the first few days on the island with their guards up, and rightfully so. But as time wore on, the four had almost completely let down their barriers to the lull of the sun and sea.

Arianna supposed that hers wasn't *fully* down, though, and that was at least comforting. In fact, she appreciated the jolting reminder that their peek into one of the great Golden Wars had given her today.

It kept her focused. She knew she'd need her warrior's heart soon enough.

"I suppose you're right," she said. "We're safe… for now."

She curled over on her side and stroked Solza's fur, letting the motion calm her back down.

"We shouldn't kill more fish than necessary," mumbled Demetrius. "The land would retaliate." He chomped into a pink fruit and placed the pit neatly in a pile by his sleeping space.

"Not that again. The land is *not* going to retaliate," said Jeom, rolling over to glare at him. "We're human, and we rule the land!" He placed his hands behind his head and smiled up toward the open sky.

"We rule nothing and no one," said Arianna, quietly, careful not to disturb Solza. "Anyways, there's no one to rule here, even if we wanted to. We're completely alone on this island."

"Stranded and safe all at once," said Lessa as she lazily flicked her finger back and forth—a whizz of electricity danced in the air above her with a well-practiced spell.

"Perhaps we should discuss what to do now..." she added. "We haven't made a single plan, and after that spectacle, I fear we've been shrugging off our duties too long."

"Our problems will still be there tomorrow," said Demetrius with a playful moan. "No need to rush a future that leads us back into danger, I say. It'll come soon enough."

"We're lucky to even have a tomorrow," said Jeom. "And I'm sure we'll remain that way. We deserve it."

"Don't tempt Fate, brother," said Demetrius. "She's a fickle thing."

"Yeah, we shouldn't leave anything else to *luck*," said Lessa. "Least of all our getaway from this place. I don't care about how we got here anymore, but I think it's time we start thinking seriously about our options to leave."

"I agree," whispered Arianna, the sky suddenly resembling the desert graveyard far too much. "It's time to go."

"*Hush*, girls," said Jeom, a finger to his lips. "Or the gods may realize their mistake and send us straight to the grave in our sleep for such talk of leaving this heavenly place."

Arianna let out an exasperated sigh.

"I don't even know where to start this time," she said, the weight of their 'stranded' problem really sinking in as she gathered the strength to finally face it. "But Demetrius is also right... we owe it to ourselves to just rest. One more night at least. It's not like we can do much this second anyhow."

She was again resigned to the easier option, relieving her mind of the frustrations of having to problem-solve their escape for just one more moon—Lessa mumbled her agreement.

"No argument there, sister!" said Jeom. "No argument there."

His words trailed off into a silence where she knew his mind had rolled back to visions of darker days; the sorrowful memories came in thick and heavy waves for them all, never truly allowing them to rest from their duties as guardians.

It's better this way, Arianna thought.

As long as they lived, and as long as their memories lived, they would be Guardians of Gold. And after Keeper Kassime's selfless sacrifice, no matter how much it hurt at times, those experiences were something she'd never want to forget.

Wake, eat, duel, play, sleep—that was life in this oasis, numbing the harsher, deadlier lives they had before.

But time kept ticking forward, pushing the future closer until there'd be nothing left to do but confront it. Nothing could last forever, and Arianna was certain this gifted sanctuary was no exception to that steadfast rule. They were guardians, and they had learned time and time again that knowledge and magic came with a price.

How soon would they have to pay for whatever grand act brought them here in the first place?

Never forget.

That mantra banged inside Arianna's head, like the giants' drum, drawing their battle nearer until ultimately they'd come face-to-face.

THE MOANS OF THE DYING woke her, as they often did here.

Usually, it was just a dream, a nightmare… perhaps. But, this time, they were Jeom's—and they sounded closer to dead than dying.

Before Arianna could even open her eyes and shake off her sleep, she knew that the darkness had caught back up with them, broken through the protective bubble of their island. It seemed as if only yesterday she had stared into the blackened eyes of Sir Vladamor as he nearly choked her to death, but weeks had already gone by.

Though Arianna had destroyed any hint of something dark taking part of her soul, they still had a lot of work to do before they could say the same about the darkness walking the Olleb. It was everywhere, threatening to take over.

Her eyes shot open, hazy with dreams still lingering in the background of her mind—she tried to focus on the sound of Jeom's voice, searching the place where he slept.

He was gone.

Embers burned in the fire now, smoke rising into the air and stinging her eyes and nose as she squinted to see. Night had fully settled, the beaming moon bouncing in all directions across the rainbow of glass stones. And the wind wrapped around her, not welcoming and warm but with a slight, foreboding chill.

For a moment, Arianna thought she'd imagined the sound of his cries. But when she again looked around their camp, she saw only the shadow-covered faces of Lessa and Demetrius sound asleep. *Jeom, where are you?*

Her heart pounded in her chest, heavy, like the giants falling to their knees before the King—Jeom was missing. She heard the moan again, and she knew without a doubt that the deep voice belonged to him… groaning with a sound that could only be caused by tremendous pain.

Arianna scanned the area and had to do a double-take as her eyes settled near the water. For a second, she quite considered that a dream still clung to her reality, because what she saw made no sense at all.

Spotlighted under the moon, there were two people standing quite still.

It was as if she looked upon a horrifying enchanted portrait…
and one which undoubtedly included Jeom Kane.

Everything about the moment was vivid and alive, yet radiating a sense of pure danger. Blackened waves roared in the background, and dark shades of color glared off the sand in the moonlight—eerie yet surreally beautiful.

But the oddest piece of this vibrant nightmare was the young woman who clung desperately to Jeom, wrapping her body across his as if they could be long-lost lovers.

Arianna couldn't see her face.

The woman held one arm around his waist as he remained pressed up against her, and one gently laid around the back of his head. Her fingers caressed his neck in the most compassionate of ways, as if she cared for him deeply.

Arianna shook her head, just to make sure this wasn't her imagination. But no matter how hard she tried to force her mind to see differently, there was no denying that Jeom was standing with what looked to be a *naked* woman on the beach.

She might have thought them only stealing kisses in the night… if not for the glimmer of blood dripping down his skin, smearing the woman's glowing white skin and covering the glass-stone beach below.

Jeom didn't seem to struggle as her lips stayed glued to his neck. His cry turned to a whimper, and then there was no sound at all.

He was paralyzed in her hold, limp as she took on all his weight to keep him up—a mystery in and of itself, seeing as Jeom was three times her size.

The woman looked toward the moon, peeling her mouth off his skin; her lips were smeared in his blood like a liquid lipstick a highlife might own. She ran her tongue across them as it dribbled down her chin, appearing to savor the taste and the wind on her face all in the same second.

Is she drinking his blood?

Arianna shook off her shock and put on her warrior mind before she fully understood what was happening—all she knew was that Jeom was in trouble. And whatever was going on, he needed her help right now.

"Wake up!" she whispered to Lessa and Demetrius as she jumped to her feet.

She didn't have time to wait, leaving them to come to their senses on their own.

She grabbed a sword and rushed to Jeom's defense.

"What *are* you?" she said, finding her voice as she came closer to the pair—the woman swiveled her head to face her. "Leave him be!"

This is no woman at all…

She heard the others begin to scramble awake farther back down the beach, but Arianna had a feeling that they wouldn't be of much use anyway. With the dangerous way this thing looked at her, she had no idea what might happen next—but she was certain it wasn't going to be pleasant.

As their eyes met, Arianna couldn't help the gasp that came out of her mouth; she was momentarily stunned by a piercing silver stare, as if precious metal were stitched to the woman's pupils.

"What's going on?" she heard Lessa call from behind her.

"*Be quiet,*" said Arianna through her teeth, barely moving an inch as she kept her gaze on the enemy.

She was reminded of the moment in the Nicora Forest when she had first come face-to-face with Solza's mother—the look that this woman gave her sent shivers to her core just the same.

It was as if an animal had spotted her for the first time. A vicious, territorial beast unforgiving of anyone who might interrupt its intimate dinner. And just as Arianna had treated Solza's mother with the respect of a powerful warrior, good or bad, she would give this person, this *animal*, the same respect.

For she wasn't sure at all what they were up against.

She raised her hands, *slowly*, as the woman considered her, Jeom still in her grasp.

"I'm not going to hurt you," said Arianna, laying down her sword. "We're not looking for a fight. Please, just let us heal his wounds."

The woman gave such a wicked smile that it made Arianna instantly reach back for her weapon. But before she could even take a step forward to try to fight for Jeom, before she could even think of what to do, a humming sound came from this monster's smiling lips.

Arianna froze in her tracks—against her will—entranced and paralyzed all at once.

The animal drew Jeom in closer still, latching back on with its teeth; all Arianna could do was watch… utterly engrossed by her mere presence, despite that she was killing her friend.

Red flowing hair covered most of her face and tumbled down Jeom's back in waves of bright crimson, like tumultuous fire flecked with gold that consumed him without forgiveness. Arianna noticed her lips too, pressed against his skin; they were bright pink and splattered with his dark, red blood.

Unable to even blink, she was still gawking at her when the predator finally pulled her teeth away from his neck. Simultaneously, Arianna felt her mind released from the supernatural grip—she stumbled forward.

But even though she could move again, she wasn't quite sure what to do.

The woman tossed Jeom to the side without any effort, his body falling like a pile of rocks to the ground with a thud. He was barely alive, and Arianna couldn't see how he could possibly survive long enough for her to help him; from the look of it, he only had moments to live, and her instincts told her that this fight was going to last much longer than the time he had left on this earth.

The animal turned to face her.

13

SYRIFINA MYR

THE CREATURE WAS NOW IN FULL VIEW. Her body glittered with tattoos of silver snaking all around her chest and lower body, like strings of fine yarn were embedded in her skin. As she swayed under the moonlight, the silver slivers seemed to shine and shift through a kaleidoscope of colors—blue, purple, red, gold, and then back again.

She wore no clothing.

Nothing at all covered her skin except for those shining tattoos, swirling across every inch of her body. Only long, luscious locks joined them; red curls fell over her shoulders, longer than Arianna had ever grown her own, releasing a shimmer into the very air around her every time she moved.

And even without Jeom in her clutch, there was something completely animalistic about her, something void of humanity that made Arianna's fear heighten to a new level. She was reminded of Grinda Risso, one unafraid of death, one who lacked empathy or compassion and only thirsted for blood—that was the worst trait in an enemy, and this person certainly embodied it to the fullest.

Arianna glanced back at Lessa and Demetrius to see if anyone had a plan for retaliation, hoping her expression told them to be extremely cautious; Demetrius took that as his cue and didn't hesitate a moment longer to run to Jeom's aid.

The woman moved so fast then, faster than humanly possible, leaving a silver gleam in her wake.

Arianna wondered if even Sano could have kept up.

One second, she was standing by the edge of the water, hovering over her kill. And the next, she was up on the grass near their campsite, holding Demetrius by his neck so that his toes barely scraped the ground.

He scratched at her hands in vain, choking out for her to let go; she squeezed tighter.

Arianna watched in horror as his green eyes bulged from his head. His face turned an odd color as he tried to form a plea on his lips.

"Stop!" cried Lessa. "Ara, we have to do something, now."

With Lessa's scream, the creature seemed to snap out of its concentration. She threw Demetrius to the side, and his body bounced across the glass beach until he finally lay still by his brother.

The next thing Arianna knew, the woman was crouched down in front of Lessa, staring her square in the eyes. She was so close to her that the fiery strands of her hair fluttered each time Lessa let out a frightened breath.

Arianna could hardly think or move. She felt like she only need blink and all her friends might be dead by the hands of some unknown rival.

Lessa hadn't even had the time to get up from where she slept, still on her hands and knees—every inch of her vibrated with nerves. Her hair fell down around her face, and beads of sweat grew on her forehead as the woman silently observed her. Just when Arianna thought she might bare her teeth again, the creature offered Lessa a soft smile instead, less menacing than before.

It could've almost been an endearing expression, if not for their unfortunate predicament. Slowly, she reached out to push the hair from Lessa's face and caressed a finger across her cheek. Then she leaned forward, appearing as if she might kiss Lessa on the mouth, lips covered in Jeom's blood as they were.

Lessa cringed away with a whimper, squeezing her eyes shut.

What in the gods' names is it doing now?

Arianna shook off her stupor and ran back toward the campsite. She steadied her sword at the creature's neck, preparing to strike, yet knowing her skills as a warrior probably wouldn't do her much good in this battle.

With the next intake of breath, the monster had whipped around and caught the blade between her bare hands.

Arianna couldn't even fathom what type of blood ran through her veins to make her so strong. A sword so finely crafted and so infinitely sharp, stopped by just the palms of her hands. *Impossible…*

She tried to pull it back, but this creature of the night held on tight, observing Arianna with the most peculiar expression as she struggled to regain the weapon—it was as if she was trying to figure out what she was, just as Arianna was trying to figure out the same about her.

The woman squeezed the edges of the sword and yanked; Arianna lost her grip on the hilt, nearly toppling forward with the force of the pull.

She stared up in disbelief as her sword was dangled tauntingly before her eyes, its bright silver metal complementing the monster's markings as if they had been crafted from the same material. The creature stepped closer and let out a hiss, another seducing sound that made Arianna nearly forget her dying friends.

Lessa crawled away to help Jeom and Demetrius while Arianna kept her focus.

"Sano, hurry!" she heard Lessa call from up the beach.

The creature stopped hissing, attention drawn to the little monkey bolting from the trees where he'd been hiding, almost mimicking the speed of the woman—Sano's movement created a gust of wind that made her hair dance all around her, like the arms of an aggravated flame.

When he laid his paws on Jeom's neck, a glow grew beneath them, surely leaving silver scars in their place; Arianna relaxed some as Lessa signaled that he would be all right. Then she turned to tend to Demetrius.

But it wasn't all right…

This creature could kill them all, rip them to pieces in seconds if she truly wanted to. Invincibly strong, faster than physically possible, and skin impenetrable to a weapon such as Solomon's swords—how could they have any hope of surviving such a fight?

Arianna let her head fall back to see the stars, blurred behind giant clouds.

We don't.

She sensed Solza's presence at her side, offering her just the reenergizing courage she needed to face this foe.

"Who are you?" she demanded, drawing the woman's focus away from Lessa and Sano and back to her. "What do you want from us?"

The creature straightened her back, still as stone now as she considered Arianna for a long moment.

When she finally spoke, her voice was just as bewitching with words as it was with a hiss or a hum. "I am Syrifina, mermaid of the seas of Olleb-Yelfra."

What does she mean… mermaid?

Arianna's mind immediately went into an even bigger frenzy. She had read little of Golden Age creatures, but she knew that 'mermaids' were one of them. But nothing of what she remembered from her studies had described what they were facing now—the main fact being that mermaids were *supposed* to be creatures confined to the waters.

Syrifina spoke again, in the most enchanting voice that had ever touched Arianna's ears.

"Your fear is not misplaced," she said, her silver eyes steadfast on Arianna as she dragged the tip of her very own sword across the beach in a mocking manner. "Tell me, child, what is your claim?"

Her expression turned to pure anger as she glanced toward where Jeom and Demetrius lay. Then it shifted into what *might've* been disbelief, watching as Sano and Lessa healed them.

Arianna couldn't be sure what was going through this thing's head, but she knew she needed to try to keep her focus to give her boys a fighting chance.

"My claim?" she asked, really not understanding.

She had tried to sound strong, but she couldn't help it as her words shook in the presence of such power.

"Your *claim*," repeated Syrifina, her words as sharp as the blade in her hand. "Who are you and *why* are you here on my island? Answer well, for I won't waste time on many more questions."

"My name is Arianna Belvedor," she said quickly, pausing only a moment to think. "I… I don't know why we're here. It's a question we've been asking for many suns." With Solza by her side lending her confidence, she knew at least one thing she wanted to make clear. "All I know is that my fight isn't with you."

It's with King Devlindor.

Arianna felt a burst of bravery, remembering the last all-powerful being who had threatened her life and that of her friends. She lifted her chin high, no longer cowering.

She had escaped the wrath of a necromancer, so some blood-

sucking mermaid wasn't going to stop them now. And since Arianna was certain Syrifina was a creature from the Golden Age,
and not some mythical monster from her nightmares, she
wouldn't hesitate to call to her magic this time should she strike
again.

She still had more weapons up her sleeve.

An even more beautiful sound filled Arianna's ears as she
found her nerve—Solza's mighty roar filled the night air as their
minds connected, sending a powerful message straight back to
this creature as the earth rolled beneath her feet.

They'd come too far to let some outside evil stop them from
upholding their duties as guardians; this was not their end, but it
was their final wake-up call… their final warning.

It's time to go. Arianna felt the flicker of magic flare again in
her heart, and she knew the time for rest was over, this gentle
existence settling into the past with so many other life chapters
behind her.

The creature fell to her knees, losing hold of the sword as she
tried to find her bearings.

"We're not looking for a fight," said Arianna again as the
earth settled back into stillness. "We meant you no offense by
being here."

She knelt down to pick up her sword, grasping the hilt with
a sureness that it wouldn't ever be ripped from her hands again.

"But we will gladly oblige if you should insist further," said
Lessa, firmly, coming to stand beside Arianna, Sano perched protectively on her shoulders.

Arianna looked Lessa over for a moment; Jeom's blood
stained her skin and the anger from almost losing their boys
shook her arm all the way through to the bow and arrow she held
at the ready.

She glanced over her shoulder and let out a sigh of relief.
Almost.
Demetrius and Jeom were helping each other up, readying

for battle should it come their way; Jeom called to his weapon, the small tube expanding into the powerful Axe of Crissy, and Demetrius went to get his staff.

They joined the girls, all gathering around Syrifina in a circle, their weapons in hand; she appeared dumbfounded for a split second. But with a flash of a smile to acknowledge their challenge, she moved again like the wind.

"Where did she go?" said Demetrius, pointing his staff in all directions as he turned in circles to try to spot her.

"Over there!" said Lessa, lifting her bow.

They all spun around to find Syrifina perched upon a stone that rose high above the tall grasses that surrounded their campsite. The moon shone down brightly on her skin in this position, so her tattoos glowed—flawless and frightening, all wrapped into one pretty package.

"Speak now, *sorceress*," said Syrifina, giving Arianna the floor. "You've piqued my interest. Why have you disgraced our oasis with this filth?"

She spat the words toward Jeom and Demetrius.

"What do you mean 'our'?" Arianna felt an uneasiness again twist in her stomach.

Syrifina snickered. "It means just that," she said with a smirk, lifting her hand as if to present a gift.

Arianna's breath hitched in her throat as her gaze drifted toward the ocean to follow Syrifina's gesture. Many other eyes, silver as the glinting sword in her hand, glared back at them from what looked to be faces distorted by the shadowy waves of the night.

"I try to liberate you and your sister from their tyranny, and you meet me with fear and fight. Such strange creatures, you humans. Quite strange." She cocked her head, observing Arianna with an odd expression. "Though, I wonder now if you need liberating at all, with the avatar race at your side. And two at that... what luck must you have to win such a prize?"

In a blink, she was off the rock and crouched right behind Solza, stroking her fur. Arianna jumped back, swiveling her sword in her direction.

Solza didn't move at all, didn't protest as she normally would with strangers; Arianna could sense she was on edge, but she remained calm, giving her hope that this creature could be handled.

At the very least, Syrifina had not yet decided to kill them—they still had a chance to prove their worth and avoid more bloodshed for either side.

"You're really a mermaid?" mumbled Lessa, lowering her weapon a bit.

She took a small step forward from beside Jeom, who had yet to recover his courage in the face of this monster; Arianna wondered if she, too, was becoming entranced by this creature's magic.

"I've read stories about your kind."

Arianna shook her head a little, her lips pressing into a thin line. *Not entranced. Just more curious than cautious.*

Syrifina laughed with such a gentle sound that Arianna could have assumed her just an innocent girl.

Such a deceitful creature, she thought.

"There's nothing left in the written word that could ever do justice to my sisters and I," she said with the cockiness of someone who quite obviously enjoyed attention. "Don't disgrace me with such talk."

She was back on the rock now, offering Lessa a warm smile. Then she jumped and was at eye level with Arianna, so close that she could smell her sweet breath on her face and see the freckles on her perfect, round cheeks, eyes fixed to hers.

Arianna felt it then, the flare of silver flash across her own, the scared emotions and the dangerous power threatening to surface without command. *At least it's there… if I need it.*

She hadn't felt it in quite some time. But she knew, without a doubt, that if she called, it would come with a fire.

"Why, you are an *interesting* human, I must say." Syrifina circled Arianna like prey. "Different than most I've encountered who've had the misfortune to stumble across the Island of Idris. You've much unreasonable courage, it would seem, in the face of certain death—"

Arianna stiffened, the others fidgeting.

"I offer you this. Perhaps, I shall tell you my story. It's been such a long time since I've had such the pleasure… and even less time since I've done so and let the listeners live." She giggled a sound like tinkling wind chimes. "But you may yet."

"And what is our part of the deal then?" said Arianna, her sweaty grip tightening around her weapon. "So that we may live?"

She felt the wind again on her face as the mermaid moved, slowing near a frightened Jeom and Demetrius; she picked them apart with her eyes as they cowered away.

"You must tell me your story," she replied, still regarding the boys—her gaze landed on Jeom's axe as he held it out. "It looks as if it might be quite an exciting tale yet, even for an old soul like me." She smiled, turning back to Arianna. "If you please me, I just may let you go."

But when she looked again toward Jeom and Demetrius, Arianna saw something there that was all too familiar in the creature's eyes—hatred and a longing to kill.

She recognized it because she'd felt it not very long ago herself; she wondered what it was about the Kane brothers that sparked such ire in Syrifina. And what was it about her and Lessa that made her pause her attack?

"Do we have a deal?" she purred.

"How could we refuse?" said Arianna, signaling for everyone to lower their weapons.

"Wonderful!" Syrifina clapped her hands, the shrill sound making Arianna's skin crawl.

She began pacing around the beach.

"Now, how to introduce my tale?" she mused, tapping her

chin. "I suppose the beginning is normally the best place to start…"

Syrifina stilled and looked up to begin, the four listening intently as another piece of the magical world unraveled before them.

"A thousand years ago, I walked this very land. This was my *home*. I was part of a small tribe called the Myr. I had three brothers and five sisters and was the eldest of them all, though still quite young, if you can imagine."

She looked them up and down.

"Not much older than you are now, I daresay. And in my time, true *sorcerers*—" she said the word with a hiss, scowling at Arianna "—were revered creatures nearly extinct to myth, holding power unlike anything else. Able to cast, control, and create such incredible, unimaginable things. They lived alone, and people sought them out only in great need. It was a different time than even in the Golden Age, where magic was of common practice and the world had combusted with enchanted life… but it was a simpler time. Much simpler than now, especially for you humans. Driving yourselves into more darkness and despair each passing day."

"So… you used to be human then?" asked Lessa, already enraptured by the story.

Arianna thought she might sit down cross-legged in front of her while she spoke as she lowered her bow further. She knew, despite the dangerous circumstance, that Lessa saw this as an almost inconceivable opportunity to learn.

Arianna focused more now as well, remembering that, because they were guardians, whatever words were spoken next would forever be part of their collective knowledge, something remarkable they could contribute to that history.

Syrifina nodded with a solemn look in her eyes.

"Long ago, I had a human form. But that girl is dead," she said with finality. "She is no more."

"SYRIFINA!" SAID AN ELDERLY MAN. *"I've told you time and time again not to go near the waters at this hour. The tide is high. The sea will be the death of you if you're not quite careful. Get back to work now. The day is yet long."*

"Of course, Father," said Syrifina. *"I just wanted a look."*

She gazed longingly toward the sea as the waves crashed toward the shoreline, seeming to roar out her name to come closer. But Myr people weren't voyagers of any kind and steered far clear of such unknown depths.

They were simple people, not needing nor taking anything more than their island could provide.

Syrifina, young and fierce with spirit, could have sat there for hours watching the waves, if she were ever allowed. But she had responsibilities as the eldest daughter, and staring ruefully at water didn't ever seem to make the list of important chores.

She scurried up the bank and back into the trees to collect the fruits and vegetables for the evening's meal—as routine.

Slowly, she went about the paths she knew well, taking her time to choose only the freshest berries or ripest apples for plucking. Still on the edge of the jungle where the sand touched the grass, she could hear her young brothers playing in the clearing near their home. And familiar tunes reached her ears on the wind as Mother hummed through her day's work.

Every passing sun felt the same, little in the way of surprises… and her worries began to catch up with her now that she was expected to settle in for the same future as her parents. She was older now, soon to be married off to another from their growing tribe.

Her thoughts spiraled with the expectations weighing on her shoulders; in a matter of weeks she would be wed and expected to provide more daughters and sons to carry on the Myr Tribe legacy.

And what a boring legacy, *she thought.*

She was the only suitable young woman for marriage. Her four sisters were just children yet and would probably end up in matrimony with one of their own brothers. The only other eligible women on the island had ailments barring them from carrying on their line.

This was her life, this small world she knew, but it wasn't everyone's world…

Syrifina knew there were others far across the island or nearby over the sea. There were many lands stretching across Olleb-Yelfra that they had procured knowledge of—but the Myr Tribe kept to themselves, as was tradition for centuries before, and for probably centuries more to come.

For what reason, she was unsure. But this was the life she had been given.

Mother always said that ancestors knew best; their knowledge and experience was to be respected.

Still, her mind always wandered to the waters, to the freedom in its vastness and to the mysteries it most surely held. Her world was made bigger by just the sheer imagination of its secrets and of what might lie beyond the waves.

As she found herself moving closer and closer to the shore once again, absent-minded all the while, suddenly grass no longer touched her feet and sand engulfed her toes.

Just as swiftly as the scenery had changed, the voice of a man startled her—so much so that she dropped her fruit basket, berries and apples bouncing every which way.

Syrifina dived after it, the sand scratching at her skin as she tried to gather them before the waves could wipe them away. The wind picked up then, her wild, red hair whipping about so fiercely that she could barely see. When she pushed the tangles from her face, a helping hand offered her the last piece of fruit; she looked up to meet the face of the man who had startled her.

He appeared to be a fisherman ashore. Or a pirate, perhaps?

Either way, he was no Myr man at all, so this was quite a surprise, indeed.

He offered his hand for her to take, but she didn't dare accept. Father and Mother would be irate should they know she had such an encounter with an outsider, and a male at that.

His language was not of her world, but he looked at her strangely, as if he couldn't look elsewhere if he'd wanted to.

No man had ever looked at her in such a flattering manner before. At twenty-three, she'd become less and less desirable. Most girls would be married already with hordes of children to call their own. But Syrifina had always fought that life. She wanted nothing but to be loved, like the oldest fairytales promised—not a future arranged for convenience.

The man gently laid the fruit back in her basket. He was handsome, something dangerous and alluring about his demeanor. She could barely meet his eyes without feeling her skin run hot. Snatching back the basket, she hiked up her dress and ran back into the trees.

Alas, she couldn't help but glance back...

He was still there, watching her go—hand lifted to his heart with a smile stretched across his face.

Syrifina didn't stay away long.

Her curiosity was too consuming to make what Mother would call the 'right' decision. She came back to that very spot the next day, and every morning thereafter, for nearly a month—and the man always came, too.

One day, soon after their first encounter, he had pulled her so close to him that she thought they might melt into one. Their lips had locked in a passionate kiss, and in that moment, she was his and wanted nothing else in life than what this surely was... true love; Syrifina wanted to stay with him forever, and that was her plan.

Soon after, he stole her away to a cove on the beach, and she experienced the touch of a man, her love, for the very first time.

She gave herself over fully to him, and afterwards she fell asleep safe in his arms, never happier.

When she awoke the next morning, he was gone. And in that agonizing moment, her life changed forever.

"AS THE MONTHS PASSED ON, my belly grew big with child. *His* child," said Syrifina with a lost look. She moved a hand to her stomach. "I was forced to tell about the foreigner from across the sea who had used me in the worst of ways, leaving me pregnant, forsaken, and alone."

"What did you *do?*" gasped Lessa, eager for more.

Arianna had to admit that this was quite the exciting change of pace from their monotonous days in paradise, but she was still very aware of who was speaking.

What will happen when her story ends?

"My family banished me for my betrayal," she said. "I had to deliver my baby, unaided, in the woods. I could give her nothing but a name."

She bent her head low.

"Maddison Myr, you live forever in my heart."

"You have a *child?*" said Arianna, awed that a creature that seemed so far from human had ever loved anything or anyone at all—let alone produced a warm-hearted soul such as a baby.

Her gaze was again drawn to the water; there were others nearby whom she probably also loved dearly.

"*Had,*" snapped Syrifina. "Don't interrupt me." She composed herself. "I wanted a life for my beautiful, sweet Maddison, so I left her at the edge of another village in a different part of the jungle. I'm certain her life was long and good. It was the right thing to do."

"I don't understand," said Lessa, shaking her head. "If you were human, how can you also be *this*? A mermaid… an entirely different species than humans, from what I've read. One can't just transform like that, right?"

Syrifina threw her head back and laughed.

"Child, I didn't just *transform*. I am the beginning of the line. Any mermaid, past or present, is a creation from me." She stood taller. "I am the *original* mermaid."

Lessa's mouth fell open, and Syrifina couldn't have looked more satisfied at her surprise.

"Now hush. The story is almost at an end."

Arianna didn't miss Lessa's expression, full of excitement.

Here before them stood not just any magical creature but the start of some of the most bewildering and powerful magic Arianna had so far witnessed on her journey across the Olleb; this woman's age reached so far back in time that she could hardly comprehend it—before the Golden Age, before even mermaids *existed*.

Somehow, Syrifina Myr was the beginning of a magical race, and Arianna had to hear more about her origins.

"With nothing left but to search for my revenge on anyone that had ever given me the false hope of true love, I went to see the sorcerer of the island," she continued. "I begged him to curse the man who had ruined my life, to give me that peace. He asked me only one question…" Syrifina paused, softening her gaze as she stared into her past. "'Are you willing to give your life to this revenge?'"

Arianna identified with her words on a deep level—she wasn't sure what her answer might be should she be faced with such a question now.

"And you were… right?" whispered Lessa.

Syrifina nodded. "I said 'yes' without any hesitation, and I don't regret it for a single second. The sorcerer whispered a phrase in a language unknown to me at the time, giving me a strange, blue tonic to drink. Then he said to me this, and I shall never forget a single word—"

"MYR PEOPLE ARE DIRECT DESCENDANTS of the Goddess of the Sea," said the sorcerer as Syrifina finished swallowing the tonic. "You have Her Grace's blood running deep in your veins. Go to the sea before the moon falls. That is where you'll find your true strength. Then you shall be granted twenty-nine moons to take this man's life. It must be done before a full cycle completes, or the spell will reverse and you'll lose your strength."

"Thank you," said Syrifina, setting down the cup.

As she did, the sorcerer grabbed her by the wrist, drawing back her full attention.

"Once you take his life, the spell will be complete and you shall have your revenge," he said. "Though, I must warn you, it will come at great cost. Once his blood touches your lips, you'll never be able to return to the world you once knew, though you will always have it in sight."

"I never want to return!" she growled, wiping her mouth of the potion.

"That may be so now, but from my long experience, I can assure you that revenge always comes hand in hand with regret. It may be yet a greater pain to watch your world go by without you, never being able to join it or live a normal life again. I've known similar tortures." He sighed. "Alas, I offer you this choice."

The sorcerer spoke in riddles, but Syrifina didn't care about anything other than her task at hand. She had already downed the potion and sensed her body transforming from the inside out.

She felt faster, stronger, smarter… more alive than ever before.

"I never wanted to be normal in the first place," she said, reveling in these new sensations.

Syrifina reached the ocean just as the sun was rising, her soul tugged toward the water by some inexplicable force. It was as if her instincts guided her there to hide, for the sun seemed to put a drain on her newfound energy.

From what the sorcerer had said, she knew that the water would be her safety net, her nourishment. She could sense that in her bones, and as soon as her skin touched the sea, an amazing transformation took hold—she let it overcome her.

Her legs morphed into the tail of a beautiful, fishlike creature. And breathing in the water was the deepest, most energizing breath she'd ever taken in her life. It was in this moment—as a human life was lost and something else was born in its place, not bound to land but to sea—that the world would soon come to discover its first 'myrmaid.'

14

THE SOUL OF A STAR

"BUT, WHAT HAPPENED NEXT?" said Lessa, hungry for more. "How does the story end?"

"Duh," said Jeom, speaking for the first time since the attack; he sounded so weak, and Arianna assumed that Sano's magic to recover a person's blood supply did not work quickly. "She obviously got her revenge."

He narrowed his eyes at her.

"Didn't you?"

"Quite right," said Syrifina with a hiss, setting her glare on him. "You're not as useless as you taste."

She turned her attention back to the girls.

"It wasn't but a week before I found the pirate's boat after scouring the seas. I remembered the deep, orange sail, quite unique on the waters. Almost like the setting sun. When he laid eyes on me, I think I might've frozen from fear. I had waited so very long for that moment, and suddenly I was that *stupid*, pathetic girl again, waiting for him to return."

She shook her head.

"But he just couldn't stop staring at me… and then I realized that whatever human emotion I was feeling inside, I could now easily turn it off. And that's exactly what I did." She laughed, flipping her sparkling hair, and Arianna recoiled from the delicate noise that promised bloodshed. "I needed only call his name, and he came to me without question."

She moved close to Demetrius, curling one of his wavy locks around her finger as her mind drifted elsewhere.

He bit down on his lip with a shaky smile, trying not to cringe away.

"He dove into the sea to rescue me from the waves. I remember his crew, screaming for him to return, throwing out the net for us both," she said in sort of a nostalgic manner. "He moved to kiss me with the waves crashing all around us. Alas, my lips found his neck instead, his veins calling to me, filling my head with an intoxicating aroma."

She inhaled deeply, as if remembering this distinct moment in time.

"The blood tasted so fresh and sweet, quenching a thirst I didn't even know existed until there was no more left of him to swallow. And as soon as I unlocked my teeth from his skin and let the sea claim his body for a proper pirate burial, I felt the human part of me slip away forever. And this new, *strong*, part of me solidified in its place."

She squeezed her fists together and Arianna thought the sea grew wilder with her words.

Syrifina looked back toward those unforgiving waters, the dark waves hurling themselves toward the shore—her sisters somehow stayed stone still, waiting, watching.

"Seduced to his death," muttered Demetrius, he glanced at Jeom, but he averted his gaze.

"I had my revenge," said Syrifina, firmly, "and in doing so, I am forever bound with the sea, restricted by its limits yet strengthened by its magnitude." Her attention remained steadfast on her sisters. "I was able to share my new life though, gifted a new family."

"What do you mean, 'family'?" asked Jeom. "How many more of you are there?"

Arianna nodded to the beach, and so he looked beyond Syrifina for the first time since he'd awoken; his hand flew to his neck—two scars shone where her fangs had pierced his skin, like two tiny, silver gems.

"A mermaid's kiss can transform a female into one of the same, gifted with godlike powers born from the soul of the sea," said Syrifina. "Our bite, however, is not so sweet. I'm sure you can attest… *Jeom*, is it?" She licked her lips again at him, and he brandished his weapon. "I freed my sisters from their wretched lives, so the Myr Tribe lives on with a female bloodline. We don't need males to procreate. We only need them to satiate our unique appetites."

Lessa gasped. "That's why you tried to kiss me before!" she said, aiming her arrow again with such a warrior's skill that Arianna almost forgot her gift was as a healer.

She was no longer curious. She was angry.

"What are you talking about?" asked Arianna, cocking her head to the side.

"I mean, she *tried* to kiss me," screeched Lessa. "Turn me!" She pulled back on the bowstring. "Why?"

"Any woman, sorceress or otherwise, would *kill* for such a life as this," retorted Syrifina, taken aback at Lessa's reaction and clearly offended.

Her demeanor also shifted to one of defense, so Arianna put a gentle hand on Lessa's arm to lower the bow. They weren't out of this yet.

"To never die, to be young and beautiful forever," said Syrifina. "Who wouldn't want such a life? You'd never feel the loss of love again."

"That isn't true," mumbled Lessa as Syrifina ranted on.

"I was offering you eternal life," she growled. "We cannot be killed!"

"Have you tested that theory?" spat Jeom, coming to Lessa's defense.

Syrifina offered him a tight smile, the look in her eyes wild. "I welcome you to give it a go," she said, softly.

She puckered her lips as if to blow him a kiss, and he began to seethe with rage.

With one look at Jeom, Arianna knew something was about to go sideways—Syrifina lunged for him, knocking everyone else off their feet for how swiftly she moved.

But Jeom was ready, his grip on the Axe of Crissy sure; he shouted a phrase that Arianna had only heard him use in the attic of the palace during their lessons. And seeing him now, she was thankful, at least, that he had never practiced anything more than defense with them when wielding his weapon—his power over the axe appeared to have a strong link to his emotions, just like her magic.

"*Protelium ahortor!*"

He slammed the butt of the weapon to the ground, and a golden shield burst out around it, hovering over him and Demetrius like an impenetrable bubble. "Kassime, that's for you, brother."

Syrifina's sisters inched closer—Arianna kept one eye on them.

The ancient mermaid cried out, banging on the barrier for entry; it wouldn't give under Jeom's focus, but his muscles bulged with the effort to hold the magic. And he gritted his teeth every time Syrifina threw her body against the barricade.

Alas, the girls were on the wrong side of this spell, left to face the volatile, man-eating mermaid alone.

Lessa grabbed onto the sleeve of Arianna's cloak and pulled her to the side; they locked eyes with the boys, panic connecting them all.

"And, what of your child, then?" blurted out Arianna to try to sway Syrifina's attention—she knew Jeom's magic wouldn't withstand her strength. "You mentioned a Maddison. Did you fate her to join the ranks of the sea as well?"

Syrifina turned her rage on Arianna, a menacing expression on her face; they were suddenly eye-to-eye.

Syrifina lowered into a crouch, as if she might pounce on her like the wild animal she was.

Arianna sucked in a breath but stood her ground nonetheless, praying Syrifina would restrain herself from ripping out her throat. She thought if she even attempted to lift her sword or call her magic, the mermaid surely wouldn't hesitate—they didn't stand a fighting chance against the wrath of Syrifina *and* her sisters… not without a little luck.

"I didn't curse my dear child to this life," she said, practically foaming from the mouth. "The human Myr bloodline lives on through other names, other daughters, but live it does! I make sure of it." Her stare locked in on Lessa's deep blue eyes and then moved back to Arianna. "She was my one blessing in this wretched life. I watched her grow wise and old, never once heartbroken. And the day she died, her children and grandchildren set her body aflame at sea, as ritual for islanders of Idris. I got to say a proper goodbye… and I daresay she produced some good in this world."

"So, you admit it, then? You've been cursed!" said Jeom, feeling braver from behind magical protection.

With such a speed, she threw herself again against the golden barrier—Arianna saw it falter this time, his look of courage quite fleeting.

"Every life has its own blessings and curses," she purred, sway-ing her hips as if in dance as she circled the boys. "This is the life that I chose."

"Well, it's not what I would wish for myself," said Lessa.

Syrifina turned to her.

"So be it," she forced from her lips. "I always offer a choice, as was the courtesy to me."

She placed her hands on her hips, assessing them all—Ari-anna could see the wheels turning in her head about what to do next.

"I bore of you now," she said with a pout. "And a deal's a deal. Tell me at once how it is you came to be here, or I shall kill you."

"We were trying to escape King Devlindor's necromancer in the Black Sand Desert," said Arianna without thought, trying an-ything to appease this creature's obvious need to be entertained. "And our magic… it just went awry. I couldn't control the power Solza gave to me, and—"

She thought again of that addictive magic surging through her veins at the moment she'd become one with the earth. She called to it now, bringing it closer as Syrifina appeared to size them up for dinner.

Arianna knew by now when a predator was about to pounce or when a challenger was about to strike. Half her training with Solomon had been in developing such skills—if she could see it coming, she'd have a better chance at defending against it. *'One step ahead leaves you alive and the other dead,'* Solomon would say.

She couldn't help it as her mind wandered to him and his lost soul. What would he say now, to see her in such a predicament as a face-off with a mermaid?

"And then we had to leap for our lives," said Lessa, jumping in as Arianna lost her words. "There was a massive crater in the earth from where a meteorite had fallen over a year ago, the only

place to run from the desert collapsing in on itself. We just...
jumped. And when we opened our eyes, this was where we were."

"Atop that hill to be exact," said Demetrius from behind the breaking barrier—he pointed up toward the tallest cliff on the island.

"That's impossible!" said Syrifina, straightening her back. She narrowed her gaze at all of them, as if to will a different truth from their mouths. "This island has been cloaked with some of the strongest magic in the world. Well, this small piece that's left of it anyways."

A sad expression momentarily shadowed her face.

"And not just with my protection. Many have contributed to keep this piece of the Olleb safe from the destroyers of your kind. It's a *sacred* land. You couldn't have just ended up here... *Unless*—" She tilted her head, staring at the hill.

Jeom faltered under the weight of his magic, his shield reversing with a '*snap*' and leaving him and Demetrius uncovered.

Lessa pulled in a sharp intake of breath.

Thankfully, though, Syrifina was no longer interested in them. She floated her eyes closed and sniffed at the air. Then she sucked in a deep breath, blowing it out with a sigh of such satisfaction that it made Arianna tremble. Or maybe it was the glare of silver locking back in on her.

"I haven't tasted such magic in quite some time," she said— she took a slow step toward Arianna, a fiery excitement in her voice.

"What are you talking about?" she said, her nerves creeping back under her skin as Syrifina neared.

She moved again on the wind with her next step, grabbing Arianna by the wrist so tightly she thought it would break—she was frozen in her hold, cringing away as Syrifina sniffed the air around her.

Arianna lost the grip on her weapon, the sword falling to the ground.

"It's subtle, yes," she said, softly. "But, oh, I can taste it."

She shoved her hands into Arianna's pockets, searching for something.

"What the—"

As soon as Syrifina had grasped whatever it was that she was looking for, Arianna found herself on the ground.

She peered up from her hands and knees to see Syrifina holding up the blue stone she'd discovered back in the crater; she held it against the backdrop of the night sky, a look of such admiration in her eyes.

"You don't even know the power you possess, child," Syrifina breathed in awe, angling the stone so that it was illuminated by the moonlight.

Arianna had kept it in her pocket for so long she had almost forgotten it was there; it dazzled with a sparkling blue, glimmering like a star itself.

"What is it?" asked Demetrius, too intrigued to keep a safe distance, craning his neck to see what was in her hand.

Arianna gawked too, realizing the stone held much more complexity in detail than she had originally thought—the light of the moon revealed a different side of the stone than she had noticed upon first examining it.

"This is the soul of a *star*," said Syrifina, seeming to be lost in the stars herself. "And not just any star, it would seem, but a *mighty*, fallen one. Such a beautiful soul. You can tell by its journey map." She angled it in different directions, each time the moonlight illuminating more depth. "It must have lived thousands of lives! I haven't seen one like this in centuries."

"What do you mean, the 'soul' of a star?" said Arianna, getting to her feet, cautiously edging closer for a better look.

It appeared the stone *had* somehow come to life under the moon, rippling with stroke upon stroke of what looked like thousands of golden strings locked inside its glittering shell—crisscrossing to create what Syrifina had deemed a 'journey map.'

Undoubtedly, it pulsed with a heart of its own.

"A warrior of the skies," said Syrifina, beaming at it, "shining its light down from a place that no man nor magical creature has even had the hope to conquer… not until death."

She became lost in her thoughts again, and Arianna wondered if a part of this eternal being didn't yearn for such an adventure as death—something that she could now, presumably, never have.

"Some say that stars are really the souls of noble creatures and humans of Olleb-Yelfra," whispered Demetrius. "That when we die, our spirits collect in the heavens to watch over the world, to protect those left living."

Syrifina gave a small nod. "No one and nothing is *truly* immortal, now are we?" she said with a hopeful look. "We shall all join the stars one day, I'm sure."

Her head snapped in Arianna's direction as she clamped her fist around the stone.

"For one to possess something so rare is almost unthinkable," she said in an accusatory tone. "Such a strong soul isn't relinquished without cause nor care. If this is in your possession, it's because it was fated so."

"I don't understand what you're saying," said Arianna, truly confused now. "How could it be fated? I simply plucked it from the dust out of curiosity." She felt her eyebrows furrow. "And how does this have anything to do with how we got here?"

"This stone is not just any stone, child," said Syrifina in a bout of frustration. "It's a life force! And for some reason, it chose you."

Arianna wanted to bury her head in the sand. "Chose me for *what?*"

Again she had supposedly been *chosen* for something much bigger than her understanding. And again, the knowledge she still had left to acquire in order to master magic was put into alarming perspective.

Syrifina just shook her head with a tinkling laugh.

"I suppose we'll find out soon, now won't we?" she said with a strange smile as she considered her. "However, it is said that the soul of a star can grant its chosen master just three wishes of equal merit, from one soul to another. If it allowed you to find it, then it belongs to you. Use it wisely, child. This is a rare gift beyond recognition. Its magic far outstretches anything you'll ever encounter again in this world. It's not bound by our earthly laws."

"Are you saying that this rock is the reason we ended up on the island?" said Lessa, mouth agape.

"I'm saying," said Syrifina in a whisper, "that her heart's greatest wish was granted." She pointed to Arianna. "From one soul to another. If I'm right… which I'm sure I am… you have just two wishes left."

"Is it true, Ara?" asked Demetrius with a dumbfounded expression. "Did you make… a *wish* to bring us here?"

Arianna thought back to that moment, shaking her head.

"I don't know…" she said with a shrug. "Not consciously. Though, I suppose I did pray we'd all end up somewhere safe, that it wasn't our end. But not outwardly."

"I think we were all wishing that one," said Jeom.

"And thus we were plopped into some magical, protected, off-the-map haven? Makes sense," said Demetrius with a little laugh to himself.

Syrifina still held tight to Arianna's stone.

"Ah!" she screeched, her fist opening—it dropped to the ground to lie with the other rocks of the beach; Syrifina's palm was glowing red.

"It… it burned me," she cried out. "Why, that's the first time I've felt pain in centuries!" She began to laugh wildly then, dancing in circles, her arms out wide, with unconstrained excitement.

"It must use protective magic like the Axe of Crissy," whispered Jeom, stepping closer to Arianna. "It belongs to you."

"Indeed it does," said Syrifina with a snicker, her dance coming to an abrupt halt; Jeom stiffened. "Though... I daresay I can't fathom why such a wondrous gift would be bestowed to someone so—"

"So *what?*" Arianna fought her impulse to test this wicked-mouthed creature in a fight now that she had new magic on her side.

Syrifina laughed her musical laugh again, throwing her head back—it seemed as if the sea rippled with the sound, her control over the water mystifying but undeniable, nonetheless.

"I would say, undeserving. But I suppose that your story isn't yet finished, now is it?"

Syrifina then scooped up some glass stones with one hand and magically manipulated a string of water with the other, until the glass and water melded into one. The result was a beautiful, slim chain, nearly invisible to the untrained eye. But as it caught the light, it shifted back and forth between the colors of the beach, just like the waves of the water.

At its center, the soul of the star was fastened tightly.

"Sorceress Belvedor," said Syrifina, "it is your turn to speak again. I'd hate for you to waste your next wish on saving your life twice over, and I don't think you have enough wishes left for all of you." She gripped the necklace, dangling it there as if it were a treat—or a trap.

Arianna didn't feel tempted to take it; it was hard for her to believe that this little rock she'd found at the bottom of a crater in the middle of the desert held power enough to grant her heart's desires three times over.

There must be another explanation...

She sighed.

And yet, I'm a Guardian of Gold. Maybe this is all the explanation I need.

She considered the idea, and it did seem to fit right in with this new, peculiar life she'd adopted. After all, she was speaking to a blood-sucking, land-walking mermaid…

"What words do you wish I speak so that we can keep our lives?" said Arianna after a moment, hoping for a hint of how to please this monster.

Her heart began to beat faster as she waited for Syrifina's next demand, her life and that of her friends in the hands of another once again.

"Convince me that your lives are worth something to my beloved Olleb," said Syrifina. "Convince me the same as you've persuaded the stars and the sands that this world's magic hasn't been thoughtlessly wasted on mere *humans* without a rightful cause."

Her eyes darted to the avatars, the necklace, and then back to Arianna—she knew that she saw the flicker of magic there as well.

"It shouldn't be too hard seeing as you've convinced the gods of the sky and earth. Now, it's time to convince the *sea* of your worth. And on behalf of the Beloved Mother, I'll be the one to decide if it's a price worth paying."

Arianna took a deep breath, gathering her fighter's spirit from where it had been safely stored this easy month on the island. She glanced to the others for reassurance—Demetrius lifted his palm, the golden dragon shimmering there, with Lessa and Jeom nodding their approvals.

"Very well," she said with courage. "Our story begins here in fact." She gestured to her friends. "We are Guardians of the Golden Age. Like you… in a way. It's been made our duty to protect the Olleb and uncover the truth that once was, shed light on the many lies that bury her."

"And how do you suppose to accomplish this?" said Syrifina, arms crossed at her chest.

Arianna's mouth twitched up in a smile, feeling her next words burning to be released. "We're going to kill King Devlindor, set the balance straight," she said, firmly. Then she laughed. "Well, we're going to try anyways."

A silence lingered after her voice had died away, and Lessa,

Jeom, and Demetrius shifted awkwardly where they stood—this bold and dangerous statement they'd declared together on the day they landed here had undoubtedly slipped to the back of all of their minds, pushed aside to make way for deliciously simple days.

Alas, it had been made quite clear tonight that they couldn't, or *shouldn't*, stay on this island forever; Arianna had to show her face in the real world once again, and that face was being hunted to the ends of the earth. It was kill or be killed at this stage, little choice even left in the matter.

Arianna laughed to herself, thinking that the whole point of freedom was to be able to *choose* one's fate. But this path had been thrust upon her, and the only choice she'd since made was to accept it.

It was the first time such a statement about their challenge against the King had been voiced to someone outside of their group, but they all stood as one behind it, more solidified as friends than ever. Since they had been forced to flee South Luose, their lives snatched out from underneath them, the only option left was to stand up and fight. *Win or die.*

It was in this moment that Arianna felt her power finally rise to the occasion, and she knew it would make for a fantastic show to hopefully win over even the likes of the original mermaid of Olleb-Yelfra. She didn't need to say the words aloud... she felt them settle in her core.

Levantis bora!

With her hands raised, the stones of the glass beach lifted high into the air—it appeared like a blanket of jewels blotched out the sky, dazzling them in a rainbow of sharp colors with the moon's rays spilling down through the cracks.

Solza's eyes glowed bright, rivaling Syrifina's metallic gaze, as she and Arianna harnessed the best of both their powers. The force of the wind joined them, beating heavily around the vicinity as Lessa and Sano showed off their strengths too; the boys grasped hands in affirmation of the girls' powerful demonstrations, Jeom's axe sparkling with the electric magic of the Crissy dragon's essence and Demetrius' smile sparkling even more with faith.

And although there was still much left for them each to learn and discover before they could accomplish the goal they set out for, it was, at least, solidified in this moment as they stood together—the Four Corners, united as one.

"We're going to end King Devlindor's reign," said Arianna; the stones of the glass beach collapsed back to the ground with a deafening sound. "*That* is our destiny, and Olleb-Yelfra knows it."

15

DESTINY BOUND

"KILL THE *KING?*" SYRIFINA SAID with a gasp. Her lips twitched up into a smile. "I'm quite shocked at such a declaration from ones so young."

She twirled a strand of hair along her finger as she spoke.

"The power on your side is surely impressive, I must admit. But his control is tight… why, even I have had such tantalizing thoughts as to try my luck, for fear he might one day try to eradicate us as he's done the rest of the magical world. Alas, thoughts they remain."

"Why hasn't he gone after your kind?" asked Demetrius.

"Because we fled instead of fighting," she said. "We keep to ourselves near this island and away from Saindora to evade his attention." She shrugged. "I don't think he likes the water much because we've lasted quite long."

"Pity," growled Jeom under his breath.

"Tell me something, child," said Syrifina, tilting her head toward Arianna, "others much older and wiser have tried and failed at what you've declared is your destiny. What makes you think you're even worthy of such an honor?"

"I… I don't," said Arianna, shaking her head. "Though every step I take seems to shove me further down that path, no matter how much I try to run from it."

She stepped forward, weaponless and confident.

"I'm not running anymore. It's fated, as you say, and so I'm going to face that fate, come what may."

She looked to her friends, each offering her nods of encouragement.

"This is what *we* choose now. Not him."

"Then you *choose* death," said Syrifina with a giggle.

"Says you who have done nothing more than hide beneath the sea, scavenging for blood!" said Jeom.

"*Jeom*, be careful," whispered Lessa.

But he was on a tangent now, not to be stopped until his breath ran out.

"We've been given the gift of guardianship from people who have actually made sacrifices," he added. "Something you seem to know very little about!" His muscles bulged, spit flying from his mouth. "Our duty is to protect the Olleb, just as much as you've assumed the responsibility to protect this island. And we're not shrugging it off nor hiding beneath the water. If death finds us before our goal is met, so be it. At least we can say we *tried*." He narrowed his gaze. "Let Death come."

"Watch your tongue, infant!" snapped Syrifina, her silver tattoos seeming to glow brighter with her anger. "Or I'll rip it from your mouth and you can meet Death here and now."

Jeom squared his shoulders, not backing down. "I only speak the truth. Is that not what you wanted to hear?"

Lessa and Demetrius were both holding their breath, and Arianna glanced to her sword on the ground; everyone was preparing to defend or fight back should this hot-tempered mermaid attack again.

A snarl escaped her lips, and she bared her teeth like a wild jungle cat.

The voice that came out of her next, though, was *much* calmer, as if two different personalities were enclosed in the same ancient mind; Arianna pondered that maybe there were. Maybe, after centuries of living, one could adapt to their situations at will, be who they wanted to be at any given moment.

Syrifina sighed, her fury dissipating along with her breath.

"It is sad what that tyrant did to poor King Damas, though. He was such a good man, wasn't he?" said Syrifina, almost to herself. "It was a time of peace under his rule. I used to roam the waters near the Palace of Saindora, but they've grown so cold now, I just can't bear it."

It was as if she had transported back to her past, and Arianna wondered what she saw there, wishing she might share her memory with them as the giants had done.

"I loved walking those beaches at night. White, soft sand beneath your toes. Waters clearer than any crystal." She stared into the dark sea, nodding. "And my sisters and I respected King Damas and his laws. We never killed more than necessary and only targeted pirates or scum alike." She looked to Arianna, a pleading expression on her face. "We kept his beaches *safe*."

"I'm… sure you did," said Arianna, trying and surely failing to appear genuinely supportive.

Jeom rolled his eyes.

"*Ahh*, but the City of Saindora," Syrifina cooed, hardly noticing them anymore; she brought her hands to her heart and spun in a circle. "Vines dripping from big balconies, streets overgrown with scented flowers, and so many different colors decorating the town, like a fairytale, if you will."

"We don't know much of fairytales," said Lessa. "But it

sounds wonderful… magical."

Syrifina's smile vanished.

"It used to be," she said. "But now the flowers don't grow there, and the sea is blackened with despair."

"Much like the Four Corners," mused Demetrius with a tight smile. "Do you know of it?"

"I know a thousand years' worth of things, darling," said Syrifina. "The sea doesn't go there. Only ice."

"Then you know why King Devlindor created it, of the prophecy?" said Arianna, wanting to yank every sliver of knowledge from Syrifina's mind.

"I see now…" she said, considering them with a bemused expression. "You believe you are the catalyst to the Golden Rule igniting, the spark which could bring about the King's demise?" She put her hands on her hips, touching eyes with them all. "You *really* do think it's your destiny, that it's quite literally written in ink?" No one replied.

Syrifina cackled.

"Let me give you one piece of advice," she said, turning stone-faced again—Arianna could hardly keep up with her ever-changing state. "Never trust the written word of anything, even prophecies and rules of gold. Ink has distorted many things over time. You may find that a word is written that you *think* you understand, but when strung together with others, there's a puzzle to be solved and no right answer. He who reads the writing defines the meaning for himself, just as he who writes it." She looked to the sky. "The conclusions of men rarely align to perfection, if ever at all." She chuckled to herself. "A woman though…"

Syrifina made a sound like a purr of satisfaction; the words she spoke next were unlike anything Arianna had ever heard before—a soft slur connected each one in a spellbinding fashion, as if they rolled along a wave of water, a language certainly unknown to their world.

She set her gaze on Arianna, as if trying to see straight into her soul to find out if she had what it took to make good on her promise.

"I won't be the one to stop you from trying to decipher one of the longest-standing rules of time," said Syrifina. "It's everyone's right to draw meaning where they can."

She smacked her lips.

"The modern world has not always lived in peace alongside magical creatures, as was in the Golden Age or even in my earliest time, but we were accepted, *known*, better understood and left alone. Now—" She shook her head. "Now, we're almost *extinct*. That is why we protect the Island of Idris. It's a safe place for all that King Devlindor has tried to erase, and we will protect it until the end of time. Even if that means we must one day fight."

She glared again at Jeom—Arianna would be utterly shocked if he lasted the night for how much Syrifina loathed him.

"And when you say we?" Demetrius had a sheepish look on his face; he was trying to make himself small. It was clear he had much he wanted to ask Syrifina, so intrigued by her presence, but also didn't want to end up in his brother's shoes.

"I mean me, my sisters, *and* any magical creature that resides here or should one day find refuge on this land."

Arianna felt the familiar chill of eyes burning at her back.

How many magical beings makes up Syrifina's 'we'?

"This place may be much more alive than I thought," whispered Demetrius to Jeom, gazing around.

"Quite," said Syrifina with a smirk. "And I'd like to keep it that way. Magical things are good at hiding, but rest assured, we *see* you. We've been watching you for some time now."

She swayed back and forth, to the beat of the sea.

"My sisters and I can control the currents to an extent, and we're smack in the middle of an ocean, no land on either side. No ship nor lost swimmer has ever found it before because of Myr magic. I've taken every precaution to protect what is left of Idris... yet here you are."

She stopped swaying, her glare again piercing.

"If you're a threat, I shall discard you now." Again, the black waves seemed to dance with her tongue.

"We're no threat!" said Lessa. "If you say this is a safe place, then that's why we've come. That's what we wished for when we fought the King's necromancer, nearly to our deaths. We've proven ourselves enough. We wish to *help* magic thrive."

"You survived Vladamor?" screeched Syrifina. "Now I'm truly fascinated! You might as well have led with that." She cocked her head to the side, drinking Lessa in. "Your story isn't dull, that's for certain. But still… do I let you live?"

She tapped her finger to her lips.

"We can help you protect Idris, help you to restore the balance to the world so that more than just this island can flourish," said Demetrius, throwing caution to the wind as he grabbed her attention. "We could work together to bring life back to the land."

Syrifina considered him for a moment, seeming to warm to him despite her judgment of the male species.

"Your hearts appear to speak a truth, but the truth can only be known when it is known," she whispered. "You shouldn't make promises you're not certain you can keep. But I tell you this, I cannot deny that the Olleb has her eye on you, and I won't be the one to test her verdict."

Arianna chewed on her lip and gave an internal sigh of relief.

"So… you'll help us, then?" Her voice came out more eager than she'd intended. "Can you help us to get off this island?"

"I certainly am able," said Syrifina, raising an eyebrow at her. "But I do not offer favors to strangers. If you want my help, you must first give me something in return. Otherwise, I won't risk meddling in your fates."

She glanced to the water again, and Arianna noticed the other mermaids were inching nearer, their perfect faces clearer than ever now.

"And though I'm convinced of your *potential*," she said, "I'm not so sure my sisters will agree in time for you to survive them all."

Arianna's good feeling quickly turned back to bad—the last thing she wanted was to come face-to-face with any more of these quick-tempered creatures.

Such a deceitful woman.

She didn't trust a thing about Syrifina Myr.

"Name your price," said Jeom before anyone else could answer.

"That's the smartest thing you've said all night," said Syrifina, winking at him. "What I want is that you first deliver on the promise you've already given. Prove yourselves and ensure that the Island of Idris is *truly* protected. Especially since you lot clearly leave a trail of destruction on this warpath you've created. Only then will I help you continue your journey away from here."

"How do you suppose we do that?" said Demetrius, looking to the others.

Syrifina shook her head back and forth, her hair shimmering red. In a flash, she was in front of Demetrius, staring deep into his eyes.

Arianna could practically see him becoming entranced by whatever invisible magic she possessed, so drawn into her that he couldn't even blink.

"*Something* is killing my sisters," she whimpered, glancing back to the sea as her serious persona switched to one of vulnerable and scared in the passing of a second.

She let out a moan of sadness, and Arianna swore she even saw a tear glisten on her cheek; it was hard to tell for how much she naturally sparkled. Demetrius leaned closer in.

Jeom put a hand on his brother's shoulder, pulling him to arm's length, so Syrifina released her hold over him.

"It's as if the Olleb is purging us from this world, like we don't belong anymore in this magicless time. We're... *dying*," she said. "And I don't know why! Save us. Use your powers to stop this from happening so we can keep protecting the oasis. Only then shall we protect you too."

"Would that be the worst thing?" said Jeom. "Maybe the Olleb would be better off without leeches roaming the waters."

Syrifina growled.

"Would you not kill an intruder who threatened your home and its inhabitants?" she barked at him. "And you're still alive, aren't you? Any creature on this island, my sisters included, could have done away with you lot by now. But we haven't. Nothing is pure good nor pure evil, my race included. And just as I see the unfortunate benefit of keeping the *male* species around, my sisters and I have been watchers of the sea and protectors of magic for thousands of moons." Her lip quivered with rage. "We were meant to live forever, and so we shall, as long as forever may be."

"But… how can you even be killed?" whispered Lessa. "I thought you were invincible? Immortal?"

This time, Syrifina had the decency to look somewhat humble.

"Like I'd give away my one truest secret to the likes of children for nothing. Hardly!" She scoffed. "Promise me you'll try and save us. If you can accomplish that, I'll tell you anything you wish. But only then."

"I give you our word," said Arianna.

"Ara, what are you doing! We should discuss this first," snapped Jeom. "She's talking in circles. We can't trust that snake. We can get off this island ourselves."

"You're the one who said 'name your price,'" she snapped back, hands on her hips.

"*Yeah*, and her price was to put an end to whatever godsend is doing off with these monsters." He gaped at her.

"Jeom, what other choice do we have?" said Demetrius, interjecting before an argument could ensue. "There's no exit sign, no map to get us off this island. We can't just stay here forever and let reality keep passing us by. We have to get back and make a plan, and we need her help to do that." He pointed to Syrifina as the four all tried to come to a decision together.

Lessa nodded and squeezed Arianna's hand.

"We'll do our best to help you," she said, addressing Syrifina. "We're Guardians of Gold, and your kind is a part of the magic we've vowed to protect."

"Fine," mumbled Jeom, kicking at the rocks on the ground. "But let it be known, my vote was 'no.'"

"Very well then," said Syrifina with a slight bow of her head to signify the agreement.

This was a deal Arianna wouldn't dare to break.

Before she could even think her next thought, Syrifina had placed the crystal-like necklace—with the soul of the star at its center—around her neck. The chains of the watery glass were ice cold against her skin, but the stone was entirely warm, as if she could feel it slightly pulsating against her chest with the fire of life.

"You have a deal," she whispered. "Help us, *try*, and I'll make sure you and your friends get off this island."

"Alive?" asked Jeom, sarcastically.

"Alive," Syrifina said with a laugh. "Maybe we could even part as friends." She blew him a kiss.

"Not likely," he grumbled, shrugging it off.

"Once my sisters and I are safe, you may continue your quest. This, I *promise*," said Syrifina. "And a mermaid never breaks such an honorable thing."

Arianna was a bit taken aback by the statement; she had never considered once over the last two years that she was on a 'quest' toward anything but escaping oppression. But somehow the word seemed to stick. *Quest.*

She finally had discovered a specific mission in life, and even though she didn't quite know where they'd end up or how they'd get there, she felt so satisfied with finally knowing her purpose. It wasn't just *her* freedom from oppression that mattered, it was the world's—and it was on her shoulders now to remind the Olleb that magic still existed.

Syrifina extended her hand, and she took it without hesitation, the deal solidified in that moment. The mythical mermaid's skin was stone cold as her fingers wrapped around her palm, and Arianna had a sickening feeling that she couldn't have let go… even if she'd wanted to.

16

TRANSFORMATIONS

THEY ALL LISTENED INTENTLY now as Syrifina spoke of the Myr Tribe's one vulnerability—she had come to learn, long ago, that if a mermaid was unable to return to water by the time the sun fully rose in the sky, she would cease to exist.

"The terrible and excruciating loss of one of my sisters in our earliest reign under the sea taught me this harsh lesson. Even *we* are bound by a set of rules," she said. "Though ancient they are. The sorcerer who created this gift—"

Jeom coughed. "Curse."

Syrifina cleared her throat, pursing her lips. "The sorcerer who gave us this *gift* tied us to the sea, and so we're also strengthened by the moon, as is water."

"How could you be on the verge of extinction, then?" asked Demetrius, scratching his head. "I mean, if you're aware of your one and only weakness…"

Arianna knew he, like Lessa, was truly fascinated by this creature who ruled a piece of the Olleb that many had barely even glimpsed. The sea had so many treasures yet to be discovered, and she saw them sparkling in his eyes; Arianna thought even Syrifina had started to grow a sort of fondness for Demetrius' show of respect, or at least a tolerance—his sheer kindness and plain interest in her visibly dented her frozen heart.

"That's just it," said Syrifina, giving him her full attention. "I have no idea. This is…"

She ran her fingers through her hair, appearing uncomfortable with the thoughts on the tip of her tongue, and with the subject of dying.

"I think there is something dark at play. My poor sisters, it's as if one by one they're just going *mad*. Suddenly, they can't breathe the water's bountiful breath, and they…" She let out a sob, covering her face with her hands.

"They what?" asked Lessa, reaching out to console her.

Not at all wooed by Syrifina's story, Jeom followed Lessa's hand with his eyes, as if he might jump to her rescue at any moment should Syrifina suddenly bite.

She shook her head, her lips trembling as she said, "They take their own lives."

Arianna's heart was pained for even the blood-sucking mermaids in this instance.

"The worst possible end," she uttered, thinking of the ghosts of Jacob and Damon, the innocent souls forever sealed in the Vanishing Tunnels, fated never to move on to a peaceful rest—and all because of the King.

It's not fair. Everyone should have freedom in death.

She shivered then as another thought occurred to her.

Do the ghosts of the Myr sisters also roam the seas?

Syrifina let out another exaggerated moan. "It's just not like them," she said. "They were so happy with me."

Jeom scoffed and Arianna thought Syrifina might go back on

her promise and rip off his head, jumping back into the sea before anyone could even notice he was dead.

"But how?" said Demetrius, gently. "How did they…"

"When the sun is at its highest, while the rest of us dream, those bitten by this tragic destiny take themselves out of the water to the driest part of the land." Syrifina gazed past them to the trees. "Too far for any of us to be able to risk dragging them back to safety by the time we realize they've gone. It's as if they *want* to die. And so… they do. Turned to dust after centuries of life."

"Maybe the time of mermaids is just up," said Jeom, curtly. "You speak much of fate. Maybe this is what the Olleb wants."

"How dare you speak of my departed sisters with such little regard!" Syrifina's angry personality came back to life with the snap of her teeth.

She was behind Jeom in the blink of an eye, sniffing at his neck, sucking in his aroma.

"I shall sink my teeth back into your neck the next time you speak," she whispered near his throat. "And this time, I won't let you go until the last drop of blood is drained from your body. Do I make myself clear?"

Jeom still grasped his axe, squeezing its staff even tighter. But he couldn't possibly be quick enough to use it. Their weapons were worthless against Syrifina without magic running through them—and right now, his was only an axe, its Crissy magic appearing dormant with his master's attention focused on the mermaid.

"Jeom," said Lessa, offering a shaky smile and remaining composed. "I know you're angry, and you've every right to be. But we can handle this. You have to stay calm now, and *quiet.*"

She gave him a reassuring look, and he took a deep breath.

"All right," he said, averting his eyes. "I'll shut up."

"You're better off letting your witch make the decisions, *human.* You're not advanced enough to be speaking among such intelligence anyways." Syrifina shoved him forward.

"I'm not *just* human," said Jeom, stumbling. He whipped around and puffed out his chest. "You've no idea what—"

Arianna and Demetrius both locked stares, gawking at one another. *Did our Jeom just brag about being something other than only human?*

"Do finish that sentence." Syrifina had such a malicious smile on her face that not even Arianna would've spoken. "Go on, test me."

Lessa merely touched Jeom on the arm and his lips clamped tight; there was something happening there, and Arianna was eager to find out more… if ever a good time presented itself.

She stepped in between Syrifina and Jeom, ready for this death dance to end. "For this deal to work, no harm can come to my friends, Syrifina. None. Do I make *myself* clear?"

Syrifina smirked, crossing her arms at her chest and releasing her aggressive stance. "Your bravery amuses me, girl."

"Glad you find me funny," snapped Arianna, feeling her cheeks run hot. She stood her ground. "So long as you can keep your end of the bargain, laugh away. But if you or anyone, or *anything*, so much as touches a hair on our heads while we're stuck on this bloody island, the deal is off. And it's your sisters who will pay the price in the end—" she looked to her friends for support "—because I'm *sure* we can find a way to help them. We tend to be very lucky in this area, as you've well seen, so we're your best hope."

A low, rumbling growl rose from Syrifina's throat, like the sound Solza might make when she was deciding whether or not to pounce.

"Very well," she said after a long moment. "But my, *my*, you aren't very trusting, are you?" She grinned, showing off all her pearly white teeth. "Good girl. Maybe you will live to see the end of this dark era."

She turned to her sisters; they were practically at the edge of the shore now, their eyes glowing with the magic of the sea. A beautiful, delicate hum sounded from Syrifina's lips, and the girls, one by one, sank beneath the waves and out of sight—but never out of mind.

Arianna knew they were only a call away should something go wrong.

"There," said Syrifina, stopping her melody just before Arianna and her friends had a chance to become bewitched. "My sisters won't be coming ashore anytime soon. You needn't worry over them. They can feed elsewhere."

"Now that that's out of the way," said Lessa with an awkward laugh, "do you have a plan in mind to help us get started?"

"Yeah… it's not as if we can just go down and investigate," said Demetrius, fiddling with the stubble growing on his chin. "I'm assuming you have some sort of idea on where we can begin our investigation."

Syrifina's eyes fell on the girls, and surely something wicked played in her mind.

Arianna's stomach twisted in knots. She raised an eyebrow. "What are your intentions—"

"You'll need to see an incident happen for yourselves. Stop this atrocity at the source, before…" Syrifina's face went even whiter. "Before it happens to me. Before our race is wiped out for good."

She turned her back to them.

"If I should die, then all my creations will swiftly follow. We would cease to exist, and the seas of the Olleb would be open to worse monsters than us."

"So—" Jeom did not speak another word as Syrifina spun back around just to glare at him.

"So… what does that mean, exactly?" said Demetrius, finishing his brother's sentence. "How can we see?"

She softened, turning to him. "The only way you can help us is by visiting our lair for yourself." She looked to the girls. "You'll need to transform."

"Transform into *what?*" said Arianna, her voice coming out in more of a squeal than actual words.

Her eyes dropped to Solza and all the times this word 'transform' had dangled around her avatar's existence; it didn't make sense, that a physical form could actually change into something else. Even her Aridyn identity had only been a façade. Neither she nor her friends had physically changed in any way with Keeper Kassime's potion.

Arianna just couldn't find the imagination to grasp this piece of the magical world, even as it came from the mouth of a mermaid.

Syrifina only smiled.

"After your transformations and the problem is… eradicated, then—and only then—will my sisters and I lead you across the sea to the next city. Our currents will guide you to safety," she said. "The City of Zambienth isn't far from here. You'll need your own transportation, of course, but I'm sure you lot can figure that out on your own, yes?"

"I thought this deal meant keeping our feet on dry land," mumbled Demetrius, shaking his head. "We can't… become *mermaids,* if that's what you mean!"

"A truer statement has never been spoken, boy," said Syrifina with a barking laugh, nearly buckling over. "This gracious offer is only for the *women* in your clan. It would be a disgrace to my sisters to give the male species such power. If I had it my way, I'd drain you both of your lifeblood right now."

She stated this so casually that Demetrius' expression snapped back from excited to scared.

"You lied to us…" said Arianna, balling her fists at her sides. "Tricked us! We can't agree to this."

"Well, you already have. And this is no trick, sorceress," said Syrifina, walking toward her. "This is me keeping my promise, and you must keep yours."

"No, absolutely not," said Arianna, putting her hand up.

She looked to Lessa for help, both of them completely taken aback.

"We can't just leave Jeom and Demetrius here, and what are the risks?" said Lessa, appearing to calmly contemplate the choices—or lack thereof.

"And even still, what about our avatars?" added Arianna, spiraling. "We'd never separate from them. *Never.*"

"What about them? They're *avatars!*" spat Syrifina, growing impatient again. "They will turn to accept the sea, just as you must. It's in their nature."

"What do you mean by that?" Arianna thought Lessa might actually be losing her cool as well; trying to talk to Syrifina Myr was like a never-ending Talis Churry riddle.

"Avatars are shifting creatures," she said, gesturing toward Sano and Solza. She spoke slowly, as if talking to young children. "They control the natural elements, and they are the most revered species in the magical world, even more so than the Myr, I regret to say."

She rolled her eyes.

"Earth, air, and *water* are all quite natural to them. Fire is the only one that is of a rare occasion, but you needn't worry over that." She counted something on her fingers. "There's been only thirty or so avatar-dragons in my lifetime, and it's been a rather long one. Once one crops up, though, their species catches on just like the fire of their breath. Personally, I don't miss them much, so who cares."

She waved the thought away with the flick of her hand.

"However, the other elements are all perfectly capable for any avatar, including yours… unless you lack the skills as a master."

She threw her head back and let out an exasperated sigh when she was met with blank stares.

"I really don't get it… why the gods would bestow such gifts to you." Syrifina spoke to herself, tossing her hands into the air.

"They will *shift*, for they are born from the purest natural elements… of the purest magic."

"But, please, what do you by mean *shift?*" asked Lessa, glancing to Sano. "We've read about this before, but we just don't understand—"

"There isn't the time for this!" shouted Syrifina, her temper unleashed once more.

She was up in a flash and took both Solza and Sano by their necks—she dragged them across the beach as they whined and struggled against her strength.

Solza sank her claws into the ground, the glass stones in her path spraying out in all directions. And Arianna could hardly see a thing as gusts of wind blew the sands into the air, Sano releasing a terrible screech.

But their fight wasn't enough to deter such a powerful creature as Syrifina Myr.

"Don't," cried Arianna, running after them with Lessa and the boys in tow. "Let them go!"

Syrifina was too fast and too strong, and she had ages of experience beyond the young guardians or the young avatars. By the time the four had caught up to her, she'd already been holding their animal companions under water for so long that they visibly struggled for air, their bodies convulsing—moments later, they went slack, Syrifina letting them sink away beneath the sea.

Solza, no…

Arianna couldn't feel her anymore.

"They'll pass on to the next life now," said Syrifina. She stood back from the waters. "No need to worry over them. Let's move on."

LESSA CUPPED HER HAND over her mouth and fell to her knees, crying out for Sano as Jeom tried to console her.

Arianna could only stand and stare at the place where Solza had vanished beneath the water… seeing nothing, hearing nothing.

"What have you done?" she whispered as the loss hit her. She unsheathed the dagger at her thigh and lunged for Syrifina. "You killed Solza!"

Arianna wanted to plunge Aurora straight into Syrifina's iced-over heart, but the mermaid was too fast to surprise and Arianna was too distraught to focus.

Syrifina caught her wrist, the tip of the dagger an inch away from her chest.

I was pretty close, at least. Arianna didn't care if she died now. Not if it meant trying to avenge Solza and Sano.

Syrifina snickered. "Even if that blade touched my skin, it would only break into pieces," she said, squeezing Arianna's wrist as her weapon still sought to meet her chest.

Arianna grasped the vibrant winged guard with both hands now, using all her strength to push forward.

"I'll take my chances," she growled, feeling the buzz of magic tingle across her skin and electrify the dagger.

It lit up with such an energy that Arianna wasn't sure what she'd released inside of it.

Syrifina screeched, eyes wide.

"A dwarf-forged weapon!" She let go of her, jumping several feet back. "Such annoying little creatures."

She considered Arianna and the others with something of both disgust and curiosity.

"I'm shocked at all the luck on your side, truly. Maybe if you were older and wiser, it might even be enough to win a battle over me. But alas, you are not."

Syrifina lunged at Arianna, forcing her to relinquish her grip on the dagger. In another swift move, she was behind her, pinning her arms back so tight she thought they might snap right off.

"Just you wait," she purred in her ear, patting down Arianna's hair as if she were a child to be consoled. "If they're strong avatars, a tiny swim might do them some good."

Arianna gritted her teeth as Syrifina's lips nearly touched her skin; her breath was cool and crisp, not warm as was natural. And she couldn't help the shiver that rolled all the way from her neck to the base of her spine as her voice rang headily in her ears.

She was busy contemplating all the ways she would like to end Syrifina's long-lasting life, eyes cast to the ground, when there was a loud splash of water.

Arianna looked up, expecting to find Syrifina's sisters dancing on the waves; instead, she saw something entirely splendid—a dolphin with gleaming black skin and a silverish-white underbelly jumped out of the sea, an arc of glittering water in its trail, before landing gracefully back down, the resulting splash reaching toward the shore.

"Look!" cried Lessa, wiping the tears from her eyes and pointing excitedly—a bright white sea turtle emerged on the sand. It was enormous, with a silver-lined shell and big, orange eyes.

"Solza... Sano?" gasped Arianna.

Syrifina let her go.

She stumbled forward onto her hands and knees as the dolphin swam as close as it could get, smiling up at her with electric, blue eyes.

'*Eyes never lie,*' Kassime had once said.

He couldn't have been more right; Arianna recognized the distinct slash of yellow across one bright blue eye, completely unchanged from the first day she had found her. It was Solza.

She thought if Keeper Kassime could be with them now, he'd probably have howled for joy at such a sight, to see an avatar *transform*—an expression that was now utterly clear.

"Sano, is that really you?" sang Lessa, getting her feet wet as she ran to where the water met the sand. She bent down to lay her hand on the turtle's shell.

"The scroll…" said Demetrius, unable to contain his excitement. "Jeom, the scroll you found in the attic! It all makes perfect sense now."

"They actually turned," whispered Jeom, mouth agape.

"You're quite welcome, children," said Syrifina, holding her arms out wide, as if they might run into her embrace.

She came to the edge of the water to admire her success.

"Looks like they just needed a little push. Now… to the matter at hand."

She turned to face them, seeming as commanding as ever with the two avatars waiting in the shallows.

Arianna thought of her options; either take the offer from Syrifina—who, despite being terribly flawed in her actions, so far hadn't killed them and had simultaneously forced their avatars to the next level—*or* fight. She looked to Lessa for reassurance and saw her offer a single nod.

Arianna squared her shoulders then.

"We won't go back on our promise," she said, accepting Syrifina's challenge. "I'll go with you to your lair. The others can stay behind."

"I'm not letting you go alone," interjected Lessa as Arianna walked to the water to get a better look at Solza.

Jeom caught Lessa by the arm, but she shook him off, running to catch up with Arianna.

"I'm going with you," she said, firmly.

"No… it should be me," said Arianna, facing her. "I'm the one who landed us here in the first place. My problem to fix."

Lessa was glaring at her, arms crossed at her chest—she wasn't going to budge.

"She's right, Ara. You shouldn't go alone," said Demetrius. "Jeom and I will be fine by ourselves. I know what plants to eat, and he can start working on a boat to get us off this damn island. We'll survive all right, and you'll both come back… because you'll be able to protect each other."

"No!" said Jeom. "This is an absolute mess."

He waved his hand at Syrifina.

"What of these creatures? They'll kill us in the night without one of the girls here. Lessa should stay."

"Jeom, I will *not*," she said, firmly. "This is my decision, and nothing you say will change that."

Jeom caught Arianna's eye, desperation and worry written all across his face. But Lessa had made up her mind, and she wasn't going to be the one to try to change it.

"On the soul of the sea, I promise that I won't kill you," said Syrifina.

Jeom made for Lessa's hand again to pull her back.

"Let go of me!" she said, yanking it away.

He looked wounded.

"I'm not yours to *save*," she said in a gentler tone, blushing as all attention settled on them. "We each have a part in this, all right? We can't get distracted from the true goal, and this is a risk that I'm willing to take to help us reach it. Can't you understand that? I can't let her go alone."

Arianna felt so much gratitude toward Lessa in this moment—she didn't want to be alone.

"If it were reversed," said Demetrius, "you know it would be the same for us."

Jeom let out a deep sigh, trying to find his calm, the nerves and anger plain in his expression.

"Right," he replied, resigned to her decision. "Just… don't stay gone too long."

"We won't," she said with a soft smile.

"Come, it's nearly light," said Syrifina. "We must hurry."

Arianna and Lessa hugged the boys and promised a prompt return.

"Stay safe," said Jeom, not wanting to let Lessa go; he kissed the top of her head.

Arianna gave Lessa a sidelong glance when they walked away.

"I'll explain later," Lessa whispered to her.

The girls met Syrifina near the water where their avatars were waiting nearby. At her instruction, they stripped down to their undergarments, passing the boys their most precious items for safekeeping.

Syrifina took their hands and brought them to the water's edge until they were all up to their waists; her silver tattoos began to frantically shift through all different colors, as if they had a mind of their own.

"How does it work?" said Arianna, finding her footing; her skin prickled as the waters wrapped around her.

"A kiss will turn you, a bite will hurt you," Syrifina said as if in song.

"But how do we turn back?" asked Lessa, slowly lowering herself into the water.

"It happens at will, child. A very *strong* will." Syrifina looked to the sky and saw the full moon shining down. "You're lucky. This night the moon is strong, and so shall you be. You have twenty-nine days before the next full moon to decide your futures, just as I once did. However, should even a drop of blood touch your lips, the spell will be solidified forever, your humanity forfeited. There is no undoing that once it's been done. Stay focused, for the urge will be all-consuming." She smiled, almost reassuringly. "If it's your destiny to return to the earth, then so you shall."

Arianna's heart began throbbing in her chest. *Destiny... so fickle. Who knows what she might decide next?*

She remembered Jacob's words in the tunnels at the beginning of this adventure—if he could only see now what a tangled mess her destiny had become. It seemed as if she tempted death and failure at every opportunity, with more fantastic ways to fail as time ticked on.

"Are you ready?" asked Syrifina, submerging herself almost fully in the water and swimming further out.

Arianna's eyes widened as she saw what appeared to be a beautiful fishlike tail dancing in the waters behind her—it shimmered gloriously with the markings that had once covered Syrifina's body. And her hair now matched the sunrise as the moon began to lose the fight for its right to the sky.

"Now *that's* a mermaid," she heard Demetrius say with a whistle from the shore.

"We can do this," said Lessa, drawing back Arianna's attention—she always knew when she was second-guessing something. "We're guardians. Who better than us to have the strength to change back?"

"She's just so manipulative," whispered Arianna, thinking that Syrifina had yet to give the full picture of what they'd agreed to. "We have to be careful."

Lessa nodded, grasping her hand tightly. "As long as we stick together, we'll be fine."

They waded deeper into the shallows to meet Syrifina Myr, the original mermaid of Olleb-Yelfra, in her domain.

We will survive.

"We're ready," said Arianna with one last look back to Jeom and Demetrius.

Syrifina had no more words to say—she took Lessa's hand and gently pulled her close, placing a kiss on her lips. Then, Arianna experienced it for herself, the second kiss of her lifetime, gifted to her by a proven enemy and a Golden Age creature of the Olleb.

17

A MERMAID'S KISS

Arianna's reflexes told her to fight or flee; she cringed away from Syrifina on instinct, though her lips remained pressed against hers. The way she had envisioned a kiss had always been so different than what she had thus far experienced. In the imagination of her past, it had always been with Liam... and she thought it would be so much warmer.

Now, here she was, her first kiss stolen during a frigid, desert storm, shivering all the while; her second taken by the likes of Syrifina Myr, with breath as cold as ice—it was like receiving a kiss from the Blancoren Mountains themselves.

After what seemed like ages, Syrifina's lips parted from hers, magic sparking between them to signify a powerful change. Arianna felt her whole world shift, as if someone had taken it and spun it upside down.

A blanket of frost wrapped around her body, inching over every crevice of skin, from her belly button to her toes, hardening her from the inside out. She felt as if the water encased her in an icy shell. Then… she realized that it actually was; when she opened her eyes, the waves had completely engulfed her, churning and whirling around her with a life of their own.

She felt the magic, the water, grip her lungs next—she inhaled deeply, more deeply than ever before.

The watery shell fell away with a splash.

Arianna had to steady herself, a sudden flow of foreign energy whizzing through her body. So many new strengths vied for her attention, her senses amplified in every way.

Colors took on a radiance that her eyes had never known, and there were things she didn't even have words for floating on the surface of the water and dancing in the air. She could feel every fiber in her bones, every grain of sand between her toes, every lick of salt in the water around her—it was a state of overwhelming bliss.

"What's happening?" she heard the boys calling from afar.

She didn't care to answer; she was fixated on examining her new self—her body was covered in tattoos, just like Syrifina's, except that hers took on the color of a brilliant red paired with silver.

And, now that she and Syrifina were one and the same, Arianna realized that her colorful new features weren't even tattoos at all. They were the strands of her actual lifeblood, now on the outside of her body and just as alive as anything had ever been.

She ran her fingers along one of the lines as it twisted across her skin, feeling its warmth and energy. They moved ever so slowly, like enchanted caterpillars scuttling across her skin for a colorful display—a fiery red and a mesmerizing, magical silver.

"Your transformations highlight your truest natural elements within," said Syrifina; her voice truly sounded like a melody now with this new heightened sense of hearing—otherworldly, in fact.

Syrifina flipped her tail in the water so that Arianna could see her bright, metallic scales, flickering from one color to the next under the growing light on the horizon. Hers were a medley of colors, every shade trying to take a turn in the spotlight.

Arianna understood that Syrifina must equally embody all the elements then, a pure magical source; she supposed that was because the mermaid line had begun with her.

Lessa was still at her side, admiring her own transformation; Arianna thought her a perfect match to the sea, covered in crisp cerulean and silver strings of lifeblood.

Though tails of shimmering scales replaced their legs and their hair tumbled down their backs with an elegant, unnatural length never achievable in their human lives, Arianna distantly thought that they were still who they ought to be… somewhere deep down—they were still Arianna Belvedor and Lessa Thur, escapees of the Jar, evaders of the High King, Guardians of Gold.

But a slight tingle of fear in her heart conveyed to her that in sacrificing their human forms, some very important pieces had been pushed to the side to make room for these enhancements.

Arianna ran her fingers along her neckline and felt that fear dissipate just as soon as it had come; the soul of the star was still fastened tightly to its chain, reminding her of their purpose, keeping her tethered to the life and the identity she had fought so hard to gain.

She reached toward Lessa, and they clasped hands. It was only a small sign of unity, but it assured her that they were still in this together, mermaids or not.

"By gods, you're actually… *fish*!" screeched Demetrius from up the beach.

He ran forward to get a closer look; Jeom was right behind.

"Mermaids," said Syrifina, pursing her lips. "And how beautifully they've taken to this state, hmm?" She clapped her hands, swimming around the girls approvingly.

Demetrius nodded, clearly awestruck, asking them a billion questions at once about how they felt.

But Arianna couldn't concentrate, her eyes stuck again on the colorful new veins snaking across her skin.

"Something's… wrong," she stuttered; her lifeblood glowed brighter, an uncomfortable warmth beginning to radiate from them. "Something's happening to me—"

A terrible cry ripped from Arianna's throat, startling even Syrifina as sparks of color exploded all around her; everyone, including the ancient mermaid, quickly found their distance.

It felt as if all the bones in her body were breaking at once, bursting inside of her. And she could literally see her newly won tail fading into nothing just as fast as it had come.

With her very next breath, the bliss from only moments before fell away in one agonizing rip.

JEOM AND DEMETRIUS RAN toward Arianna, splashing into the water as close as they could get.

"Nothing like this has ever happened before," Syrifina said, gasping, as Demetrius took Arianna in his arms, trying to soothe her. "It's as if she's rejecting my magic!"

"What do you mean?" yelled Jeom as Arianna convulsed in his brother's arms, shrieking out from the pain—his voice hardly carried out over her screams.

Arianna felt as if she were drowning. Only moments ago, breathing in through the water had felt as normal as anything… now she was choking on it, desperate for air.

She thrashed like a speared fish, frantic to keep her head above the waves and coughing so much water up. Then the pain began to ease until there was only the memory of it.

"What *was* that?" she murmured, regaining her focus.

Arianna felt drained of all her energy now, Syrifina's magic wholly severed.

"I honestly don't know," said Syrifina. "In all my time, I've not seen a single girl reject my magic."

She couldn't stop gawking at her.

"A few have refused the gift, yes, and even fewer have turned back at will during their first cycle, but these are rare occurrences. Nothing like *this* has ever happened. It's as if your own magic is protecting you from the transformation instinctually."

She examined Arianna with an expression that *almost* resembled fear.

"You'd have to be very strong… to reverse something like that," said Syrifina, an accusation in her tone.

"She is," said Demetrius with sincerity, still holding her upright and stroking her hair.

Arianna smiled at him and then found her footing, wading in the shallow waters with him close by. Solza swam to her side, nudging her gently with her beak.

"Thanks, Solza," said Arianna—she could already feel her energy boosting with the avatar magic. "That was horrible."

She shivered, the before comforting night waters now cold and unpleasant.

"Are you all right now?" said Jeom, his worry palpable.

Arianna nodded. "I think so," she said. "It felt like the time we drank the poison that undid our identity charms. Maybe worse… like I was purging the magic from my body." She glanced to Syrifina, shaking her head. "There was nothing I could do. It just didn't *stick*."

A soft clump of sand balled beneath her feet as her toes touched the bottom, and a part of her was very glad to have those toes again—even if she was baffled as to the reason why.

"It did for me," she heard Lessa say.

"Hmm?" said Arianna, still absorbed in the riddle as everyone hovered around her to make sure she wasn't hurt.

"It stuck," she said.

Lessa's voice sounded so sweet, *too* sweet, that Arianna

thought she'd never heard such a beautiful sentence in her life. Turning around, she gasped at the sight of her friend.

Seeing Lessa now with purely human eyes was even more astonishing than when she had looked upon her as a mermaid—Syrifina's beauty paled in comparison next to her stunning transformation.

She seemed to be made of stone, her body unmoving as the sea splashed softly all around her; Arianna and the boys shifted uncontrollably with the heavy weight of the waves.

Marble white skin shone in such contrast to the dark blue waters, glistening as the early light touched down. Designs of blue and silver strands painted her flesh and created metallic scales for a tail. And her hair was long, floating out in strings of wavy gold, as if the sun had graced her with an extra dose of color.

More stunning still, Lessa's eyes boasted her signature bright blues, yet they were even more captivating now as they took on a new piercing color—the sea had surely stitched its reflection to her pupils, shifting back and forth between silver and cerulean, just as water.

"Are you all right to do this alone?" said Arianna, feeling unsettled about their plan now; it was already half fallen apart.

She waded closer to her, but something kept her from getting too close.

Lessa was Lessa… but *wasn't*.

This was a terrible idea.

The adrenaline and courage from earlier quickly faded back to fear, seeing her friend as she was now.

"Never better," breathed Lessa, a smile forming as she acclimated to her new body.

Her hand rested calmly on top of Sano's silvery shell as she stared back at Arianna and the others, clearly not really seeing them; with just her breath, the waves grew wilder.

She was teeming with power, and Arianna was sure that was all she could focus on in that moment.

She wondered briefly if all mermaids experienced a similar influence on the sea, or if Sano was aiding in Lessa's new, extreme control over this element. There was so much still to learn—Arianna considered only now, as panic cleared her mind of its bravery, that maybe they ought to have thought a little harder before accepting a deal with a known monster of the sea.

"Gently now, dear. You haven't yet drunk," said Syrifina. "You won't be as strong as you may think... as you could be."

"Don't!" shouted Jeom. "Don't drink anything they give you. Don't trust them, Lessa. Remember why you're doing this, for the guardians. We have to do our duty."

Jeom waded toward her, but she remained unmoving, unfeeling.

"You're one of us," he said, desperate for a reaction from her. "Family!"

The way he said the word made Arianna feel sick to her stomach.

Lessa didn't seem concerned in the slightest.

"Figure out what's going on with them quick, Les," said Demetrius, trying to seem hopeful. "Come back to us soon, all right, love?"

He spoke in reassuring tones, as if he might spook a child should he raise his voice louder.

Syrifina looked at them all with curious eyes, surely seeing them for the first time in a different light.

They didn't want to let Lessa go, *their* sister.

"I'll keep an eye on her," she said, sincerely. "Don't worry. I just care about saving my family, not stealing away yours."

Something in the steadiness of her voice made Arianna believe her... somewhat; Syrifina's priority was to save her own sisters, and that was a fact.

But the slight smirk—the silent appraisal and approval of her newly created mermaid—was enough for Arianna to wholly regret agreeing to this in the first place. They had risked Lessa's life, and there was no telling what the outcome may be.

She would be all on her own.

Jeom reached for Lessa's hand, trying to force her to focus on him. With the snap of her neck, she locked eyes with his. She began to speak, this time in a purr... a sugary, seducing sound lacing her words.

"I can hear your heart beating for me," she whispered, leaning closer to him, her tail flicking in the waves.

"It will always beat for you," he said, pushing the hair from her face.

Arianna watched as Lessa's eyes followed his hand *too* closely, like an animal stalking its prey. She caught his wrist in her palm, holding it steady near her mouth.

"Les," said Jeom, cowering away as she tightened her grip. "You're hurting me..."

Lessa forced his wrist closer, first to her nose, sucking in the scent, and then slowly to her lips. Her eyes glowed a bright silver then, and Arianna saw two perfectly sharp teeth waiting to sink into his skin as she opened her mouth.

"Stop! You'll kill him," screamed Arianna, splashing toward her. "And you'll be turned for good. You can't!"

The real Lessa seemed to break through the mermaid barrier in that moment, her eyes flashing back to a breathtaking blue. She scrunched them closed, as if to ward off a headache.

"Les?" said Jeom, his voice trembling. "It hurts."

With the catch of her breath, like she'd realized her error, Lessa shoved Jeom away so hard that he flew backward into the water. Demetrius rushed to help him, and Arianna waded toward the boys to make sure he was all right.

And honestly, right now, she was terrified to be near Lessa.

We need to get out of the water.

"Please," said Jeom, staring at Lessa still. "Don't go."

"We must, my daughter," said Syrifina, swimming to her side and stroking her arm. "You'll feel more yourself when the scent of mortals isn't filling your head."

An eerie melody weighted the air then, floating straight up from the bottom of the sea—the Myr sisters surrounded them.

Arianna didn't need to be a mermaid again to know that they were calling for their sisters to leave; the sun had nearly made a full appearance now.

Lessa and Syrifina backed away slowly toward the never-ending horizon, the stealthy bystanders of the waters sinking back beneath the sea; only the ripples in the waves suggested they had been there at all.

"Control your thirst," said Arianna, calling after her. "Don't give in. Remember who you truly are, and fight for it!"

She felt so helpless, scrambling clumsily against the waves to get one last glimpse of her best friend. Her heart pounded wildly and she stayed unblinking, wanting to prolong the inevitable in any possible way.

"You promised to return. One week, you hear me?" she yelled as Lessa began to lower her body beneath the water too. "One week, or I'm coming after you!"

"I'll try," said Lessa, her voice uncharacteristically cold and unpromising.

She didn't even look back before she and Syrifina submerged completely, Sano following faithfully behind. A silvery-blue tail was all they could see before the waters stilled. All was quiet with the risen sun.

18

LEFT BEHIND

"LESSA!" ARIANNA COVERED HER EARS as Jeom's booming voice echoed across the waves. "Lessa, don't go. Don't go!" He plowed through the waters, but it was too late. She was gone, swallowed by the mammoth abyss that was this ocean.

"What are we going to do?" said Demetrius, coming to Arianna's aid—she was still quite weak.

He looped one arm around her waist as they both wobbled across the pebbly shore to dry land.

"It was one thing that you two would have each other, but now… I just don't know. I don't have a good feeling about this."

"No, I should be there with her," said Arianna. "I thought I might be strong enough to withstand whatever games Syrifina surely has coming, but I never thought Lessa might have to do this on her own." She gazed back to the sea. "It was all-consuming…"

She placed a hand on her forehead, a raging headache settling in as if she'd drunk her weight in wine; she recalled the feeling of pure ecstasy just after her shift from human to mermaid, remembered how little she cared to think of real-world matters as her heightened senses and powers took front and center.

"What was?" asked Demetrius.

"The transformation," said Arianna. "I know that I looked different on the outside, but the inside changed as well. It was sort of like how we assumed the personalities of the new identities back in Luose. Eventually, it was hard to separate that person from who we were... *are.*" She put her hands on her knees to steady her spinning head. "It will be hard for Lessa to do that twice."

She thought of all the things that being Aridyn had taught her—how to act like a proper highlife, confidence under the eyes of her superiors, becoming a guardian, and being a better warrior. Her highlife mask had brought comfort to her in a time of much distress. And if Lessa felt the same about her Lilith identity as she did about Aridyn, Arianna knew this would surely be a more painful separation than the first.

Arianna had felt it, even if just for a moment, that the mask of a mermaid weighed a lot heavier on the heart than a mere potion.

"I don't think we'll ever truly let go of them," said Demetrius, looking out to the water as his reflection stared back; Arianna knew that he imagined the lost face of his Darrios identity there.

"No, I suppose not," she said. "But this... this was much stronger than that. It felt more *permanent.*"

Demetrius' face wrinkled with concern. "Nothing is permanent."

"I hope you're right," she whispered back.

"I won't listen to this!" said Jeom, his emotions exploding.

He stormed up the beach, eyes to the sky. The moon was completely gone now, the burning rays of the sun glowing across the horizon in its place, creating a strip of bright orange that dented the black.

"Jeom," said Arianna, laying a hand on his shoulder. "We'll figure something out. It's going to be all right."

"Don't!" he snapped, rolling out from under her touch. "Just don't. This is all your fault, you know? You only ever think of yourself."

She shrank back, unwelcome tears swimming in her eyes. But, for some reason, she didn't feel as intensely as he did about losing Lessa to the sea.

It just didn't seem to be her reality yet.

Only hours ago, she had awakened to find Syrifina on the beach, sucking Jeom of his life. And in even less time, the Golden Age had unfurled further with the history of Syrifina Myr and the beginning of her magical legend soaked in water and blood. Then their avatars had shifted to creatures of the sea, just a prelude to her and Lessa's own unthinkable transformations.

Now, both Lessa and Sano were gone, leaving them stranded on an island named Idris that had been deliberately wiped off the map long ago, hidden from the King.

Arianna pressed her fingers to her forehead again, squeezing her eyes shut. It was too much information to get in mere hours, and she couldn't find the focus to address the inconceivable loss of her best friend—*refused* to.

There were just too many other things in her mind that seemed much easier to comprehend at this moment.

"That's not true. It's not her fault," said Demetrius, standing at Arianna's side. "Certainly, none of us would have chosen this option, but it was a necessary risk. Remember, brother, it was either fend off Syrifina's sisters or prove our worth. We wouldn't have lasted the night."

"We could have taken her," said Jeom. "We should have at least tried! What if she doesn't come back? Do you realize, she might *not* come back?"

"Syrifina could have ripped us all to shreds before we even

had time to reach for our weapons. She almost killed you, Jeom," said Arianna, treading lightly. "Don't forget that. This isn't a wasted effort. And had her sisters come for you and Demetrius, we would have had no way to defend ourselves."

She let out a deep sigh.

"She may not be our friend, but I do believe that if we, if *Lessa*, can keep our promise, Syrifina will keep her end of the deal and get us off this island. We must trust her. We've no other choice but to wait."

"Lessa is the smartest one of us all," added Demetrius, nodding to himself. "Think positive, brother. I'm not worried." He tried to speak with confidence, but his words still shook. "She'll be back by high tide, I'm sure of it. She'll figure out what's killing the mermaids, and then we'll be back on track in no time."

Jeom gave a single, forced nod, but Arianna didn't have to read minds to know that his thoughts were anything but positive... surely they echoed her own.

Standing there without Lessa felt so odd, utterly wrong; in this moment, when it was already too late, Arianna understood why Lessa had always been so strongly opposed to her separating herself from the group. She felt it constricting in her own heart now, the loneliness settling in without the one person she trusted the most by her side.

Not to know if she would ever return was a tormenting thought—Arianna decided right then and there that *when* Lessa did return, safe and sound, she would apologize profusely for ever having put her through similar suffering.

Demetrius had a point too, though.

Lessa was the wisest addition to the group, and if anyone could solve a mystifying puzzle such as a suicidal pack of mermaids, it was her.

"One week," said Arianna, squinting toward the now sparkling waves as the sun glared off the water. "She'll be back. You'll see." She twisted her fingers around the chain on her neck; Jeom stalked off toward the jungle with his axe.

"Where are you going?" called Demetrius.

"To build a boat!" He disappeared into the trees.

AS THE SUN ROSE HIGHER, the trio had trouble returning to sleep and instead tried to find a semblance of the peaceful, make-shift home they had experienced over the last several weeks—alas, now it seemed like penance.

Demetrius took to the forest to gather what food he could find; Jeom ceaselessly chopped wood to blow off steam, the Axe of Crissy slicing easily through the old trees; and Arianna took over Lessa's job to spear fresh fish for the group.

In her solitude, she went to where Lessa's longbow lay forgotten by their campsite. She picked it up with care, the delicate weapon feeling so strange in her grasp—it was much lighter than her swords, the weight distributed in such odd areas. But she realized what a treasure this must be, gifted to her by Keeper Kassime on behalf of her Master Churry.

She lifted one of the arrows into place, pulling back hard on the bowstring. She aimed, tried and true, as Lessa had taught her.

Arianna, of course, had a warrior's training; her arms didn't shake. But she couldn't quite find the trust nor confidence in this weapon as she did when she handled her swords. Without them, she felt as if she were missing limbs—the metal blades extensions of her hands, almost a part of her actual, physical being.

This bow was just like any other weapon to her, a lifeless instrument to be handled. *But not to Lessa…*

This was *her* physical extension, and Arianna would treat it with the same respect.

She recalled the attitude in the Warrior's District, as if General Ivo were there whispering in her ears—archery and arrows were for cowards, for those who liked to climb high and steer far clear of any battle.

How ignorant we were.

She knew now that they were meant for the intelligent, the calculated, the *clever*. Waiting unseen in the trees for one single moment to release and strike their opponents dead, no time for even a last breath—that was the arrow, and that emulated Lessa in every way.

She would figure out Syrifina's riddle and fight whatever magic was attempting to overcome her.

Lessa will return.

Arianna tugged the bowstring tighter and released, relishing the exciting, foreign feeling of the arrow doing the bulk of the work for her, of trusting in it and just letting go.

"Don't be gone long, Les," she whispered. "We can't do this without you."

When the disturbed sands had settled in the water's depths, Arianna saw a silver fish flopping atop the seabed, caught beneath the arrowhead, as good as dead—its school swam away in alarm.

Arianna couldn't help the twinge of a smile that crossed her lips as she imagined Syrifina pinned beneath her weapon, lying for dead at the bottom of the sea she loved so dearly; if anything happened to Lessa under that water witch's watch, anything at all, that's exactly the fate she'd ensure Syrifina Myr—the monstrous Mother of Mermaids—would meet.

19

CRAFTING HOPE

"I CAN'T TAKE THIS ANYMORE!" Arianna had barely fluttered her eyes open to the morning sun when Jeom's roaring voice greeted her. She pretended not to stir as he and Demetrius bickered for the thousandth time about their options.

"Time is up," he said. "We have to get off this gods-forsaken heap of rock!"

He kicked a plank of wood, grumbling curses to the wind.

"Jeom, please," said Demetrius, taking a deep breath to try to call the calm within; Arianna didn't know how he did it.

He tucked his unruly hair behind his ears.

"We should count ourselves lucky and trust that Lessa and Syrifina will keep their word. She'll find her way back to us. Besides, she has Sano to keep an eye on her. There's still time."

Jeom shook his head.

"Your optimism has worn on me," he said. "I'm tired of waiting. We can't just sit here and rot. We should do something. We should be out there looking for her! Otherwise, it'll be too late. Lessa can't—"

"Can't what?" retorted Demetrius. "She's just as much a fighter as Arianna and smarter than us all combined. And where are we going to go? What would we do?"

"Well, I've been thinking…"

"Thinking what?" Arianna yawned, making herself known.

She pulled her robes over her shoulders and twisted her hair into a braid as she approached the boys. It was chillier today, new clouds rolling in on beautiful pillows of purple and gray. Even so, Arianna was tiring of this oasis quickly, and the fact that it was probably going to pour down rain for once would only add to her urgency for a change of scenery.

She was just as ready as Jeom for this break to be over and to continue their duties as guardians—whatever that meant at this stage. She felt like she needed to sink her feet back into the real world, see other people, if only to ensure something still existed outside of their bubble.

Has the world continued on without us?

Jeom took a deep breath. "I've been thinking… we shouldn't just sit here and wait for someone to get us off this bloody island," he said, much more rationally. "Especially not some two-faced mermaid who already had a go at our lives."

"And how do you suppose we could go about leaving?" said Arianna. "*Swim?*" She threw a handful of berries in her mouth and shook Solza awake.

"The boat's nearly ready," said Jeom, curtly.

Demetrius crossed his arms. "That's what you said last time."

"Water filling up to the top every time we test it out is a pretty clear sign," said Arianna, growing tired of this argument. "That boat isn't ready for anything but sinking, and we're probably better off just waiting right where we are." She waved her hand toward the sea. "What if Syrifina sabotages our getaway and hurts

Lessa for breaking our promise? She probably has eyes on us during the night, and the deal is surely not completed yet, if Lessa hasn't returned…"

Jeom howled to the sky, throwing up his arms.

"That deal has nothing to do with us anymore and everything to do with Lessa! If you would both help me more, rather than stockpiling food as if we'll be living here for years to come, the boat would already be done."

"We've been through this…" said Arianna with a sigh. "We don't know how long we will be here. We can't leave anything to chance, least of all food."

"But we can leave *Lessa* to chance?" he snapped back; Arianna felt the sharp stab of guilt pierce deeper, but she kept her expression unreadable as he continued. "The moon's cycle is winding down faster than we can blink, so if we don't do something soon, Lessa could be lost to us forever. She really could."

Arianna had to admit that things were looking gloomier day in and day out—she had kept so much faith when Lessa first left, so assured that she'd return in just one week…

That week had come and gone, and there was still no sign of her; the end of twenty-nine days was fast approaching. Even if she hadn't drunk any blood yet, soon it wouldn't matter.

"When we first landed here," said Jeom, drawing her and Demetrius back in with the gravity of his tone, "I was just as burned out as the rest of you, what with everything…"

Arianna didn't have to take two guesses that 'everything' meant Keeper Kassime's death and the swift end to their luxurious guardian lives; the topic had slowly come back into discussion as time started to make their wounds a little less tender. Although, talking about the loss of loved ones, as well as their coveted life, didn't nearly amount to the pain of the possibility of losing Lessa—something that seemed to be more of a reality each passing moon.

Jeom cleared his throat. "I chopped so much wood just to

pass the time, and eventually I started building, *creating*," he said. "I started filling every moment with work to keep my mind from wandering. We all did, I suppose."

He paced around their campsite.

"I carved out these benches, made arrows for Lessa, and now this boat." He gestured to the lump of wood on the sand.

"What are you trying to say?" said Arianna, watching the sky as a sliver of lightning snaked across the brooding clouds.

Jeom wasn't one for so many words, so she knew whatever point he was trying to make was very important to him.

"I'm saying that I made a difference in the situation by doing *something*. We all did. We made it work, and it was good for a while. But now, it's our duty to do something again. If we just keep standing around twiddling our thumbs and waiting for Lessa to find her way back, we'll miss our opportunity to help her if she needs us."

He pressed his hands together in a prayer-like fashion, his eyes boring into hers.

"I can't believe I even have to persuade you of this. You said *one* week, Ara. You said one week or you'd be out there."

She pursed her lips, wanting to say so many things and shout back so many defenses, but she knew it wouldn't matter—Lessa was gone, and they each had their own way of dealing with it.

She opened her mouth to reply just as a loud clap of thunder cracked overhead; they all jumped.

"We better find some cover," said Arianna, ending the discussion.

Jeom visibly slumped—he looked to Demetrius for support, but he just stayed silent. They'd been through this too many times to count since day one of Lessa's absence, but leaving Idris to find their friend was a double-edged sword. It could also mean abandoning her, and Arianna wasn't ready to face any more guilt for losing Lessa than she already did.

What if we lose her forever?

At least, if they stayed put, they knew what their chances were. But tackling the ocean was a big gamble.

Jeom closed his eyes, taking a deep breath before angrily snatching up his things; Arianna and Demetrius gathered their essentials and followed him to a spot they had discovered in their earlier days on the island.

They walked between swaying trees with giant leaves and followed a river to keep their bearings before finally coming upon the mouth of a small, hidden cavern; they had to squeeze into the tight space to hide from the oncoming rain, an awkward position to be in, forced to face each other.

As the clouds opened wide and the rain poured down, Arianna absentmindedly watched the storm unfold, her knees pulled into her chest, as huge droplets of water fell like a sheet over the cavern entrance. Its loud, pounding rhythm seemed to mimic her foreboding thoughts.

"We can't leave," she finally said, frowning. "Lessa wouldn't leave us behind, and we won't leave her."

She fidgeted with her necklace—it took on an eerie glow in this dim setting.

"Face it," said Jeom, curtly. "We know that if she doesn't come back by the end of this moon cycle, she'll be a mermaid forever. That's how the magic works. She's been gone for eighteen days already, and the rest are ticking by fast."

"Sure, but—"

"Did you ever stop to think that if she doesn't keep her promise to Syrifina, who knows what our fates will be? We're completely vulnerable here." He rubbed at his neck.

Arianna had honestly never lingered on that possibility because her faith in Lessa was so strong. But she could not ignore the silver marks forever bonding Syrifina's sharp teeth to Jeom's skin. *Mermaids are innate killers.*

"I actually think he has a point there," said Demetrius, chewing on his lip. "She… she's not back yet, and I think our chances of seeing *our* Lessa again are slimming. She'd understand if we left to protect ourselves. In fact, she'd probably demand it."

Arianna couldn't hide her shock as Demetrius spoke his doubts out loud for the first time.

"Not you too!" she said with a groan. "And what if she does come back?" Her voice was loud over the rain. "What if she comes and we're not here? Have either of you thought of that outcome?"

A somber silence fell over them as no one seemed to have an answer. But then, a light seemed to cross Demetrius' face, and he perked right up. "She'd find us!"

"How do you mean?" said Jeom.

"Think about it," he said. "She has the powers of a mermaid right now. I'm sure she could track us in the water. It's not like we would get very far on that small of a boat, anyways. Whatever land is out there needs to be close by, or we'll just run the risk of starvation or worse fates."

"I didn't think of that…" said Jeom, scratching his head.

"Of course not." Arianna rolled her eyes. "It's not as easy a plan as you might have imagined."

Demetrius continued before Jeom could retort.

"Syrifina said herself that Zambienth wasn't far off. We could leave Lessa a message here." He shrugged his shoulders. "Who knows, maybe she'd make it there before even we did."

Arianna mulled this over for a moment.

"That's hard to argue," she said after a long while. "And you're right—" she could feel Jeom perk up beside her and couldn't bear to stress him out further "—I think Lessa would understand. If it was just me, I'd probably stay. But Syrifina doesn't have an issue with females. You boys are at high risk if anything goes wrong, and the closer we get to the end of the moon cycle, the more chances are that things didn't go as planned… unfortunately."

She choked out the last word, remembering Liam's deadened gaze as Solomon struck down his blade; she just couldn't think of

Lessa as dead to her too, so she veered right away from that idea.

"*So*, you finally agree, then?" said Jeom, his voice coming out in a nervous squeak. She found it funny that he awaited her permission to do anything at all—she wouldn't have awaited his—but it made her love the Kane brothers that much more to know that they valued her leadership so highly.

I can't let them down anymore.

It was as if all Jeom needed was to be moving, planning, doing something in order to feel like he was helping the situation at all; Arianna couldn't fault him for that. In fact, when they had first met, that was exactly what he had been doing to free himself of the guilt of killing his friend during his Free Falls. He was 'creating' away his pain in the Inventor's Zone and plotting out a new future that might rid him of it.

"I do," said Arianna, trying to channel her inner-Lessa. "But we need a proper plan. We can't just go out to sea on a whim."

"What about my compass?" said Demetrius, pulling it from his robes and holding it in his hands. "We'll follow it toward the South Star, just the same as before. We were heading straight for Zambienth the last time we used it, so it'll have to lead us in that direction."

"Oh, you're a genius, Demetrius!" said Jeom, glowing.

His excited laughter filled the cavern; Arianna had missed it so much.

And she couldn't help but crack a smile too—she had completely forgotten about that wonderful gift from Tobias.

"All right, this is a start. But how long until the boat is actually ready?" said Arianna, raising an eyebrow at Jeom.

"It's about done," he said, suddenly very interested in a rock. "Maybe a few more days… a week, possibly?"

"A week works for me," said Arianna, trying to push her hope to the surface. "Let's do it! Let's get off this island and go find our girl."

OVER THE NEXT SEVERAL DAYS, tension and hope seemed to run hand in hand as the three struggled to create some semblance of a plan to get them to Zambienth and find Lessa on the way. For the most part, they were coming to the realization that they had no control over anything—not whether they made it to Zambienth nor whether Lessa was found in time to reel her back in from Syrifina's dominion.

Truly, it was up to the waves.

Still, they diligently worked together to put the finishing touches on the boat. And what a magnificent boat it had turned out to be—the Crissy magic had lent its charms and Jeom showed off his truest creator talents through the woodwork.

"For all we know, Lessa has already drunk some poor bastard's blood and is gone for good." Jeom huffed as Demetrius packed up the now finished boat.

Jeom's optimism and negativity were interchangeable by the hour.

"We don't know that," said Arianna, her swords dangling at her sides. "Now, would you *please* focus already?"

She and Jeom had taken a break from readying their getaway to practice-duel away some stress.

But his temper never improved, and Arianna kept taking hard blow after blow.

With his next swing, his axe sparked with magic; Arianna quickly conjured her own in defense just to be able to withstand the force.

"We're done here," she said between heavy breaths—she sheathed her swords and wiped the sweat from her brow. "I'd like to make it off this island in one piece, if you don't mind."

Jeom was about to respond when Demetrius interrupted them, walking over with a worried look on his face.

"What is it?" said Arianna, cautiously. "What's happened?"

She could tell Jeom was also bracing himself for bad news.

"It's the compass," he said, frantic. "It... it isn't working."

Jeom was barely holding it together. "What do you *mean* it isn't working?"

Demetrius handed it to Arianna to examine—the compass was the heart of their plan in order to lean on something other than just blind luck. *It has to work.*

To her dismay, the compass' arrow seemed to have a mind of its own, flitting from one direction to the next in an inexplicable fashion, completely gone awry.

"I think it's this place," said Demetrius, running his hand through his hair. "Syrifina said the island is cloaked with strong magic to hide it from travelers. It's no wonder it doesn't work here. Her spells are probably interfering with it somehow." He bowed his head. "But if we don't have the compass, I don't know how we'll have any hope of reaching Zambienth now..."

"We wouldn't," said Arianna, abruptly. She balled her fists at her side. "That takes our chances down to impossible."

It would be too risky to make this voyage without any guidance at all. They only had room for enough food and water to last a few days, maybe a week, in the boat. And without the compass it'd be even more of a gamble than to wait for Syrifina to come back with her teeth bared.

She glanced to Jeom full of regret, afraid to even meet his eyes. "Jeom, I'm sorry, but—"

"No!" he screamed, snatching the compass from Arianna and staring at it as if to will it to work again; he squeezed it so tight Arianna thought it might crumble in his palm.

"I'm so sorry, brother," said Demetrius, seeming lost for words. "We all wanted this plan to work."

"It's not fair," said Jeom, his hands trembling as he fiddled with the instrument.

Arianna knew he must understand the implications of this,

but he was inconsolable—he threw the compass toward the sea with all his might.

Arianna's heart sank into her stomach as she watched the compass fly through the air before meeting the water with a splash.

"Jeom!" said Demetrius, looking after it in shock as it fell to the depths of the water—the waves washed it away. "How could you do that?"

Silent tears started down Demetrius' cheeks, and Arianna couldn't help the sorrow welling in her chest. This moment seemed to have broken their very thin layer of hope in the most complete way.

"I'm sorry," Jeom choked out, giving Demetrius a tormented look; he embraced him in a short hug and then ran off, leaving Arianna and Demetrius alone.

Arianna stared blankly off into the sun as it began to lower in the sky, sinking beneath the waves as Lessa had done not so long ago—the moon rose in its place.

And every time it showed, there was a bigger slice missing, mocking them with a giant grin on its face; it reflected her own heart too, each night a piece of it missing.

Lessa had always said that they couldn't survive without Arianna. But what she apparently didn't know was that they couldn't survive without her either—she was a sort of glue, always keeping the peace, always in everyone's favor.

Now she was gone, and they were falling apart.

Demetrius walked off with his thoughts, and Arianna stripped off her sheath and clothes so that she was in her undergarments. She stepped into the warm waters to clear her mind of this pain. If she closed her eyes, she could imagine she was safe and sound in her utopia.

She let her head fall beneath the waves to try to picture herself there. But the water was much harsher here than in her long-gone hot springs, scratching at her skin and tasting of too much salt.

She looked back and saw Solza sitting on the beach, looking at her oddly, watching her; Arianna had come to learn that the snow leopard was her preferred avatar form, could sense her strong connection to the earth. Solza had turned back to her earthly body, not long after Lessa's disappearance, in a magical display that had shocked and awed them all.

But, in this moment, she needed her avatar's companionship—and she knew Solza could sense that, too, as she willed her to join her in the waters.

"Solza, will you come with me?" she asked.

Solza pranced down the beach, her fur shimmering under the moonlight. When her paws met the water, the avatar magic took hold in a stunning demonstration, transforming her back into a remarkable creature of the sea.

Arianna thought she might never get used to watching such magic occur. Avatar magic was unfathomable to her, even as she continued to witness more levels to it.

She wished she and Solza could share minds again, that she could wander the waters freely and unencumbered with her eyes. Alas, she had tapped into Solza's sight only once before and had little idea of how to do it again.

As Solza took on her new form, the gleaming skin of a dolphin bounced back and forth across the frothy waves—Arianna grabbed hold of her fin and down they went, the water rushing up to meet her in a swarm of bubbles.

With one big breath, she let the sea engulf her and wash away her troubles, Solza swimming as fast as she possibly could. And when Arianna grew short of air, Solza would instinctually know; up they'd go again, repeating the routine.

Arianna kept her eyes open, the water blurring her sight, burning, but the moon was high enough in the sky that its shine reached down toward the bedrock; she could see everything if she didn't go too deep.

Under the waters of the Olleb, the sea grew colder the farther away from Idris they got. And strange creatures, *dark* creatures, roamed the waters if they journeyed too far. But Arianna was used to this unknown terrain by now—since the day Lessa had turned, Arianna and Solza had been scouring the ocean for any trace of the mermaids.

I never break a promise, Les. I'm going to find you.

The boys didn't have a clue about her escapades; she always returned with a heap of fish for supper once the sun finally set and the sea darkened. This search was something she had to do alone. And not just because the boys had no way to keep up with her under the water… but because it felt like her responsibility.

If anyone was supposed to be the leader of this group, it was her, always dragging her friends into messy situations for this reason or that. And though Arianna wouldn't allow herself to feel the full guilt of admitting out loud that she felt responsible for this loss, she could admit it with screams underwater.

She knew with a certainty that if she didn't bring Lessa home, she would never forgive herself for leading such an innocent soul into the dark.

Where are you, Lessa? Tell me!

It was then that she spotted something on the bottom of the sea floor, and when she surfaced this time, she knew it would be the last.

With the compass in hand, she waded into the shore, water still up to her waist.

"Jeom, Demetrius, come quick!" she called out.

"What is it? Are you okay?" Their voices melded together, both running out of their hiding spots to meet her in the water without hesitation.

Arianna's heart warmed at the sight of them—no matter their tensions, they still very much cared for each other in the way that she assumed families should. They could get through this together with just one last dose of hope.

"It's the compass," said Arianna, holding it in her palm. A

huge smile stretched across her face. "Look, it works! We just have to bring it off land, outside of the island's protective magic."

"It works?" Jeom's large brown eyes widened in disbelief.

Arianna smiled wider.

He ran to meet her in the shallows and lifted her into the air, swinging her around in circles as water splashed all around them. "It works. It works!" he shouted, hugging her tight.

"Are we ready then?" she asked, laughing dizzily when he placed her back on her feet.

Demetrius jumped into the water too, taking the compass from Arianna to inspect it.

"As ever," he mumbled, wiping the tears from his cheeks when he saw the arrow pointing steadily toward the south.

Arianna looked toward the boat, already packed with their belongings.

"Let's leave now, then," she said with a heavy heart. "Tonight. We shouldn't waste another moment."

Demetrius nodded in agreement.

"She'll find our message at the campsite should she return," he said. "We left it in plain sight."

"I hope so," said Arianna, her gaze lingering on the shore. "We just have to have faith in our plan."

"All right then, come on!" said Jeom. "No use worrying over anything else. Fate can decide our future now. It's finally time to go."

The three embraced as a group and then began final preparations, clearing their campsite of any last belongings. When they were ready, they pushed the boat into the water and everyone jumped in.

The boys handled the finely crafted oars to start, so Arianna sat in the back of the boat, gaze lingering on their temporary home—the creations Jeom had constructed to make their short-term stay a little more comfortable would stand the test of time. And she hoped that no other lost souls would find themselves on

Idris to ever put them to use in the future.

They had also gathered the brightest stones on the beach and ordered them so that they spelled out 'Zambienth' in big letters… should Lessa ever come looking. Though, as they got farther away, the island shrinking quickly into their pasts, Arianna couldn't help the pressing thought that since Lessa hadn't returned to this beach already, when or if she did, there was a good chance that she might not be *their* Lessa anymore.

The Island of Idris grew smaller in the distance, Solza swimming diligently by their side as Demetrius guided their direction with his compass in hand.

20

LESSA MYR

LESSA HAD ALWAYS BEEN one for climbing, for the adrenaline she felt when she rose higher and higher, but there was a freedom in life underwater too—it satisfied her yearnings in more ways than one. It felt as if this were the missing piece to her life all along, the hunger finally satiated that had always lingered in the back of her mind.

Such a freedom.

It was the type of freedom she craved when she climbed to the highest heights. Or when she had snuck around the districts, night after night, mapping the Vanishing Tunnels for an escape even before discovering Arianna by chance.

Freedom.

Why follow Arianna Belvedor into endless battles when she finally had what she desired? Why want for that sad life again? Right now, she didn't have the answers as the most selfish parts of her mind rushed to take over her attention.

She had never taken a more nourishing, revitalizing breath as the one she inhaled under the sea, and she had never felt her muscles work so fully and completely than they did now, propelling her through the waters. Her eyesight was impeccable, and no aerial view could compare to the wonders she had seen during her journey through this watery world with Syrifina Myr as a guide.

She had laid eyes on the magnificently mysterious and surely ancient beasts that roamed and ruled the depths of the sea—they moved slow and steady, deep beneath the world, never bothering to trifle with the worries of a life above water.

Wild, wiggly plants of striking colors swayed back and forth with the currents, and she had danced with schools of silver fish, finding a sort of kinship with them in nature now. She whizzed through sunken ships from ancient times, and she explored sands dotted with gold and other lost treasures, enough to fund the lavish lives of a hundred kings. But material things mattered to her in no such way anymore, not when she felt so nearly complete all on her own.

She had come face-to-face with creatures of much greater size than herself in her exploration, and though their sharp teeth could have normally ripped her in half or had her swimming for safety, *they* steered far clear of her in this domain—and it only ever took one look.

She was the predator of the sea now, the conqueror of the territory, a fierce and worthy opponent that no monster lurking in the waters would dare challenge. She was the mysterious creature inhabiting this enchanted, underwater world, ruling it with no fear of competition.

Lessa recalled faint memories from her days in the Learning Center, of drawings and readings of the types of creatures populating the vast seas, known to sink boats on occasion—she pushed those teachings to the side to make room for new knowledge. She was invigorated by her surroundings, and nothing would stop her from exploring every inch of this infinite new playground.

But the most significant new sensation that had come with this transformation was that Lessa was no longer afraid; fear had been removed from her selection of emotions once she'd turned to accept the sea. The only thing she could truly sense of fear now was how faint her wish to turn back was... in a way, that scared her most of all.

"WE CALL THIS EMPRESS ISLE," said Syrifina as she and Lessa made their way to the surface after an exhilarating swim.

Time was lost to her, but Lessa was sure at least a day had already passed—she'd seen the waters lighten from below, presumably with the touch of the sun, and then darken again as it set. She had even felt her energy ebb and wane with the pattern of the moon.

"This is your new home," said Syrifina, a huge smile stretched across her face as she ushered her in. "The Myr Tribe has grown to be a large and loving community of the sea over the centuries. My sisters shall welcome you with open arms."

Lessa saw the dark waters begin to lighten, twinkling like there were stars dancing on the surface. When she broke through, the sight was so dazzling that it took her breath away.

The walls were a glittering dark blue, sweating with beads of water, and the area was decorated with jewels that even King Devlindor himself could never hope to attain. The floors glistened like bronzed mirrors in a dark room, and springy, bright orange and green flowers grew thick between the cracks, wrapping around all sorts of interesting treasures.

Lessa also noticed a large opening at the top of the cavern—it appeared as if a portrait of a magnificent sky, complete with a vivid, yellow moon, had been painted on a vast ceiling.

In its entirety, this hidden cavern was massive, an underwater palace; Lessa was sure there was much more waiting to be explored, noticing several water-drenched pathways in the vicinity.

"No man has ever set foot here in a thousand lifetimes… and *lived*," explained Syrifina, unabashedly boastful. "And they never will."

Lessa took pause at Syrifina's words as she drank in the scenery, noting the addition of skeletons scattered haphazardly across the floor. It made her wonder… *Just how many souls have met their ending by the likes of a mermaid?*

It was also made quickly apparent that fish and other creatures of the sea steered far clear of Empress Isle, here, where the true predators lurked. Alas, most staggering of all was the gathering among the cave.

Ready to greet them—on the sides where the cavern sloped inward and sitting atop large, jutting stones—was the most beautiful collection of women Lessa had ever laid eyes upon. It was as if Syrifina Myr had multiplied into a hundred different forms, all just as alluring and wicked as the first.

Syrifina slid onto one of the large stones, her skin no longer touching the water; her tail morphed back into legs.

Lessa gawked, staggered by the transformation. The other mermaids—in both human and sea-faring forms—kept their eyes on her, though their looks weren't nearly as welcoming.

Reproachful murmurs rolled off their tongues in whispers, but Lessa could hear every word, crisp and clear, with her heightened senses. Lessa's skin prickled and her muscles tensed, unable to stop this new body from readying to defend itself as they openly criticized her.

"Syrifina, *again*…" whined one girl with brown skin and tight curls brushing her shoulders—her lifeblood seemed to shimmer back and forth between silver and gold. "We're supposed to hold a vote. Don't you remember the last poor soul you led into the lion's den?"

She snickered, blowing Lessa a kiss.

"This happens once a decade," said another with a sigh, lounging in a pool of water, splashing her tail about; she let out a hiss toward Lessa from beautiful, pink lips. "How do we know this girl deserves to be one of us? And at such a time of despair… we can't just replace those we've lost."

Flushes of pink enveloped her silver tail, and golden locks hung down her bosom; she flicked her hand back and forth over the waves, the water twisting in delightful shapes at her command.

Lessa turned in circles, staring up at the women who glared down at her. They came in so many variations that she assumed Syrifina must've scoured the entire world just to have a sister from every part of the Olleb—some were pale white, others with skin as black as the night, and everything else in between was accounted for.

Lessa watched them closely, absorbed with each mermaid's lifeblood displays, all shining silver yet with their own unique color melodies to match. She met their eyes, one by one; it wasn't hard to see the dangerous animals behind the beautiful mermaid masks… she felt just the same on the inside.

Though, Syrifina had been right. Here, she didn't find the need to drink blood or an urge to hurt anyone.

Out of sight, out of mind.

With this newfound concentration, the goal at hand seemed to come back into focus. She could feel some of the Lessa she knew returning to take control. *Some*, but not all.

"Sisters—" said Syrifina, standing; the seducing hum of voices came to a stop.

She waved her hand toward Lessa, and the pool beneath her bubbled up gently into the air, placing her upon a watery pedestal. Her majestic tail flicked back and forth in a rhythmic fashion, and Lessa started to find a comfort in it.

"Sisters, calm now," she said, sternly. "Join me in welcoming another mermaid to our clan." Eyes narrowed and more unsupportive hisses filled the air.

Syrifina stood up straighter, slowly turning in a circle so that all attention was on her.

"Let me remind you all that though we must agree on your selections to *my* tribe, who I decide to turn is not, and never will be, a discussion." Her hands balled into fists as her angry persona replaced any excitement there before. "I am your queen, your *mother*, and I make the rules here. Lessa is one of us now, and I daresay she shows fair entitlement to the gifts of the sea more than most of you. She's a great addition to our legacy and has already proven to be exceptional of sorts." She pointed to Sano who hovered in the water nearby. "*And* she brings with her an avatar on the tide! What say you?"

"Welcome, sister," sang one of the mermaids with ivory skin and jet-black hair. Dark purple veins coiled around her body; she took Lessa's hand in her own and planted a kiss on her lips before blowing another to Syrifina.

Syrifina smiled, accepting the offer with a graceful nod. Then she moved out of the way for the rest of the welcoming ceremony to commence.

"Welcome, sister," said the others in an echo—with so many enchanting voices laced together, it sounded like a song.

The girls nearest to her took turns to greet her in the same, intimate fashion while the ones farthest away blew only gentle kisses to the air instead.

"Welcome, sister," they each said again.

Their words seemed to strike a nerve with Lessa, as if jolting her awake from a daze.

These are not my sisters…

"Thank you," she stuttered, somewhat confused.

Atop the bewitched watery pedestal, her mind began to flood with foggy memories of Arianna and the Kane brothers. She kept her gaze down so as not to lose concentration on them.

She locked in on Sano. He was floating idly by in his sea turtle form in case she should need him. Their connection remained undisturbed and felt even strengthened by the pulse of the sea; as their minds linked, Sano reminded Lessa that she was among enemies, not friends—the images of Syrifina sucking Jeom dry of his blood and tossing Demetrius clear across the beach flew back into her thoughts at full force.

This was not her family, and she needed to remember that Syrifina wasn't on her side. Not yet, anyway... She had struck this deal in order to rescue her friends and ultimately have the chance to free a badly beaten Olleb-Yelfra, so she had to see it through.

There was no time to play with these tricksters, but Lessa could feel it in her gut that the ancient mermaid could be satisfied in more than one way—if Syrifina had another motive at all, it would be that Lessa never returned to her friends and was added to her collection of beautiful monsters.

Though her friends were counting on her prompt homecoming, it felt as if a heavy veil had been fitted to her skin, to her mind, like she was wearing a costume that pressed on to be everlasting; if Lessa didn't concentrate on who she was, she could slip away permanently... of this she had no doubt.

The voice that came out of her next shocked even herself as she struggled to resist this new world around her.

"Thank you," she said again, slightly bowing to Syrifina. "I am so humbled by the honor to be welcomed as one of your sisters this night, but you needn't worry that I disrupt your legacy." Her eyes were still locked on Sano's, feeling his healer powers somehow revitalizing and sobering her human mind and spirit. "I'm not going to stay very long... I've come here to help."

"Why would you ever choose to go back to that life?" snapped Syrifina. "Look at you! You're a goddess of the sea now, and you would throw it all away just to help your mortal friends?"

"Syrifina, I'm grateful for your gift," Lessa replied with caution, "but I have a duty to uphold, and not just to my friends but to you and to the Olleb. I'm a Guardian of Gold, first and foremost. I've taken a vow, just as you've taken similar oaths to protect this magical life under the sea."

"You mean to say that she hasn't drunk?" another whispered sharply. "She's no Myr. Not yet!"

Syrifina's smile tightened as the other mermaids put their defenses back up, and Lessa could feel the bond of sisterhood snap away—a dangerous wall being put up between them in its place just as suddenly.

"That's quite right," said Lessa, finding the courage to face them all as she tore her gaze from Sano, knowing his magic was with her still.

She felt the lull of the water rock back and forth with her mind, lowering the bubbling pedestal she sat upon back into the water with ease. Sano swam to her side, and she placed a hand firmly atop his shell to demonstrate their bond.

The mermaids seemed shocked at the magical energy that rolled off her then, Sano giving her a much-needed edge and proving Syrifina's statement; she knew in this moment that their connection alone could be her key to survival in this new world and finding her way back to where she belonged.

"I'm not a Myr. I am a *Thur*," said Lessa with a smirk. "Now, tell me…" She turned to address Syrifina as the waves rocked behind her. "How may I help your family so that you can help mine? A deal's a deal."

PART THREE

21

CITY OF SAND

OUT ON THE WATER and under the dark of night, Arianna was again reminded of the desert. Except here, she felt the environment was much more manageable in a way. The waters had been kind to them.

Too kind, she thought.

Given the stories she'd read of sunken boats and beasts as large as ships, she had expected the journey to be rocky at best.

But the only waves they encountered were far from troublesome, pushing them faster along the currents toward the South Star. And the only beast that roamed the waters was Solza, as far as she could tell. It was as if the Goddess of the Sea herself guided them safely to where they needed to go, and Arianna desperately hoped that she'd lead Lessa in the same direction.

She let her hand graze the water just as Solza surfaced again; sometimes she even wondered if Solza wasn't the one to thank for their safe voyage across this unknown territory, never straying too far from the boat. After all, her avatar was learning to master this element now, and if she had powers anything like what had been gifted to her by the earth, Arianna was sure that bringing calm to the sea would prove a simple task.

She thought of another who now had the power to tame the waters… Lessa still showed no sign of returning to the guardian life. And the strenuous journey had taken them far longer than expected, making this the twenty-eighth moon.

Just one more night left to get her back.

As fate would have it, they were stuck in the middle of the sea, laying all their hopes on a star—Arianna grasped the blue stone at her neck and tried to remember just exactly what a star was capable of.

There were many times she had wished for Lessa with her hand wrapped around that stone, but it hadn't ignited the power Syrifina claimed it possessed. Arianna was still a believer, though; she could feel its power resting on her skin. She just didn't know how to tap into it the way she supposedly had during their escape from Sir Vladamor; in the search for Lessa, it proved useless.

As Arianna's eyes drifted over the deep blue of the tranquil waters, a reflection gazed back at her, blurry with the subtle roll of the waves. This time, she knew without a doubt who she saw— the darkness wasn't overwhelming her mind any longer, and that was something to rejoice about, at least.

Alas, it had been replaced by something darker, surrounding them from the *outside.* A constant evil tried to squeeze out the light all the time, weighing down on her and her friends as they tried to overcome it at every turn.

Down with the King.

As much as the darkness still engulfed their world, Arianna had learned now that there was a light bright enough to dent it. But those lights were scattered—all around the Olleb it would seem—and they would need to come together to fight the dark- ness away permanently.

There's still hope.

She skimmed the waters as far as she could see under the moonlight, and Arianna noticed what looked to be tiny diamonds stitched to the shadows, dancing on the waves; it was the stars reflecting off the water. The sky was littered with them tonight, and the South Star was indeed the brightest of them all, leading the rest in their victory over the night.

She hoped that, by the end of this, the world might reflect a similar image.

Arianna's attention was pulled away from her musings then as a low hum touched her ears, coming from Jeom. As she listened to the words, a chill tingled across her skin. His voice a slow, slurring sound, the subtle tones of the dwarf-language came to the surface as he sang a song that brought life to some of the feelings locked in her heart:

> *Oh, buried souls of men too bold,*
> *Entombed here at the earth's plea,*
> *Their bones glitter, and the dead whisper,*
> *The Black Sand Sea wants company.*
>
> *An eye to the sky, day and night,*
> *The South Star is my guiding light,*
> *Bones may glitter, and the dead may whisper,*
> *But the Black Sand Sea, she can't have me.*

His voice died away into a whistle to replace the words he couldn't remember, but Arianna heard them repeating over and over in her head.

The Black Sand Sea, she can't have me.

"It's lovely," she said. "I haven't heard you sing since the Four Corners. Where did you learn that?"

"From Eli," he said, solemnly. "He had a song for everything."

"That he did," said Arianna; she doubted he was still alive to sing.

The hours again passed in silence. Then the sun began to rise. *Day twenty-nine.*

Demetrius thrust himself to the edge of the boat, making it rock dangerously—Arianna and Jeom both yelped.

"What are you doing? You'll capsize us," said Arianna, pinching her cheeks to wake herself up; no one was able to get much sleep in their current situation.

Demetrius leaned over the side as far as he could without falling in.

"I see something!" he shouted, his compass in hand.

"Not again…" Jeom groaned.

Arianna closed her eyes, unwilling to be tricked into the same illusions as she rowed the oar over and over in sync with Jeom. Her arms ached, and she became hot as the sun started to peak above the earth, welcoming the splash of water on her exposed skin to cool her down; she was burned to a crisp by now, and she could see where her skin had darkened incredibly around the shining silver scars on her shoulder, almost as if she had left the island as a different person altogether.

"I swear it," said Demetrius again. "There's land ahead!"

Arianna lifted her head with the little energy she had left and forced herself to follow the line of Demetrius' shaking finger—there was a bulge of rocky shoreline.

"Brother, I think you're right!" said Jeom with a whistle. "*Finally.*"

A smile broke wide across his sun-dried lips, and the boys both cheered loudly.

"Come on," said Arianna in a bitter tone, not joining in on the celebration. "Let's get out of this wretched boat."

Though she was elated at the prospect of land, she couldn't help but feel dread tied with it—if land was what they had found, then where was Lessa to greet them?

She glanced down at the water to see the shimmering silhouette of Solza swimming nearby in her dolphin form. The water rippled with her swift movements, teasing her; Arianna was in such a tired state that her mind kept tricking her, making her think that Lessa might surface at any moment.

"She can still find us," said Demetrius, laying a hand on her shoulder, knowingly. "We'll wait. There's one more day."

His voice was soft and reassuring, as it normally was, but they were empty words; Arianna hated that the only thing in her power to do now was hope.

"We'll wait," she said with a nod. "As long as it takes to know that she's safe… in whatever life she chooses to live."

As the wind picked up and the waves grew strong, this last bit of the journey proved more challenging than the rest. They rowed faster to the shore, battling their way to dry land.

Arianna felt pulled in two different directions, her muscles shaking from the exertion it took to combat the thick arms of water trying to push them back out to deep sea. On one hand, she had quite enjoyed the chance at exploring the ocean—undiscovered territory and a journey that seemed never-ending, untold surprises only a dive away. But on the other, land was safe and welcome, offering a warmth that could never be achieved with water on one's skin…

I grow weary of the sea.

With one last push of the oar, she let herself finally relax as the boat met the shoreline after the break of the waves.

"Nice work," said Demetrius, hopping out with a splash; he guided the boat the rest of the way, Solza nudging him along until it was too shallow for her to swim any farther. "Out you go!"

He opened his hand for Arianna to take, and she joined him in the shallows.

The water came up to her knees, soaking her parched skin.

"*Ahhh.*" It was an instant relief.

It felt so good to even just stretch her legs and plant her feet on somewhat solid ground—she thought she might take off at a run and never turn back.

Instead, she took a moment to enjoy the way the wet sand clumped beneath her toes while the boys dragged the boat to shore.

"Well, this is familiar," said Jeom, scooping dry grains into his hands—the sand fell from his fingers in black curtains.

"I think we've finally made it full circle," said Demetrius, pointing up.

"Talk about a detour." Jeom shielded his eyes against the sun, following his brother's line of sight.

The land they had found sloped upward, so it was easy to spot the giant pyramids looming down over them.

"The City of Zambienth," said Arianna, her mind flashing back to darker days where Sir Vladamor took front and center. "I wonder if the necromancer made it here as well?"

Demetrius took a deep breath. "Let's hope he had other plans."

Arianna shook the thought away as Solza shifted forms; the avatar seemed to float out of the water on a cloud of her own magic. She pranced up the shoreline to sit on a rock, now an elegant snow leopard.

The sun illuminated her on the beach as if she needed a stage to stand on, and she had noticeably grown during their many weeks of rest on the island; Arianna knew that the transformation to a water-element creature had somehow strengthened her avatar's body and soul, matured Solza in the same way that she felt herself maturing as time went on.

She took in the rest of the scenery—a short coastline with the tide rolling in, and long, gray cliffs stretching across it; Arianna supposed if they followed their rocky paths up and up and up, they'd eventually find the main city and the people who undoubtedly inhabited it.

She pondered how often Zambienth citizens might venture

to this beach. *Never, I pray.*

They were still fugitives, and now they were back in the open, a highlife prize for the taking.

The stark white pyramids glared harshly under the rising sun, seeming to connect from one to another, like a puzzle that fit perfectly together—an elevated world above the sand.

Jeom jabbered excitedly, pointing to the different types of architecture he could spot from this viewpoint.

"See there!" he said. "Every structure meets the next, big or small. I bet there's corridors and pathways that could get you all the way from one end to the other and everywhere in between."

"It's like a maze," said Demetrius.

"Exactly," replied his brother. "And I'm sure there's loads of secrets hidden in there."

"Why is that?" said Arianna, hands on her hips.

"Well, this architecture was created to eliminate privacy," said Jeom, clearly in his element. "The pyramids sit high, overlooking the desert so that its dwellers can see who is arriving by all sides. And it's an open-style build, you see? Every archway, every window, is open to the fresh air." He waved his hands about. "I'd wager there are even pathways indirectly connecting the street cleaner's house to the keeper's palace if you mapped it."

He pointed to the tallest pyramid and drew an invisible line from there to the other side of the city, where buildings began to shrink considerably in size.

Arianna saw his point. Surely, this was the residence of the Zambienth Keeper, keeping watch with a bird's-eye view.

"With that kind of close quarters and defensive lifestyle, I'd be surprised if there weren't a few secret staircases built into sheds leading to a vanishing tunnel—if you know what I mean?" Jeom laughed, nudging Arianna in the ribs.

She shook her head, smiling to the ground as she considered his statement. *If there are secrets, we'll need Lessa to help us uncover them…*

Her heart sank just as quickly as it had lifted.

"I bet you're right," said Demetrius. "I wonder what the City of Sand is hiding?"

Arianna had to squint to get even a glimpse of the city life. She saw what looked to be people dressed in light-colored robes busying about, rushing across carefully carved archways or traveling through twisting corridors that bridged one pyramid to the next. A new day had just begun, and the city woke with it, just as it would be doing right now in South Luose.

From this outside view looking in, Arianna began to see the chain reaction of King Devlindor's rule. Though Zambienth clearly had its own personality, one small look revealed an identical behavior to that of the city she'd most recently fled—Arianna imagined there was a place for public gatherings, like the Garden… a fine palace with exquisite chambers fit for highlifes alone, and a tavern with a young citizen tending to its many patrons just to make ends meet.

There'd be newly freed slaves trying to figure out what freedom meant for them and masters fiercely attempting to sharpen their new apprentices. Worse still, there was certainly a keeper chosen by the King, inflicting severe punishment where necessary and maintaining some version of the Luose Dungeon where people would waste away in the dark.

I see right through your veil.

On the surface, this city was bright white and shining, but the sand it was built upon was as black as the soul of the King who ruled it from afar—this city and the next, all those from here to the edge of Olleb-Yelfra, were nothing more than bandages dropped over a deeply infected wound.

"What now?" said Demetrius, the tremble in his voice taking them all back to the torturous task at hand.

"We wait," said Arianna, gazing toward the sky.

The silence was deafening, all hearts shouting out for Lessa. Then Jeom's rumbling stomach broke the quiet.

"I hate to say this…" said Demetrius, averting his eyes from his brother's. "I want to wait for Lessa more than anything, but we can't just sit around here and do nothing. We've no energy left to do anyone any good, and there's no more food. We need supplies, and we shouldn't waste time in case this beach doesn't prove as solitary as it looks."

"What do you suppose we do, then?" snapped Jeom, his stomach grumbling again and betraying his stubbornness.

Arianna couldn't help but notice his recently adopted foul temperament toward his brother. Normally, he reserved most of his outbursts for her.

Demetrius shrank back a little but held his ground nonetheless, evidently unsurprised by his reaction.

"All I mean to say," he said, softly, "is that this isn't Idris. We're not surrounded by trees or plants that can feed us, and there's no spring waters here to drink from." He patted his belly. "I'm simply stating a fact. We're *hungry.*"

Arianna stepped in, seeing the heat rise to Jeom's face as his stomach gave another embarrassing rumble.

"He's got a good point," she said. "We'll have to find more food soon. We've been eating rations for too long, and we need our strength now more than ever."

Demetrius nodded, glancing toward the sharp cliffs rising tall around them; they offered nothing in the way of a trail. But the glistening rocks gifted them a striking backdrop, at least, swirls of gray and white layering atop the black sand.

Arianna looked longingly at Solza—she playfully pounced at the birds daring to land on the beach in her vicinity as they hunted for crabs. Her avatar had all the energy in the world.

Alas, even with her magical boost, Arianna was fading fast.

We can't find a way to help Lessa, or anyone, if we starve to death.

The Island of Idris had provided them safety in so many ways, a break from the stresses of a normal existence; food was plenty, the water was clean, the location was stunning, and they had been cut off from humankind, completely protected by ancient magic.

Now, Arianna felt the cold wrapping back around her, even under a hot sun. They were no longer in a safe place—they were being hunted, the war for freedom refreshed just as soon as they had reached land.

"Well, how do you suppose we do that?" asked Jeom, clutching at his stomach, resigned to the fact that he would eventually need to eat to cure his sour mood.

"Listen," said Arianna, fully intending on continuing their search, "I'll stay on the beach with Solza and watch our belongings. Use some of the money we took from Godfrey and go to the city. Scope it out and come back with some *real* food. I'll be fine here, and by the time you're back, I'll have had plenty of time to do one last underwater search for Lessa."

During the days confined to a boat, their secrets had all been aired, nothing much else to do but talk; Arianna had confessed her fruitless searches for Lessa and the guilt she felt over her loss. Much to her surprise, the boys hadn't let her bear the burden of it all, despite some of the harsh words that had passed between them on the island—they agreed to support one another to the end, no matter what happened tonight…

"Are you sure that's wise?" said Demetrius. "We've barely eaten a thing on this journey. You won't have energy enough for that kind of dive. It's unsafe."

"Don't worry," said Arianna. "Solza gives me all the strength I need. I'll be careful. Just wear your robes and keep your hoods up. It's safer for you to go and check out the scene. I'm the one they have eyes out for. We'll go from there. Oh, and take these!"

She rifled in her bag and then shoved two papers into their hands.

"Our citizenship proof?" said Jeom. "But—"

"Nobody will recognize you," she said with a shrug. "Jaxin and Darrios only existed in South Luose, so it's a small risk here that anyone might have met you. Just in case, you'll have identification if you need to show it. It's probably your best chance to not draw any attention."

Demetrius looked to Jeom. They both nodded, tucking the documents away in their cloaks.

"All right," said Jeom, his shoulders slumped. "We'll bring back food and water and see if we can find out anything useful. It's been some time now, but I'm sure if Vladamor has blown through town, we'll hear about it."

"And we can make a camp under one of these cliffs for the night," said Demetrius, pointing to an area nearby. "Nobody will bother us at all once the tide comes up."

"Sounds like a plan," said Arianna, passing them their shoes; they quickly readied for the trek. "Now go. You still have a few hours before nightfall."

They placed their belongings into the boat, hiding it safely behind some rocks and out of the water. Then the boys made their way up the winding cliff, taking care to pull on their hoods to hide their faces.

"And *don't* kill anyone!" Arianna shouted after them.

She heard grunts of agreement from Jeom, but she doubted that was a promise. Demetrius, on the other hand, had long since taken a personal vow against killing—she never had to worry much over him.

She watched them struggle up the steep slants of rock. It was strange to see the green and purple of their cloaks fluttering about on the wind; the practical robes of their former lives were now the only thing that kept them warm at night, the luxuries of the palace life gone. The only reason they even had these at all was because of Lessa's foresight to pack the essentials in her magical Luose bag for emergencies.

Lessa... What would they do if they had to go on without her?

The boys darted around the cliffs with care, back and forth

on a path Arianna could barely see. Several minutes later, they waved down at her to signify the worst was over; Arianna waved back before they disappeared on an obscured path toward the City of Zambienth.

The lump of numbing fear in her chest grew wider; she felt completely alone, not knowing if Lessa would ever return or even if Jeom and Demetrius wouldn't be walking straight into a trap, gone forever to her too. There was not a day anymore when she could convince herself that everything would end up all right from one minute to the next.

The moment they had fled the Four Corners was the moment they knew their lives would be forever uncertain. Every day would be a risk, every choice could be the last; that was the life they had chosen, whether they realized it or not at the time. And after so many trials and tortures, Arianna wasn't sure if any one of them could ever be convinced again that life could be any other way— even if they lived forever.

Lessa, come back.

THE SPLASHES OF SOLZA in the water startled Arianna out of her thoughts before they could turn to more sinister themes.

"Coming!" she called, tearing off her robes and tying up her long, unruly hair.

She dove into the warm sea and latched onto Solza, the avatar's slippery skin glistening as bubbles of water ran past her fins and tickled Arianna's face. Off they went, as routine, in search of their lost friend.

The sun beat down brightly today, making the water so clear that she could see straight to the bottom.

As usual, there was nothing more to find but swarms of colorful fish and hills of sandy, sparkling terrain in this underwater world, though changed from white to black—it was surely never a dull sight… but also never quite what she was looking for.

Just then, Arianna urged Solza to follow the flick of a silvery tail, her heart beating wildly as she thought it must be Lessa. She tried to call out, but her voice was lost to the sea.

Solza swam faster, pulling her along for the ride, the rush of water around them intensified as magic gave them a boost.

Inevitably, they caught up. But when it turned to face them, to Arianna's dismay, it was not Lessa at all.

Out of the darkness, she saw what looked to be a giant fish on first sight, much larger than Solza was in this dolphin form. Though, as it came closer, she recognized a mouth lined with sharp teeth and a silver tail streaked with red, as if a fire had broken out under the sea and this creature had swum right through it to be one with the flames.

Out of the few beasts that Arianna knew roamed the watery realm, this was one of the worst—a *shark*.

Next to a mermaid, she was sure this would be the most feared monster of the sea, a terrible creature that many fishermen had encountered in ill-fated trips and not escaped from whole.

Arianna froze and felt her own fear jolt into Solza, still clutching her fin—she couldn't help but wonder in this terrifying standoff if Syrifina hadn't morphed into this creature herself, a shark of the sea with a fiery passion to stop them from ever seeing Lessa again.

The shark circled them slowly, its big, probing eyes always keeping them in sight.

Solza rushed forward in a show of strength, forcing Arianna to lose hold of her; she floated helplessly behind to watch.

The shark welcomed the battle, swimming fast toward them, its mouth open for the kill. But as the shark advanced, Solza opened her mouth too—Arianna could literally see a shield of powerful sound spread out in front of her, clearly throwing the shark off balance… angering it more.

She was stunned once more by her avatar's talents.

A tangled, undersea duel began.

Arianna's air supply was thinning quickly, though. She had to try to reach the surface now, the sun dancing like a teasing light on top of the water.

It proved so much farther than it looked.

Every time she kicked her legs, she felt as if she might sink back down at any moment, the weight of the water growing heavier as her lungs longed for a breath.

Moments later, Solza was underneath her, pushing her fast toward the surface; Arianna coughed as they both broke through the waves.

She choked on the revitalizing air, letting Solza guide her back to shore.

"You were very brave," said Arianna in clipped breaths. She caught Solza's electric eyes. "You've got more fire in you than any other creature, I'm sure. More than some senseless shark."

They nuzzled in the shallows before Arianna beckoned her out of the water, fearing the creature could return; she worried now, more than ever, for Lessa's safety with such things lurking in the seas.

Solza effortlessly changed form, back into the bright-eyed, furry-coated snow leopard she knew best.

"Don't worry, girl," said Arianna, still so much wonder in her heart in the face of such magic. "We'll find them both."

She could sense her avatar's concerns—not just about Lessa but Sano as well; Arianna had a fleeting hope that whatever link Solza and Sano shared might well be the link to bringing them both home, though she wouldn't voice it.

She squeezed the water from her hair and let the falling sun dry her clothes, watching in contempt as a full moon slowly began to rise in its place. She counted on her fingers, but there was no denying that this was their last night to find Lessa.

Tomorrow a new cycle of the moon would begin again. And if Syrifina spoke a truth, Lessa would be bound to the life of a mermaid forever.

Arianna observed the sky in silence, waiting for the boys to return; for now, all that was visible of the rising moon was a mere shadow behind billows of dark gray clouds, the South Star even hidden from view. It was clear, though, that once the sun finally set in just a few short hours, moonlight would engulf the land— and if Lessa didn't return before the moon solidified its place in the sky, Arianna was sure she'd never want to see the sun again.

22

THE KANE BROTHERS

"WAIT FOR ME!" he heard Demetrius call.

Jeom took the steps two at a time, his long legs having no trouble to climb the steep stairway they'd found after navigating the cliffs. Looking back, he saw his brother was already far behind.

Begrudgingly, he slowed his pace.

"Hurry up," he yelled down to him. "We can't waste time."

Jeom rested for only a moment to take in the view, the sun a deep red as it began to lower in the sky, dancing over the blue waters.

"Where are you, Lessa?" he whispered to the wind.

"All right, keep up now," chimed Demetrius with a laugh as he hopped past him. "Don't keep us waiting!"

He waved Jeom along, and soon they were at the top of the cliff looking upon a city that seemed to be chiseled from mountains of white stone. Giant pyramids stabbed toward the sky, all different sizes decorating the land for miles.

Jeom was awed by the structures—this city floating above the sand, built to perfection as it edged toward the sea like a warrior in search of the horizon.

"What should we do now?" he said, scratching his head.

The area seemed to stretch out magnificently for as far as his eyes could see. And the closer they got to entering, the more details that unfurled; winding pathways and open-air tunnels connected each building to the next as if giant worms of granite crawled across the earth, willingly, into the hungry, white beaks of enormous birds from every direction.

Standing there, Jeom truly felt like a dwarf. He wondered even if this place hadn't once been touched by the magical influence of his fallen brethren.

He patted the Axe of Crissy at his belt, concealed in a tube that looked nothing more than cheap tin, a truer treasure than many rulers had ever had the blessing to possess.

How did I get to this place?

Despite this good path he tried to lead, this brave man he'd tried to become since ridding his life of slavery, he never felt on the inside as sure as the others seemed to look on the outside—as *he* tried to look on the outside. *Kill the King?*

He shook his head of such a monumental thought, but it found a way of always snaking back into his mind. The idea didn't make him feel brave and powerful, or like his life was full of meaning. It just made him feel scared, and weak, and *vulnerable*—as small as his dwarf kin had physically been.

He felt ashamed for even thinking so weakly when the dwarves had obviously been strong, so courageous, to stand up for what they believed in. And he had vowed to stand up for them, too, to stand up for the Olleb and rid her of the King.

But he was just so *scared.* Scared of dying, scared of feeling so strongly about anything, scared of losing people he had only just realized he loved. His friends, his family—*Lessa.*

If I had never loved at all, would that have been better?

Secretly, at times, he prayed for the past to return.

Though, of all the chapters in his life, Jeom most relished the one he had led in South Luose as Jaxin; he felt the crumpled citizen certificate in his pocket, burning, a painful reminder of all the things he'd always wanted and probably would never have again.

Master Gansevurt had taken him under his wing, inducted him as a legendary Creator's Club member, setting him on a path to a grand life as a master creator. There was also Keeper Kassime, holding open the door to a colorful, magical opportunity to be a Guardian of Gold at the very same time—a protector of knowledge from a lost age.

Of course, Jeom understood what this meant to his core, to be a guardian. He really, *truly* did, but he just couldn't help that selfish part of him wanting back the safety of the place that had come hand in hand with such a wonderous responsibility.

For an entire year, the keeper had insisted that their focus should be only to learn and protect knowledge for the sake of someone else. That hopefully, years from now, that someone would take the reins and end King Devlindor on their behalf and the behalf of all those who had fallen before them.

Even his thoughts of Keeper Kassime's loss, though sad as they were, couldn't help but be centered around his own desire to go back to their safe, comfortable life that once was; it wasn't the most noble of wishes, but it was the securest. Others had suffered around them, but he and his friends had not. They had been highlifes with magic to aid them and anything they desired at their fingertips, protected by status.

Now they were on the run again, weak from hunger, missing a friend, and completely defenseless in a new, unknown city. *Kill the King?*

Jeom scoffed out loud for having supported such a goal.

How could they expect to kill anyone in this state? How

could they avenge anyone, protect anyone when they couldn't even protect themselves?

King Undoriamus and the dwarf tomb he'd left behind so long ago now flooded his mind—he'd left no other legacy but supposedly him, Jeom Kane, Slave Twenty-Three of Creator's District.

He might have cried right then and there, caught between this never-ending sea and the city, if Demetrius hadn't been around to witness it.

Alas, the tears he held tight to were not for the death of the dwarf people—he'd already felt and dealt with that pain the best he could for a family he'd never known, a magical inheritance he didn't think he deserved. No, he wanted to cry because King Undoriamus and all his people's sacrifices were the least important thing on his mind.

He wanted to cry over the greedy piece of himself that no one knew existed but him, the one that wished he'd never met Arianna in the first place and that none of these problems had ever even fallen into his lap.

He gazed to the water, the waves calmer than ever. There was still no sign of Lessa—he wanted to cry for her too. He wanted to shout to the sea for her return… but he'd tried that already and it hadn't worked. He wanted to scream at himself for being so absorbed with her now that he could no longer focus on the bigger picture, the one Lessa had understood so clearly when she let Syrifina give her the kiss of death.

Kill the King? How could I ever even dream of doing such a thing… without you?

Jeom shook his head, imagining once more a life that didn't include Arianna Belvedor, or Demetrius, or Lessa, and he just couldn't fathom it one bit. He knew, deep down, that the worst, heart-wrenching pain in the world was worth the fleeting, happy moments he had been privileged to have with his new family, even if the future proved their time together painful and short.

He had fought for all of them, and he would die for all of them too. That was love, and he would have to keep reminding himself not to try to wish it away—for now he knew that wishes could come true, even at the most uncertain of times.

"Let's go," said Demetrius, snapping Jeom out of his mind's plunge into darkness, urging him forward. "Don't let your thoughts consume you. She will be okay. Let's just keep going."

THEY FINALLY CLEARED THE HEIGHT of the cliffs, so Demetrius led the way down across a maintained path. They entered a torchlit tunnel that spanned a small stretch of water and, eventually, reached what appeared to be the main entrance; they slowed to assess the situation.

Two guards stood at a gate—from there on, a bustling city seemed to expand out in front of them.

"Identification," said the city guard, holding out his hand in a bored voice, not even bothering to look up. When they both hesitated, he lifted his eyes.

He seemed to tense when he found Jeom towering over him.

"*Identification.*" He tried to sound sterner, squaring his shoulders.

"Here you go, sir," said Demetrius, pulling out his boyish charm and the highlife swagger that Darrios had bestowed upon him.

He handed over his papers, and playfully nudged a stone-faced Jeom in the ribs to do the same.

"Sorry, my friend here is a little slow as of late. The journey across the desert was a long one. Do you know where we can find a market?"

The guard looked him up and down and then unfurled the

documentation Keeper Kassime had gifted them as part of their guardian initiations. After a long, agonizing moment, he seemed to relax, nodding to the other guard.

"Jaxin, Darrios," he said. "From the Twin Cities? You're a long way from home."

Jeom winced at the name, at the man he wished he were. Jaxin was more of an empty shell now, and he would have to fully shed that skin someday.

"This place can be hectic for newcomers, 'specially at night if you don't know your way around the Burrows," the guard said.

"The Burrows?" Demetrius peered over the guard's shoulder, trying to get a better look; Jeom could tell he was excited to see what this place was all about.

A little part of him was, too, but it didn't feel proper to be excited about anything right now.

"Right you are," said the guard, handing their papers back. "That's what we call all the tunnels like these cutting through Zambienth. They burrow under the city in some places and through nearly every building you come 'cross. I'd be damned if you don't get lost on your first day here." He chuckled. "I'm betting you're lost already if you found this entrance. Most travelers taking the desert route come in from the other side. This entrance is used mainly by those who arrive by ship."

Demetrius gave Jeom a questioning look; they hadn't seen any ships on their climb…

Jeom wished he hadn't been so absorbed in his thoughts that he hadn't bothered glancing to the other side of the sea. Would they have spotted ships in a harbor?

That would be a sight to see.

He made a mental note to check on his way back *and* to make sure their camp wasn't too close by.

"And food?" he grumbled, his stomach rumbling along with his voice.

"Head straight down this path," said the guard, pointing up

ahead. "See that archway some ways up at the end of the tunnel?"

Jeom peered past him over the heads of people rushing this way and that—a huge archway rose above the street. Intricate carvings decorated every facet of the structure, complete with the crests of all four districts paying homage to the City of the Four Corners.

"No matter how far we get," said Jeom, glaring at the golden snake in the center, "the Jar reaches to the ends of the earth."

He noticed large trees planted all around the archway, as if a small forest had gotten lost in the middle of the desert.

"They must've imported some of those plants," said Demetrius, standing on his tiptoes to see. "No *way* they'd grow naturally here."

It was practically the Garden back in South Luose but with a dry, desert flare.

The memory of the brutal whipping Eli had endured at the center of the Luose Altar gave him a jolting reminder of why their goal was what it was. *Kill the King.*

Someone had to do it… so why not them?

"Once you reach that, you're in Arch Alley, a huge marketplace," said the guard. "You'll find something there. Just make sure you got coin."

He eyed Jeom with nothing short of suspicion.

"You mean, like this?" he barked, shaking a bulging bag of gold at the man.

Jeom shoved past him then, unable to resist the cocky personality of Jaxin, a respected highlife of South Luose; Demetrius profusely shed gratitude onto the guard, tossing him a gold piece as he slunk through the iron gate at Jeom's side.

"When you get to Arch Alley, don't linger!" the guard called after them. "I hear the keeper is on one of her rampages again. She'll spot new blood a mile away and drain you of it."

"Let's just get some food and get out of here," said Jeom, a shiver rolling up his spine—he'd already been drained of enough blood by an evil woman, and he wasn't about to let go of another drop.

Demetrius fell in step by his side. They lifted their hoods and blended right into the bustling crowds as the tunnel was replaced by an uncovered black, sandy path. They walked in silence, rubbing shoulders with the citizens of Zambienth as the arch seemed to grow closer and closer.

Strange, pointy cacti reached out at them from all sides of this wall-less tunnel, stretching in through the open spaces and tempting them to touch. Beautiful, bright flowers decorated the arms of the prickly plant life, and Demetrius steered Jeom far clear of them.

"One touch from that and we'll be in search of the Well Center," he said, nodding to a striking blossom. "Don't let the hand fool you to forget what arm it's attached to."

Jeom looked closer and saw sharp, yellow thorns that dripped with natural poison, camouflaged in the petals of the feathery flower.

As the tunnel receded, the archway opened up into a wide area—Arch Alley—just as the regulator had promised. From there, the pyramids truly towered over them, larger than the giants from the lost memory.

There were so many paths to take, bridges from one pyramid to the next.

Looking around, Jeom realized that the sea even crept in and out of the area as well, feeding this dry city with much-needed water.

When they reached the center of the alley where the arch stood, he realized what the guard had meant—a crowd gathered here today, and he was certain he knew why.

The archway was made of thick stone and decorated in long garlands of pink flowers. It had been strategically erected in a central point of the city where many tunnels surely led, curly trees and dusty, maroon bushes surrounding it.

Directly in front of the arch, now visible up close, were low steps made of thick glass. They encircled what looked to be a pond, shimmering in the middle of the desert city like a mirror atop the sands. And the way the stairs held tight to the pond at its tip made the structure seem as if it were a pyramid in and of itself, though small among the giants.

Inching closer for a better look, Jeom peered to the bottom of the water and found the striking image of a gold, coiled snake glaring back up at him. Then he noticed not coins for luck littering the floor of the crystal-clear waters but gleaming bones.

Although glittering glass and sparkling water stole the show, this was the King's land, need they be reminded.

A hush grew over the buzzing crowd, everyone looking up to the top of the glass stairs where a platform provided room to stand by the edge of the water—to the watchers from below, though, it looked as if those atop the platform could walk on water.

A fierce woman with black skin, dark eyes, and hair braided tightly to her scalp stood proudly on the edge. She wore stark, white garments that showed off her stomach, legs, and arms, her muscles sculpted to perfection. Gold, chunky, jewelry dazzled around her neck, and she wore a single sword strapped to her hip.

"City regulators!" she called down. "Bring me the treacherous thief, *now.*"

Her voice was sharp, not to be disobeyed in the slightest, and Jeom suddenly felt an overwhelming sense of gratitude toward Keeper Kassime—he'd somehow found the strength to retain his kindness, even while bearing the burden of such a vicious role.

He glanced up to see citizens hanging out of windows and off the edges of the tunnels crisscrossing in the sky, all trying to get a better view of what was sure to be a gruesome public punishment.

Jeom and Demetrius observed in horror as two large men carried a young woman up the stairs. She kicked and screamed the entire way, but she was so thin and weak it could have hardly made a difference.

"Who is she?" one man asked, Jeom tuning in to the murmurs of the crowd.

"A girl from the palace kitchens, I think," said another. "Pity, but I'm glad it's not anyone I know today."

"Right you are. But yes… such a pity," said an older woman. "She barely made it a year by the looks of it."

Their voices were low, shaking. But this was the way of the world. This was what had come to be known as 'normal,' and there was nothing anyone could do but accept it and go on living—if they were lucky.

"This thief shall not even be dignified by name at today's punishment," said the keeper.

"Please," screamed the girl, her gray robes fluttering in the wind like a scared bird caught upon landing. "Please, it was just a loaf of bread! I was so hungry."

"Well, I hope it was a satisfying last meal," said the keeper. "Nobody steals from me, from *my* home, and lives."

"But you were starving us!" she yelled, her voice cracking as she looked to the crowd for help. "She was starving us! I'm a citizen too. I earned my citizenship *too*, and you made your kitchen staff eat the scraps off your glamorous table." She bowed her head. "It was only bread!"

The keeper struck her, and Jeom could see the blood fly from her mouth as the sharp, heavy rings on her hand dug into the girl's skin. The girl looked up, breath coming heavy, still struggling from the weight of the regulator at her back.

The keeper gave a wicked smile, happily letting her teeth show.

"You're not a citizen anymore," she said. "Now, you'll be nothing but *bones*." With that, she gave some sort of signal lost on Jeom. Everything happened so fast.

The regulators restraining the girl released their grips, thrusting her into the keeper's arms; it almost seemed as if she might console the terrified girl in a hug, say that it had all been some cruel joke.

But with the sharp inhale from the bystanders, Jeom knew that the true outcome would be something awful.

The girl was too shocked to do anything but stare into the keeper's big, dark eyes with her fingernails digging deep into her strong arms.

The keeper effortlessly shoved her backward with one hand—and that's when Jeom saw the dagger in the other, dripping with fresh, innocent blood.

The girl stumbled across the platform and the crowd went silent, waiting for something worse as she let out a shaky cry. Her hands covered the place where the dagger had been, blood staining her palms and darkening her silver robes.

"Enough of this!" said the keeper. "Enjoy your punishment." With a kick, she sent the girl flying backward into the pond with the golden snake waiting at the bottom.

Jeom's breath caught in his throat—she hit the water with a splash, her screams diluted as she sank.

For a second, the girl floated there with blood streaming eerily from her wound; Jeom thought she'd surely put up a fight before she drowned.

What a cruel sentence...

He pitied her terribly, resisting the urge to jump in and rescue her; she reminded him so much of their innocent Lessa, her blond hair floating out in a train behind her and blue eyes bulging, overwhelmed by the heaviness of the water.

"By gods," choked Demetrius, clutching at his sleeve. "Brother, this is madness! I can't bear to watch."

Demetrius pulled him away through the crowd, following the lead of others who had turned their eyes away, not willing to witness such horror that would surely haunt their sleep for years to come.

As Jeom was yanked back to the present, away from his

thoughts of Lessa, he realized that the pool wasn't filled with water at all—it was some kind of toxic liquid, an *acid*, eating the girl away. Before they could fight their way through the crowd and away from the punishment pond, her body had vanished as if she had never even existed.

Jeom's eyes stayed wide and unblinking as her bones sank slowly to the bottom of the shining, glass floor, seeming to fall right into the snake's open mouth, its sharp fangs at the ready. And though he couldn't look away, he knew he wouldn't stop seeing that image for a long time to come.

"Jeom, let's get out of here, please!" cried Demetrius, breathless; his brother had lost himself, panicking.

"Take a breath," said Jeom, his voice solemn.

Demetrius placed his hands on his knees, trying to pull the air back into his lungs in a corner away from prying eyes.

"What is this world we're living in?" he said after finding his calm, tears shimmering in his eyes.

Jeom sighed, looking back to the arch. "This is the King's world," he said.

He had needed that harsh reminder of the real reason there was a need for guardians at all, of something bigger than him; he couldn't let selfishness or greed stand in the way any longer. There was more at stake than just his feelings, of even Lessa, and of the others he called family. *Every* innocent life mattered.

"We can't forget what we're fighting for."

Lessa, don't forget.

Demetrius shook his head. "Never," he said. "We can never forget." He grabbed Jeom's hand. "Hail to the World."

"Hail to Olleb-Yelfra," whispered Jeom, pulling Demetrius to his chest.

Under the setting sun, they put their focus back on food and back on Lessa. They passed underneath the archway and into the depths of Arch Alley—it seemed the commotion from the punishment ceremony had done little to disrupt the day.

The market was flooded with people, and in no time, they had their packs filled with plenty to keep their bellies full for the next few nights of adventure. They also learned from gossiping passersby that the city keeper was called Val Yahindi, and they should never wish to meet her—though they had quickly established this on their own.

With the coming of night, and bursting with stories to tell Arianna, they headed back through the tunnel and gate where they'd entered. Oddly though, there were no guards around to question their motives this time.

"Well, that's convenient," said Jeom, cocking his head to the side as he surveyed the area.

"I wouldn't be so sure," said Demetrius, pointing to the nearby bushes.

There lay the earlier guard with what looked to be a large bump on his head, slumped over and out of view. Someone had obviously attacked him; Demetrius threw down his staff and ran over to check to see if he still lived.

"Looks like he's still breathing," he said with a sigh of relief—he pulled out the tiny jar of healing gel he and Lessa had concocted together on Idris. "*Helthra saludis emencia.*"

Though Demetrius didn't have clear powers to speak of yet, he believed in himself more than anyone and diligently recited the words that Lessa had taught them all for emergencies… *just* in case they made any difference at all when he spoke them.

"Will he be okay?" asked Jeom, scoping out the tunnel. "I wonder what happened."

"I think so—"

Demetrius suddenly shouted out in what sounded like anger or surprise, a scuffle clearly underway. Jeom rushed to his aid, finding a man in the black-hooded robes of a city regulator struggling to keep his brother pinned to the ground.

Jeom grabbed the intruder by his neck from behind, pulling him off Demetrius and squeezing tight.

"You have bad timing," growled Jeom, practically seething, as the man clawed at his hands for freedom. "I promised I wouldn't kill anybody today, but I'm feeling a lot less than forgiving right now."

"Wait!" said Demetrius, reaching for his staff and getting to his feet. "I threw the first punch."

He stormed over to the man and ripped off his hood to reveal a face that Jeom knew well; he threw the man to the ground, staggering backward in surprise as Demetrius held the sharp end of his staff to his throat.

Elijah Neve—the traitor who had left them in the desert for good, taking with him their secrets of magic—had somehow come back into their lives once again.

"You!" roared Jeom, glaring down at Eli and clenching his fists. "Give me one good reason not to kill you right now."

"*Jeom*, it's just not worth it," warned Demetrius through gritted teeth, but he looked angry enough himself to make a life-ending strike, still holding his weapon threateningly at Eli's neck.

"I believe Arianna would say differently," said Jeom, stepping forward, wanting so badly to take out all his anger on him.

"Just hear me out," said Eli with a shaky voice, slowly standing and dusting himself off.

Demetrius pursed his lips but lifted his staff, standing by Jeom's side.

Eli let out a sigh of relief. "It's good… I'm glad…" He cleared his throat. "It's good to see you both again," he stuttered, a wavering smile on his lips.

"How did you find us?" asked Jeom, cutting him off.

"I was sent here to help," said Eli with a more serious look. "I was sent here on behalf of the Guardians of Gold."

23

CALLING A LOST WITCH

HEARING THE TUMBLE OF ROCKS, Arianna looked up to see what must have been Jeom heading down the cliff's jagged pathways. "Thank the gods you're back!" she called, instantly relieved. "How did it go? What's Zambienth like?"

She was eager for a distraction and hoped she'd get the chance to one day see what was known to the Olleb as the 'City of Sand.' Her curiosity nagged her to explore more, but she had to be smart and put her focus on Lessa now.

She ran to meet the boys but stopped cold in her tracks, finding Eli strolling down the beach behind them.

"You!" she gasped. "I don't believe this. What on earth is he doing here?"

"Ara, please," said Demetrius, holding up his hands.

She knew that look—that 'just listen' look she didn't ever care for and had yet to tolerate under such circumstances.

Arianna was beside herself with shock and anger at the sight of him. Not to mention his terrible timing. She didn't want to waste a single second dealing with him when Lessa needed them now more than ever.

His intense, green eyes sparkled with anticipation as he got closer, reminding her of the time she'd set her gaze on Solza awakening in the Luose Well Center; she remembered becoming lost in the avatar's exotic beauty, striking black and white fur and a deep, innocent stare—as if she hadn't just put her through the worst pain of her life. Oh, how she had hated Solza then, hated the beautiful sight of her and loathed herself for thinking she was beautiful at all.

Watching Eli get closer, with the confident stride of a warrior, she despised herself for thinking the exact same thing. Except she couldn't even begin to imagine how they would ever have as happy an ending as she and Solza had found.

"Don't do it," called Jeom, half-heartedly.

But she had already made up her mind long ago in the desert...

"You left us!" she screeched, hurling herself toward him.

Before Eli could even open his mouth to voice whatever excuse she was sure they all had at the ready, Arianna grabbed her swords and lunged at him with the full intent to stop him from breathing—he was a threat to the guardians with the knowledge he held, a traitor. Not to mention that he'd almost indirectly killed Arianna *twice* by abandoning her with no means of survival in hopeless situations. And looking at him now, she had trouble remembering what good she'd ever seen in him to begin with.

Demetrius and Jeom dodged out of the way as she prepared to cut right through Eli's center; Eli dived for anything he could use as a weapon to block her, finding Demetrius' staff in closest range and snatching it from his hands.

Her blade landed hard against the wood, the only thing separating Eli from death.

Arianna grimaced, wishing she and Lessa hadn't magically enhanced Demetrius' staff and wishing she had more energy to give to this battle; she'd spent it scouring the waters for Lessa and proved a weak opponent now. Nonetheless, she swung her swords to the beat of his weapon.

Arianna could tell he was going easy on her, and that maddened her even more. Eli was as strong as ever, fully returned to his warrior ways, swiftly blocking blow after blow.

She wasn't a fool, and neither was he—Eli knew she was tired, and she knew he was just waiting her out.

"You left us there to die! I told you I'd kill you if you betrayed us," she yelled as they met again in the middle, her swords and his staff pressed up against each other. "You betrayed us after we saved your life."

She shoved off him, throwing him a kick to the stomach.

He groaned, hunching over.

"I know," he said with a cough, jumping out of the way as she swiped her blade at his neck without mercy. "And I'm sorry. I just wasn't ready to understand the truth yet, but I am now."

Arianna chose not to hear him, though his words rang in her head without welcome. Fighting him with all her strength and growing slower and more distracted by the second, she couldn't hold off the tears beginning to pool in her eyes—and along with the tears, her true emotions began to emerge from somewhere deep down.

Frankly, it wasn't really Eli that she was angry with at all.

"She left us…" she stammered, crumpling to the ground, no more energy left to give to this battle.

Eli dropped his weapon to the sand and ran to Arianna's aid; the boys stood back a safe distance, watching quietly.

He knelt down beside her, laying a hand on her shoulder.

"I heard about Lessa," he said. "It's going to be—"

"Don't!" she snapped. "Just *don't* say another word. You have no idea what's going to happen." She shoved his hand away.

Eli let out a deep sigh and sat back on his knees.

"All right… well, you must try and eat something," he said with a gentle tenor, observing her as she struggled to catch her breath, sweat dotting her forehead.

"*Eat?*" Arianna wanted to snap his neck. She couldn't think about food at a time like this.

"Yes, eat," he said, nodding toward Jeom and Demetrius, who held up a loaf of bread as some sort of peace offering—her mouth watered. "I know what it's like to go hungry. You don't want that now. There isn't time."

"What do you know about time?" she said, curtly. "What do you know about anything? You've no business being here! So you should go before I change my mind about killing you."

Arianna crossed her arms at her chest, not permitting herself to meet his eyes as hers still swam with tears. Instead, she glared at the boys, trying to decide whether or not the bread was worth her dignity.

"I *know* that you've only got hours left to find Lessa," he said a bit more sternly. "I know that if you don't find her in time, she'll forfeit her life in more ways than one. Jeom and Demetrius filled me in on everything. And I know that if you don't *eat,* your magic will be useless."

That drew her attention—*what does he know of the workings of magic?*

"I'm here to help, Arianna, to earn back your trust. Please let me."

She scoffed, glaring up at him, unable to resist the lure of his stare.

"Remember, I'm forever in your debt," he whispered, holding out his hand for her to take. "Even more so now, and I intend to pay up… for as long as it takes."

She couldn't help her temper softening a little bit, wandering over past moments with him. She had once cared something for Eli, so his leaving without warning had stung badly. He had added to her loss, and she hated him for that, hated admitting that she'd let anyone else have a piece of her heart when it only seemed to make her all the more vulnerable.

How she wished she could go back to more ignorant times when he was just a boy in a tavern singing to a guitar—all he did was remind her that that life had been a lie all along. That boy had been a regulator hunting them, and when given a second chance, he had abandoned them in a desert.

Now, here he stood, asking for a *third* chance to prove his worth, to prove that he could be trusted in another desperate situation; Arianna wasn't ready to give out that deal, but she was ready now to let him speak. He seemed to know something about Lessa, and she wanted to know just exactly what it was. They were running out of options.

"Fine," she said, getting to her feet, ignoring his extended hand. "I'm listening."

She pulled on her robes, beckoning Solza to her side to help renew her energy. Then she stormed over to the boys, snatching the bread from them—they couldn't have looked more guilty.

"So speak!" she said through a mouthful, still glowering toward Eli.

"Ara," said Demetrius, stepping forward. "It's Lessa…"

There was something in his eyes, something of hope or fear sparkling there that made her take pause.

"What about Lessa?" she asked with caution.

"You need to trust Eli now," he said with a pleading expression. "He has an idea. You must listen to him and do as he says, or we may never see her again. Do you understand?"

"But listen to him about what?" She raised an eyebrow, waving the bread toward Eli. "How could he even help? He's a nonbeliever to start! What does he know of mermaids… or *magic?*"

She spat the words at Eli—sure that they would force him to shrink back into the hole he had crawled out from. He didn't even flinch. It seemed he had somehow found a way past his aversion to such themes.

What's changed since we last saw Eli?

"We wouldn't have brought him to you if we didn't think he could help," implored Jeom, looking at Eli with reluctance. "I trust him just as much as you do, but you have to listen to him now. It's really our last chance, whether it works or not. We're out of time."

He had his hands in his pockets, rocking from side to side as his eyes glued to the clouds, his nerves plain; Arianna followed Jeom's gaze and saw the darkened sky and its clear threat looming over them as the last bit of sun fought to stay visible.

The night was growing thicker now, and time was not on their side; the boys wouldn't waste their breath on Eli if they didn't think what he had to say was important.

"I don't trust him in the slightest," she said, walking to Jeom's side and laying a gentle hand on his arm. "But I trust you."

He squeezed her hand.

"So what is it then?" said Arianna, whipping around to face Eli. "Speak now or be gone. I can't stand the sight of you."

"Well," said Eli, wiping the sand from his pants as he stood. "It's a spell, actually…"

Arianna smiled, cocking her head to the side as she considered him.

"Is this supposed to be some kind of joke?" She itched for her swords again as the bread settled in her stomach, giving her back just enough energy that she thought she could go another round.

Eli squared his shoulders, and she saw again that confident, assertive side of him she was sure had been squashed during his time rotting in the Luose Dungeon. She thought if they weren't in this situation right now, maybe she'd find that he had completely healed over all these months. Maybe he *was* that Eli she had first met in the tavern, just as strong and collected as he proved witty and cheerful.

But then she remembered the girl she used to be and knew that would never be true—loss and pain changed people from one second to the next, choices hardened them forever, and there was no going back.

"I believe you now," said Eli. "I've come to believe in the magic you tried to show me in the desert, and I'll convince you to trust me in time. For now, please just do as I say. I know this can work… because someone much wiser than me has been using it to try and find you and Lessa."

Arianna tensed. "What do you mean, find us?"

"Later," he mumbled, pulling a crumpled parchment from his pocket and handing it over. "This *has* to work."

Arianna took the parchment from him, reading it quickly.

"Who gave you this?" she said, unable to hide the surprise in her voice.

"Nobody gave it to me," he said. "I wrote it down to try and memorize, to help the—"

Jeom exploded, his face going pale from anxiety as ominous shadows grew over the beach with the hovering darkness.

"Ara, we don't have time for this!" he said, his voice thundering out. "Just read it, all right? Read it now! The sun is almost fully set. Demetrius and I don't have your kind of magic, so it's all up to you." He was shaking with fear each passing second that the moon rose higher.

"Yes, all right," she said, nodding to him. "I'll read it."

Demetrius gave her a supportive smile, whispering something in Jeom's ear that made him visibly relax—in a way, his brother was to him like Solza was to her, she thought.

Arianna put her attention back on the scroll, reading the description aloud. "Calling a lost witch?"

"That's right," said Eli, chewing on his lip. "It's supposed to, well, I don't know exactly. It's supposed to help you contact someone lost, someone with close magical ties to you, I think."

"But how—" She saw Jeom fidget in the corner of her eye.

"Please, Arianna," said Eli, laying a hand on hers. She flinched, his touch unwelcome. "There was a time where you trusted me, and you saved my life. We've both been through so much together since that moment in the forest long ago, and I know that leaving you like that in the desert was cowardly. I was your guide, and I made a promise to you that I broke, fleeing with your secrets. But I know how precious they are now. I know who you *really* are, and it's my honor to serve your cause, to serve the guardians… starting with this."

Arianna was taken aback by this statement of fealty, and even more so by the fact that it seemed he knew much more about magic and the Guardians of Gold than she thought they'd given away—who was this mystery person who had guided Eli back to them?

"Lessa helped me recover," he added, a passion behind his words. "She's the only reason I'm a resemblance of who I used to be. She healed me with her remedies, with her magic, from the inside and out. I owe her everything, just as I owe you. *Please*, let me help."

She looked him up and down and knew that, even if he seemed back to normal on the outside, the scars on his soul were surely still there—just like her own.

"Well, we have nothing left to lose, I suppose," she said, skimming the parchment. "It looks like a simple spell, but you never know what magic will bring."

She considered the wisdom of Solomon, Keeper Kassime, and Talis, and how magic proved time and time again to have a mind all its own; Arianna took a deep breath and readied herself for one final attempt to bring Lessa back. Alas, she was far from certain what this new magic might conjure up.

"Please, work," she whispered to the sky, the South Star visible again from under the clouds, suspended above them like a beacon of light. "*Please.*"

"What do you need, Ara? Let us help, if we can," said Demetrius.

Arianna thought over all her lessons and knowledge of magic gained thus far, remembering the night she had attempted one of her very first spells as a last hope to find a way out of the Vanishing Tunnels. When she couldn't do it alone, Lessa had grasped her hand to recite the spell alongside her—to their astonishment, an enchanted emerald light emerged, guiding them safely to where they were meant to go.

Stronger together.

"Everyone take hands," she said, hurriedly, letting the parchment fall to the sand as she held her palms open.

Jeom and Demetrius came to one side of her, already holding hands. Then she looked to Eli.

"*Everyone,*" she said. "If you have even a trace of magic in you, I need it now. We have to work together."

She felt Eli's warm hand fit into her own.

"Right," she said, eyes cast down as an unexpected heat rose to her cheeks. "Solza, you stand close too."

Linked together, the four stood to face the water as the final orange haze of the late sun died behind the vast expanse of the sea, sinking beneath the water the same way Lessa had done the day she turned to follow Syrifina Myr into the dark.

Arianna momentarily closed her eyes to try to find some peace within her mind. When she opened them, she felt again the magic beating beneath her skin, just waiting at the surface to explode. She had to control it this time, had to master the magic within with a Lessa-like charm—or it could master her, and nothing good would come from losing control right now.

She turned her head slightly, looking to Eli; he grasped her hand with confidence, gazing back at her with such courage. In his eyes, she saw the reflection of her own, glowing silver with power.

Arianna half expected him to let go from fear and run as he

had before. He didn't—he gripped tighter, stood even taller, ready for whatever came next.

In some inexplicable twist of fate, Elijah Neve had come to accept that magic was a part of this world. And if he could do that, Arianna could accept his help now.

Her voice rang out loud above the crashing of waves, a spell rolling off her lips and carrying off into the wind:

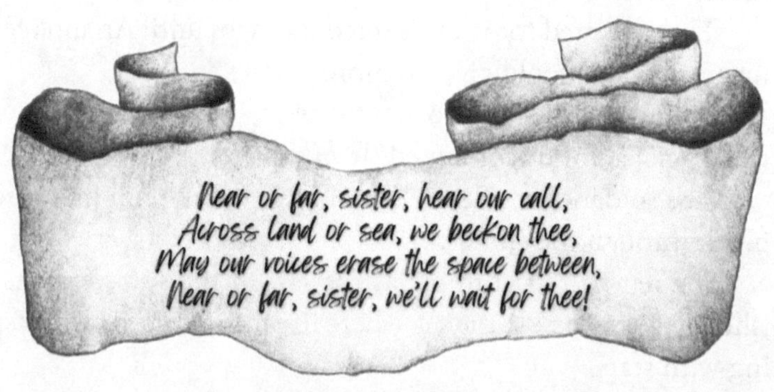

Arianna looked out to the waters, but they stayed calm and steady, nothing to suggest Lessa would surface soon.

"It's not working," she said, growing frantic.

She felt Jeom squeeze her hand tighter.

"Try again," he urged in a shaky voice.

Arianna nodded, resigned to speak the words once more, but she couldn't help the doubt flooding her mind; she had let herself hope again, let herself believe this one last effort might achieve something. Still, taking another breath, she forced herself to chant the spell again.

This time, as she started, Jeom's voice rang out beside her, strong and steady, booming across the open air; Demetrius and Eli were quick to follow.

Soon, they were all practically singing out the words across the sea, over and over, until their voices ran dry. Arianna felt the magic grip her, filling each word with a power unknown to her, as if magic was wrapped around each letter, guiding their call out into the world on a mighty search.

She imagined the words whizzing about to every corner of Olleb-Yelfra in their quest for Lessa.

But would they find her?

Would they beckon her back in time before she was permanently sealed as a Myr sister rather than their own?

They chanted for what seemed like ages until Arianna felt the magic ebb and could give no more.

"I think all we can do now is wait," said Demetrius. "I felt the magic, all of us combined. It *has* to work."

"It's so dark now," said Arianna, seeing the full moon finally break through the clouds.

She felt herself crumble as the last of the sun's embers vanished in a strip across the sea where fire met a dark navy sky sparking with stars.

There were only moments now before all hope would be truly lost—if it wasn't already.

Arianna heard Demetrius and Jeom sniffle beside her and felt the tears beginning to flood her own eyes again as they all watched, with aching hearts, the most picturesque and saddest sunset of their lives.

"You can only see the stars with the help of the night," said Eli, eyes pinned on the South Star suspended directly above the sea. "There's still time."

24

GATHERING AGAIN

SILENCE JOINED THEM for a long while, seconds that seemed to stretch into hours as they waited. But nothing happened.

"She's not coming," said Jeom, shaking his head. "She's not coming! We've lost her."

"At least we tried," whispered Arianna. "We really tried."

She bent down to hug Solza, burying her face in her fur as the tears could no longer be held back; Jeom turned from the edge of the water, beginning to walk away, and Demetrius covered his eyes with his hands.

They just couldn't bear to watch the end.

"No, no, no!" Jeom cried out. "This isn't right."

"Just wait," said Eli, his hand balled into a fist as if he might will a different outcome.

Arianna saw him staring so certainly at the waters, praying, maybe just as much as them, that Lessa would break through at any moment and come back.

But it was over… it was done.

"Don't you hear that?" He walked to where the water met the sand.

"Hear what—" Arianna's heart started beating faster as her ears picked up on the subtle tones of what sounded like a hum, so soft and so beautiful that she thought she might fall asleep where she stood as it echoed around them.

Jeom turned, lulled back to the waves along with Demetrius—they all wiped away their tears and focused in on the sound. Something was happening.

"There!" said Demetrius, pointing frantically to the water. "No, over there!" He moved his arm in the opposite direction. "I swear… I *saw* something."

"I don't see anything at all," said Arianna, standing up from Solza and staring intently at the sea.

Then her eyes caught where the water began to ripple, and just as suddenly, she saw what appeared to be the shadow of a beautiful woman, head moving with the drift of the waves.

Her hair floated out behind her in strings of golden yellow, fighting the black color the sea had taken on in the deepening night. And her eyes were a striking cerulean blue, as if the water itself had capsuled there.

"Lessa!" screamed Arianna, running forward to the edge of the water.

"I heard your call," she replied, softly, not moving an inch.

Arianna saw the flicker of magic streak across her eyes and the swoosh of a silver and sapphire tail splashing behind her.

"Time is almost up," said Jeom. His voice sounded so desperate, and he looked on the verge of jumping into the sea to drag her out if not for Demetrius holding him back. "You have to get out of the water. Come back to us!"

Lessa didn't reply as she observed them, swimming closer to the beach until Arianna could see her clearly.

"I don't know if I can," she said, sucking in a gulp of air.

"There's too much temptation."

Arianna could see Lessa was fighting something, suppressing an urge that was strong and clearly trying to take over. She recognized the same, determined look in her eyes that Syrifina had shown the day she'd found her drinking Jeom's blood.

She looked *hungry.*

"If you don't come out of the water before the moon is at its peak, you'll be stuck like this forever," said Arianna. "*Please*, Les! Just take my hand. You're so close."

She reached forward, slowly, not wanting to scare her. There was something so fragile about this moment—one wrong move and Lessa could disappear beneath the waves forever. They'd never see her again.

Arianna felt her truly slipping away before her eyes, could sense that she just wasn't ready to come back yet. She began to panic, not knowing the right words to say to sway her dearest friend away from the tides.

A deep voice drew Arianna's attention… and it wasn't from Jeom, Eli, or Demetrius.

"Lessa, what do you think you're doing, child?"

The voice gripped at Arianna's heart so much that she thought she might cry out.

At first, she was sure she'd imagined it from her past, conjured it up to help her in this moment of need. But as the sound also seemed to penetrate Lessa's cold exterior, she was certain this had nothing to do with her imagination.

Spinning around, she found none other than Master Talis Churry walking up the sandy beach to stand beside her; he looked aged, his beard longer and whiter, and he seemed more crumpled than usual. But that light in his eyes, the magic twinkling at the ready, made her more thankful than ever for his presence.

If anyone could knock some sense into the smartest girl they knew, it would be Talis; she almost broke down at the sight of him, hugging him around the waist.

He laid a hand on Arianna's shoulder, relieving her of her duty to Lessa.

"Save her," she whispered before stepping aside to stand with the boys.

"Master Churry?" said Lessa, a quizzical expression crossing her hardened face.

Arianna swore she heard a crack in the cool, smooth voice she had adopted in her mermaid form.

"In the flesh," he said, moving closer to the water.

He sounded nothing less than the master that had helped introduce them to this magical, wonderful, terrifying world—stern and kind in one fell swoop.

"Do not shrug away your honorable duties for a life such as this, girl," he said. "I've taught you so much better. You *will* get out of the water."

His voice was colder, sharper than Arianna's could have ever been toward her friend, but she was sure that Lessa's heart had iced over too—he'd have to do better than that.

Lessa shook her head, but her curiosity seemed to draw her in closer still. Arianna could see clearly now the colorful lifeblood pulsing across her skin, shimmering like an artist's delicate strokes to create the wisps of wind on a mural.

"I don't want to hurt you," she said. "Any of you. But if I step out of the water, I will kill you all. I'd *have* to. The thirst is stronger than ever this night. I've resisted for so long, but I can't anymore. I… *won't.*"

Her words came harsh and threatening; Arianna couldn't help but take a step back, remembering Syrifina's infinite strength and lethal bite.

If she so desired, Lessa could rip them apart before they even had a chance to think of how to stop her.

The silvery-white shell of what could only be Sano emerged alongside her, his orange eyes popping out of the water ever so slightly, as if scared at what might happen next; Arianna could feel Solza's energy surge, calling out to him.

Lessa's hand rested on his shell, steady, no intention of letting him nor herself join them on land.

Arianna had a strong, reassuring feeling that if Lessa had truly turned and given away her humanity completely, her avatar would cease to exist. For, theoretically, she'd be dead—and avatars could not live without their masters.

Lessa's still in there... somewhere. She grasped Demetrius' and Jeom's hands.

"I'll take my chances," replied Talis.

He lifted his arms into the air, and Arianna watched in awe as strings of electricity snaked around them, disappearing before she could even wrap her head around this new show of power from Talis Churry.

"Hand me your dagger," he commanded to Arianna, holding out his hand expectantly.

She didn't hesitate to obey, pulling it from the sheath at her thigh and tossing it over.

He momentarily examined it with something of recognition, and then he gave her a thankful nod. "Now stand back everyone. This won't be easy."

Arianna did as he said. "What do you mean?" she asked, pulling the boys back with her. "What are you going to—"

Talis used her blade to cut open the palm of his hand, gritting his teeth as it sliced easily through his skin.

Arianna looked up to see the monster completely take hold of Lessa in that moment—she sniffed the air as the smell of his blood met her nose, sharp fangs flashing as a hiss of warning left her mouth.

"You'll lose her!" she shouted as she ran forward, attempting to cover up his wound; as soon as her skin met his, Arianna crumpled to the ground, a numbing sensation running through her bones. Her eyes remained open though, watching the horror unfold.

Lessa rushed toward the shoreline, focused on Talis, her blue-silver tail morphing back to legs under the watch of the night sky. But when she came upon the beach, she stopped cold right in front of him—it was as if she had run into a wall.

"Barrier magic," Arianna mouthed; she knew the spell well.

Lessa howled in anger.

"What's he doing?" asked Jeom as Eli and Demetrius helped Arianna up, pulling her to a safe distance.

"Just wait," whispered Talis, concentrating. "Come on, girl. Have a go at me!" He beckoned to Lessa, eyes wide with anticipation, sweat gathering at his brow.

Lessa lunged forward, again and again, throwing all her weight against his magic. Then she froze.

"What's… happening to me?" she shrieked, looking down at her hands.

With her next breath, a fierce scream ripped from her throat, head tilted toward the now brightly shining moon—Lessa's body had begun to change.

The lifeblood flowing on the outside of her skin seemed to melt off and float away like strings of colorful paint adrift in a breeze, and the magical mermaid sparkle she had attained dripped off her like the water she was so fond of. Then, a cocoon of bright silver light encased her body.

They all stared upon her now, mute from shock and fear—it was clear that Lessa was, undoubtedly, becoming human again.

"A mermaid who has not yet drunk the blood of a man cannot walk on land until she does. Otherwise, she forfeits the magic," Talis explained, releasing his barrier spell with a heavy sigh of relief.

"But how could you have known that would work?" stuttered Arianna, finding her voice.

He twisted his beard on his finger, laughing to himself.

"You learn a few things in old age," he said. "There's always a loophole when it comes to magic."

Arianna's eyes were drawn to the wound on his hand as it began to heal with a wordless spell; he handed back her dagger.

"Though, I certainly wasn't expecting to have to combat mermaid sorcery when I tracked you lot here." He placed his hands on his hips, narrowing his gaze at her. "You girls have *a lot* of explaining to do!"

"Wait… she's really human again?" interjected Jeom, mouth agape as he slowly stepped up to investigate.

Talis nodded. "That she is."

Arianna and the boys gazed down upon Lessa with dumbstruck and saddened expressions; she was undergoing what appeared to be an excruciating transformation.

"I just thought she would've been able to *choose*," said Arianna, shaking her head. She turned to Talis. "I thought that she would've chosen to be with us. Syrifina never said—"

"Lessa always had a choice to get out of the water before the full cycle completed," said Talis. "Alas, the lure of the mermaid life is strong, especially for one who has such an uncertain future ahead."

He shook his head, considering his apprentice.

"I don't know how you found yourself in such a predicament, but the battle she entered was not an easy one. I'm sure this Syrifina neglected to tell you that the longer one lives as a mermaid, the harder it is to fight that carefree existence." There was a mix of fear and fondness in his eyes as he gazed at Lessa. "Nevertheless, she did return. She *chose* to follow the light back to life in the end. You know all about that, Ara."

He smiled, laughing a little to himself.

"We just needed to give her a little nudge in the right direction. Though, I wonder… how were you even able to coax her this close to land? That was a feat in and of itself."

"It was Eli, sir," said Demetrius. "He tracked me and my brother down somehow. When we told him about our desperate attempt to locate Lessa on the seas, he shared a spell he said the guardians had been using to try to find her and Arianna." He let out a sigh of relief. "I guess it really worked after all."

"Is that so?" said Talis, turning his attention to Eli.

Eli shrugged, averting his eyes.

"Well, if that's not luck, then I don't know what is." Talis patted him on the shoulder. "Good work, son. It seems you were certainly the right man to send to collect them from the beach."

"What?" Arianna eyed Eli with nothing short of confusion.

"The guardians felt when you all landed here," said Talis. "Mermaids though… I never would've imagined."

"Thank you, Master," said Eli with a bow before Arianna could question further.

"So… Syrifina didn't technically lie, then?" Jeom was still trying to work out this puzzle as Lessa continued to change back before them.

"No, she just gave half-truths," spat Arianna, enraged just thinking about it.

Talis nodded, his expression serious. "It seems that I'm one lesson too late, but *never* trust a witch of the water. A mermaid's tongue is slick. If Lessa didn't drink by this final night of the moon cycle, she would have died in those waters anyway. And if she hadn't walked on land, she would be a mermaid still."

"You really don't think she would have come out on her own?" said Demetrius.

"I think it very unlikely she would have gotten out without your help. Even our Lessa isn't that strong," said Talis. "A creature of the water has a natural aversion to the land, and one's nature is not easy to fight."

They all looked down to her.

As Lessa's screams ebbed and the cocoon of magic fell away, her transformation back to her human form was finally complete.

Talis knelt down to help her, catching her in his arms before she could hit the sand. "It's all right," he said, wrapping her in his cloak. "You're home now."

Lessa blinked open her eyes, and Arianna instantly felt a glow of happiness—those were definitely human.

"Master?" She was staring at Talis with such bewilderment, as if trying to decide whether or not he was real. "I'm sorry… you're always getting me out of trouble," she murmured before passing out.

Talis pushed the wet hair from her face.

"That's my favorite thing about you," he said with a chuckle. "Ah, ole boy, good to see you too! I thought you'd be nearby watching over her."

Sano had joined them on the beach, already transformed back to the monkey they all knew and loved; it was as if no time had passed at all.

"All right, I'm too old for this," Talis huffed, struggling under Lessa's weight. He beckoned to Jeom. "You look strong. Think you can handle her, son?"

Jeom shook off the daze that had settled over him, coming to Talis' aid.

"Yes, sir," he said with confidence, hoisting Lessa into his arms; the way he gazed at her was with nothing short of deep affection, and Arianna was sure Talis saw it too.

"You're okay," whispered Jeom, planting a kiss on her forehead. "You're home."

Demetrius and Arianna shared a knowing glance.

"Fine work," said Talis. "Now, let's get you all somewhere safe. We've much to discuss, don't we?" He turned to Arianna. "How did you let her turn into a mermaid of all things?"

"I'm not sure where to even begin," she said with a laugh, relieved in so many ways to have her family back in one piece.

Demetrius giggled as Sano came to land in his arms, just like old times.

"Well, we have a long walk ahead of us, so why don't you fill me in on everything since I last saw you in the districts." He gestured to Demetrius and Jeom. "Maybe start off by introducing your new friends… guardians too from the looks of it?" He raised an eyebrow at her.

Arianna grinned, shaking her head. "I don't know if any walk is long enough, Master Churry."

Even just saying his name struck her as impossible…

How are we together again, all of us now?

Magic—she knew that was the answer, somehow.

They all gathered their things from the boat to follow Talis to wherever he had planned for them, and Arianna turned for one last look at the sea.

The moon was high in the sky now, perched atop the waves and cleansing the dark night with its glorious light. The clouds of earlier were now far off in the distance; it was the first full moon since they had lost Lessa nearly a month ago.

As she gazed on in wonderment at their journey, Arianna spotted the unmistakable silver eyes of someone watching her.

"Syrifina," she breathed. Her lips pressed into a thin line as they locked eyes—she sat calmly in the waters, fiery hair floating out eerily around her.

The mermaid's mouth twitched up into a smile as soon as her name was spoken.

Syrifina bowed her head low, as if out of respect, and Arianna knew that their deal was finally done; if she knew Lessa at all, mermaid or not, she had figured out what was happening to the Myr sisters, just as they'd all agreed. On top of that, she'd found her way back home.

But Arianna considered that Syrifina now officially owed *them* a debt in return—she and her friends had escaped the Island of Idris against all odds and without any help from the mermaids… as was promised.

'And a mermaid never breaks such an honorable thing.'

Arianna promptly returned the gesture, bowing her head with all the politeness she could muster. As she did, the waves rolled threateningly around Syrifina—the power of the sea was an element Arianna had gotten to know quite a bit better with so much time surrounded by water.

"Until we meet again," she said with a deep exhale, feeling her magic course stronger.

Syrifina remained steady against the hurling waves, her eyes burning bright with understanding.

"Until we meet again, Sorceress Belvedor." She blew her a kiss on the wind before she sank under the sea.

As Arianna watched Syrifina Myr disappear beneath the next wave, her sugary, seducing voice filled the air in her wake, singing the words of a spell she had surely only just learned.

"Near or far, sister, I'll wait for thee."

25

A SECRET GARDEN

ARIANNA BROUGHT UP THE REAR of the group, eyes glued to Jeom and Lessa as everyone climbed the steep cliffs, leaving the beach behind. As they rounded the corner, the vision of water was finally replaced with something different, the City of Zambienth in their futures.

She soaked in the view as they walked, circling away from the beach and heading inland until the earth they stood on became strangely flat, pyramids jutting up from every crevice of the dry, sandy land. Arianna felt so exposed here, as if anyone might look down and recognize her from afar.

Talis escorted them through the main gates on this side of the city. Near the gates, she noticed several guards had been knocked unconscious, moved to the side to make for an easy getaway—or, in this case, entry into the city.

As they carefully stepped over their bodies, she decided not to question it as Demetrius tucked a gold piece into the robes of one of the snoozing regulators.

"Stay close, Solza," she whispered to her avatar, taking in their new surroundings with caution.

She pulled up her hood, keeping her head low as they zigzagged between the quiet streets of the sleeping city.

Her face was papered everywhere here, just like her beginning days in South Luose. Except this time, Jeom, Lessa, *and* Demetrius joined her in the 'Wanted' posters.

"We didn't get a chance to mention before, Ara, but we think Vladamor must've passed through here, reigniting the search," said Demetrius as street lanterns spotlighted their detailed depictions.

His fingers traced the lines of his face on a poster, his frown and lost look telling Arianna that the reality of their situation was solidified for him in this moment.

"Or Solomon," she breathed—that flicker of fire grew again in her heart, uncomfortable and hot, hungry for revenge.

The silver twenty-two and the bright red cloak of her former life peeked up from ripped parchments, half-buried beneath the sand or tacked to the walls of the tunnels. And the glow of their lantern light illuminated her eyes.

So familiar...

She had always pondered who might have provided her description to the first painter. Who had been responsible for this portrayal that would be replicated a thousand times over? For this was the hundredth parchment she'd seen with her face painted on it, and the resemblance was truly uncanny.

Her best guess was reserved for the one person who knew her better than anyone yet was no longer on her side—Master Bell.

As they walked deeper into the city, pyramids blocking out the view of the moon, she couldn't help but feel discontented by more than just her former master's hand in the King's hunt for their heads; Zambienth felt so foreign. She had grown used to the stacked buildings in Luose and giant trees hovering just outside the city gates, visible from every corner.

The difference here was jarring; there was little for plant life, just sand on one side and water on the other. And the city looked like jagged, white jewels grew out from the land.

South Luose, on the other hand, had constructions similar to her home in the districts, more relatable to the life she'd always known.

Her imagination exploded with all the possibilities of what they might discover here when everything already seemed so different, expanding even further to consider other cities of the Olleb. *What might they be like if two cities in the same corner of the world are so vastly different?*

Talis whispered words to Jeom and Demetrius, drawing Arianna's attention. He introduced himself as Lessa's district master and inquired about their journey since the Jar.

She was eager to question him, too, wanting to understand how he had come to be in Zambienth in the first place and to learn how he and Eli had been acquainted.

The last any of them had seen of Talis had been in the Warrior's District more than a year ago at the Free Falls. And Eli was last seen fleeing on the back of his horse across the desert before they had even known anything about Syrifina Myr and her pack of vicious sea sisters. Yet, here they were—familiarized with each other in more ways than one.

How had this happened?

As Talis and Demetrius began a lengthy chat about the Agrarian's District, Eli fell in step with Arianna.

She observed him through her peripheral vision and noticed his skin had darkened since she'd seen him in the desert—the tattoos on his arms, abstract lines wrapping across his body, stood out less noticeably than before.

And his hair was shorter, though brown waves still bounced over his shoulders.

There was also something about his eyes, brighter than normal—that had everything to do with a newcomer to magic.

Eli hadn't fought against a necromancer or an army of skeletons, and his friends hadn't been casualties of the feud between good and evil. He didn't yet know the dangers of the enchanted Olleb-Yelfra, but Arianna was sure that if he stuck around this time, he would quickly learn.

She and her friends had faced unfathomable horrors, all conjured up by the same magic that gave him enthusiasm now. And it would only grow worse as they positioned themselves more openly against the King.

"What's this city like?" she said, breaking the silence as different tunnels and pathways crisscrossed above their heads.

It made her dizzy trying to figure out which path might lead where.

"Dry," said Eli. "Not like South Luose. There's not much green here. Well, except…"

"Except what?" Arianna turned to see him fully—the sight of him still made her so livid.

She didn't understand his role in all this and didn't trust that he should have any at all. How was it possible that their stories had intertwined yet again?

"You'll see," he replied, hands in his pockets; he walked with more pep than before.

"I suppose so," she mumbled. "Anyways… I do owe you my gratitude."

"How's that?" He raised an eyebrow.

Arianna let out a long exhale, some of the stress from the day dissipating along with it.

"For what you did for Lessa," she said, staring at her feet. "If not for you, who knows what would have happened."

He shrugged. "It was really the least I could do," he said. "Besides, I'm not the only one you should be thanking."

"I've already given Talis my thanks—"

"It wasn't just him," said Eli. "You'll understand soon."

"Right, as you've mentioned," said Arianna, turning away and closing the door on any more conversation.

It was the dead of night now, and Jeom still held Lessa safely in his arms with Sano protectively perched on his shoulder. She dangled there, head nuzzled into his chest and feet hanging over his arms as they walked.

Arianna didn't even see her stir once to suggest she could walk on her own. *Jeom must surely be exhausted…*

But if he was, he didn't show it.

Talis steered them far clear of the city center, keeping them to the tunnels—the Burrows—as Demetrius had explained. Anything of the city that Arianna could see along the way had been distorted by the dark of night; she longed to know what might be uncovered by the sun.

"Where are we going?" she asked no one in particular, her patience waning as they rounded another corner.

She was sure if she were on her own, she'd get terribly lost, the Burrows a tangled web of paths branching off in every direction.

"Almost there," said Talis. "Better to show you than try to explain another impossibility." He winked a blue eye at her.

Arianna laughed. "You haven't changed one bit."

"I can't say the same for you, little guardian." He gave a knowing smile before turning his attention forward.

"Thanks to you…" she said on instinct.

She wasn't sure whether she had meant it to be a compliment or an accusation, but it didn't much matter. This life had been fated to them, and Talis was a major piece of that fate tying together. Without him, Arianna wouldn't even be alive or have had the opportunity to escape the districts—let alone ignite a *quest* to meet King Devlindor head on.

Yes, things certainly have changed.

"How did you find us? How did you know about Lessa?" she

asked, unable to restrain herself.

"Maybe the question is, how did *you* find us?" Talis said with a chuckle.

Arianna sighed, resigned to reserving her queries for later—the riddles of Talis Churry were not something she had the energy for right now.

He would explain more in time, if he wished. And if not, there was no use in trying to pull anything from him.

"Well, whatever brought us back together, I'm so very glad for it," she said, looking on the bright side for once.

We've got Lessa back!

"Me too," she heard Eli whisper from behind.

Soon, the tunnels engulfed them in complete darkness.

"Ara, do you mind?" said Talis. "I'm a bit tired from earlier. I hear that you've had a good bout of training by now."

"Who told you that?" Again, she was met with infuriating silence.

"Fine then," she huffed, rolling her eyes. She called to the spell she'd long since mastered. "*Solza ven immito!*"

She raised her hands, as if to summon the power directly from the earth, concentrating hard—the fire came swiftly.

The corridor lit up with pink glowing flames filling several lanterns lining the tunnel walls; apart from Jeom and Lessa, they each grabbed one to carry for the rest of the journey.

"Very good," said Talis with a cheerful screech. "Kassime taught you well, I see."

"You know about that too?" she stuttered. "About... what happened in South Luose?"

"I know enough, I'm afraid."

There was such sadness in his voice that Arianna knew he must be referring to Solomon as well.

"I helped Kassime master healing and alchemy," he said. "He was a good man, a brave soul to give his life to the cause in such a way. But let's keep that for later, shall we? I want to speak of happier things now. Your magic is strong! You've really grown from when I first met you."

He chuckled to himself.

"You gave me quite the scare that night. And then you didn't want to believe in magic when I told you I was a sorcerer. My… to see you now with such light in your eyes."

Arianna smirked. "What a fool I turned out to be."

"Quite the contrary," he said with a firm nod. "You're a fool no longer. However, now that you've nearly mastered magic, you need to master your mind *and* control. That will be the greatest of challenges."

"What do you mean?" she asked, thinking of all she'd already done to conquer the realm of her dark thoughts. "My mind is under control… trust me."

"Don't get cocky, now," said Talis. "You've only studied a year outside of the Jar, and your enemies have been at it for centuries. Just think, if they know what spell you speak with your tongue, how could you possibly ever have the upper hand?" He tapped his temple. "Now, if only you could master all that magic using the wordless voice of your mind, then maybe you could catch them by surprise."

He snapped his fingers and Arianna's torch blew out, leaving her momentarily blinded. He snapped them again and the flame returned with a '*pop.*'

"Solomon was a great master of this," he said. "I daresay he taught you something to lay the groundwork, hmm?"

He carried on ahead.

"You do have a point," she muttered to his back—and if she didn't know what spells were being cast on her, how could she defend against them? *There's too much still to learn!*

They had to hurry and catch up, before the King caught up to them. But Arianna didn't want to linger on memories of Solomon Bell.

Although… now that she was forced to think about it, it was clear that he had been training her, or *testing* her, for such a skill using the 'meditation' words during duels and too many lessons to count.

Solomon, you trickster. How lies come so easy to you, I'll never know. At least this one proved in her favor.

She pondered then over her recent battle with Sir Vladamor, how she had felt the magic materialize in her mind without her voice to guide it. It had unleashed on the desert in a devastating fashion, driven by fear and emotion.

She had lost control then, and it had almost cost them their lives.

"Magic isn't meant to be controlled," said Talis from up ahead, as if reading her thoughts. "It is meant to be accepted. Once you master that, your greatest powers will come."

Arianna didn't respond, but his words sank in deeply.

Who will be my master, my teacher, now?

Solomon had taught her a great many things that she wished not to remember, if only to shield against the pain.

But his teachings would be with her always, creating the foundation of the woman she had grown to be and the future that she now raced toward with the flame of magic lighting the way.

THEY DIDN'T SPEAK AGAIN until they came upon their destination, Talis guiding them deep into the bowels of Zambienth. Occasionally, the pathways would resurface above ground and Arianna could catch another glimpse of the city.

Everything seemed to take on a glistening white color, and she noticed strange animals ambling about, quite like horses but with humps lining their backs and mouths gone lame. She'd also seen what she knew to be called 'lizards' scuttling up the walls in haste, their tongues licking at the air.

Not many people were out this night but flames burned in windows of what she assumed to be sleeping quarters, and every now and then she'd hear the echo of voices from hidden places. Talis stayed calm, so she did too; nobody was looking for them here, and the farther down they went, the more isolated it proved to be.

"I think Jeom was right," whispered Demetrius, falling back to walk with Arianna. "This infrastructure is perfect for hiding secrets."

"I wonder what Talis is hiding," she whispered back, curiosity tingling her nerves.

"Ah, here we go," said Talis after a long while, holding open a small, jagged door. "Follow me everyone. Quickly now."

With the whoosh of his hand, instantly, the flames of their lanterns went out, thrusting them back into darkness; all Arianna could see were Solza's electric eyes and the silver scars glinting on Jeom's neck where Syrifina's teeth had left their mark.

Instinctively, she reached around to feel for the jagged slashes of the scar on her own arm where Solza's claws had once dug in deep—these were permanent reminders that all her truest friends carried now, proving that not one of them was exempt from magic's claim.

Talis disappeared through the door, which seemed to melt in as one with the tunnels, and everyone else followed right behind him, reaching out their arms to guide them in the dark.

"What is this place?" asked Jeom as they entered a dimly lit chamber, keeping his voice low as Lessa shifted in his arms.

"This is where the resistance gathers in Zambienth," said Talis, gesturing to the space around them. "Most major cities have a guardian gathering place… or *used* to. We won't really know until the end."

"The end?" Arianna was met with more silence.

They stood in a small room filled with moldy-smelling plants.

Between the six of them and two avatars, they were tightly crammed in; Arianna couldn't fathom that anyone, guardian or otherwise, would want to stay here for long.

She preferred the beach.

"This is where you gather?" asked Jeom, turning up his nose without shame.

She knew he must miss their luxurious palace attic even more right now—this place paled in comparison.

"Still so much to learn." Talis chuckled, moving farther in. "Not everything is as it seems, least of all a guardian safe space." He smiled. "You lot should know that by now if Kassime had you in his grasp."

Arianna jumped as a new voice joined them.

"You didn't think that little attic of yours was the only hideout, did you?"

"Tobias!" she screeched, pushing past everyone. "Oh, I'm so glad you're all right. I thought—"

"It's good to see you too, miss," he said, tipping his hat with a smirk.

He seemed to have appeared out of nowhere, blending in with the dark; Arianna gave him a big hug, overjoyed at seeing her former chauffeur and friend in one piece.

"This skin suits you much better, Arianna," he said. "Glad to see you haven't shifted again."

She blushed—it sounded a bit funny to hear her real name from his mouth, Aridyn now buried in the past for them both.

"Don't worry, we *all* got out of Luose all right," he added. "They weren't after us yet. They were after you, and they didn't linger."

"You mean, *Solomon* didn't linger," she said, a bite to her tone.

He nodded, a sad look in his eyes; Arianna supposed that Tobias had once known Solomon as a guardian and friend too. Her master had disappointed many more than just her.

"Glad to see you're all right, mate," said Demetrius, shaking Tobias' hand. "Here, I've held on to this for you. It got us safely through a desert *and* a sea, if you'll believe! We can't thank you enough."

He handed him the compass.

"*Ah*, I see, and looks like it brought you right where you needed to be in the end." Tobias beamed. "Just as we had hoped."

Arianna, Jeom, and Demetrius all shared a glance. *We?*

Tobias looked at the treasure fondly before pushing it back into Demetrius' hands.

"It's yours now. A gift that I daresay you'll need again one day."

Demetrius couldn't have been more grateful if he tried, overjoyed at such a gesture. But Arianna didn't miss when he glanced at her with another question in his eyes, the same one running through her mind. *How much help had the compass truly been on their journey?*

Arianna examined the trinket that had gotten them across more than one sea, as it were. Then her eyes widened as she noticed, for the first time, that the inner workings of the tool faintly shone with the same dazzling colors that could only be bestowed by aura and ora stones, glowing even in the low light.

A ring, a compass, and a dagger? All forged with identical properties found in Undor?

It could not be a coincidence, and she filed the thought away to address later, along with all the other burning questions weighing on her mind.

"So… what happened after the fire?" asked Jeom.

Tobias took a deep breath. "Long story short?"

Jeom nodded, shifting Sano onto his other shoulder.

"Once it was made clear that Solomon was lost to the Shadow Resistance and that he'd compromised the guardians," he said, "those of us out of hiding made quick plans to flee South Luose before any more of his regulators could scout the place."

Tobias nodded to Talis.

"Cyn made fast work of getting word back to Talis in the Healer's District, and then we all made our way here. This was always the next gathering point in case of such a… crisis. It's the closest hideout to the Palace of South Luose that we know still exists. And with the guardians so disbanded, Solomon shouldn't even *think* that you would come here. Not without Kassime guiding you."

Talis tensed at the mention of his name, arms crossed at his chest.

"We've been waiting on you for weeks now. Been on vacation, have you?" added Tobias, trying to lighten the mood.

"Something like that," said Demetrius, rocking back and forth on his feet.

Arianna was just relieved that the others had gotten away at all. "And… the attic?" she asked.

She and the boys all held their breath.

"It still stands," he said. He shook his head. "But it's in the control of Solomon now."

"You mean, King Devlindor," growled Jeom. "He'll know all our secrets."

"That's hardly all, my boy," said Talis.

"And we'll get it back one day," said Tobias. "But that's the least of our worries right now."

"Not to sound ungrateful," said Jeom. "But the attic was a lot more comfortable than this…" He cleared his throat. "What do you call it?" His eyes scanned the rotting plants drooping from the ceiling and frowned, drawing laughter from both Talis and Tobias.

"You must've made a *grand* highlife as Jaxin," said Talis.

It was apparent that Talis knew a lot more about their Luose lives than Arianna had at first assumed. She wondered how well he and Keeper Kassime had kept in touch over the years, wondered how many letters may have passed between the pair.

Or had someone else kept him so informed?

"Come on," said Tobias. "The others are waiting for you."

"Others…" said Arianna, glancing around in confusion. "Cyn? Is she here somewhere? Is she all right?"

Tobias gave a warm smile.

"And Master Tayshin?" she added, elated by his reaction; his smile vanished, and he lowered his head so that his hat covered his eyes.

"Master Tayshin couldn't join us," interjected Talis. "He has other duties to attend to. You needn't worry over him now." Of course, though, she did.

Solomon had been her foundation in everything, the rock her strength was built upon. And when that foundation had been ripped out from beneath her, Master Tayshin had given it back.

He had renewed her willpower to survive her most recent and trying battles. Her new, unlikely master had honed her skill and shaped her mind into something more. He'd challenged her in a different, sharper way than Solomon had ever achieved, helping her to stand on her own two feet.

Timing and predicament had all certainly aided his teachings, but nevertheless, he had instilled in her something Solomon was never able to accomplish yet had always encouraged—*humility*.

For all its worth, Arianna had never quite been humble.

Only when she had become a highlife did people stop challenging that characteristic in her—all *except* Master Tayshin.

He had made sure she'd stay humble to the end, whipping the sense right into her with the flick of his sword. A year later, she'd found out he was not just a master warrior to be respected but a founder of the Guardians of Gold to be revered.

Jeom interrupted her thoughts.

"And what about Eli?" he said, glaring back at him. "How did he come to find you?"

"Much like you, I suppose," said Talis. "A lot of luck and a little magic."

He winked, and Arianna saw Eli fidget under the attention. Jeom opened his mouth to retort, but Talis held up his hand. "Now, wait here."

With that, he turned his back on them, the moment for questions over.

Arianna jumped as another new voice filled the space; Talis was speaking to someone she hadn't noticed before, sitting there among them all the while.

A small, old woman hunched over a table tucked away in a corner, scribbling diligently on a piece of paper. Her hair was wild and matted with dirt, and she wore spectacles over her eyes that made them look double their size. She looked up to find Talis staring down at her, tapping his foot.

"What can I do for you?" She seemed annoyed at the disturbance, and Arianna realized this place to be some sort of establishment. "In the market for medicinal herbs, or cooking maybe? I've got a good selection of radishbulbs this month, if you're interested."

Demetrius sniffed at a little potted plant on the table nearest to them, wrinkling up his nose.

"I think it's some sort of greenery," he whispered. "Wonder what we're doing here?"

Arianna shrugged, just as curious as the rest of them.

"*Really?*" said Talis, seeming flustered with the old woman. "We were just here! These are the guests I spoke of."

"There are rules for a reason, Churry," she said, crisply, pulling down her glasses to glare at him properly. "Now, what can I do you for?"

Talis let out an exasperated sigh and then shoved his palm in her face, putting it up close to her eyes as she squinted at it from beneath her glasses.

"Rowina," he growled, impatiently. "Won't you *please* grant us entrance to the Greenhouse?"

Arianna noticed for the first time that he too had the gold

dragon imprinted there on his palm—only visible to those who shared the same bond.

Does that mean this woman could be a guardian too?

Rowina tilted down her glasses to examine his hand and then gave a curt nod.

"And you can speak surely for all who accompany you, under threat of penalty?" she asked in a serious tone.

"That I can," he said with confidence.

"Right this way then." Rowina stood up from the table; she was so short that it barely looked as if she had changed position.

Talis nodded at Arianna and the others to follow—they all shuffled deeper into the dingy, narrow space until they came upon a wall made purely of vines hidden at the back.

When Rowina lifted the sleeve of her robe, Arianna swore she saw the old woman bore the same guardian mark as they did; she pressed her palm against the vines, and a gold light emanated from her hand.

Arianna watched in awe as the bright green vines reacted to the sure guardian magic, moving like snakes and sparking with their own mysterious charms. They wiggled and wormed apart until they created a new formation—a door.

"After you," cooed Rowina, batting her eyelids mockingly at Talis; she scooted back to make room for him.

He scoffed and then pressed both hands against this gateway of vines. The plants then engulfed him entirely until he disappeared altogether, sucked into the wall.

"Not *again*," grumbled Jeom, looking back to Arianna for reassurance.

She giggled, knowing he thought of the first time she and Lessa had forced him to step through an enchanted green wall; he sighed and then walked in after Talis, Lessa and Sano in his arms.

One by one, everyone vanished, until Arianna and Solza were all that was left. But before they could follow, Rowina grabbed her by the arm.

"So, you're Arianna? *The* Arianna Belvedor... of the Warrior's District?"

"That's me," she replied in a shaky voice.

"Well, I suppose it's something of an honor then," she said with a slight bow. "We've been waiting for someone like you for quite some time. Go on now." She urged her forward. "Haven't got all night, dearie."

"Thank you... I think," said Arianna, placing a hand on Solza's head. "Come on, girl. Together."

She stepped through the enchanted door with her avatar at her side—it was a terrible sensation, like all the air was being pressed out of her lungs as the plants tangled around her body.

The vines seemed to have a mind of their own, and limbs to go with it; Arianna imagined that green arms and hands were pinning her down. The last she saw of the dingy room was Rowina walking back to her table, placing her head in a book as if nothing at all had just happened... as if a group of people hadn't just disappeared through a wall of vines.

EVERYTHING WENT BLACK, and just as soon as Arianna had time to panic, she felt all the air being forced back into her body. She opened her eyes with a gasp.

"Welcome to the Greenhouse!" sang Tobias. "Our little reprieve from the desert. You'll be spending quite some time here, but there's a lot to explore. Don't worry. You won't have a moment to get bored."

Arianna was momentarily stunned, experiencing quite the same feeling as when she had first laid eyes on the true City of Undor. A vast balcony spread out before her with a door at her back, and there was a tall, swirling staircase at her front, decorated in the same bright green vines that had brought them here. When she raised her eyes up, she could tell that if she climbed the stairs higher, she could look out over the city, the secret chamber coming to a point far above their heads—just like the other pyramids of Zambienth.

To add to the wonderment, glass stretched out all around her, farther than she could see, to create this picturesque guardian hideaway.

Following Tobias' lead, Arianna stepped down the stairs with care, unsure of where to look first. It was as if the Island of Idris had been bottled up beneath the city, untamed and magnificent, an underground hollow of glass brought to life with all the green of the earth.

She glided down the steep spiral staircase, her attention swayed to a huge structure that the steps were wrapped around; it reached down all the way from the top of the pyramid to the bottom and looked to be a glass cylinder filled with the sparkling black sand of the desert.

Most spectacularly, it encased a massive blue flame flickering inside like a lantern, filling every inch of this underground chamber with a natural light that made it seem as if they were still in the outdoors under a brilliant night sky.

"It reflects the natural weather patterns," called Talis from below. "You can thank Master Tayshin for that gift."

Arianna was stunned, the truth of her new master's strength in magic put into shocking perspective—as well as how much he still had yet to teach her.

She made the final descent, coming to stand by the boys.

Four wide corridors ran through each side of the pyramid, connecting to the massive, open area where they stood; and if this was anything like the Luose palace attic, Arianna was sure there would be much more to discover down each one.

She couldn't wait to start looking around.

Though glass walls surrounded them on all sides—the base

of the pyramid clearly sitting far beneath the earth as the desert reached high above their heads—the light of the giant flame made the black sand twinkle all around them. It was as if they were shrouded by an endless sea of stars, giving off the illusion that this chamber might extend on into an unexplored universe.

Arianna even saw that the firebugs of her past filled the space somehow; an entire ecosystem thrived beneath the desert in defiance here, like some sort of fantasy meadow.

"It's protected by magic," said Talis. "Same as in South Luose." He pointed up, signaling to the top of the pyramid. "We can see everything that goes on from in here, but they can't see us."

"But how does so much grow here?" asked Demetrius, careful to keep on the designated paths as he drank everything in.

"Those additions were an extraordinary gift from an extraordinary and very dear friend," he said, closing his eyes for a moment, as if to savor a memory. "Alas, her identity isn't mine to share. Maybe you'll meet her someday."

It reminded Arianna so much of the greenery in the attic where Demetrius used to seclude himself, so much beautiful life fighting away human influence; there was even a large, silver tree with maroon leaves growing at the center of it all, as if a forest had taken back the land, nature staking a claim as ruler.

She recognized it almost immediately. *A tree from the Nicora Forest!*

She was curious at how it could have possibly found itself in the middle of a desert, so far from home.

More notably still, a small lake accompanied the tree, and vibrant flowers sprouted along the sides—there was a buzzing about this place that Arianna was drawn to, life in the middle of a desert where there was typically none.

"I don't understand how any of this is possible," breathed Demetrius, mouth agape.

"My boy, anything is possible," said Talis, tapping Jeom on

the shoulder. "Put Lessa down here, please. I'll need to have a look at her."

There was a plushy, elegant couch surrounded by plants that Arianna had barely noticed in this setting. In fact, if she looked closely, there were many furnishings fit for the comfort of humans hidden all around so as not to disrupt the nature of the Greenhouse. They seemed to melt into the background, placed in a perfect, secret garden.

Jeom laid Lessa down carefully and sat by her feet, not taking his eyes off her.

"Glad to have you back," whispered Arianna, peering down at her, wishing she would open her eyes so that they might enjoy this moment together.

"Will she be all right?" Demetrius patted her head.

"She'll be stronger than when you left her," said Talis. "Eli, won't you take them to their sleeping quarters now? It's quite late, and tomorrow we have an early assembly."

"Yes, Master Churry," he said, starting toward one of the corridors. "Follow me, everyone."

"But, Talis—" said Arianna.

"The time for introductions is tomorrow," he said. "Lessa will be fine. Sleep well tonight, for we have much to discuss with the sun."

"Yes, sir," she grumbled, signaling to Jeom and Demetrius to join her.

Eli led the way as they passed many chambers with closed doors, covered in vines or dripping with garlands of flowers like everything else here—Arianna was eager to open every single one of them to see what secrets they might find.

Minutes later, Eli pushed open a door at the end of the corridor and escorted them inside; four large beds lined the room.

"You'll all have to share a room for now," he said. "The Greenhouse is a bit crowded at the moment." He smiled, reassuringly. "See you in the morning."

He shut the door to their chamber and left them alone.

"What's going on here?" said Jeom, plopping down on one of the beds as soon as Eli was gone. "Will Lessa be all right?"

"I know she will be," said Arianna, giving him a hug around the shoulders. "You did good. We got her back, and Talis will give her a good round of healing. *Trust* me. He might love her more than you do."

Jeom reddened, beginning to fiddle with his thumbs—she hadn't meant to say the word 'love,' but secrets were unfolding here, so why not this one.

She giggled and so did Demetrius, everyone relaxing for the first time since they had watched Lessa disappear beneath the water.

"What do you think this place is though?" said Jeom, gazing around the room.

"You heard what Tobias said," replied Demetrius. "It's another hideout… for the Guardians of Gold."

Jeom shook his head. "Yeah sure, but—"

"I know what you mean," said Arianna. "This isn't any normal hideout, not like the attic. This place has definitely been built with different magic… *stronger*."

Her eyes flicked to Solza, remembering the beginning of their desert adventures when she'd revealed her unfathomable powers of bringing life back to the deadened lands.

"Well, what do we do?" asked Demetrius, rubbing his eyes as Jeom let out a big yawn.

"I think we just sleep," said Arianna, recognizing how tired they all were. "We're safe for now. Talis, we can trust him. We'll figure out more tomorrow."

She crawled into a bed and called for Solza to join her, unable to fight the weight of sleep any longer as they cozied up together. Closing her eyes, she felt something of real happiness and relief finally settling her mind's worries. They were safe, *and* they had gotten Lessa back.

For now, that's all that mattered. Whatever new mysteries were left to be discovered under the desert could wait until morning, though she was certain there would be many more glittering secrets to find.

26

THE RESISTANCE

ARIANNA WOKE TO WHAT COULD only be the sound of Cyn bickering with someone. But Solomon wasn't there anymore, so she wondered who had taken his place. *Please don't let this be a dream.*

Eyes hazy with sleep, she looked around to find the others still slept soundly. Not wanting to wake them, she dressed quickly and tiptoed down the corridor to investigate with Solza at her heels; her caretaker's voice grew louder and louder, leading her right into a narrow chamber where several people had gathered.

Arianna stopped in the doorway to spy.

"We need a plan," said Cyn. "Who knows what Jon has gotten himself into this time. We can't just wait around for him to show up and save the day."

"She's right," said Tobias. "With Kassime gone and Solomon turned, everything we've built is crumbling. We have our memories back now, and we knew this day would come again, but this time it just feels so… fragile. We *have* to protect them. They're our only chance."

"Only chance for what?" whispered Arianna, stepping out from the shadows.

Now in full view, she saw that everyone was sitting around a large, stone table; and the room they were in was quite sophisticated for an underground hideout, portraits of important-looking people lining the walls.

Besides Cyn and Tobias, Arianna recognized Talis and Eli there too. She was shocked to also find the face of Gabriel among them, the sweet-tempered barkeep from South Luose and former partner to Mya, before Eli had taken her life—he offered her a small smile.

She couldn't find the energy to even process this strange addition to the guardians, just glad they had all made it out of the city safely. There were, though, several other new, tired faces joining the ones she knew well. Men and women seemingly of various backgrounds, including the old woman, Rowina.

She felt her cheeks redden with all eyes on her, so she averted hers to the empty seat at the head of the table. Directly behind it was a portrait hung in a rusted frame as a centerpiece, overcome with vines of green blossoms so that it almost became one with the nature-covered wall.

I know this painting…

It was the exact same one of the young guardians in the palace attic library, the start of it all. So much had changed since then, already a year ago now—Arianna was starting to see herself, Demetrius, Jeom, Lessa, and their avatars in the same painted pattern.

They were the young, hope-filled guardians now, though she still didn't fully grasp what that even meant. True understanding could only come with time, experience, and answers from any one person at this table… if they cared to be less than cryptic as was Talis' unfortunate preference.

Arianna and her friends had finally accepted their role in this, decided on who they were supposed to be and what they were supposed to do. But their mutual decision hadn't come full circle yet; the real, dirty truth of what they had stepped into was always kept at bay with close calls, shiny new magic tricks, and intriguing Golden Age history. All very distracting from the horrors that surely lay in their futures, should they come even close to achieving their goal.

As Arianna looked on, thinking of the faces in that portrait that were forever missing from this room—thinking of Keeper Kassime's death and of Solomon's absence—her mind vividly conjured the same image of her friends and their avatars, contemplating past moments in a different, darker light.

What if Lessa *hadn't* come back, a mermaid for good? What if Jeom *had* fallen through the ice in the City of Undor, swallowed whole by Blancoren? What if the skeletal army *had* been too much for Demetrius to withstand with no defensive magic on his side? And what if she herself *hadn't* risen from the dead for a second time, fought off the darkness, when Sir Vladamor had snuffed out her life, the light?

We'd all be dead… Gone.

Arianna knew by now that luck would only get them so far, and she wondered if, in the end, this quest they'd set out on would be worth it.

She wished she knew what had happened all those years ago to tear the guardians apart, because she wanted to stop it from happening again, to prevent any more lives from being lost.

"Oh, Arianna!" cried Cyn, jumping out of her chair and running to her. "Oh, honey, give me a hug." She wrapped her arms around her and pulled her close. "I'm so happy to see you. I'm so, *so* happy you're all right. It took you too long to find your way here. We thought—"

"It's good to see you too, Cyn," she said. "I'm all right. I missed you." She hugged her back before gently pushing her to arm's length. "How did you know we'd end up here?"

She tried to remain serious, willing herself to demand answers from her elders once and for all—her overdue reunion with Cyn would have to wait a little longer.

"The compass." Tobias proudly stood up from his chair; he bowed slightly.

Arianna returned it upon instinct, her adopted highlife mannerisms now just as much a part of her as her recent history as a slave.

"It's a guardian relic," he said. "That one is laced with strong directional magic to keep its holder on the right path."

"A guardian relic?" She cocked her head to the side.

"Indeed," said Tobias. "We all received them upon induction as Guardians of Gold… in the old days. Sadly, they're most likely scattered now, many lost."

"But what are they, *exactly*?" she asked, determined to form some kind of understanding before someone interrupted.

"Well, they can be many things, in fact. But all guardian relics share in that they're conduits for astral journey. They symbolize our journey to open the door to a better world." He gestured to everyone in the room. "Some have other unique gifts, too, like the compass. That is, *if* you can tap into the heart of their magic."

"Aurora?" mumbled Arianna—she slipped the dagger from its place at her thigh and held it in front of her with shaky hands, remembering the day it was gifted to her in the Jar.

"Seems that you've had a proper initiation after all," said Rowina, craning her neck to get a better look.

An old man she didn't recognize laughed.

"Kassime wouldn't have done it any other way than proper," he said.

"Kassime didn't give this to me," said Arianna, looking up. "Solomon did."

There was a moment of silence, all eyes flicking to the portrait, to Keeper Kassime staring down at them with his favored smug grin. But Arianna knew his real face now—the face of Ferlon Ragaric was burned in her memory, and *that* wasn't who was painted there.

He had given his entire life, and more, to their cause long before many of these younger guardians had even joined the ranks, including her and her friends; Arianna wouldn't be leaving this table until she knew exactly why.

Cyn gave a sad nod. "I remember the day. Bell gifted that to her at the start of her apprenticeship under him."

Just the mention of his name caused a stir at the table, and Arianna again became distracted by the pain of having to think of him at all. Her grasp tightened over the blue hilt of the dagger, the black blade sparkling in the low morning light—the enchanted flame of this pyramid told Arianna that outside it was going to be a bright, sunny day.

As she studied the weapon, fingering the curves of the winged beast that made up the guard, she considered it with a new mind.

These must be the wings of a dragon…

Since a guardian had gifted it to her, it was an easy conclusion to make—both were inherent protectors of the Olleb.

She had always felt there was more of a story to this weapon, and finally the pieces were falling into place.

Had Solomon parted with his rightful guardian relic because he wasn't a true guardian at all?

Arianna wished she could tear the answers from him, understand his darkened role in all this in order to move forward.

"Does it do anything special?" said Eli, his curiosity palpable.

"It's saved my life a few times, so I'd say yes," she said, fixated on the golden streak that intersected the black jewel in the middle of the pommel; it had always seemed so familiar.

Her eyes found Solza's, and she suddenly knew why—that streak of fire belonged to her avatar as well.

A prickle grew up her spine as Arianna made this association;

she was sure there was much more to uncover with both her avatar and her guardian relic.

Could they somehow be connected?

She shook her head, looking back to the dagger, yet another puzzle unfurling just as one was solved.

"I'd say, it's *quite* special," she whispered to herself. Then she put her attention on the faces she knew and trusted. "But why didn't you just tell us to meet in Zambienth? We could have ended up in any number of places. This was just luck. We can't keep putting our faith in that."

She pursed her lips, trying to command respect from these teachers of hers who still always treated her like a child.

"Faith is sometimes the key component," said Talis, his stare boring into hers, as if to impress his wisdom on her mind forever.

Arianna recalled how Solomon had swayed Talis back from the depths of his despair, drove him again toward the light to fight in its name.

Though all for nothing, it would seem.

Still, it was because of Solomon's renewed 'faith' that Talis had returned to the fold.

"They couldn't tell you about our hideout here in case you were intercepted by Bell," said Gabriel. "We couldn't risk it with the Luose palace being compromised. There are only a few safe guardian gathering houses left in the Olleb, and now probably even fewer. There's no telling how many of us remain."

Arianna felt her heart grow heavy as Solomon's wicked face grew larger in her mind's eye.

"We've cloaked this place with strong magic." Talis looked around the chamber. "He may search for it just to rule it out in the King's hunt for you, but so much time has passed, he'll have doubts it still exists when it can't be located again. It's grown considerably, though, since I was last here."

He said it as if this secret garden had a magical mind of its own, budding at will; Arianna assumed that it did.

"Rowina does a great job at maintaining it," added Tobias, tipping his hat to her.

"That she does," said Talis. "Anyhow, it would have been too risky to tell you our next move should you have been caught. Instead, we put our *faith* in magic to guide you to us."

"The spell…" said Arianna, glancing at Eli.

He offered her a knowing nod.

"We recited it daily," said Cyn, clasping her hands together with a shy smile, "hoping you girls would feel the magic in your hearts and follow it here… hoping you were still alive."

"Whether or not that worked, thankfully the compass never lets us down," said Tobias. "It's notorious for bringing guardians together. When the holder is in close enough proximity to others, it gives off a blast of magical energy. As soon as you hit the beach, we sensed it."

It all clicked for Arianna then, how Eli knew exactly where to find them and why Talis had come to join them so quickly.

"It's so good to see you've made it safely, dear," said Cyn, squeezing her shoulder. "We were on the verge of putting out a search!"

Arianna gave her a solemn smile, so relieved to see her again too.

"Oh, I am sorry, though… I'm so sorry. That Bell." She shook her head, lip quivering. "I just don't know—"

Talis came over and guided Cyn back to her seat before she could work herself back up.

"There's nothing we can do about Solomon," he said. "Let's save that grief for later. Right now, we need to think of how we can protect the Guardians of Gold and all we've built. He'll be going after everyone now that Devlindor has caught wind of us out of hiding. He knows our secrets and has surely shared them with the rest of the King's shadows."

Arianna nodded.

"I saw the additions to the 'Wanted' posters," she said. "Lessa and Demetrius have been added to the list in exchange for the highlife reward."

"I just cannot believe that Bell went dark, a part of the Shadow Resistance!" A woman she didn't yet know pounded her fist on the table. "He trained me by his own hand."

"Well, believe it," snapped Arianna, her temper taking over. "Master Bell *is* dead."

A hush fell over the table.

Talis led Arianna to a place by his side, introducing the new faces as he went.

She took her seat, leaning back in her chair with Solza hovering close by—it was hard not to notice all eyes remaining on her, though, observing her intently as if she might give a speech. She felt inclined to say something after introductions were through.

"It's nice to meet you all," she said, just to fill the awkward silence. "So… what's the plan, then?"

Rowina scoffed. "Well, isn't *that* the question."

"Don't mind her," whispered Gabriel. "She's been a little fussy with so many visitors lately. They call her the gatekeeper here in Zambienth. She never leaves this post."

He snickered and Rowina flashed him daggers for eyes.

"So, you're the slave that caused our king to finally get off his throne and leave Saindora?" said a brusque man called Sergios; he had a goatee curling on his chin, an accent that Arianna couldn't quite place, and something warm about him that made her instantly disarmed. "I hear he even made an appearance in the Jar!"

"I am not a slave anymore," she said, folding her arms across her chest. "And he is not my king."

There were murmurs across the table, some nodding in agreement and others staring at her with plain curiosity. She knew that, by now, fragments of her story must have reached far and wide—surely everyone was intrigued to know more.

"I see the courage that must have gotten you past the ruthless gates of Blancoren," said an extremely tall woman she now knew as Margery. "He is also *not* my king."

Arianna met her eyes, and she saw reflected in them the same ferocity that she felt in her own heart.

"Nor mine!" said Rowina, slapping her hand on the table, her glasses tumbling to the floor as she stood.

Arianna was startled by the old woman's intensity. The others quickly joined in.

"Nor mine!" they all repeated, the statement echoing across the room as everyone took to their feet.

Arianna stood too, catching Talis' eye as he grinned approvingly.

"Would you like to do the honors?" he asked.

Without hesitation, she placed her fist across her chest. "Hail to the World," she sang. "Hail to Olleb-Yelfra!"

The other voices around the table followed her own in a welcome chorus, the first time she'd heard so many banded together behind the same, treasonous goal. And as they all recited their declaration as Guardians of Gold, Arianna's gaze pinned to the opposite wall where a plaque hung, so similar to one she'd seen many times before in her first guardian sanctuary, the attic library—it was the Golden Rule, the prophecy of old.

When their voices receded, they all settled back in their seats.

"Now that pleasantries are over, what do you propose we do?" asked a skinny man at the far end of the table.

Arianna remembered Talis calling him by the name of Vance; he had an intellectual quality about him, as if he'd always know just what to say next.

"Miss Belvedor has nearly brought down our entire practice with her carelessness," he said with a bit of a hiss. "We lost Kassime over her! And now that Solomon has turned, we're surely all being hunted. Who knows if there's anyone even left in the other regions. It's only a matter of time before he digs the Greenhouse back up."

"This is nobody's fault," said Gabriel, sharply. "Least of all

Arianna's. Yes, Solomon's betrayal is a tragedy, as is the loss of our friend, but things cannot be as they once were for the guardians. We have to embrace this change and work together to overcome it. We need a new way forward."

He offered Arianna a kind, supportive smile as she gathered the courage to address them with the words burning in her soul.

She took a deep breath and then cleared her throat.

"I've learned that we can't force our future to be any certain way," she said, "even if we're *certain* of who we're supposed to be and how we're supposed to get there. A new path has been carved for the Guardians of Gold, and change *will* come. We can't continue going one way when life is so clearly guiding us in another direction." She spoke these words with a heavy heart—owed to someone much wiser than her but who would never stand with them again.

"Wonderful advice," said Vance, challenging her. "But how do you suppose we do that, huh?" He looked to everyone at the table. "Do any of you have any bright ideas?"

Nobody replied, everyone looking anywhere but at Vance and Arianna.

"That's what I thought." He huffed, crossing his arms.

"May I?" said Arianna, glancing at Talis for permission to continue; how strange it was to be in such a discussion with elders from all walks of life.

Emotions were clearly running high right now—they were scared. Everyone at this table may have held a guardian status, but they weren't exactly all on the same page yet.

Talis twisted his beard around his finger, deep in thought, nodding to her to speak.

"My friends and I were trained as guardians by Keeper Kassime over the last year," said Arianna. "I don't know all of you, and, obviously, we're quite new to this heavy responsibility. But in our short apprenticeship under him, we took an oath to protect the knowledge of the Golden Age, to protect the most precious pieces of the world which the King seeks to bury forever."

She looked back to the portrait.

"Now, I know how Kassime felt about our responsibilities to learn and *store* such knowledge, to continue passing it down to others until one day someone strong and worthy could defeat King Devlindor and put the world back right."

Arianna stood up from her chair, fists on the table.

"Kassime died for his duty, for his dream, and for the future of Olleb-Yelfra." She jabbed a finger at the table, growing more passionate. "Well, the future is *now*, and I intend to see his dream through to the end."

Vance scoffed, shaking his head as he leaned back in his chair. Others shared his incredulous expression, not ready to take her very seriously—this only made Arianna feel that much more determined to be heard.

Talis remained quite silent while Margery and Rowina considered her intently; their reactions alone told her she had, at the very least, a chance to sway them to her side. Arianna didn't need any more proof of what her responsibility in life was, but *they* did. And she intended to give it to them right then and there.

She and her friends had been distracted for long enough, their course led astray by fairies, necromancers, giants, mermaids, and more. Their world had exploded into a maze of options and choices—challenges and mistakes—since escaping the Jar. And yet, Arianna recognized, without each trying experience, she would have never earned this moment to address some of the last remaining Guardians of Gold.

Now that she'd found the right path to follow, she would do her very best to steer the others in the same direction… if they wished to finally act.

"It took me quite some time to come to this conclusion myself," she said with more fervor. "In fact, Kassime's death is what made me realize what I'm meant to do with my life—"

She bowed her head for her fallen teacher.

"I'm not perfect. I didn't wake up one day expecting to flee the Four Corners or to discover magic. *But* I did. And all thanks to a guardian." Arianna smiled at Talis.

She stood up straighter.

"And my friends and I never intended to assume the identities of highlifes, to become guardian apprentices, to battle the King's right hand in a desert... and win—"

There were gasps from a couple of people, and she nodded her affirmation.

"—*or* survive a mermaid's prejudice, of all things." She paused for effect, holding everyone's attention as she proudly stated their unlikely triumphs over the last several weeks. "And yet, here we are."

Nobody responded, breath hitched all around as everyone ate up the first true recounting of the tales of Arianna Belvedor since she'd escaped the Jar and caught the King's eye.

"These victories were all achieved with the help of friends, teachers, avatars, and Olleb-Yelfra herself," said Arianna.

She clutched the stone of her necklace, knowing she held her destiny in her hand.

"The time for passively hoarding knowledge is over. King Devlindor will come for us just like Vance said, and if all we do is nothing, he'll surely smoke us out from this glamorous hole quickly. We can't stand for anything if we're dead!" She touched eyes with each of them. "Hear me now. We *must* fight back."

Master Lethander's words echoed in her heart. The people in this room *could* be the first makings of the army they needed to win back the Olleb; and if her own people, fellow guardians, wouldn't follow her into battle, then who would?

"If King Devlindor has the chance to wipe us from the earth, who will ever stop him? Who will right his wrongs and make room for magic once again in this world if not for the Guardians of Gold?" implored Arianna, in one final push for action. "What we need now is an army to end his regime... to end his Shadow

Resistance once and for all."

"Are you mad?" said Sergios from down the table, his warmth vanishing. "You make a thrilling speech, child, but it's empty words without a plan. How do you suppose we go about that? Half of the guardians are dead, and the other half are on their way to the grave with Solomon surely hunting us like the wolf he is." He ended with a string of words in a language Arianna couldn't understand, but from the sound of it, they weren't very nice.

"What we *need* is to hide," said Cyn, fear in her eyes. "Make new protection spells and find new safety dens until we can strengthen ourselves again."

"Kassime never would have agreed to this," said a woman named Iris, who, up until now, had yet to speak a word; a dark scar sliced from her chin to her chest, and there was something in her eyes that told Arianna not to cross her.

Some people at the table began nodding their agreement with those who voiced such reservations—some, but not all.

Arianna felt her cheeks run hot. Still, she wouldn't accept defeat in the face of their doubt, for what would that prove?

Absolutely nothing. Be brave!

"Kassime would want us to protect ourselves and our knowledge," said Rowina, coming to Arianna's aid. "He sacrificed his life for that."

"Ferlon *Ragaric*," said Arianna, internally thanking Rowina for giving her a push back on track, "sacrificed his life to save me and my friends so that we could escape from Solomon's wrath. He believed in us and our gifts, and he died to protect us." She pressed her palms flat upon the table. "His duty was to protect and share knowledge of the Golden Age. *Ours* is to try and save the Olleb. We do him no justice if we don't ultimately rid this land of the darkness that's been allowed to spread unchecked for so long. We can't just sit back and wait for someone else to save us."

She felt herself grow taller, locking eyes with all those who challenged her stance.

"You can, but I won't."

"*We* won't," said a voice from the doorway.

Arianna looked up and caught her breath as she found Lessa there, Sano wrapped around her shoulders, a normalcy she'd long since prayed to see again; Jeom and Demetrius were standing protectively by her side.

"Lessa, you're all right!" said Arianna, running to her.

"I'm all right." She offered her a small smile.

"When you didn't come back—"

"I'm here now," she said. "And I'm not going anywhere."

Arianna drew her into a long hug, and Sano jumped off her shoulders to join Solza, the young guardians finally reunited. As they all grasped hands in a moment of solidarity, she knew they would stand by her now through anything—and the day had finally come when they would need to voice their beliefs to others outside of their tightknit family, together.

It was time to let it be known that they intended to truly fight for their freedom, no longer willing to run or hide behind magic. They would resist the King's control and would live or die in doing so.

"Ready?" she whispered to her friends.

She felt supportive hands at her back as she turned again to address the table.

A strong gust of wind burst through the room, startling everyone as there was no part of this chamber open to outside elements. And the blossoms framing the portrait of the fallen guardians began to grow into the most glorious flowers Arianna had ever seen—the avatars were showing their full support as well.

"This is our legacy, the destiny that we've chosen and the one that we believe the Olleb is guiding us toward," said Arianna, feeling the burn of magic start in her eyes. "Together, we're going to bring down the King and his castle."

"Or we'll die trying," said Lessa, standing tall at her side.

It was the first time Arianna had really heard her speak since they'd recovered her from the sea, and she noticed she'd adopted an edge that definitely hadn't been there before. There was such confidence behind her statement; Lessa's usual sweetness had been replaced by something stronger, more assertive.

Arianna was just glad that Lessa was still *their* Lessa, edgier or not. The boys declared their agreement.

"Well, I'll be damned!" said Sergios, slapping Vance on the back. He buckled over from the force. "So, it's true then? With two avatars on our side, the prophecy can surely come to pass!" He gestured to the plaque that Arianna had spotted earlier. "We could be looking at the beginning of it all, folks."

"I sure hope so," said Margery, a dazed expression crossing her face.

Iris stayed silent, but there was something resembling a grin growing on her lips.

Cyn began to sob, Gabriel trying and failing to calm her down. "I'm just so *p-p*-proud…" she stuttered into a handkerchief.

"I have only faith," said Talis, observing Lessa with such pride.

"That's what we said last time," said Vance, shaking his head; even still, he seemed to also be won over by the extraordinary magic on their side, his attention locked in on the avatars.

Rowina craned her neck to get a better look at them. "And are those *really*—"

"Avatars," said Tobias with a sureness. "I've seen them in action for myself, and now so have you." He slammed his hat onto the table, and Arianna jumped, not used to seeing him so forceful with anything when he'd been bowing at her for so long. "Why are we even still discussing this? This is what we've been waiting for."

"I support every word," said Eli, gawking at them—Arianna refused to meet his eyes. "We should fight the King."

"Slow down now," said Talis, raising a hand for silence. "You young ones are always so impatient. It looks like we can all agree that sitting back while Devlindor destroys this land isn't an option anymore. It's gone on long enough."

He looked across the table for any challengers—there were none.

"Wonderful, but we need to think the next steps through. We can't just go knocking on his door and ask him to politely leave." His brow furrowed. "We need a plan."

"He's right," said Cyn, collecting herself. "The last time we rushed into battle, there was a terrible price to pay."

This statement seemed to shake Tobias' confidence away, his eyes flicking to the portrait as he leaned back in his chair.

Arianna suddenly remembered the details of the attic perfectly then; she grasped onto a single memory from that eye-opening past—the day she learned of the Guardians of Gold.

A young, innocent Solomon Bell had smiled down at her from the very same painting, encouraged her to be the best she could be and learn as much as she was able to in that gifted moment of peace. It was the strongest of reminders that anything was possible… that, together with those she called family, she could defy the King's rule and *truly* take her freedom.

"What happened to everyone? What happened to the rest of the guardians in that portrait?" said Arianna.

She traced the lines of the dragon on her palm as her eyes glued again to Solomon's; this time, though, his depiction didn't give her hope… it gave her more of a reason to want to fight back.

"What turned you from being guardians who take action to so passive and scared?"

Talis twisted his beard again, a grave look clouding his eyes—a hush fell over the room.

"It's a long story," he finally said, his voice shaking. "The short version is that the death of loved ones can cause you to re-think your strategies… if such strategies caused their deaths in the first place."

"We all know well about death," said Arianna, tersely, refusing to let this subject go twice. "There's not a single soul living
today that doesn't, given the King's laws. And it's what keeps
shoving us forward." She gestured to her friends. "This is our plan
because of the loss of loved ones. And the death of a golden world
that could have been ours if not for a greedy royal."

Demetrius squeezed Arianna on the shoulder in support.

"Sir, Kassime told us that you tried to take on King Devlindor
once… but that the plan failed," he said, gently, looking to Talis.
"We know many of you were lost. Maybe if you told us what
happened back then, we could prevent it from happening again."

"The only way to prevent death is to not go running straight
toward it," growled Iris.

"Find your calm," said Rowina, glaring toward her from
across the table.

Iris locked her gaze on Arianna, challenging her.

"You realize that any decision or action which leads us to directly challenge the King *will* result in death, right?" she said,
matter-of-factly. "Many of us will likely die before finding the
chance to even stand face-to-face with him. And whose honor
will that be? Yours?"

She folded her arms across her chest, snickering.

"His powers are greater than anyone in this room, including
you and your friends, *combined*. And his supporters, the Shadow
Resistance, won't do you any favors. Those are the facts. How do
you plan to defeat a monster like that?"

She lifted an eyebrow at Arianna, waiting for an answer—
when she couldn't form a response, Iris scoffed.

"You will not be the first to try, but you'll be the first to die
publicly for it. I don't care if you have avatars on your side. It's
not enough! You're just children experimenting in a world we've
been studying for ages."

"And he has an avatar too," mused Margery.

"Children do not battle necromancers and *live*," said Sergios.

"But they are children, nonetheless," said Vance, tapping his fingers on the table.

Arianna wasn't ignorant to these brutal facts, but she had accepted them, lived through them. It was the only way. If they were ever to meet the King and challenge him properly for their freedom, the Olleb's freedom, the path toward him would not prove easy.

Alas, Iris' words could not be unheeded—there would be more bloodshed on the way to the King, possibly from those closest to her; and if not her friends, then whose?

Blood is blood, a dear sacrifice to be paid.

"We need to know what happened," said Jeom, jumping in to Arianna's rescue, ignoring Iris' bleak portrayal of their futures should they continue down this path. "If we're going to do this… create a strong, fool-proof plan, and try this again, then we need to know what went wrong in the first place. So, tell us, dammit!"

He was growing angry again—this time, though, instead of Demetrius whispering words to try to calm him, Lessa took on the role.

"What went *wrong*?" snapped Talis, getting to his feet. A cold laugh escaped his lips. "What didn't go wrong, you mean."

He looked to the other elders and nobody protested, but Arianna could feel dread hovering around the group, everyone readying themselves for an unpleasant trip to the guardians' past.

"Go on, Talis, they have a right to know. They're all one of us now," said Tobias, a solemness shadowing his face.

"They deserve the truth," agreed Cyn. "Jon was going to tell them sooner or later anyhow."

"I suppose you're right," he said, glancing to Iris—she looked away.

He took a deep breath and sat back down, signaling for them to be seated too.

"Thank you," said Arianna as she and her friends all settled in the empty chairs, filling the spaces of those lost before them.

"I deserve no thanks in this story. None of us do." Talis spoke with such a firmness that it made Arianna cold; she was both afraid of and eager for the understanding that the conclusion of this story might bring. "All our gratitude will always lie with your master, Solomon Bell."

Arianna couldn't help her sharp intake of breath at this statement.

"No matter what path he chose to take after that day," said Talis, "Solomon is the reason there was any hope left for the guardians to rebuild with." He closed his eyes, and Arianna heard murmurs of agreement around the room. "Listen closely now, children, for our fallen dragons deserve your full attention if you wish to be privy to their last moments of life."

27

A MOMENT IN TIME

"THIS DOESN'T FEEL RIGHT," said a young Solomon Bell, thinking out loud. He had a map unfurled out in front of him, moving pins all around to try to see the picture that would least likely get them killed.

Talis thought he might even back out if he weren't such a proud soul, but it was far past that point now.

"Nonsense," said Talis. "We're ready for this. You're ready. Keep your head on straight, brother. We're almost through it." He patted him on the back, and Solomon gave him that subtly grateful look they'd long since mastered by now to hide their emotions.

Talis was older than Solomon, sure, but brothers they proved to be—if not in blood, then in spirit. A healer and a warrior, much to teach one another and much to learn. They had grown to be fast friends, two unlikely souls who found each other outside of the Jar, drawn to the magic.

Upon first meeting Solomon Bell, Talis was already a guardian, already in the know. He had watched closely and carefully to see how Solomon could measure up, and, thankfully, he hadn't let him down. It wasn't long before Solomon had earned a rightful place as a Guardian of Gold with strong, magical talents of his own and a courage and drive unlike anything Talis had yet to see in the others.

What's more, the companions this new recruit had surrounded himself with after earning citizenship possessed other valuable and unique strengths to complement his own; he had helped steer a spirited, young, and eager group straight into the open arms of the Guardians of Gold.

Solomon, Ferlon, Cyn, and Nico—a warrior, creator, healer, and agrarian—each joining the ranks of the guardian resistance not long after the 205th Free Falls. They were almost what the world needed to break free of the King's hold.

Almost.

"What doesn't feel right?" asked Master Tayshin, coming into the room and peering down at the map alongside Solomon. He took a swig from a flask, alcohol dripping onto the parchment and forever smudging the ink that outlined a map of the Golden Age terrain.

Master Jon Tayshin was a virile man, muscles bulging from every crevice, except for the soft belly inevitably growing at his middle from too much ale over too much time. Talis thought him a bit of a brute, but he had demonstrated his strengths and his loyalty well. And despite the man's lack of manners, Talis believed in his revolution without reservation. He believed in him—their leader.

As he watched Solomon and Master Tayshin discuss the battle to come, Talis reflected on first meeting Master Tayshin in the South Luose Well Center; he had been just a young healer's apprentice at the time with not yet an inkling of magic. Nevertheless, Talis had proven himself a natural healer without the aid of spells, so Master Tayshin had his eye on him at first sight.

Warriors of the Olleb found themselves in the city well centers more often than any other trade. For Master Tayshin, being one of the foremost master warriors and trainers in South Luose, it wasn't a surprise that Talis would eventually tend to him as a caretaker-in-training. He remembered fondly the day that Master Tayshin would change his life forever—the day he learned of magic.

MASTER TAYSHIN STUMBLED into Talis' well room, a deep gash on his leg gushing blood. He was blue in the face from pain, gritting his teeth to keep from crying out.

"Boy, you had better fix me up quick!" he said. "It's not in my cards to die today. I've plans to give the kid that did this to me a whooping when I get back."

But young Talis wasn't one for quick work.

He was slow and methodical, calculating everything down to the tiniest detail. Little did he know that a much wiser man was calculating him all the while.

He worked the wound over carefully, feeling Master Tayshin shudder with every movement.

"It's going to take a bit of time to heal such a deep cut," Talis replied. "I'm sorry but looks like you'll be here a while, sir. Do you want me to send word to someone to cancel your duel? I can have a messenger ride out."

"In the King's name…" he growled. "Give me that prillyberry juice over there. I'll show you how it's done."

"But, sir, I don't think the best course of action now is prillyberry—"

"Lesson number one," said Master Tayshin. "When in doubt,

prillyberry juice is always the best course of action. Its simplicity mixes best with magic.”

Talis hesitated, not quite sure of what he’d meant by ‘magic’ in the least. He recalled the word from old fairytales children whispered about in private during his past district life, but, surely, this master trainer wasn’t speaking about such a forbidden theme—all fantasies born from the imagination were prohibited under the King’s laws, because they were lies. Talis shook his head of the thought, knowing he must’ve misunderstood, and he didn’t dare say one word about it.

Master Tayshin continued barking his demands without even a pause for breath, so Talis let the shocking moment slip away and hurried to fetch the prillyberry juice.

“And bring me some of those too,” he said, pointing to a shelf lined with jars that Talis had yet to even explore.

He stood back now and watched as Master Tayshin quickly concocted a foul-smelling remedy, prillyberries as the main ingre-dient. “Lesson number two.” He turned serious, waving Talis closer. “A little magic goes a very long way.”

Talis felt his heart skip a beat, for now he knew he had not misunderstood anything.

A highlife talking so openly of such things was incomprehen-sible. But before he could question him, or decide if he should even question anything at all, Master Tayshin spread the prilly-berry paste all over his wound.

As he did, he whispered a phrase both foreign and pleasant to Talis’ ears, “Helthra saludis emencia.”

Though Talis didn’t understand these words at the time, he had felt it in his heart that they were special; something small sparked in him then that would soon grow to be a large and life-altering blaze—this had been the first sound of delicious magic to his ears, and he would come to fully believe in the existence of it not long after this day.

“What did you do?” he asked in an awed voice. “What were

those words you spoke just now?"

Talis saw the paste seemed to be working at a much quicker speed than normal, the concoction appearing oddly electrified, as if it had been somehow energized by Master Tayshin's very words—butterflies began to flutter in his stomach.

"Healer's magic," he said, matter-of-factly. "Would you like to learn?"

With just that one question, Talis knew this would be a turning point in his life. He could feel the choice tickling something deep inside of him.

Backward or forward, he had to decide now.

One minute, he was going about his day under his normal caretaker apprenticeship, and in the next, a renowned master warrior was asking if he wanted to learn about magic—a word he couldn't even quite grasp and a taboo topic per his king. But what gave him certainty of the right decision was what he could see with his very own eyes and feel in his soul.

His mind, which was eager to continue learning more than most, was hungry for answers; somewhere not so deep down, he was ready for more than this arbitrary existence and post-slavery placement he'd been handed.

"Yes," he stuttered. "I'd like to learn very much."

"I thought so," said Master Tayshin, getting to his feet as if he hadn't just done the impossible.

His blood smeared the tiles, proving that he had.

"Now, I'm off to give someone a beating. I'll send for you tomorrow." He narrowed his eyes at Talis. "Until then, not a word of this, you hear? Tell no one."

"Yes, sir," breathed Talis, eyes wide and watering.

"That will be 'Master' to you from now on." Master Tayshin extended his hand, and Talis took it without hesitation. "Your life just got a whole lot more interesting, son. Welcome to the Guardians of Gold."

WHAT MASTER TAYSHIN HAD SEEN in young Talis that day to compel him to offer such a wonderous opportunity was never divulged. Yet, tomorrow had come and gone; now Talis Churry was a changed man, a magical man, and he had never once regretted his choice.

"The plan is simple," said Master Tayshin, snapping Talis back to the present with a slap on the back. "Sneak into the palace and kill the King while he sleeps. A sleeping king is vulnerable, *weak*. And a weak man can certainly be killed."

He mimicked a knife to his throat, and Talis reflexively cringed, thinking of how much blood would soon be spilled—he spent so much of his time trying to keep that from happening or cleaning it up. *What a sure waste*, he thought.

Though Talis had never been one for dueling, a healer at heart, he could hold his own with a sword, if necessary. A friendship with master warriors like Jon Tayshin and Solomon Bell hadn't been without its perks.

He preferred the bow and arrow over anything else—a weapon that offered a clean kill if you aimed it just right. Swords felt too theatrical for him. If he absolutely *had* to end someone's life, then from a distance and with one strike was his preference. He took no pleasure in killing and would rather put his efforts toward prolonging life.

Nevertheless, Master Tayshin was one of the greatest warriors the Olleb had seen in centuries, and Talis had never taken a lesson from him for granted. He was lucky that Master Tayshin had stuck around long enough to lend his skill, not traveling as much as most other master warriors did; he never strayed too far from his home in South Luose where the colder climate and forest terrain suited his temperament best.

"A sleeping king is still a king that has withstood many nights without dying," said Talis, brushing long, dark hair from his face.

"And one must wonder as to how…" added Solomon, biting his lip. "It seems *too* easy."

Master Tayshin laughed, shaking his head at the pair, always having each other's backs.

"Son, this will be far from easy. But the only way to move forward is one step at a time. Standing still is the hard part, and we've been still long enough. We have an opportunity to leap forward now, so let's take it. This is the moment we've all been preparing for."

He grasped Solomon encouragingly by the shoulders and looked around the room, all eyes on him now as everyone's nerves came to the forefront to be seen.

"The time to take back our Olleb has come!" he said, addressing the gathering of guardians. "Who's with me now?"

There was a resounding "*I*" across the attic library—Solomon's voice joined in as an unenthused mumble.

"Everything will be *fine*," said Talis, taking a deep breath and lifting his chest high so that he felt slightly braver. "You'll see." Inside, he echoed Solomon's sentiments.

Solomon was key to this plan succeeding—if he was feeling unsure, everyone else certainly would be too, and that was anything but reassuring.

"I wish I didn't have to stay here," said Ferlon, pouting, already much accustomed to the face of Keeper Kassime and the Luose palace life that came with it. He crossed his arms at his chest as he paced around the table, sword swinging at his hip. "You lot get to have all the fun. I'd love to pay the King back personally for having to constantly enforce his evil laws just so we can survive."

"We need you to stay put to help smooth out the aftermath," said Master Tayshin. "You'll assume control as Keeper Kassime once the King is dead. You're a strong leader with this identity. It's a good match. The people will follow you."

Ferlon gave a resigned nod. "Everyone follows Helix Kassime," he grumbled.

"You won't have to be Keeper Kassime for much longer, my friend," said Nico with a chuckle. "Besides, he suits you a heck of a lot better than that old grump, Ragaric."

Ferlon cracked a hard-won smile. "If only you hadn't gone and volunteered me to be a guardian, *Bell*." He turned his glower on Solomon. "Right mess you've gotten me into!"

"You mean lording over the rest of us is starting to wear you out, is it?" said Solomon, raising an eyebrow. "Could've fooled me." His contagious laughter filled the room.

Nico began to mock Ferlon too, drawing more laughter still—he pranced about the library with his chest puffed out and head held high. When he snatched the thin, silver crown from Ferlon's head to use as a prop, nobody could contain themselves.

Soon, all the guardians were cackling right along with Solomon, and even Talis felt his mood lighten; Ferlon's permanent scowl on the face of Keeper Kassime made the entire show that much more enjoyable.

"We need to keep a strong foothold in Luose to sway the ignorant into the light before they can wander off any further from the Jar," said Master Tayshin, trying to quell his own laughter and calling their attention back. "Ferlon, you're as strong as they get! As long as you're in South Luose, you must be Kassime. But once we solidify control, you'll be on your way to the next city wearing your true colors. No more hiding. Just you wait."

"It's my own fault," said Ferlon with an exasperated sigh. "I should've steered far clear of that one."

He nodded to Solomon, rolling his eyes.

"I didn't tell you to go getting into trouble!" said Solomon, throwing up his arms in defeat at a conversation they'd all heard enough times to have memorized.

"*No*, you just dragged me into it, per usual," said Ferlon with a sly grin, seizing his crown back from Nico and placing it neatly on his head. "And I wouldn't have had it any other way." He turned more serious. "Though… you are lucky you can serve the guardians with your true face. It can weigh terribly heavy on the soul to be someone else all the time. Don't ever take that for granted, Bell."

Solomon's smile tightened.

"I'm not sure which is worse," he said, "serving the King as somebody else, like you, or having to make room for a wolf in your real skin."

His eyes were cast down.

Ferlon patted him on the back. "I guess we'll find out one day," he said, solemnly.

Talis stood near the fireplace with Ferlon and Solomon by his side, peering up at the brand-new portrait Margery had forced them all to stand still for in order to mark this momentous occasion; it was the fiftieth anniversary of the Guardians of Gold since Master Tayshin had given his purpose an official name, the beginning of what they hoped to be the end of the King's reign. Not everyone was squeezed into the portrait, but the ones he knew the best were certainly there—so to Talis, it was a priceless treasure.

"Tomorrow, I leave for Saindora," said Solomon with a steady voice, looking to Talis. "You and the others will follow in a fortnight." He shifted his gaze to Ferlon. "And you'll be waiting here to pick up the pieces once you hear word." His statement somehow made it all the more real.

"That I will." Ferlon gave a slight bow of the head. "Take care of yourselves out there. I'll be waiting impatiently to hear of your safe return."

"We'll be just fine," said Talis—hoping with every positive thought that those he had helped recruit as guardians would not be marching alongside him to their deaths.

The three friends downed one last drink together by the fire, trying to sway the conversation to happier times and hopes of a brighter future.

"Ferlon…" mused Solomon. "You remember our first meeting at the tavern in Draminet?"

"How could I forget?" he replied with a grin. "You and Cyn were quite the pair. She really stole my heart, that one."

Solomon's eyes flicked over to Cyn, and he beamed; she was undoubtedly giddy from wine, giggling to herself as she helped set out trays of food, slapping away eager hands.

"As she did to all the lads in those days," he said. "Still does, I daresay."

"Think she's all right… with everything?" asked Ferlon.

"No, but she'll be fine," said Solomon, nodding to himself. "She's stronger than the rest of us anyhow. If anything does go wrong, she'll be waiting for us at the meeting point with supplies. I don't want her to be part of anything that goes on in the palace."

Talis and Ferlon agreed, both glancing her way.

"And what about Nico?" Talis asked Solomon; he spotted him tiptoeing around Cyn, plucking food right out from under her nose. "Have you decided yet? He's not much of a warrior, but I'd hate to be the one to try and stop him from coming with us."

"He's savvier and more stubborn than anyone in this room," added Ferlon, shaking his head. "That's a *bad* combination. It'll be more trouble than it's worth to try and get him to stay behind."

"I have to agree," said Solomon, chuckling a bit as he looked toward Nico. "I thought you could keep an eye on him, Talis? He's unpolished with a sword, but his spirit is truly a valuable asset. He could come in handy when all is said and done. Everyone else has already been teamed up, and I'll be on a separate mission… as discussed."

Talis and Ferlon didn't respond; it was all too unfathomable to say out loud anymore, but the plan was set in stone—by Solomon's hand King Devlindor would die, while the rest of the guardians would remain focused on securing the palace.

The conversation ended as Nico strode over with mugs filled

to the brim with more ale.

"What are you girls whispering about over here?" he asked, passing them around.

"Just who's going to babysit you during the ride to Saindora," said Solomon with a smirk.

Nico, always so hotheaded, stood on his tiptoes, his height not even clearing Solomon's chest. "Say that again!"

Talis always thought his voice sounded shockingly deep for how small of a man Nico had turned out to be.

"I *hope* you didn't just use the word 'girls' as synonymous for weak again!" Iris shouted at him from across the room. "Don't make me come over there."

Nico was hiding behind Solomon quicker than Talis had ever seen anyone move.

"*Sorry!*" he mouthed to her from a safe distance.

Solomon peered down at him and smiled, ruffling up his hair.

"Wait…" stuttered Nico, tilting his head to the side with an incredulous grin. "Do you mean that I'm in?"

"You're in," said Ferlon. "So simmer down!" He let out a huff, rolling his eyes. "Glad I won't have to be the one to put up with you."

He tapped his mug to his before taking a swig, Nico still with a dumbstruck look on his face.

The young men broke out into more much-needed laughter after that; Nico hugged Ferlon, Solomon, and Talis around the waists, ecstatic to be included on the hunt for the King's crown—despite some of their initial reservations.

"All right, lads and ladies, gather 'round," said Master Tayshin, vying for everyone's attention again. "I've plucked you all from your lackluster lives and brought you together as Guardians of Gold. Now, it's our chance to repay the Olleb for gifting us her magic, even under such trying circumstances."

His words were a bit slurred after hours of celebrating the sure victory to come, but everyone stood front and center to hear from the man they would soon follow into battle.

Many guardians from every corner of the Olleb had found their way to the South Luose palace attic on this night, forty-odd faces to witness and celebrate their first act of true protest, the severest *treason*, against King Devlindor. Half of those gathered (some portrayed in the portrait and some not) would march together to the High City in just two short weeks, following in Solomon's footsteps. The rest would head back to whatever corner of the world they had come from to await word—triumph or defeat?

"This is our last gathering before what is sure to be a life-changing event!" Master Tayshin raised his cup. "Hail to the World. Hail to Olleb-Yelfra!"

They all raised their cups too and roared out the mantra with fervor—then they rushed toward the food and what seemed like such a promising future.

TALIS RAN THROUGH THE PLAN over and over in his head on the long trip to Saindora.

Solomon had wormed his way quickly into the King's favor after Master Tayshin had put him to the task years ago, not long after Talis had guided him into the fold; in no time at all, he was dubbed the King's Wolf of the East and one of his most trusted warriors. He had returned to the High City some weeks ago now to prepare for the arrival of the guardians, but he'd left his doubts behind for Talis to hold on to.

Talis had been to Saindora before. He remembered the journey well, the way the palace started out as a small pinprick with the beach and busy harbor as a thick border—time had not

changed a thing as the carriage bumped along toward their destination in the dead of night.

As they got closer, the Sea of Saindora snaking in and out of
view alongside them, the palace seemed to grow taller and more
foreboding. It was a massive, white, sprawling figure that swelled
atop the land, the town crawling down beneath it in stacks until
an abrupt stop at the surrounding shores. And even in the dark,
the pale exterior of the palace appeared glaring and harsh under
the moonlight.

"So this is how ole Bell has been spending his time?" whistled
another young and eager guardian brought on not long after Solomon and his friends.

Talis thought him a gentle spirit with no magic to his name,
but he was just as ambitious as the others when put to the test.

"Don't sound so jealous, Tobias," he said. "Living a lie is
hardly living, regardless of your sleeping quarters."

There were eight of them in this carriage, several others following behind; it was unbearably warm, the tight space only allowing room for fear to spread as all eyes glued to the windows—
they were almost to the city gates.

In a past that seemed not so far away, Talis had spent time in
the High City to support Solomon's duplicitous efforts; his friend
had waited for an opportunity to try out for a position as a Saindora Palace regulator, and he had earned his black cloak with
honors, proving himself unparalleled with a sword.

King Devlindor couldn't wait to sink his claws into him after
such an enthrallingly bloody performance. And over time, it became more than evident that Solomon was a reflection of the
young, fierce spirit the King saw in himself.

Ultimately, after tutelage from Sir Vladamor and many blessings from the King, Solomon was granted the name 'Wolf of the
East' and a place on the King's Guard after he had protected him
and Princess Elisa during one of the more recent civil wars—wars
where people like the guardians had tried to fight his oppression,

though without knowledge of the strong magic that could have aided them. Those wars were marked in the history books as rebels wanting nothing more than to take power into their own hands, the reality of it scraped under the rug, buried with the other monstrous lies of the monarch.

But as the years wore on, such rebellious outbreaks ceased—the Four Corners grew stronger than ever, solidifying King Devlindor's sovereign rule.

It was now that the guardians would strike back, during this lull of fragile peace the King felt so sure of.

Master Tayshin had been the start of it all, the one who had slowly formed what was now the Guardians of Gold over time. He was an old soul, magic keeping him youthful, and he came from a long, esteemed bloodline with a rich family history—one which led him to uncover a wealth of knowledge that the King sought to hide and destroy.

He was a few generations removed from the purge of the Golden Age, but his family had left a glittering gold trail for him to follow back to the magic. And that's exactly what he did; he carefully accumulated what information he could of a magical world that he had just barely missed the chance to take part in, endeavoring to share it with other promising souls in hopes to build out a new and better future.

Talis thought about his piece of that goal now as one of the original Guardians of Gold, a healer rescued from a dead-end life to help show others the way the world could be, to help heal the Olleb of its infectious wounds. And there were six other carriages crammed full of guardians ready to storm the King's palace in the night and take back their country alongside him—a new future was about to begin.

Solomon had informed them well of the tricks of the palace. There was a lightly guarded entrance they planned to use to penetrate it; King Devlindor would be so taken by surprise that there'd be no way he could stop the oncoming slaughter.

Sir Vladamor was also now surely far away from Saindora this night, investigating a matter they had fabricated to lead him astray, conjured up by the magical genius of Margery and Vance combined; the guardians would deal with the monsters separately, for together they were an unbeatable force.

TALIS WAS THE ONLY ONE who had ever stepped foot in the Palace of Saindora before, except Solomon, so he took the lead, Master Tayshin close behind. He looked back one last time, seeing Tobias and Cyn; they waved him off in good spirits, tasked to keep a lookout and to ready the carriages at the meeting point for a quick escape if necessary.

He offered them a faint smile in return and then tested the side door Solomon was supposed to leave unlocked; it swung open with ease, and they all stepped inside a dimly lit hall.

The click of his shoes sounded so loud on the marble palace floors, making him feel so visible. But the regulators meant to guard this entrance had already been dealt with; they were slumped over on the ground.

Solomon's doing, of course.

He wondered about the location of his young friend on this dark night, if his part of the plan was going smoothly.

"Let's go," he said, sliding the golden mask down over his face.

Everyone followed in his footsteps, Talis leading his comrades down the halls he had memorized—they'd rehearsed this very moment countless times before in fields and forests, but now that he was here, it hardly felt real. Eventually, though, he located the main foyer, a vast open area with a rainbow-jeweled chandelier that danced with firelight.

"This is the place," whispered Talis. "You know what to do." He lifted his fist to his chest to wish everyone good luck.

The touch of Master Tayshin's calloused hand on his arm in goodwill woke him up to the task at hand. He watched him slink down a different corridor, sword drawn, several guardians flanking him.

Talis ushered everyone except for Nico to go on ahead, observing closely as they veered off in different directions. Black cloaks fluttered out eerily behind them, material chosen specifically to blend in with the King's regulators—though instead of golden snakes stitched on their backs, they boasted dragons.

Everything was going according to plan.

Alas, Talis couldn't shake the fear that had settled in his gut upon splitting off from his friends—his chosen brothers and sisters—branching out in order to weaken other potential threats besides the sleeping royal.

They had all whispered quick goodbyes and good lucks to each other, men and women who he would never hear the voices of again. Guardians who would lose their lives in the mere moments after the separation, their magic sucked back into the oblivion the King had crafted.

For, of all the situations the guardians had prepared to face, they hadn't been forewarned of the seer.

Talis could still hear her screams clearly in his memory, her cry for help echoing throughout his mind; she coaxed him astray, and he followed her hypnotic voice all the way down to the lower level of the palace, Nico at his heels.

When he first laid eyes on Ophelia, he became immediately entranced by her beauty, his thoughts swayed by just her presence. Tears swam in her clouded eyes, chains shackling her to a luxurious room—an elegant prison in the Dungeons of Saindora.

"Release me," she cried, her delicate voice ringing in his ears as she reached toward him. "Please! There's still time."

Before Talis could even reply, she spoke the answer to the

question floating in his mind.

"I am named Ophelia, the King's imprisoned seer," she said. "True, you don't know who I am, but I know you, Talis Churry. Quick, free me now! Time is running out. You can ask questions later… if you live."

"Time for what?" stuttered Talis, lifting his mask from his face, his heart drumming faster inside his chest.

Nico hovered in the doorway, trembling by his side.

Something told Talis not to trust this Ophelia, not to become entangled in her sure web of lies. He had read plenty of the seer species and knew they told half-truths to their own advantage while the endless secrets of the universe—past, present, and future—floated in their minds. It was a gift and a curse, a single bloodline passing down the ability of all-knowing sight and the blindness that came with it forevermore.

"Time for you to escape with your life!" she replied, straining against the shackles at her feet.

Blood pooled beneath the metal tearing at her skin, dripping to the plush featherbed she sat upon.

"The others are surely dead by now. The King knows you're here. I foresaw this rebellion long ago, and I had no choice but to warn him. I have *never* had a choice."

Talis' eyes grew wide as the shock and comprehension of her words settled around him like knives stabbing at his skin.

Please, let these be lies!

"I speak a truth," she said in response to his thought.

"Does the King know who we are? Does he know us by name?" His voice ricocheted throughout the beautiful chamber, filling his own head and distracting him from his duties.

He feared for Solomon who had betrayed King Devlindor in plain sight; if his treason were ever revealed, he was sure to face a fate worse than any death.

Ophelia shook her head.

"I was only given a future sight filled with masks of gold,

dragons coming to fight with fire… *magic*," she purred. "Nevertheless, the King has been patiently waiting for you, preparing. He has desired for so long to snuff out the guardians before you can spread any more of your flame. Now, that day has come. But you still have a chance to survive, Talis Churry. You and I, together, can escape with our lives."

Dark brown hair hung in waves down her back, and she was dressed in an almost sheer gown as she pleaded for Talis' mercy, tears streaming down her cheeks—it was a dreamlike setting. A beautiful nightmare.

Before he could think of how to respond, her eyes began to glow bright with magic, seeing something he could not; Talis couldn't look away, staring at her in horror as he tried to comprehend her warning.

"We have to keep moving," said Nico, snapping him out of his daze. "I don't have a good feeling about this."

"No, let me out!" Ophelia screamed at the top of her lungs, the echo vibrating off the walls as the silver magic fled from her eyes.

She fought even harder against her restraints, and Talis thought surely they must be laced with strong magic to render such a powerful being helpless.

"Don't leave me here. I *will* not forget this!"

Talis let Nico pull him back into the hall before slamming the door to her prison shut as her threats and screams fought to follow them.

"We always have a choice," he whispered, knowing she would hear.

With the seer locked away, Talis could think clearly again.

Different voices joined them now in the still air of the palace, shocking him and Nico back into action. Screams for mercy and of pain—of sure and agonizing death—came loud from every direction; the guardians were under attack.

As Talis and Nico raced back up the stairs and toward those

crying out for help, all went unnervingly quiet. When they rounded the next corner, they both froze where they stood; the bodies of their friends were strewn across the floor, each one mutilated beyond recognition by both magic and weapon.

"No, this can't be!" cried Talis, dropping to his knees.

Nobody lived—the amount of blood spilled on the marble floor told the true story of that.

His eyes filled with tears that he could hardly feel, his whole body numb with sadness and confusion. "No, this was all a mistake... I must find Solomon."

He looked to Nico who had also crumbled to the ground, trying to wake one of their friends. At first, Talis thought it a futile effort, but then the faintest movement caught his eye. To both their disbelief, there was at least one survivor of this massacre—Iris was barely alive, the dark residue of magic still smoking off her skin.

Talis ran to join Nico at her side; he lifted an emergency healing potion from his robes and forced her to drink.

"*Helthra saludis emencia!*" He and Nico recited the spell together, willing her to live.

"This is just a quick fix," said Talis, hurriedly. "You have to get her to Cyn now, or she won't survive."

"I can't just leave you," said Nico, fear in his eyes.

"I said go!" roared Talis, not to be disobeyed by his young friend. He couldn't stand the thought of losing him, too. "There's been enough loss here. Take Iris and warn the others so we can get out of this alive. I'll go and find Solomon, but if we're not back soon, you must leave without us."

Nico stood, a strange look in his eye.

"It won't come to that," he said. He shifted his attention to Iris. "*Levantis bora!*"

Her limp body lifted into the air with the spark of his magic, shadowing him closely as he ran to find an exit.

Talis knew now that the seer had spoken a terrible truth, their plan foreseen by Ophelia probably long before they had thought it up themselves. With King Devlindor in the know, they had been no match for the ruthless royal with magic on his side.

He picked himself off the floor, the blood of his friends staining his cloak and his shoes. Then he called his defensive magic to the forefront and made his way to the meeting place he and Solomon had agreed upon, deep in the palace. Alas, the halls were crawling with monsters now—the King was no longer sleeping, and Talis knew with a sickening certainty that just one bite from the provoked snake would be fatal.

"Talis!" called Solomon from out of the darkness in a panicked voice. "What are you still doing here? You must've heard."

When they reached each other, Solomon's grave expression under the light of the torches lining the walls made Talis grow even more numb.

"The plan has failed. The King knows you're here, and Sir Vladamor is roaming the palace searching for blood."

He yanked him down a dark corridor without warning.

"Stop!" said Talis, pulling back. "We can't go that way. The necromancer has already left his mark. They're all dead… gone. If there's no other way out, I lay down my sword now."

"Over my dead body you will," said Solomon, shoving him down a different path—somehow Talis knew he meant that. "There's always a way. You taught me that, Churry."

"In here!" came the hushed voice of a woman.

"By gods… *Princess*," said Solomon, his twin swords dangling at his side; Talis couldn't help but notice that blood dripped from the blades, and he wondered who had felt his unforgiving swing tonight. "What on earth are you doing in this wing of the palace? You're supposed to be in your chambers. It's too dangerous for you here. I was going to come for you after—"

"There isn't time," she urged. "If you want your friends to live, the ones who are left, you must follow me now. My brother or Vladamor will sniff you out in minutes."

Talis looked at Solomon with a quizzical expression, but there was no time for an explanation as Princess Elisa—the King's very own sister—led them through the dark maze of hallways to an unknown destination.

She looked like a silver animal lost in the night, her hair glistening with an alluring glow. And she wore a white nightgown that fluttered out behind her as if a ghost of the castle guided them to safety. *Or*, more probably, their deaths.

In all his dreams, Talis could have never thought up such a moment as this… Princess Elisa Devlindor, saving them from the wrath of her brother and king.

Solomon was entranced by her, that much was certain. He held her hand tightly, eyes glued to her back as they raced down hall after hall. When they turned the next corner, Solomon maneuvered her out of the way of danger so fast that Talis almost missed the gesture at all.

A group of regulators blocked their way, weapons raised.

"Your Highness," called the regulator in the lead, cautioning his men to halt, "you shouldn't be out of your chambers right now." He glanced to Solomon and then to Talis with his eyebrows raised. "There are intruders roaming about."

Solomon swiftly pointed one of his swords at Talis' back, shocking him silent.

"I've rounded this one up," he said, firmly.

"Is that so?" replied the regulator, gripping the hilt of his blade tighter.

"Yes, this *filth* was attempting to take the Princess hostage," said Solomon. "I was escorting her back to safety before coming to rejoin you in the hunt for the treasonous scum."

When the regulator didn't release his hold on his weapon to let them pass, Solomon let out a sigh.

He released Talis, guiding him and the Princess protectively behind him. Then he readied both swords—each were dazzling specimens, jeweled guards and the sharpest of blades that would make a lasting impression on anyone who might find themselves at the wrong end of either.

"I suppose you've caught me then," he said, twisting the swords at his side. "Are you *sure* you're ready for this, boys?"

"Traitor! I knew you were a snake from the minute you joined our ranks," shouted the regulator.

"A snake, hmm? I think King Devlindor might call that a compliment."

Solomon puffed out his chest so that the golden serpent of the King's Crest shone clearly across his gleaming black armor.

"And yet, I am a wolf by his standards." He cocked his head to the side. "So… which bite would you prefer? The wolf or the snake?"

The guard turned red with anger. "Call for Vladamor! Call for the King!"

"You know that I cannot allow this," said Solomon in the most menacing voice Talis had ever heard come out of his kind-hearted friend. "As the King says, a wolf chooses his pack, so I'm deeply regretful to inform you that you can no longer be a part of his service."

Talis witnessed then the full strength of Solomon Bell, the Wolf of the East, that had so quickly won the King's approval. He spun around the regulators with ease, his swords electrified with magic as he tore them apart—they never stood a chance.

"Hurry!" said the Princess after the slaughter was done, her robes splattered with blood.

She guided them deeper into the palace, eventually stopping before a towering door; she pressed her palm against it and it swung open.

They tumbled inside, engulfed in darkness as the door slammed shut behind them.

"*Solza ven immito*," she said softly—the lanterns on the walls buzzed to life all around them.

Talis and Solomon stayed close to each other as she led them down a long flight of stairs and through a vast hall; it was cluttered with boxes stacked high to the ceiling, and shelves lined with books and parchments all sat with a thick layer of dust.

"What is all this?" whispered Talis as they entered a small chamber.

His query was ignored as Princess Elisa's focus was elsewhere. She seemed to be searching frantically for something, tearing open box after box.

"Ah ha!" she shrieked, smiling as she skimmed a parchment. She turned to Solomon, pushing the scroll into his hands. "I knew he kept it here. Take this and go. Herein lies the proof."

"I can't leave here now, Elisa," he implored, caressing her cheek.

She looked back at him with pleading eyes, her hand pressed atop his. "You must… if you stay here—"

"Our plan has failed," he said, shaking his head. "I must keep my status with King Devlindor, or all of this will have really been for nothing. If I vanish, he'll know I was part of the rebellion."

When Solomon removed his hand from her face, blood was smeared across her fair skin; he gazed at his palms in horror. "Talis," he choked out, "I can never atone for this."

"What do you mean?"

Solomon looked up with watering eyes, searching for forgiveness—Talis couldn't bear to see him this way, to see what this night had broken in his strongest ally.

Solomon pushed the scroll into his hands, the blood staining the outside of the parchment. Perplexed, Talis tucked the scroll safely in his robes, waiting and fearing his response.

He averted his gaze. "The King was by my side when our friends entered the palace, ordered me to attack," he said, head bowed low. "I had *no* choice. I couldn't get word to anyone in time. I was able to slip away from him, though, in all the chaos. To find you… to try and save anyone else."

Talis was momentarily speechless, realizing that the death of many of their friends was likely a direct result of Solomon's sheer skill and determination to keep their collective secrets.

"Solomon, it isn't your fault," he said, sternly, trying to keep his voice from quivering. "We all knew the risks of coming here. If you hadn't lifted your sword against the others, Kyrone and his necromancer would have killed them anyways, along with you. At least a handful of us still live. Maybe we can rebuild… one day."

"I did not let them suffer," he said in barely a whisper. "The ones who faced me."

"Brother, I know they're at peace now," Talis said with conviction, "and I know you have their forgiveness, should you ever seek it." His voice cracked and more tears escaped his control. "I pray I'll have it, too, for my part in leading them here."

Solomon clutched at Talis' robes, and Talis returned the embrace in a moment he wished might never end. He didn't want to let him go, didn't want to face this bleak reality.

"I won't let you die here too," said Solomon. "You can live if we hurry. Elisa, how do we get him out of here? There must be a way."

"There is, follow me," said the Princess—she led them to another chamber and uncovered a small opening in the old wall. It looked to lead to a long tunnel.

"I discovered this forgotten passage when I used to roam here as a child," she explained quickly. "This cellar used to be part of the Saindora Dungeon, but the King has long since sealed this section off… for privacy. You can follow it directly out to the front gardens."

She looked up to Talis, meeting his eyes for the first time as she passed him a torch. "You should hide your face until you're far from this land."

He nodded, pulling the gold mask back over his eyes and lifting the hood of his cloak up to shield his identity.

"Thank you, Princess," he said. "Please, keep him safe."

He squeezed Solomon's arm, but there were no words left to say in consolation. They each wore expressions of tortured understanding, hoping that they'd both survive this nightmare to meet again one day.

As Talis hovered in the mouth of the tunnel, Princess Elisa turned and kissed Solomon square on the lips. "At least you tried," she whispered before hurrying out of the room.

Talis averted his eyes, no space in his mind to comprehend that his friend had just kissed the Princess—a *Devlindor*.

"Get to the carriages," said Solomon. "Let the others know what happened here, and do not risk sending word to me of your future plans. I will be in touch one day soon… if I can."

"*When* you can," said Talis.

They embraced one last time in a strong hug, but as soon as Solomon began to lean away, Talis froze with his arms wrapped around him; he was staring directly into the eyes of the King, who stood in the doorway of their chamber.

"Let me go!" Talis cried out. "I won't let you get away with this."

Solomon was momentarily confused by Talis' outburst, but then all the blood drained from his face with understanding. Talis clung to Solomon tightly now so that he wouldn't be able to free himself if he'd wanted.

"I owe you my life," he whispered in his ear, feeling Solomon shudder from fear—he knew what was coming.

Talis called to his signature spell in full force, sending waves of electric magic all throughout Solomon's body. Talis could already see the scarring on his skin as his friend cried out in pain, and his own hands could hardly stand the magical burn, shaking uncontrollably. He threw Solomon a hard kick to the knee so that he buckled to the floor.

They locked eyes for only a moment before Talis had to run, but he knew Solomon saw the unspoken apology there.

I had to make it look convincing.

In many magical ways, Talis was stronger than the Wolf of the East; this had been the only way he could think of in a split second to salvage the King's trust in him in order to save his life.

Talis prayed to every god in his knowledge that the show had worked. Otherwise, Solomon would be in an even worse position than their fallen brethren.

Solomon watched him go, paralyzed with watering eyes as King Devlindor came to his aid.

"Bell!" called the King, rushing toward him with his known animal companion, Raja, at his heels—a powerful creature that had taken shape as a jaguar, one the guardians had already determined to be an avatar of legends.

Talis raced through the tunnel, clutching the torch. He didn't get far before the mighty roar of the avatar jaguar joined him, causing the ceiling to cave in behind him in waves; he narrowly escaped being buried alive, making it to the meeting point where Tobias and Cyn still waited by the carriages.

"What happened?" cried Tobias, running to him from across the field. "Where is everyone?"

Talis just shook his head back and forth, trying to catch his breath. "If no one else is here, then no one else is coming," he said, gravely. "We must go, now." He glanced around. "Wait… where's Nico and Iris? They didn't show?"

Cyn opened her mouth but nothing came out.

Talis took another deep breath, trying to hold it together.

"We have to go," he said.

Tobias readied the horses.

"Wait, look!" said Cyn, pointing. "More are coming."

Talis expected to find the Shadow Resistance racing after them. To his relief, instead, he saw Nico limping toward the carriage, Iris still hovering behind him. And now both Master Tayshin and Sergios were also by his side.

"What about Solomon?" said Master Tayshin, out of breath and covered in blood as he reached them.

"He'll live to fight another day," said Talis. "I pray…"

"Anybody else?" said Sergios, frantic, holding his hand over a deep gash at his hip. "Did anyone else survive?"

"If there's anyone still alive in the palace, I'm afraid they will never leave it that way," said Talis, sounding utterly defeated. "Our time here is up. We *must* go."

With heavy hearts, they fled in a single carriage, far emptier than they had arrived. Talis watched the palace grow smaller and smaller in the distance until, once more, it was just a gleaming pinprick in the rising sun. It was then that he lost all faith in the Guardians of Gold, as did everyone on the journey home. Consequently, it was in this single moment in time that the guardians lost faith in themselves, now just a broken shell of the mighty dragon that they had sought to become—failing to fly and failing to break the Olleb free.

FAITH RESTORED

"SO IT WAS YOU WHO STOLE THE SCROLL, *Olleb-Yelfra the Fallen*, from the palace?" said Lessa, her mouth dropping open wide as she gazed at Talis with new eyes. "Is that how you learned of the prophecy?"

"The guardians have known of the prophecy since our inception." A new voice joined them from the doorway. "The prophecy will always stand, even long after Kyrone Devlindor is buried in the ground."

Arianna couldn't help the way her skin itched when the name 'Kyrone' flew to the air, unaccompanied by its proper station. She had been ingrained to bow down to the *King*. To call him by a mere name made him seem just a man.

But it was an aversion that she knew would quickly fade in time, for that king was not *her* king any longer. And if he was no longer a king, then just a man he proved to be.

All the elder guardians suddenly rose from their seats to welcome the person who entered.

"Please, sit," he said, his hands grasping the edge of the tall chair at the head of the table.

As everyone sat obediently, Arianna stayed standing, her heart thrumming a little bit faster—with joy, with fear, and with shock at what may lay ahead for them all.

"Well, if it isn't Miss Belvedor. Bending the rules again, I see." A wry smile grew across his face. "Glad to know that you haven't disappointed me after all."

Arianna let out a deep sigh of relief that she hadn't realized she'd been holding.

"Master Tayshin," she said, running to hug him. Her arms couldn't quite reach around his large belly, but she squeezed as tight as she could. "It's wonderful to see you again. I'm glad you're in one piece."

Her mind flashed back to the horrible day that had ripped them apart from their palace lives and set them on this course.

At first, Master Tayshin seemed surprised by her show of emotion, as did the rest of the room, but then the shock wore off and he let his arms wrap around her as well.

"I'm glad you're in one piece too," he said before letting her go.

Arianna hadn't known Master Tayshin for very long, and their beginnings had been shaky at best. But he had far outshone bad first impressions by now, and she was sure he would say the same of her.

She had come to find his quirks endearing and his training tactics, though harsh at times, quite welcome, with much-needed life lessons presented in each and every one.

We can trust him.

It was then that Arianna was very glad to have the leaders in her life that she did, others outside of her close family of friends that she knew she could rely on—those not corrupted by the dark pressing down on their worlds.

Like Talis had affirmed, Master Tayshin showed a renewed faith in the cause he'd carved out, and they had a renewed faith in him. In truth, if there was anyone in the entire world she had yet to thank for steering her toward these magnificent, magical possibilities, for giving her a purpose and the strength to hold tight to her swords and fight *for* that purpose, it was the man who had started it all—the master guardian who had brought her first masters into the light as well.

Keeper Kassime, Master Churry, Caretaker Cyn, and even her lost Master Bell were the products of his teachings, apprentices of the guardian founder. Therefore, no matter where her destiny led her, Arianna would always be a product of the Guardians of Gold.

And if she was being completely honest, hugging Master Tayshin felt like the closest she might ever get again to hugging the Solomon she had once known.

After Talis' story of the failed rebellion, she understood the true scars that lingered with the guardians, the innocent souls that had been lost. Solomon had fought and bled for something good, something they all believed in—he had risked his life to save the friends that he could. And the skill, wisdom, and hope he'd since passed down to Arianna had surely stemmed from this man in front of her, Solomon Bell's first master in magic.

"*Olleb-Yelfra the Fallen* is valuable not only for the prophecy hidden between the lines," said Master Tayshin as Arianna went back to her place at the table, "but for the weak man it proves Kyrone to be. Fear and greed drive his very existence *and* his actions. Such a life cannot be sustained forever. His ending will be just as catastrophic as he has been to the world."

"We will make sure of it," said Jeom, placing his hand atop Lessa's.

Master Tayshin considered the faces at the table, studying those he surely hadn't seen for a long while by the way they looked back at him, hungry for his words of motivation.

"The seer was what we overlooked in our plan," he said, his fingers tightening into a fist, "resulting in many lost lives. Ophelia is one of the biggest weapons the King has ever gotten his hands on. Because of her, we hadn't stood a chance."

Arianna noticed the way Talis paled when Master Tayshin said her name.

"And now she willingly serves him," said Demetrius, shaking his head.

"It's no wonder our highlife covers didn't last long," said Lessa, stroking Sano in her lap.

"Your time in South Luose was always limited, always a risk, no matter how comfortable and safe you felt," said Master Tayshin, glancing to Arianna. "If Godfrey and Solomon hadn't interfered, it is possible she might not have gotten whiff of your scent at all. Kassime and I, and Tobias too," he nodded to him, "had hidden for a very long time, right under her nose, with never a worry. But secrets have a way of revealing themselves, don't they? It was only a matter of time that this one came out."

Arianna's face ran hot; she had only killed one out of two for their betrayal at the Gathering. Ophelia was still out there, and she hoped to meet her again one day with a sword in hand.

"Maybe she did know about you all along though…" said Arianna, her chin in her hand as she tried to digest all this new information. "I'm no seer expert, but they're powerful, no?"

"Extraordinarily," said Master Tayshin.

"Then how could she not have known who you were in South Luose… no matter what magic you used to hide? Godfrey played a part, but surely minuscule now that I see things clearer." She nodded to herself. "*Maybe* Ophelia just never saw you nor Kassime as a threat. You all but gave up guardianship after that terrible loss, so what would it have been worth to expose either of you? Not until we showed up, dragging the King behind us."

She gestured to her friends.

"Interesting," said Talis, catching Master Tayshin's eye. "It could be, but what makes you say this?"

"Well, from the story I just heard, Ophelia will forever be his *slave*, not a willing servant, as long as she has the gift of future sight. And a slave will do anything to save their own skin, to earn a sliver of freedom. She turned on you because he was after *us*. She saw an opportunity to please him and seized it, knowing exactly how to smoke us all out."

Cyn raised her hand to interject, so Arianna let her darkened thoughts slip away.

"Be that as it may, what's done is done," she said. "The King knows the guardians are back at large because Solomon has turned, and who knows when that happened. Anything that Bell knows, we must assume the King knows too. And that puts us in a very sticky predicament."

"Sticky, indeed," said Rowina, tapping her fingers along the table as a silence followed.

"Are we? *Back*, I mean?" stuttered Gabriel from the far end of the table; his hands were clasped together and he seemed nervous, wrinkles denting his chubby cheeks.

Arianna looked at him fondly, curious to know more about his part in all of this… a young guardian who she'd previously only assumed to be a magicless barkeep in Luose. Surely he hadn't even been born yet when the coup happened, now already seventy years ago. What was his story to have unearthed the Guardians of Gold since then and position himself among them?

This train of thought only begged more questions—who else might be hiding in plain sight as a citizen of the Olleb yet with the mark of a dragon on their palm?

Master Tayshin measured Gabriel's question, sinking into the head chair. All eyes searched his for guidance once more, though his gazed remained steady on Arianna.

"Despite the devastation of that day," he finally said, "some still held faith in the cause even after we disbanded. Some believed that outside of the established guardians there were others who, like us, knew more than just what the King has spoon-fed the world. People like Gabriel."

He nodded toward him, and Arianna began to understand his makings a little bit better.

"And who here still has faith?" she asked Master Tayshin. "Anyone?" She felt the weight of her words, but they needed to be said.

There were whispers around the table, awkward gestures as eyes flicked to one another and then back again.

Master Tayshin let out a loud laugh, startling Arianna out of her seriousness. He slammed his hands onto the table; she felt Demetrius almost jump out of his seat next to hers.

"Well, you heard the lady," he barked with a smile, focusing on the elder guardians. "I know a certain fiery-hearted warrior has restored mine." He shoved a finger at his chest. "*But* what's she asking of us?"

He looked back to her.

"Because if I know you well enough, my dear, you've always got a question on your lips."

Arianna couldn't help the smirk he pulled out of her, always bringing a challenge to her plate; she was more than prepared to accept it this time.

"I'm asking you to act," she said, straightening her back. "The guardians were built on promises of protecting knowledge, of keeping the magic of the Golden Age alive."

She stood, meeting everyone's eyes again.

"Well, look around you! Just this place speaks wonders, a garden beneath the desert fit for the Golden Age herself. Magic *lives*, but it's struggling now more than ever to survive."

"You're asking us to march into another battle, another bloodshed," said Sergios, his palms open as if in prayer. "That is what you're asking."

"No, I'm asking you to fight!" snapped Arianna, eyes locked on his. "Because a battle is coming again whether or not you choose to pick up your swords."

Sergios pressed his lips into a thin line.

She turned her attention back to Master Tayshin, lifting her palm so that he could see clearly what shone there.

"You founded the Guardians of Gold for this purpose I lay at your feet. If we're meant to live up to the dragons we claim to be, we can't sit back any longer while the King and his shadows consume the rest of the light that belongs to us. Dragons fought with fire and died with honor for their rights to a thriving Olleb."

Arianna squeezed her hand into a fist, feeling the electricity burning silver in her eyes and the sizzle of magic wrapping around her fingers.

"And so *dragons* we should prove to be!"

Master Tayshin said nothing, but the smile creeping across his lips and the light in his eyes told her everything she needed to know. He rose to his feet to stand with her, fist to his chest.

The rest of the table slowly rose to stand with them.

"I guess you have your answer," he said, opening his arms out wide. "They just needed their leader to show up to remind them why we all have a place at this table."

Arianna was taken aback at his statement, but she hid well the firebugs fluttering in her stomach as Master Tayshin slightly bowed his head toward her; just a nod it was, but everyone else around the table followed the act—declaring something she wouldn't dare say out loud.

Me… a leader of the Guardians of Gold?

How could she accept such an honor? Did she even have a choice?

Master Tayshin put a hand on her shoulder and whispered, "Now, watch this."

The elder guardians all turned their palms upward, the tattoos they bore seeming to twist and sparkle to life with unspoken magic until rays of golden light sprang into the air. Joined together, the lights created a wispy mirage of a golden dragon that soared across the glass ceiling of the chamber, dancing among the starry desert sand in place of a sky.

Arianna's jaw dropped; she'd never imagined such a perfect picture of what a dragon might look like in real life. To think that they had all been wiped away, these warriors of the Olleb, was impossible to fathom while watching this magical depiction soar confidently over the room, a strong guardian for certain.

Arianna glanced around the table, laying eyes on each person taking part in this enchantment—she could feel it in her heart that the guardians were getting ready to soar again too.

And she and her friends didn't hesitate to join them.

Together, they raised their palms into the air, letting their instincts guide them; Arianna instantly felt the warmth of this strange magic pool into her control, rising into the air with her friends' to create the dragon's fiery breath.

"I found my faith in the end," said Talis as the mirage eventually dissolved, everyone again finding their seats. "You know that. Arianna, Lessa, and even dear Solomon restored that faith for me back in the districts, showed me that magic was still strong and potent in this world. That we should never give up... no matter the setbacks or losses—"

His eyes lingered on the painting, glistening as he smiled to himself.

"A life for a life," he whispered. He turned to Arianna. "He had such hope for you. Even then, I doubt Solomon could've imagined just the jewel he'd found buried in the mountains. How very glad I am that you pulled me out of the dark, child. Your rebirth into this world that night gave me a second chance as well."

Arianna swallowed the lump in her throat, unable to even force a smile on her face for fear it might come with tears.

"A life for a life," she stuttered with understanding, finding

Talis' eyes. "He saved you in the palace... helped you escape. And so, you saved me."

"Surely we're even now," he said with a curt nod, though more to himself—his attention again drifted to the portrait.

Cyn patted Talis on the back.

"That rebellion was the last of any such act against the King," she said. "In fact, the guardians never really organized again. Eventually, with things so quiet, Devlindor released Solomon of his duties to retire in the Warrior's District as a master trainer upon his request. Not so very long ago, in fact. Maybe just a handful of years before your apprenticeship under him, Ara."

"Yes, I was quite surprised when I saw him again, banging down my door," said Talis with a chuckle. "Though, not *that* surprised, I suppose. Bell always had a flair for teaching." He let out a big sigh and crossed his legs. "As for me, I returned to the Four Corners to be as far away from Saindora as possible, long before him. I put that life behind me... or so I thought."

"As did many of us," said another Arianna hadn't even noticed before. He had snuck in behind Master Tayshin, an apple in hand. "*And* to keep watch on the new troublemakers born into this world."

He winked at Lessa, and she jumped out of her seat like an electric bolt had nipped her.

"*Nico*, is that you?" she said, walking around the table to get a better look. "I mean, I never thought—"

"Right back at you, little menace!" He chuckled, tossing her the apple.

She ran to hug him.

"He was a cook in my district," she said, addressing her friends' baffled expressions. "Always looking out for me. I just never put it together from the stories Kassime told us... Nico is such a common name."

"Maybe I would've had an inkling of your magical calling if ole Kassime hadn't always been wiping our memories," he said, rolling his eyes. "Anyone Talis takes under his wing is bound to wind up a guardian, especially one with such an aversion to the rules, like you."

He smiled before his expression found something of sorrow.

"Rest in peace, Ferlon," he whispered.

"Kassime took on the heavy burden of being the only one who remembered our guardian pasts," explained Talis. "Well… he was *supposed* to be, anyways, but many of us had secretly blocked his mind magic."

He shrugged, and Master Tayshin snickered; Arianna understood that they and Solomon had all remembered well what happened back then to the guardians, never letting themselves forget a single second.

The rest, though, like Cyn, had remained in the dark.

Arianna gazed at her caretaker with affection; her heart had prevailed as a guardian during her time as a Warrior's District healer. She always looked out for her and Solomon, even without her magical memories.

"It was easier, safer, if we didn't remember," said Cyn with a quiver in her voice. "Less painful than to bear the burden of such loss of friends and faith."

"But we remember now," said Tobias. "And since our memories have returned, others have joined us. Others who were meant to find their own way to the magic." He placed a hand on Gabriel's shoulder. "There's still hope here."

"So, shall we begin?" Talis raised an eyebrow.

Margery clapped her hands, an excited gleam in her eye. "Without delay! *Oh*, it's good to be back."

Sergios turned to Arianna. "*So*, how do you suppose we get you this army then?" He was being perfectly sincere.

Before she could reply, Master Tayshin chimed in.

"An army, hmm?" He scratched at his beard, looking around. "Well, I wouldn't quite call us that, but we can certainly hold our own on the battlefield. Isn't that right, Vance?"

"Still alive, aren't we?" He had a cocky smirk on his face.

"*You* and Margery are alive because you weren't in Saindora in the first place," said Rowina, smacking her lips. "But Iris, the poor thing, now she's proven her worth."

The elder guardians all looked at her with something of pity; Arianna couldn't help but notice the haunted look that crossed Iris' hardened face, and she knew that Talis' recap of past tragic events had caused her emotions to stir. And rightfully so—it was clearly a miracle Iris had survived such an attack at all, and she had certainly earned more than physical scars as a result.

"Yeah, but we would've fought the necromancer if all had gone as planned. He just never showed up!" said Vance, looking to Margery for support. "Bastard."

"Probably for the best," said Nico. "As far as we know, he cannot be killed, so who even knows if your magic would have been enough to hold him."

Margery agreed. "I'm sure we can all stand to get back to practice. And there's certainly much to teach these young ones as well."

"I don't know about you lot, but I'm just as powerful as I was back in the day!" sang Rowina, cracking her knuckles.

She concentrated on Eli, and his chair flew into the air; he let out a howl of surprise, clutching the edges. Arianna had almost forgotten he was there, just playing a listening role among the more seasoned guardians.

"That's an understatement," said Master Tayshin, the rims of his eyes turning silver—Eli's chair settled back onto the floor.

"But if the King is coming at us with an army, we'll need more help than just what's left of the guardians," said Jeom. "I saw the number of dwarves he slaughtered in Undor." He shook his head.

"We won't be enough alone," said Demetrius, nodding.

"I couldn't agree more," said Master Tayshin. "Now, why don't I fill you in on what business has kept Nico and I away for so long? Seems like as good a time as any."

Everyone listened with eager ears as he and Nico spoke of their weeks spent journeying to several different cities in the Olleb after the South Luose attack, seeking out those they knew to be friends of the cause and spreading word of the rebellion that Arianna had thrust into motion. The two guardians had sent whispers on the wind, naming her the face of something much greater than she maybe even realized.

In two months, they had sparked a tiny fire in hopes that it would grow and grow, like the breath of a thousand mighty dragons. And though, at the time, they hadn't known of Arianna's fate in the desert after fleeing South Luose, by sharing her story, her triumphs, *and* her failures, others felt more empowered to try, too.

The King was watching, the King was *scared*, and so he sent his little wizards and witches to try to snuff out their fire. But Arianna lived, her friends survived, and everyone would soon know that truth—their fire burned brighter than ever before, and it wouldn't be easy to oppress it again.

THE KING'S GAME

TIME TICKED ON, and Arianna and her friends were further strengthened in traditional lessons of both magic and battle, soaking in as much knowledge as possible while locked away in their secret garden.

Lessa and Demetrius enjoyed every minute of their lectures, truly taking a liking to studying ancient scrolls and diving deep into Golden Age texts with the elders as guides. Arianna, on the other hand, found it too reminiscent of the Learning Center.

She, Jeom, and even Eli, who remained among them still, didn't have as much patience, itching to spend the bulk of their time in more hands-on practice.

Though Eli hadn't displayed any powers as of yet, like Demetrius, he was enthralled with everything about this charmed existence.

Arianna could always feel his eyes on her back when she conjured a spell or worked with Solza to bend the elements to her will; and as Talis had predicted, this came easier to her over time.

She had learned to connect her mind more to the magic now—if she let go of her fear of no control and didn't force it, she found that it was more willing to yield itself to her.

However, no matter their promise as budding young witches and warriors, as a group, they were mere children in the eyes of the elder guardians. Arianna had trouble keeping up with her growing list of people to call masters, teachers who patiently helped them harness their truest powers and develop their weaknesses into strengths.

With every morning, Arianna awoke fiercer, a more capable version of herself than she had been the day before—but with each lesson, she was also humbled by the amount of experience she still had yet to gain; if she wanted to defeat the King, she'd have to be better.

Thus, she didn't take one day for granted, pushing herself harder during every duel and training, knowing that one of these teachings could mean the difference between dead or alive in the end.

As the months dragged on, the elder guardians came and went, bringing with them new stories and talk of other rebellious gatherings cropping up in cities across the sea and across the sand, places they had never even heard of before. But were the stories just gossip… inspirational tales to rally the guardians into putting their lives on the line again in the hope that this time it wouldn't be in vain? Or were they *real?*

Arianna had trouble picturing that anyone outside of her little bubble could be positioning themselves against the King. Then again, if people knew a teenage slave had put up such a fantastic fight, maybe others could find the courage, too.

Master Tayshin, Talis, Rowina, Margery, Vance, Sergios, Tobias, Cyn, Gabriel, Nico, and even Iris had all come around from being passive to active guardians, all offering ideas that would someday, hopefully *soon*, form a plan. Until then, they awaited word from those Master Tayshin hoped might join their small group in the looming fight.

When Arianna and her friends weren't knee-deep in trainings of magic and war, or reading from the Greenhouse's library of Golden Age scrolls to devour all the knowledge they could, they spent their time lounging by the underground lake discussing renewed dreams of freedom. They each had quickly come to understand that being in such close quarters with so many elders watching their every move meant they were no longer independent at all—they were the young ones to be looked after.

And while their presence had sparked a new energy among the guardians to try to defeat King Devlindor once and for all, with the passing of time, Arianna began to doubt that day would ever come.

Months flew by, but the elder guardians could never agree on a plan, not even a starting point as Arianna sat through conversation after conversation. Master Tayshin guided her in the art of leadership, but she didn't have the patience for it...

That's what Solomon would say.

There were just too many people with conflicting opinions on the best way to get the job done—all she cared about was her own.

We must kill the King... before he kills us.

Arianna didn't blame them for hesitating, especially given what they'd been through the first time. In fact, she'd hesitated for weeks on the Island of Idris before facing her own fears. But now that she had, she was ready to do something about them and was quickly growing tired of being locked up in one place all the time.

Though endless corridors, rooms, and the kind of fresh air that only an enchanted garden could provide kept her sane, she felt old habits drifting back to the surface of her mind, urging her to carve her own path rather than wait to be forced down someone else's. Every morning that she woke in her bed, Lessa nearby, she was reminded of being sealed away in her private sparring room in the Warrior's District Dueling Arena, awaiting the day she would finally be able to fight for her freedom from the Jar. But that day had never really come… at least not in the way she'd always expected it would; Arianna had *taken* her freedom instead.

To add to her restlessness, they hadn't been permitted to explore the city for fear someone might recognize their faces. She longed to know what secret pathways created the deeper Burrows of Zambienth and to see another pyramid from the inside. To feel the true sun on her face instead of some magical mirage.

Though Arianna had nothing but respect for the elders who had spent their time guiding and teaching them over these long weeks, she was ready to go.

Trying always to steer her mind toward more positive thoughts, she was just thankful that they were, for now, safe. In the meantime, while she and her friends impatiently waited for the elders to decide a way forward, they would grow their skills as much as they could, studying the strengths of each guardian—and quickly coming to learn how they had earned the dragons on their palms in the first place.

Today, though, was a little different than the norm. The elder guardians didn't demand their attention for lessons, for something more important stole their focus—with the coming of night, Zambienth's annual Gathering Ball would take place, and attendance was mandatory for every 'free' person; the elder guardians had an obligation to go in order to keep up appearances as normal citizens of the Olleb, leaving Arianna and her friends to entertain themselves.

"All right down there?" called Lessa, dangling from the limb of the large tree that dominated the center of the garden.

Sano lounged with her, nibbling on a small fruit.

As Lessa's foot rocked back and forth, the waters in the lake beneath her rocked too, her power over the element incredibly controlled since her time as a mermaid.

Arianna lay on the grass next to Demetrius, her head upon his lap as he examined some new plant that had caught his attention. This was clearly a sort of haven for him, an underground wonderworld full of nature and magic, and she dreaded the day they would have to pull him from it; he was surely in no hurry to leave this place. Though, when the time came, she knew he would loyally follow through on his duty.

She glanced up, smiling at Solza, who was perched on a lower limb of the tree, lazily twitching her tail. Her eyes darted back and forth, watching Jeom and Eli intently as they dueled in an area nearby. Though it was almost indiscernible at first glance, the guardians who had created this sanctuary had also included a special area for sparring. Overtaken by grass and nature now, the stone slates were still there if one looked closely, defining a smooth battleground—to put it back into use, they had taken it upon themselves to clean up as much as possible without ruining the integrity of the wildlife that had claimed it.

Eli dueled often there with Jeom as of late. They were a proven match, each always ready to test the other's skill in a fight. And though Arianna still couldn't stomach the thought of trusting the newest guardian, she couldn't deny that Eli was a worthy opponent.

As she lay there, watching the two dance around the grounds with their weapons raised, her mind was thrust back to the day in the desert when Eli had abandoned them. She repeated his words in her head—the countless apologies he'd offered after they'd grown to be on speaking terms again—and wondered if one day she would fully forgive him.

But even now, as he swung his sword toward her friend, a part of her wanted him dead… just to be certain he couldn't betray them again.

It was common knowledge among the guardians that Eli had deserted the four friends, making his way to Zambienth ahead of the turmoil they had caused during the battle with Sir Vladamor.

Barely escaping the unstable terrain, he ended up at the Well Center where Cyn had already taken up a new station; she recognized him immediately and brought him to the guardians for questioning, demanding to know the whereabouts of Arianna and the others.

With so many guardians specializing in mind magic, his confessions had spilled without protest.

But Talis showed mercy to Eli for turning his back on their young apprentices, offering him a chance to prove his worth after he'd begged for forgiveness. Not long after, by demonstrating his loyalty with his part in saving Lessa, he finally earned the dragon at his palm as an official Guardian of Gold.

Arianna couldn't deny that he *did* seem genuinely full of regret for his earlier choices. He had opened his mind to the magic now and fought daily for her to open back up to him. The others had long since forgiven his wrongdoings, Jeom the last to follow, but they didn't understand like she did; they hadn't been betrayed so many times before.

Nevertheless, unless she killed him herself, he wasn't going anywhere anytime soon.

As time drew on, Arianna began to consider Eli as more of just an annoying reminder than any kind of real threat—there were plenty of other people out there that deserved her wrath more than him.

Jeom jumped into the air, bringing his axe down hard on Eli's thick sword, the ring a piercing sound that seemed to ricochet within the glass walls.

"Nice work," said Lessa from her perch, absentmindedly twisting Kassime's ring about her finger.

"He's hardly putting up a worthwhile fight," said Arianna, speaking of Eli; she didn't even bother to look up to see.

"Care to give it a go?" he called as he dug his heels into the ground, bracing himself for Jeom's next attack.

Arianna pursed her lips but could never refuse a challenge.

"I suppose I can't pass up the chance to whip some sense into you again," she said, tersely, moving to her feet.

"Ah, my leg's asleep now!" said Demetrius, stretching it out after she stood. "I can't feel it at all."

"You're such a baby," said Lessa, beaming down at him. "At least you've got one good one!"

Demetrius laughed, hobbling around on one foot as he tried to wake the other up.

Arianna left just in the nick of time, catching Lessa sneaking water magic tricks his way for her own amusement. She smiled to herself as she heard a big splash of water, Lessa giggling from the trees and Demetrius complaining even louder.

When she got to the dueling area, Jeom was more than happy to swap places.

"Good luck," he said, wiping the sweat from his brow.

"Ready for me?" said Eli, flashing her a smirk.

He bent his knees and beckoned her forward, twisting his blade back and forth.

He was a one-sword man—it gave him an edge in maneuvering but fewer opportunities to land an attack.

"Let's just do this," she said, tossing her cloak to the side and picking up her swords from where she had left them.

"As you wish," he said with a mock curtsy.

Eli toyed with her, waiting for her to come to him, but she was smarter than that; she mimicked each step he took—just like if she was warming up with Solomon—until his patience waned and he came dashing forward.

It was clear he was putting in more effort during this duel than he had with Jeom, darting around her with intricate attacks, more focused; Arianna appreciated it, in a warrior's way.

She knew he was still trying to win her over, and battle was important to her. Each one she took just as seriously as the last. Each one, she tried her best. Eli understood this and truly gave her a warrior's respect—because he was a warrior, too.

It infuriated her no end that he was making it so hard for her to hate him… and hard to concentrate now. His attacks came swift, never a moment to think, his agility impressive; Arianna learned something new from him then. She needed to think faster with such an opponent and become less reactive. But it was a lesson learned too late this day.

"I win," he said, surprising her from the side.

She sucked in a breath as his sword nearly found her neck—he stopped it with a skill that even she had to commend.

"That was a great duel, though," he said, sincerely, dropping his sword to the ground and holding out his hand.

With a sarcastic laugh, Arianna tossed her swords to the side and took his open hand, pulling him forward so hard that he fell off balance.

"It's not over until someone is bleeding," she said, looking down at him with a smirk. "What did *you* learn in the Jar?"

Jeom gave a hoot in the background.

"You going to take that lying down, Eli?" he yelled.

"Apologies, *miss*," said Eli, narrowing his eyes with an incredulous grin on his face, "I thought we were being sophisticated and leaving our savage ways behind. But I'm happy to oblige."

He swiped his leg toward her, catching her foot, so that she fell to the ground on top of him. They twisted around for a few moments, grappling until he finally surrendered.

"I see blood," said Arianna, Eli finding himself with a dagger to his throat. "Nice try though."

She pushed off him and walked away, unable to help the toss of her hair as she did.

Eli gave an awkward laugh, looking a bit dumbfounded as he got up to follow her back toward the tree.

"Come on, mate. Keep your head on next time!" said Jeom, slapping him on the back as they walked together.

"She sure is something," he whispered—Arianna pretended not to hear, and she made sure not to let him see her blush.

"Well, you got your work cut out for you there," said Jeom. "She did defeat a necromancer and all."

"One of these days…" he said, starry-eyed as he went to sit next to Demetrius in the grass.

He was soaking wet from when he and Lessa were goofing around, but now it seemed the fun was over; Demetrius gave them a look of caution as they all came back over to join them.

Lessa sat cross-legged at the edge of the lake, so Arianna went to sit next to her. Just then, Sano popped his head out of the water, floating around in his turtle form.

"Is everything all right, Les?" she asked, worried.

Lessa seemed changed after her journey with Syrifina, so distant at times.

"I just…" She looked again to the lake—it was eerily still.

Arianna knew she was controlling it, her newfound connection with the water element not to be trifled with.

"Please, just talk to us," said Jeom coming over. "Let us help you." He touched her on the shoulder, and she looked up at him with pain in her eyes.

"I just miss it sometimes," she said, shrugging away. "Being trapped down here, surrounded by sand… I was so free before."

"I know how you feel," said Arianna, gently—sometimes she thought Lessa might find a way to run away again if they pushed her too far. "I think we all do in a way."

Everyone gathered around her to show their support, giving Lessa the chance to be heard without fear of judgment.

"What happened while you were away?" asked Demetrius— she had barely spoken of her life as a mermaid yet, and no one wanted to force it out of her. "You know you can talk to us."

Lessa slowly slid into the lake until she was in all the way up to her neck. Nobody said a word, waiting.

Her eyes glowed bright with magic now, the lake manipulating magnificently behind her as she floated on her back with a smile on her face; Sano swam around excitedly as the water twisted and turned in beautiful patterns.

Moments later, the magic disappeared from her eyes, and her smile faded.

"I found out what was happening to Syrifina's sisters," she said after a long while, coming back to the edge to meet her friends. "It was part of the reason why I struggled to return at all. I wanted to help save them."

"What was happening?" Jeom moved as close as he could without getting wet, his hand on her hand.

"It was terrible," she said, looking back into her watery past. "We were in a place they call Empress Isle—"

Arianna was captivated by every word that followed, finally a piece of her missing time filled in.

"It was very grand at first. A week went by before anything happened. I thought Syrifina had lied, tricked us. But one night, Sano woke me. I felt as if he was calling for me to open my eyes." She gazed at him, lovingly. "And so I did, just as one of Syrifina's sisters had left the lair, swimming away. I followed her as fast as I could."

She chewed on her lip, shaking her head.

"I just knew something terrible was about to happen, but she was *too* fast. I could hardly keep up… I couldn't stop her."

"Where did she go? What happened?" said Demetrius with a wary expression.

Eli listened intently too, but he said nothing, and Arianna was glad for that; he wasn't part of their family, and he had no right to such intimate moments. But this was hardly the time for her to make a fuss over him—Lessa needed her focus.

"The sun was blazing hot, but she kept swimming higher, closer to the top of the water. I thought she would stop, but then she broke through, heading up the shore," said Lessa, choking on the last word. "I was bound to the water, so I could only watch from afar. But there was someone on the beach waiting for her. I *saw* him."

"Who?" asked Jeom.

"Vladamor," she replied, gravely.

Demetrius gasped, covering his mouth with his hand, and Arianna and Jeom locked horrified stares.

"I recognized his golden mask glinting in the sun and his gray horse from the desert. It *had* to be him."

"The necromancer… with a mermaid?" stammered Demetrius. "That's not a pretty picture."

"It gets much worse," she said, pushing the hair from her eyes. "Sano and I watched her crawl up the beach, tail dragging through the sand. It's not natural. Mermaids can only turn under the moon."

She buried her head in her arms, feet still kicking in the water, so her voice was muffled now.

"She wouldn't stop screaming, calling out for help, but there was nothing I could do. It was like she was under some kind of spell, pulling her toward him like a magnet until she was so far from the water that there was no hope of her return."

Lessa let out a whimper, lifting her head up as tears streamed down her cheeks.

"He just stood there and watched as she faded away, the sun turning her into nothing… to dust. And he had these velvet pouches, all different colors, dangling on his belt. When she died, I watched him collect her ashes in one of them." She shook her head. "She just was gone. And then Vladamor rode away as if it were nothing of consequence."

Her tears really fell then, and Jeom pulled her from the water and into his arms. "Just let it all out," he said, patting her on the back.

The lake seemed to churn viciously, her magic still connected to it; Arianna drew on her own powers to suppress the chaos so that poor Sano didn't get dizzied, but soon Lessa found her calm as well.

"Sorry, everyone," she said, sniffling a bit. "I feel loads better just telling you. It was a very confusing month without you all there with me. I missed you."

"We missed you too," said Arianna, squeezing her hand.

"You know you can always confide in us," said Demetrius, crouching down next to her as Jeom still held her tight.

"You told me once not to keep these types of feelings bottled inside," added Arianna. "Same goes for you, all right?"

Lessa gazed up at her, forcing a smile.

"Thanks," she said. "Will just take some more time to adjust, I guess. Why do you think Vladamor would do that? What could he *want* from their ashes?"

"He's a necromancer," said Demetrius, hugging his knees to his chest. "Can't be good."

"But what's the motive?" said Jeom, stroking Lessa's hair.

"Well, he has control over the dead and mermaids are creatures of death incarnate," said Demetrius, matter-of-factly, rocking back and forth as he thought. "They have essentially sacrificed their human lives in exchange for another. So I'd wager that this leaves them even more susceptible to the risks of being dead in the world of the living, like a necromancer latching onto them… wouldn't you think?"

Arianna felt her mind come alert, never having considered mermaids in such a way before—Demetrius was exactly right. Sir Vladamor could probably control their species easily using necromancy because to be a mermaid meant sacrificing one life for another, and that was the same thing as *dying*.

She felt so stupid for not connecting these dots before.

Lessa had died.

Finally, she understood just exactly why Lessa still seemed so out of sorts. She had come back to the world of the living, and Arianna knew firsthand that this was never an easy transition to make after seeing the other side. It also provided an explanation as to why Arianna's body had rejected the mermaid transformation in the first place—unlike Lessa at the time, she'd already chosen life twice over, likely counteracting such magic.

"What did Syrifina say when you told her what you saw?" said Arianna, deciding that her newest revelation would be better as a private conversation.

"She seemed unsurprised in a way," said Lessa, her brow furrowing. "She's ancient… calculated. There's so much knowledge we couldn't possibly fathom living in her mind, but how to stop a necromancer that's never been stopped before? I think if she knew, she would've said so."

Lessa sighed, pushing herself up to sit properly.

"When I told her the deaths of her sisters were of Vladamor's doing, even she understood that there was nothing to be done… for now. The best they can do is stay far from land so his magic has less effect, but who knows if that will even help." She shrugged. "I'm happy I was at least able to shed light on the situation—"

Lessa looked over to Sano with such fondness in her eyes.

"If it wasn't for Sano, though, urging me to wake, I might've never found out a thing. A mermaid's sleep is like death. Since Syrifina created all of her sisters, she could feel the loss of each one the moment they died, felt their pain. It was always too late." More tears welled in her eyes. "She believed they had wanted to die, hadn't known it was by the hand of another. When she learned it wasn't suicide, like she at first thought, that they hadn't *wanted* to leave her, I think it gave her some peace."

Arianna could barely meet Lessa's eyes, so full of sorrow. Her kind, innocent friend had walked the thin line between life and death just to witness the necromancer do another dark deed. And it only impassioned her more toward their goal.

Kill the King. Kill the King!

"What happened after you warned her?" said Demetrius.

"Well, as soon as I transformed into a mermaid, I started hearing distinct voices of guardians, ringing in my head for *weeks*." She whined at the memory. "It was unbearable! And when I heard yours added to the call on the last night…" She touched eyes with all of them. "I just couldn't ignore the magic any longer. It was so loud, so forceful. I *had* to come back, if only with the intention to shut you all up."

A sly smile crossed her lips.

"I think that the spell they used is very potent for mermaids for some reason. Whereas a human only senses this magic in their hearts, guiding them."

Arianna nodded along, knowing deep down that she had heard the call of the guardians too, urging her to find them even during their time stuck on Idris.

"And Syrifina let you go?" asked Eli, too intrigued to keep quiet any longer. "Just like that?"

"I always had a choice," she replied, softly. She glanced to Arianna. "Syrifina never lied about that part. Considering the whole reason for me turning in the first place was to find out what was happening to her sisters and stop it, she couldn't very well refuse when I wanted to leave… since that's exactly what we're going to do."

Her voice came sharp now, much of the former mermaid still present in her.

"If we kill King Devlindor, the necromancer *is* going down with him."

"Most certainly." Arianna smiled, hoping Lessa's newfound strength was permanent.

"Damn right!" said Jeom. "So glad you came back."

"So glad Eli found us in time," said Demetrius, giving him a wink.

"I can't take all the credit," he said, turning red as all eyes shifted to him. "The guardians started using that spell after I told them what happened in the desert." He bowed his head. "They hoped you were still alive and that it would guide you safely back to them. I had it in my pocket to try and learn, to try and help, but I don't seem to have magic like the rest of you."

He looked to Arianna, eyes glittering.

"Then Talis told me they thought you'd arrived, had felt the energy released from the guardian compass being in such close proximity to us. He demanded I run ahead to the beach and find you… so I did. When I bumped into Jeom and Demetrius, they informed me of their search for Lessa."

He plucked at some grass.

"That I had the spell still in my pocket was only luck."

But Arianna was beginning to understand 'luck' much better now—it was just a fancy way of saying *magic*.

There was a silence as they all let their predicament sink in; they hadn't truly defeated the necromancer yet, only wounded him in their getaway. And now they'd learned he was up to something even more sinister, stealing the lives of ancient, powerful mermaids—Arianna knew he wasn't just doing it for kicks. He and King Devlindor only did anything for one reason at all, and that was to gain infinite power.

"It's time to get going," she said, her focus set on the King.

She knew they were all thinking the exact same thing. He had toyed with their lives long enough, and she'd die before another one of them had to look Death in the face again.

"If what I'm hearing is true, then the guardians *really* won't be enough," said Eli, voicing the thing no one wanted to believe. "Not as we are now."

"No, we won't be," said Arianna, running her fingers through her hair. "We need a substantial army, and the way our elders are going about it will take us forever, I fear. But… I think I know just where to find one."

Her attention settled on the blue capsuled flame hovering high above their heads, an eternal magic that would always be trapped in the Greenhouse—in a great glass jar.

Jeom let out a loud sigh, reading her mind; he was truly intuitive when he wanted to be.

"So you want to go back, then? Is that what I'm hearing?"

He groaned, tossing his head back in exasperation before she even answered.

"You know I do," she said in a low whisper. "What other way is there?"

The fact that he had guessed her direction of thought reaffirmed it.

"How would we even get back in without getting caught?" said Demetrius, eyes wide and fearful.

"We make a plan," said Lessa, pulling herself together. "We know the goal, so we make a plan. That's what is stalling them here. They all have different goals. They're not truly unified yet, but *we* are. We can do this."

"We were meant to do something more than just wait. We did enough of that on Idris," said Arianna. "Everyone has supported us, even if they're slow to put action to it. Let's be the leaders they believe us to be. If we can't be the change we're praying for, then who can?"

"Do you really think going back there is the right thing to do?" asked Eli. "A plan for breaking in is one thing, but how do you expect to sway them to follow once you do?"

"Don't worry," said Arianna. "For that, I at least *do* have a plan. As for the elder guardians, let them follow their strengths and we'll follow ours."

"You mean… break the rules again?" Demetrius laughed. "Our greatest strength!"

"I *mean*, setting fire to them," said Arianna. "After all, they were created by the King, so let them burn."

She was already excited by the thought.

"Well, do you at least mind sharing this grand plan of yours with the rest of us this time before we go dashing into danger?" Jeom stretched his legs out on the grass, evidently resigned to the idea.

"It's simple really, something the ghost of Master Lethander mentioned to me in the desert," said Arianna. "He told me all I need to do is *show* them… the purpose of all this, I mean." She opened her palm so that a flicker of magical fire danced there—so warm, so welcome. "My plan is to give them a show, demonstrate our powers just like we did for Syrifina and the other guardians here. Then we offer them a choice, just like we were given."

"But we've never had any choices," said Demetrius, crossing his arms.

"Haven't we? Everything that led us here were choices," she said. "I chose to defy the rules until the chains ultimately broke, even though I didn't know what outcome to expect. Lessa chose to try and escape through the tunnels before any of us even conceptualized the idea. Jeom, you chose to join our fight before even knowing what it was. And, Demetrius, you *chose* to follow the light, the magic you saw right before your eyes."

She looked to Eli, understanding that even his wrong choices in life had turned out all right in the end.

"We all made the right choices," she continued, "even if they felt like the wrong ones at the time, and survived through the consequences. I want to give that to them, prove that each day they sit and obey the King, *that's* a choice. I make no promises… but they're our army, if they so choose."

"For this to work, we'll only have one shot to earn their trust," said Demetrius. "King Devlindor has his own soldiers. We've seen them, and we know what Sir Vladamor can do. I doubt he was even giving it his all. They *have* to follow us, or we'll surely die there."

Jeom waved his arms in the air to stop the conversation.

"Let me just get this straight then," he said, his voice pitching. "Are we going *back* to the Four Corners? The place where we almost died a hundred times trying to escape?"

Arianna couldn't help the laugh that burst from her lips.

"We're going back," she said, getting to her feet and pulling Lessa up with her. "But first, one last stolen adventure."

30

FREE THE FLOWERS

TUMBLING THROUGH THE WALL of vines at the top of the winding stairs, Arianna found herself back in the dingy light of the storefront they had first entered through more than nine months ago. She could hardly fathom that another year was on the horizon, but time was pushy, and it had shoved them straight toward the future quicker than she'd seen it coming.

"Follow me," said Eli, leading the way.

"Lucky they don't keep tabs on you," said Jeom, following at his heels.

Eli pushed open the creaky door to begin their journey through the Burrows—he'd clearly done this before.

"Nobody cares where a drifter goes," he said with a shrug.

"I feel like a drifter all the time," said Demetrius.

Eli laughed. "I guess we kind of all are now, but we're the best-kept drifters I've ever known!"

Nobody responded, making it apparent that everyone else

was losing confidence in the idea to explore Zambienth.

"Oh, *come* on," he said, shaking his head. "You're all ready to sneak back into the Jar but afraid to poke around this city for a bit?"

Arianna laughed. "You have a point."

He grinned.

"Just relax. Tonight's the Gathering. It'll be a mess in the city with all the preparations. They won't be focused on you. As long as we're careful, this is your chance to see what really goes on in Zambienth." He waved them forward. "Now let's get out of here before you change your minds."

Arianna felt a shiver roll up her spine as her mind transported back to that fateful night a year ago today, the annual Gathering Ball of South Luose. Her nineteenth year had come and gone, and her twentieth was literally around the corner. It seemed such an odd time to enter a brand-new decade of her life, to start back at zero when she still had so many things that felt unfinished from years prior.

"I suppose it's now or never," said Lessa, taking a deep breath and calling to her magic to light the torch in her hand. "Are you sure Solza and Sano will be okay alone for one night?"

Arianna nodded. "They'll certainly be safer than us."

Lessa offered a timid smile.

They all stumbled out of the room after Eli, sneaking their way through the dark tunnels of the Burrows.

Arianna caught her breath as the city expanded out in front of her. It was early evening now, the remnants of the sun streaking in radiant colors across the sky and casting a warm glow over the grand pyramids.

"Welcome to the City of Sand," said Eli. "It's about time you saw it properly."

Her eyes stayed glued to the pearly white pyramids and the bridges connecting them all, busy with passersby.

"It's remarkable," she said. "South Luose was so… calm."

"I can't wait to see what the rest of the world is like," said Eli.

The traveler in him was easy to spot; Arianna thought that if the opportunity ever presented itself to travel for leisure rather than necessity, she'd probably be a lot like him.

Maybe one day, she mused—when traveling was safer, a day when evil monarchs didn't roam the land.

"Where should we go first?" asked Lessa, tugging on Jeom's hand and ready to fly off her feet. "I don't even know where to start!"

"How about there?" said Demetrius, squealing with delight—he'd spotted a garden of pastel-colored cacti in the center of the market.

He darted forward with everyone following slowly behind, all absorbing the energetic scene for themselves; without the elder guardians watching their every move, they were free to really take in the city life here, to explore and relax a bit before dodging straight back into danger.

As Demetrius fawned over yet another plant species, Arianna was drawn to the centerpiece of Arch Alley—the punishment pond he and Jeom had described to her in terrible detail.

The archway was pristine this day, decorated in wreaths of glowing flowers, colors representing each of the four slave districts; there was nothing to suggest that there had ever been a brutal death here at all...

Aside from the bones at the bottom of the water, of course, which told a different, unsettling tale.

Drifting away from the group, Arianna climbed a set of tall stairs until she was standing on a low bridge with a bird's-eye view of her friends. They were parading about the city center excitedly and fit right in with the throngs of people doing last-minute shopping for the Gathering. This peaceful second of seeing her friends happy and carefree was short-lived as she spotted men on ladders cementing fresh 'Wanted' posters to the walls so that they might never be torn down.

The terror that filled Arianna's heart at seeing, as she stood out in the open, a sign calling for her head in exchange for the highlife reward was indescribable. But as the moment passed, she realized that Eli had been perfectly right before; the city's focus was on the excitement of the Gathering, and the posters drew no interest from the surrounding crowds.

In fact, it seemed that Zambienth entirely dismissed them, openly viewing them as propaganda from the High City.

Arianna had made an assumption back in South Luose that was surely solidified now—the citizens of Olleb-Yelfra would have to see her with their own eyes to believe in any of the happenings from her Free Falls Festival gone wrong. Their imaginations had been squandered and warped for so long by the King's oppression that she doubted they could believe in anything out of the ordinary without proof.

In their world, it was truly unthinkable that a slave could have escaped her chains from the Jar and that other traitors to the Olleb were aiding her; it wouldn't be easy to sway their beliefs with just a poster.

Still, she drew her hood over her face.

"The rumors have died off again, you know?" said Eli, coming up from behind.

"Does it matter?" she said, jumping slightly at the intrusion. "It won't stop *him* from coming."

"I know." He laid a hand on her shoulder. "I wish you didn't have to hide."

She turned around to face him, shrugging away from his touch.

"Me too, but you never know who you can trust," she snapped. "You taught me that lesson well."

"When are you going to forgive me, Ara?" he blurted out, shedding the calm and collected demeanor he so easily wore. "It's been the better part of a year. I'm in this now. You can't be mad at me forever."

She didn't reply, unsure of what she wanted to say.

Did she trust him? Was she just holding a grudge? The truth was, she didn't know anymore. Arianna was so used to keeping her guard up that she couldn't tell if she was being honest with her feelings or if she was just scared of being hurt again.

After a long moment, she decided she would need to let her defenses down a bit if she were to enjoy this night of freedom at all...

"I don't think I'm mad anymore," she finally said with a deep sigh, turning again to the scenic view. "I was for a long while, but I suppose I couldn't help but to eventually forgive you after you helped save Lessa."

Her eyes settled on her friend bouncing around the shops and filling her bags with useless trinkets, Jeom by her side.

"But I warned you I'd never forget, and so I haven't. I just still don't... trust you. I'm sorry."

Eli let out a howl of frustration.

"If only I had magical powers of my own. My first order of business would be to straighten out that stubbornness you're saddled with!" he said, running his fingers through his hair. "Guess I'll just keep trying."

Arianna couldn't help the smirk he pulled out of her then.

"A hard-won smile," he said, beaming, hands on his hips. "That will do for now."

"Speaking of saddled..." she said, changing the subject. "How's Phantom? Missing you terribly, I bet?"

"I think he's tired of me, really," said Eli, folding his arms across the ledge of the bridge to look down beside her. "He spends his days being pampered here in the Stables and takes turns riding with much worthier guardians than I."

"How lucky of him," she said. "The chosen steed of the Guardians of Gold." She shook her head, thinking how lucky that horse truly was. "I'm glad he's still with us, though, after everything."

"*Say*," said Eli, leaning into her line of sight so that she couldn't ignore him, "how about we go for a ride? For old time's sake? I know you fancied it… before."

"I don't know," said Arianna, standing up straighter and chewing on her lip as she mulled over the idea—she couldn't deny the thrill of that ride through the desert, to feel like she ran toward any future she chose. "I guess it couldn't hurt."

"Safer really, away from prying eyes." Eli flashed that same charismatic smile he had mastered long ago when she'd followed him to the South Luose Stables.

Though her feelings for him were certainly hardened, her faith in him was growing a little more each day that he fought for her approval; if everyone else she trusted had deemed him worthy of the most sacred secret in the world, then what good did it do to waste energy on believing something different? She was—begrudgingly, *slowly*—changing her mind about him.

"We're going for a ride!" he called down, catching Demetrius' attention. "Meet under the arch before nightfall?"

Demetrius waved them off, and Eli took Arianna's hand, guiding her across the bridge and into another corridor of the Burrows. As they made turn after turn, bumping into the rushing city people who shoved anything that could be sold into their faces, Arianna caught the last part of a tense conversation.

"Keeper Yahindi," said a woman in a shaky voice. "What can I offer you today? How about another ring for the collection? Or perhaps a necklace for the Gathering Ball tonight?"

"Are you asking me to make a choice in exchange for *my* coin?" said the cool voice of the city keeper. "I'm the only reason you can offer such choices in the first place! If not for the thriving ports of this city that I control, you wouldn't even have merchandize to peddle." She spat at the ground. "I shall take it all, if only to teach you a lesson for your ignorance."

"Yes, of course, Keeper," stuttered the woman, eyes cast down. "Take what you wish."

"Move," whispered Eli, pushing Arianna up against the wall just as Keeper Yahindi passed by them, the jingle of jewelry ringing in their ears.

His hand pressed flat against the wall by Arianna's head so that his arm fully covered her face from view; she looked up at him, cheeks running hot as she caught the way he gazed at her in this moment.

He never once blinked, his green eyes blazing into hers as he stared on, breath hitched in his throat as they waited for the city keeper to pass.

Arianna finally had to look away, so she averted her eyes to get a glimpse of the back of Keeper Yahindi. Long braids were tied at the top of her scalp, decorated with tinsels, and her black skin glistened against the white and gold of her robes. She walked like the ruthless queen of this city, but Arianna knew that queens no longer existed—only the lavishly dressed slaves of the unrighteous King.

"I think we're in the clear now," she said in a hushed voice as Keeper Yahindi rounded the corner with her guards.

"Yeah," he breathed, lowering his arm and stepping back. "Come on. The Stables are this way."

Arianna followed him closely, a little shaken after such a close call. At the same time, she couldn't help but feel a little bout of confidence come with the knowledge that she'd survived far worse than Keeper Yahindi.

Soon they entered the Stables, and Eli located Phantom in a pen toward the back—he looked as fit and plump as a horse had ever been.

"Hi, Phantom!" said Arianna, beaming. "Miss me?" The horse barely acknowledged her, and she scoffed, patting him on the head. "You're just as sweet as I remember."

"Hop on," said Eli, tightening the saddle to Phantom's back and offering to help Arianna up.

"No, not this time," she said, hands on her hips. "I learned a few things from Tobias, you know. Apprentice Aridyn wasn't just a pretty face."

She hoisted herself up onto Phantom with grace and held out her hand for Eli to join her.

"Hop *on*," she said in a mocking tone.

Eli smirked in bemusement, taking her hand. "You're always surprising me."

Arianna whipped the reins once they were both settled. "Yah!"

Phantom sped off and they took to an outer path, Arianna steering him down a cobblestone walkway that wrapped around the entire city. As they galloped away—the pyramids rising high all around them, waves splashing up against the cliffs, and the desert sands swimming into view on either side—she began feeling more liberated than she'd felt in a long while.

The warm winds brushed her face, and the setting sun made it seem like they raced straight for the beautiful, fiery ends of the earth. The vibrations of pounding hooves on stone surged through her body in a delightful sensation, as if an ongoing beat to a song she surely held in her heart. And her eyes watered with what could only be the result of bliss.

After a while, Arianna felt Eli tighten his grip around her waist—she pulled back on the reins to slow Phantom, feeling her nerves spike unwillingly.

The last time we were this close, it didn't end well.

"I think there's another storm coming," said Eli, peering off over the sea as they came to a stop on the pathway.

Arianna looked toward the water and saw giant purple and black clouds rolling over the ocean—though far away yet. Slivers of lightning through the graying sky told her that when the storm reached them, it would be a big one.

A gaggle of massive ships docked at the shore on this side of the city stole her attention, rocking back and forth with the rowdy waves. She wondered which one the guardians had planned to use in the next voyage should Gabriel and Margery get their way.

A rumble of thunder burst from the sky, startling Phantom.

"Easy, now," cooed Arianna, brushing his mane to try to keep him calm—her own anxious mind raced to the last storm she'd endured with Eli.

She scowled at him over her shoulder. "Don't get any ideas this time."

He threw his head back and cackled.

"On my honor as a warrior," he said, placing his fist across his chest. "I'll wait for your permission next time."

Arianna turned to the front so he wouldn't see her blush.

Will there be a next time?

She whipped the reins once more, and Phantom kicked his feet to the air, starting off at a run; it was the only distraction she could think of as an unbidden smile grew on her face.

At least I have someone to share the memory of the sensational desert graveyard kiss with… even if it was Eli.

"Shall we take him back to the Stables now?" asked Arianna after a while. "It's getting pretty dark."

"No," said Eli. "Let him come with us for a change."

"But there's no way we could get him in the Greenhouse without drawing attention…" she said.

"Anything is possible," said Eli in a very Talis-like tone. "I'll show you a little secret later on, but only if you *promise* not to get mad."

Arianna couldn't help the snort of laughter that came out.

"I wouldn't hold my breath," she said, wondering how many more surprises she could withstand before she truly snapped.

"Let's just go find the others," said Eli, the hint of a smile in his voice. "Trust me."

Arianna shook her head with a snicker and steered Phantom back toward Arch Alley; the others were waiting at an outdoor tavern, ale in hand, so Eli went to tie Phantom up nearby.

"We've saved some for you, but just *barely*," said Lessa, glaring at Jeom who had a big smile on his face and a drink to his lips. "Come sit!"

She was clearly tipsy, her rosy cheeks giving her away.

Arianna went to join them, trying and failing at combing the tangles from her curls with her fingers—the price of a relaxing horseback ride.

"We should be heading back soon," said Jeom, a slur in his voice. "They'll be angry to find us gone."

"They're always angry," said Lessa, giggling. "Let them moan! Besides, they won't be back for a while. The Gathering hasn't even started yet."

Demetrius held his mug up to cheers. "How about just one dance, then?"

"No, I think we should probably go," said Arianna. "I don't feel right… in such plain sight." She feared anyone who might flash their eyes her way in this crowded city center, with the 'Wanted' posters circling them.

"I can solve that!" sang Lessa, rummaging in her bag. "I had a feeling we might want to fit in. I got some for everyone."

She passed out eye masks for each of them to take. Keeping true to the colors of their districts, Eli and Arianna were handed matching reds.

As Arianna considered hers, she felt the weight of Aridyn return, the easiness of hiding. Though, when she placed the mask upon her face, tying the strings tight at the back of her head, she knew that there would never be any disguise that could truly hide who she was.

She removed her cloak, exposing herself to the city folk who had already started the pre-Gathering celebrations, dressed in dazzling clothes and jewelries representing their districts. It looked as if the City of the Four Corners had been transferred from its solitude in the Blancoren Mountains to the middle of this desert.

As Arianna took in the scene, eyes glued to the citizens floating about with not a care in the world other than the festivities
this night, a soothing melody reached her ears. Following the
sound, she noticed an area where instruments had been gathered,
surely in preparation for the late-night entertainments that would
take place after the Gathering.

There she found Eli.

Despite the crowd, he did not hesitate to pick up a guitar and
perform.

She hadn't heard him sing for some time now, but even Arianna could admit that it was always something special. When he
began, she saw him transform into something else; it appeared
that he did have a magic all his own, whether he realized it or not.

Eli could entrance people with his words, make them feel
what he wanted them to feel with just the sound of his voice. He
could truly make them *listen*.

With the strum of a single chord, the people in the vicinity
gave him their full attention. And with the strum of a second, all
went quiet in Arch Alley, passersby pausing in step just to hear
the song of a drifter. Other than his voice and the guitar, the only
thing not silent was the echo of the wind and the beat of the sea—
his guiding symphony.

Eyes averted down, Eli started slow, whispering the words to
a song that Arianna had never heard before. She realized very
quickly that this song had emerged from the confines of his
heart... because it was one that had also been restrained in her
own. And in this moment, with these strangers, it was the first
time it had ever been shared out loud.

Sucking her in, Eli's voice shook with such a passion that Arianna could feel it pulsing within her soul. It told the haunting
truth of a fate that united everyone there—and with just one look
around the crowd, she was certain that they could all feel it in
their hearts too.

Should we pity the flowers who sway in the breeze?
Or pity ourselves while we watch?
The flowers, so untroubled.
With nothing to do but sway in the breeze.

Should we rejoice as they stay rooted to the soil?
Or cry each time we see their winter freeze?
Such pretty flowers.
With nothing to do but sway in that breeze.

Oh, should we pity the flowers who sway to the breeze?
Or pity ourselves while we watch?

Eli strummed the chords louder, his voice raising with it.

I say cry for the flowers with nowhere to run!
We'll pity ourselves when they're gone.

His eyes shot open, fiercely challenging his audience as he finished, the final verse resounding across the night.

As soon as the last word left his lips, a hush fell; Arianna could sense the people around them deep in thought—their only safe place to express their true feelings.

She knew what it was like to stand where Eli stood, commanding a crowd and clearly seeing the sea of colors meant to represent the sovereign rule of their oppressor. She knew how their eyes looked once they glazed over, their memories flicking to their dead friends who had never made it past the Jar, wondering what it really was they celebrated at the Gathering Ball each year.

They stood there devotedly in red, blue, green, or purple garments, colors designated to them after being ripped away from something called a 'mother'… before being escorted into a cage where the life would be beaten from them daily—these were all survivors who had chosen to forget their origins.

Such pretty flowers, she thought.

Clapping erupted from all around, and Eli bowed, passing the guitar off to the rightful owner.

He walked back to the table and chugged his drink.

"That was *so* moving, Eli," said Lessa, hugging him. "What's it about?"

"It's about everyone," muttered Arianna, pursing her lips.

Eli gave a slight nod, meeting her gaze.

"So," he said, considering her, "are you a flower? Or are you a watcher?"

"I'm a *warrior*," she said without hesitation, "who pitied the flowers for far too long and got tired of watching them sway to the breeze." She slammed her mug on the table to kill a spider that crawled there, pretending it was the King.

A more upbeat tone started then. And with it, ample amounts of wine and ale were passed around, the people of Zambienth quick to wash away their memories of worse days.

"Let's dance!" said Demetrius, hopping up from his chair almost instantly, as if his feet no longer belonged to his body.

He swayed so vigorously that soon other men and women were twirling him around the center; Lessa dragged Jeom up to join him not a moment after, and Arianna was left watching everyone swirl about in a melting pot of colors, all coming together to form something truly beautiful to witness.

When the drums started up, she found Eli on his feet too, hardly able to resist the rhythm.

"May I have this dance?" he asked, extending his hand like the proper gentlemen he pretended to be.

Arianna hesitated at first, but when he didn't persist, she decided to take it; he knew her too well now. The one thing she couldn't stand was being denied a choice—Eli had yet to try to force his way back into anything.

"You may," she said, standing and offering him a curtsy, her highlife etiquette never to be forgotten.

They all danced well into the night, singing and laughing with each other, spinning away their worries until eventually they were the only ones left. The City of Zambienth, and all the cities around Olleb-Yelfra, would gather tonight to toast to the King—but not Arianna nor her friends.

With no one around, the young guardians tore off their masks, tossing them to the ground without remorse.

Despite King Devlindor's power and far-reaching rule, this moment was all the proof they needed to know that not everyone bowed down to the self-proclaimed monarch. And soon they'd be ready to make that point clear to the slaves of the Four Corners.

AFTER A FULL NIGHT OF FREEDOM and fun, Jeom, Lessa, and Demetrius headed back to the Greenhouse through the Burrows before anyone could miss them. Arianna, on the other hand, let Eli take the lead on Phantom, heading down a new path toward the beach on the other side of the city.

He had a secret to share.

She felt rejuvenated with life, her mind playing out the battles of her future with such gusto and success that she was sure the world would one day be set right. But the King had always warned against the use of imagination. As she let her thoughts run wild with dreams of conquering a kingdom, she considered that, in a way, this may have been his most thoughtful law—a necessary lesson to be taught.

Don't let your imagination deceive you. It isn't real…

When they reached the beach, Arianna and Eli hopped down from the horse.

"So, what is it you wanted to show me?" she said. "We should really be getting back soon—"

"There's another entrance to the Greenhouse from here," said Eli. "I think the elder guardians created it recently to make for easier work. You'll understand everything in a minute. Just wait here while I secure Phantom somewhere more private for the night. This fresh air will do him some good."

"Another entrance?" she said, confused.

But Eli had already raced off.

Arianna explored a little as she waited, wrapping her arms around herself to keep the cool night winds at bay. On this side of Zambienth, there was no busy dock or horde of ships in waiting, just a long stretch of clean, black sand—and there was something very familiar about it.

As she watched Eli lead Phantom to a more covered area where a makeshift pen had been erected for him, she spotted the boat that had marked the beginnings of their voyage to Zambienth.

"This was where we first landed!" she exclaimed, running to it.

It seemed like a lifetime ago that they'd arrived on these shores.

Arianna brushed the side of the wood with her hand and a wave of nostalgia for the Island of Idris washed over her; she just couldn't believe that this little boat had brought them safely from that paradise across this vast and unpredictable body of water that she now knew as the Sea of Saindora.

She stared out at the waters, hypnotized by memories of her past and plans for the future. After the countless hours she had spent studying in the Greenhouse, the Olleb had started to piece together more clearly for her. If she sailed toward the horizon on the line of the sun, she would find the High City and King Devlindor as her host.

One day, she'd have to take that journey—but not yet.

As she looked farther down the beach, her eyes caught sight of a different boat, or rather a *massive* ship. It was built with elegant white sails, wooden wings, and the golden head of a dragon at the front.

But it can't be…

She gasped. "*No*, is that what I think it is?"

"It's a ship," said Eli, walking back to her side. "And yes, *this* is the secret." He led her toward it, his arm behind her back. "It's what's been keeping the elders so occupied lately. It took a lot of muscle and magic to build but looks like it's nearly complete. I heard they cloaked it with spells, too, so that regular folks can't stumble on it. Not that many make their way down this side very often, but still…"

"Can never be too careful," said Arianna, finishing his thought as she craned her neck to examine the stunning creation. "I know we spoke about this as an option. I just didn't realize that they—"

Arianna's heart suddenly skipped a beat, seeing this grandiose beast of a vessel for what it really meant—this was a statement of *war*, the launch of what could someday be a fleet, a guardian army on the sea sailing toward the King and setting fire to his tyranny.

That was the real secret.

"They're going to fight!" she screeched, nearly jumping up and down with joy. She looked to Eli with such disbelief, smiling wide. "They're really going to do it?"

"It would seem so," said Eli, admiring it himself. "I'm sure Master Tayshin and the others will reveal their plans to you soon. I'll have to apologize to him later as I'm sure I've overstepped in showing you this before they were ready… but I thought since you intended to return to the Four Corners—"

Arianna reached for his hand.

"No," she said. "This is just what I needed. I was getting restless, but now I realize that I've gone and let my impatience get the best of me again. I thought we'd be stalled forever." She took a deep breath. "But this is *really* happening."

"Yes, it is," said Eli, softly. "I know you want to go back soon… but I don't think we should leave just yet. If we stick together, we could really have a shot at this."

Arianna let his words sink in—he was right.

This was one ship out of how many, or of what grand plan created out of the many possibilities they had all laboriously outlined at countless assemblies in the Greenhouse? They couldn't leave now knowing that the guardians were acting on their words from so long ago, ideas that she and her friends had put in their minds. And if they could be convinced of growing the resistance to the point of building this impressive ship for the cause, then they *could* be persuaded to join them in collecting their army from the Four Corners—their best chance was to tackle this as a cohesive group.

Arianna couldn't even blink, awestruck still.

In an instant everything had aligned. *We're going to fight!*

Despite the indecision over the last several months, she knew for certain that time and effort had won the guardians over. This vessel was a statement of their respect for her, so she would show them respect just the same.

She needed to learn from their experience and advice, not undermine it.

We're not alone anymore. We are united, all of us.

She would have to remind herself that the ones she called family were not her only friends in this fight. Others had a stake in this, too. After all, the elder guardians understood that numbers would be important to their success, for they had spent all year spreading word and trying to plant the seeds of a rebellion in farther lands. And while Arianna was eager to see those seeds grow quickly into something strong, she wanted to add her own to their guardian garden.

She decided then and there that in the morning she would call an assembly with the elders and act like the leader they had positioned her to be. Arianna would demand a full picture of the strategy forming, starting with this ship, and voice their newest idea for all to judge; it would not be easy to sway the slave districts and it would undoubtedly take more time to organize since it was such a risky endeavor, but it'd mean more people on their side if they succeeded—thousands more.

As she mulled over this new plan of action, she knew her friends would support postponing their daring adventure back into the claws of the Blancoren Mountains; for the first time in her life, Arianna Belvedor would force herself to be just a little more patient.

"Why didn't you say something sooner?" she asked Eli, her thoughts abruptly changing direction. "We've been going crazy about this for months. How long have you known?"

"For a while," he said, shifting on his feet. "I stumbled upon it during a ride. They didn't tell me, but I started picking up on snippets here and there, understanding their plans better having seen this for myself."

He let out a long sigh when he saw her frown, kicking at the sand in frustration.

"I know you don't consider me part of *your* family, but the elders do. I'm a young guardian, just like you." He stared out at the waters. "Yet… I still feel like I'm a guest in all this. I didn't want to ruin anything by blowing what was obviously supposed to be a big secret. They probably didn't want to get your hopes up until everything was fully sorted."

Arianna scoffed, crossing her arms.

"You *can* trust me, Arianna," he said, clearly exasperated with her fluctuating attitude toward him. "You can and you know it! You're just scared. This isn't just about some stupid ship or any secret." He turned away from her, fists balled at his sides. "You know it isn't."

"What do you mean?" she said, forgetting they were even fighting over a ship at all. "Scared of what?"

"You're scared of opening your heart back up!" he yelled into the wind—it was as if the words had been dying to escape his mouth for a century.

"My *heart* has no place in this war," she retorted, shaking as she tried to restrain her emotions.

"Well, mine can't be contained any longer," said Eli. He whipped around to face her. "From the first moment I laid eyes on you, and every moment since, my heart skips a beat. And no matter how far I try to run away from this madness, it keeps leading me right back to you." He stood taller, lifting his chest. "I'm not running anymore, Ara. You are my beginning and, inevitably, my end."

Arianna was stunned, not fully comprehending the confession pouring from his lips; Eli gently grasped her by the shoulders.

"Arianna, I *will* follow you wherever you go," he said. "Do you hear me? I'll earn your trust if I must die doing it. You'll have to kill me to be rid of me."

She couldn't help feeling like a swarm of firebugs fluttered in her stomach as she considered him, her cheeks running hot—she also couldn't look away.

"You're absolutely mad, you know? I don't know what game you're playing at but—"

It was then that Eli closed the distance between them, pulling her toward him so that they were almost flush against one another. As he did, Arianna reflexively reached for her dagger and lifted it to his stomach—she knew his intentions well, had seen that look in his eyes before.

"Do you forget your *honor*, sir?" she whispered, glaring up at him with scorn.

All of the memories and hurt had come flooding back—their kiss in the desert, his betrayals, their first meeting in the Nicora Forest and then again in South Luose; it was a jumbled mess of feelings as his eyes bore into hers.

They were so close now that she could feel his warm breath on her skin and outline every chiseled feature on his face under the moonlight. And his irises, they appeared now like piercing jade jewels. It was as if a mesmerizing magic spouted from Eli, urging her to lower her weapon.

Arianna remembered what it felt like to kiss him, and she'd be lying if she said it wasn't hard for her not to put down her blade and lean in. Every natural reaction told her to do so. But she needed to stay focused on so many other things, and this didn't even make the list.

She squeezed the hilt of her weapon tighter, holding on to that truth as she found the will to look away.

I don't have time for this. I don't have time for... him.

"Like I said," breathed Eli, "you'll have to very well kill me to be rid of me. And, as for a kiss—" He slowly tilted Arianna's chin up.

She pressed the dagger slightly forward, making her decision clear.

Eli sucked a hiss in through his teeth. "—I'll probably die regardless if you never allow me another one. Alas, on my honor, I *will* wait for your permission."

"Don't test me, Eli," said Arianna, pushing him away and sheathing her dagger with a shaking hand. "I won't deny we had a connection, but it's passed now. You can save your charm. If you want to truly help this war, help *me*, then you'll need to leave your feelings out of it."

She spoke a little calmer now, using her breath to steady her racing heart as Talis had taught her.

"I see how devoted you are to the guardians. They trust you, and they have no reason not to, but *I* do." She ran her hands through her hair, flustered at having such a conversation at all. "So, if you really want to show me that you're serious about all this, you can prove it by setting your heart aside... as I have mine."

Eli sighed, his shoulders sagging in defeat. He tore his gaze from her, setting it on the endless scope of stars.

"One can't prove their love by setting it aside," he said, curtly. "And if a war is coming, then love is the one thing you should be holding on to, not pushing it away. That's the *only* way you'll win. That's why you're fighting in the first place."

He turned to walk away, leaving Arianna to ponder his statement. *Love?*

She shuddered as the word bounced around her head, making her dizzier still; it was something she might have cared to hear in the past but now she couldn't even fathom the meaning until these darkened days were far behind her.

Then again, maybe he had a point…

In silence they walked, Arianna following Eli back across the beach and through the secret entrance to the Greenhouse concealed with magic inside the cliffs. She had to look back one last time to witness the dragon ship by the shore, moving with the waves. She couldn't wait for the day it might set sail—the day that would bring her one step closer to facing the King and defending the ones she *loved*, her family.

"WHERE WERE YOU?" asked Jeom.

"On the beach," said Arianna, "with Eli."

"*Ooh*," said Demetrius, chuckling.

"Shut it!" she said, tossing a pillow his way. "It was nothing." Arianna decided to save talk of secret ships and voyages to dangerous lands for the morning.

"Oh, it's *something*," said Demetrius. "Why do you give him such a hard time still? He's clearly mad about you." He lowered his voice. "And we do have some fault in what happened. He wasn't ready to see…"

Arianna was beyond tired of trying to explain her emotions to the men in her life, especially when she didn't understand them herself. Why couldn't they just focus on things like battle and magic? That's all she cared to think about.

He's right, though, she thought.

Eli had freshly experienced a trauma when she forced magic into his reality. She still couldn't admit it out loud, but she owed that man an apology.

"Because I don't have time to waste worrying about my feelings," she said. "I've done enough of that, and it's gotten me nowhere."

"*So…* you do have feelings for him then?" said Jeom, snickering.

The boys burst into a bout of laughter that filled the room, the drinks from earlier in the night clearly still messing with their minds.

"Of course she does!" sang Lessa, unable to resist adding her piece. "What she means is that she doesn't want to let her feelings get in the way of our goal. She doesn't have time to worry over love."

The laughter abruptly stopped.

Arianna bit her lip, feeling a bit guilty as she heard Jeom grumble and roll over to his side to sleep, obviously affronted.

Though their secret was well out by now, Lessa had spoken little of her close relationship with him. And only now did Arianna realize that it was because she was probably scared to— scared of falling for someone who could die at any moment, scared of being the reason they died in the first place, and, most importantly, scared of being distracted and failing the world.

Am I scared… of falling for Eli?

Fighting sleep, Arianna stared at the ceiling, snuggling close to Solza as she tried to relax and think of anything other than Elijah Neve, fellow drifter and dreamer of the Olleb. So much excitement had exhausted and energized her all at once.

With the boys now deep in a fit of snores, Arianna whispered to Lessa alone, sensing she was still awake too.

"Have you dealt with all your demons now?" she asked, thinking of their earlier chat about Sir Vladamor's sinister manipulation of the mermaids.

Lessa gave a far-off look, scratching Sano behind his ear.

"Have you dealt with yours?" she said with a bitter laugh. "Mine are unquestionably still lurking."

"Every time I cut one down, another grows in its place," said Arianna.

"What kills the monsters of the dark and keeps them dead? I'd like to know that," said Lessa with a yawn.

"Wouldn't we all," she replied. "But… I have a feeling demons die the same way that they're born."

"And how's that?" asked Lessa.

"By fire," said Arianna—she snapped her fingers, and the flame of the last light in their room was promptly snuffed out.

A GUARDIAN'S GIFT

EARLY THE NEXT MORNING, Arianna was the first to rise, the bell from the Warrior's District still ingrained in her bones to shake her awake bright and early each day, no matter what. In the Greenhouse there were no windows, only the glass pyramid at the top of the spiral staircase. And no natural light reached any of the corridors that branched away from the main area, apart from the sand that forever twinkled overhead like stars.

Yet somehow she awakened to what looked like soft rays of sun on a cloudy morning beaming through an open window… it took Arianna a moment to realize where she was and that the sunlight was merely an illusion created by the enchanted Greenhouse flame. But when she did, she was eager for a change of scenery.

She was so *sick* of 'illusions' in her life, being free and yet not truly. Thus, today, she was determined to push for a trek back into the real world they were trying to liberate—the Jar.

Arianna tiptoed out of the room as the others slept on, Solza lazily strolling behind her, headed to the main gardens. There, she took a turn around the lake to try to clear her mind. After a while, she crouched near the waters, deciding to spend a little time tending to her weapons before confronting the master guardians about the dragon ship looming in the bay or their newest mission.

First, she started with her twin swords, wiping away any hint of battle until they were so clean that she could see her reflection in the metal. Then, she put her attention on Aurora.

The black blade of the dagger sparkled like the glittering sand of the desert, and the hilt, melded with the colorful aura and ora stones, made a powerful statement that she finally understood; there had been a time where she hadn't a name for what was depicted there—a beast? A god?—but now, without a doubt, she knew it to be a mighty dragon, the wings extending out fiercely so that she had something sturdy to grasp.

Aurora boasted the unwavering symbol of the guardians, and it had been her most prized possession since her eleventh year. Whether or not it was a gift from someone she now considered an enemy, it was a true treasure to behold.

To think, I almost lost this.

Arianna smiled, admiring its elegance.

"That's a fine weapon," said Master Tayshin, startling her. He sat cross-legged in the grass by the tree as he smoked a pipe, blowing big circles out across the water. "I remember when Solomon came to have that himself."

"You do?" said Arianna, wiping it clean before going to sit beside him.

Master Tayshin blew another smoke ring.

"Of course." He chuckled. "I gave it to him. May I?"

Arianna was surprised by this detail of her dagger's history.

"Sure…" she stammered after a moment, handing it over. "The stones of aura and ora are quite rare, aren't they?"

He nodded.

"In this day and age, they haven't even been discovered," he said, examining it with something of fondness in his expression, clearly lost in old memories. "Not by anyone other than a guardian. When my family left me their treasures, there were several items crafted from these stones. I didn't need to know the history of the Golden Age to know they were precious. Their beauty speaks for itself… and their powers speak even more wonders."

"Why would Master Bell willingly give away such a gift?" Arianna couldn't comprehend it. "Especially to a slave with no knowledge of magic or the guardians?"

Master Tayshin unfolded his legs, leaning back against the tree.

"Who can say but him?" he said. "I offered the items to those I trusted most. Eventually, they became known as sort of guardian tokens, if you will. I'd wager that he trusted you to become what you are today for him to have parted with it." He shrugged. "I, for one, think it's now in even better hands."

Arianna chewed on her lip, fixated on the dagger.

"Maybe," she said, thinking of the many years gone by since the day she'd acquired it. "We came across tunnels of aura and ora after we discovered Undor, you know? It's a shame the dwarves aren't around anymore…" Her thoughts shifted to Jeom and his bizarre connection to them. "It's truly tragic."

Master Tayshin laughed, a cloud of smoke bursting from his lips.

"You *mean*, extinct like fairies, mermaids, and necromancers?" He grinned. "We know only a fraction of things, girl. It's what we *believe* that matters. And I believe there's more left of the Golden Age than we know."

Arianna looked up, considering him with new eyes. She had never heard Master Tayshin speak so optimistically before. There was quite a nice ring to it.

"I believe in that, too," she said with a smile.

He had the remnants of a young, passionate leader in his soul, that much was certain. He was someone people followed because he trusted so surely that he'd find what he was searching for. He may have lost his way for a time, but now he had returned—and, most importantly, he still held faith in the Guardians of Gold.

Just seeing the hope in his eyes gave Arianna confidence.

She and her friends had taken detours already, countless times, and some days it felt like nothing would ever turn out right. But knowing what she knew now about the trials Master Tayshin and the other elders had faced in the bloodstained past of the guardians shed a harsh light on what truly mattered—they had found a way to move forward and learn from their mistakes, looking ahead rather than behind to the unchangeable past.

Arianna and her friends would do the same, following closely in their footsteps.

When Master Tayshin finally handed Arianna back her dagger, something made her take pause.

"You mentioned about the stones' powers…" she said, cocking her head to the side. "What did you mean by that, exactly?"

"So young," said Master Tayshin, shaking his head a bit. "The stones welded to your dagger can allow you to experience astral projection. That is, if you know what you're doing." He brushed his hand through the air. "They're named for the ancient traveler spirits, Aura and Ora. Though, these beings surely wouldn't waste time traveling to our world anymore."

He gave a sad sigh.

"Astral projection?" mused Arianna, stroking Solza as she settled in the grass next to them.

"I take it Solomon never explained to you just what his gift could do, did he?"

"No, he didn't," she said, intrigued. "I understand that the dagger may, or may not, have some kind of unique ability like the compass?" He lifted his eyebrows, so she knew she was onto something. "But I haven't a clue of what it could be. And I had *no* idea that the aura and ora stones had something to do with it."

She tapped her chin as she thought.

"Although… now that you mention this, I think Tobias did say guardian relics held a connection to astral journey once. It's surely one of many on my *long* list of puzzles waiting to be solved." She batted her eyelids. "Care to help me crack this one, Master?"

He chuckled, his hand on his round belly as it shook. Then he reached forward to tickle Solza under the chin.

"Of course this would end up on me," he said after a moment, twisting his beard around his finger. "I taught Bell, so I guess I'll teach you too."

Arianna leaned in.

"When combined with the proper magic, the properties of the merged aura and ora stones can permit your soul to be released from your physical body in a controlled manner. This is known as astral projection or astral journey, whatever you feel like calling it—"

He blew a bout of smoke, and Arianna didn't miss the flicker of magic that came with it, the smoke morphing into what was unmistakably the shape of a person. It hovered over the water before disappearing in a wisp.

"Astral projection gives you an opportunity to move through other planes of existence, other dimensions," he said. "You could enter what we call the spirit world. That's why the guardian relics are so extraordinary." Master Tayshin again puffed on his pipe, smacking his dry lips. "Any other special powers your dagger might possess are up to you to discover, as Tobias and Demetrius have with the compass."

Arianna feigned writing out a list.

"And yet another mystery awaits," she said, rolling her eyes. "But wait, when you say a different world… do you mean to say that I could *travel* to somewhere other than Olleb-Yelfra?"

She squeezed her eyes shut to try to picture what that might even look like—she couldn't wrap her head around it.

"In a way, *yes*, but in many ways… no." He chuckled. "I suppose that didn't make sense."

Arianna moaned in frustration. There were too many riddles to decipher from those she deemed masters. She and her friends had gained an impressive amount of Golden Age knowledge by now, but she couldn't help but wonder on occasion if the elders sipped from some magical potion just to learn something new to confuse them with later.

"Not especially," she replied with a bite to her tone.

He scooted closer to her, tapping his temple.

"Think of your mind when you dream," he said. "It never sleeps, even when your eyes are closed, so drifting through dreams, your mind becomes connected to what's called your 'astral' body. That's why sometimes when you sleep you might find yourself in worlds quite alike yet very different from the one you know when your eyes are open."

He gestured to the gardens.

"A world that your physical body could never enter, never even *find*. A dream, a nightmare… they can at times transport you from this very world and into another without you even knowing. And when you wake," he waved his hands over his eyes as if lifting a veil, "you're right back where you began, the memory of your unintended astral journey fading away just as quickly."

"I've had quite a few vivid dreams and nightmares before," said Arianna, thoughtfully. "I certainly learned to pay attention to them over the years. Sometimes they just seem so real, but I never thought—"

"I'm not at all surprised," said Master Tayshin, matter-of-factly, "since you're so spiritually connected."

Arianna wondered how he'd drawn that conclusion but didn't want to ask any more questions until she fully understood the answer to the first one.

"I feel as if I've had this chat before," Master Tayshin mused to himself. "Solomon was a similar creature. It's no wonder he took a liking to you."

He nodded to the dagger.

"With the precious stones of aura and ora in your possession, you can control your destination within the realm of the astral plane, take charge of the entire experience without worry of losing the memory when you wake. Think of it like *controlling* your dreams—"

He snapped his fingers, and Arianna thought for a second they might transport to the moon.

"You could go anywhere in this world or another," he said. "It's a rare piece of magic to allow your consciousness to pass through realms unattainable to the heavy flesh of a human body. Alas, without the armor of your skeleton, just remember, your fragile mind becomes even more vulnerable."

"It doesn't seem possible," said Arianna with a bemused chuckle.

"What doesn't seem possible?" Master Tayshin barked—Arianna was reminded of Syrifina's short temper. "You've already attained such journeys in your dreams, so what if you could control them? It's not without hard work, of course, but you have the stones. You're halfway there!"

He visibly relaxed, and Arianna thought he just enjoyed being loud sometimes.

"Elves could attempt astral journey without such conduits to aid their magic," he added, "but it's a fine craft to master for any sorcerer or sorceress. It may take you years to get the hang of."

Arianna felt a headache coming on. "I thought giants were the only other creatures to deal with the magic of the mind?"

"Giants were revered for their skill in *one* form of mind magic, but astral projection is yet another, one that takes a mastering of many forms of magic to be truly successful. It's a combination of sorcery, elemental, and mind magic that a giant couldn't possibly achieve," said Master Tayshin. "For a novice witch, however, there are two sure ways to begin."

Arianna scoffed. *Novice...*

She knew he was waiting for her to query further, and she played right into his hand, too curious to know more not to. "How? I want to learn, Master." She forced herself to remain polite.

Master Tayshin tried to hide his amusement—he just loved to remind her how much she still had yet to grow.

"Then I shall teach you," he said a little too cheerfully. "To begin, you can engulf yourself in a warm body of water to help suppress all the senses from your physical self..."

A mischievous grin grew wide across his face.

"*Or* you can have a smoke."

"I see..." said Arianna, raising an eyebrow at him. "And how would either of these things help now?"

"*Sensorial depriva tempe*," said Master Tayshin, seeming to savor the phrase.

From just the way the words sort of chimed as he spoke, Arianna knew it was another spell to commit to memory.

"If you prepare properly by dulling your human senses enough, this spell can give your consciousness temporary freedom from the prison of your body until you master it naturally," he said. "The magic from the stones will permit you to travel and help you find your way back should you stray."

His brow furrowed with seriousness.

"Until you fully master astral projection, *never* try it without that blade on your skin, girl. If you're not careful, your soul could be lost forever."

"All right..." said Arianna, trying her best to follow. "But I'm still not clear as to where I'd be going, or why, exactly. And I only need open my eyes to get there?" She shook her head. "It doesn't quite make sense."

"It will never fully make sense until you experience it," said Master Tayshin.

He shifted his attention to one of the glass walls across the lake and moved his hand back and forth. With it, the starry sand behind the wall seemed to swirl like a vortex to a different world—far away and unreachable, yet so enthralling that Arianna couldn't look away.

"Time and space work differently without a physical body," said Master Tayshin. "You need a strong bond with whatever it is you're looking for. And remember, you'll be shifting through planes, other dimensions foreign to you."

He closed his fist, and the sand abruptly stopped swirling, releasing Arianna from her trance.

"No matter the lure, don't linger in a world not your own. You'll not be welcomed, and the longer you stay, the more susceptible you'll become to malevolent spirits."

"Where would I even want to go besides here?" she asked. "I've fought Death enough times already to know that I'm not interested in going anywhere else."

Master Tayshin shook his head.

"This isn't *anything* like dying," he said. "It's a glimpse of a different type of living." He looked up, catching her gaze. "The afterlife, for instance, is a place this magic could allow you to visit."

Arianna felt her heart quicken. "Trust me, I don't want to go back there," she whispered, recalling the boundless blackness she'd experienced in death—that *had* to be the afterlife. "Although, I do think I understand a little better what you mean… maybe."

Her mind wandered to Liam, toward the light that had guided her back to this world for yet another chance at life.

"There's also the past." He grabbed her wrist in that moment, as if to squeeze his lesson into her bones; she jumped a little in surprise. "Don't bother trying to change it. It won't work," he said sternly. "Better to focus on how your decisions at present could affect the future."

He released his grip.

"I don't want to go back to the past," said Arianna, closing her mind to the consuming thoughts of all the things she might have done differently in her life. "There's nothing left for me there."

She studied the dagger with all this new knowledge stirring in her mind, starting to get that thrum of excitement in her chest again—it was always there to greet her after a magical discovery. Arianna couldn't wait to tell the others what the guardian compass and ring truly represented.

"So… the blade has to remain on my skin—"

"Or the ethereal body could be doomed to wander another dimension forever, lost with no guidance back," said Master Tayshin, relaxing a bit as she started to grasp today's lesson in magic. "Aura and ora stones merged together act like a beacon of light in the spirit worlds, calling you home when you're ready. Reminding you of where you belong. And when your astral form takes control, the stones also act as a layer of protection to your physical self. No harm can come to your human body, and no other spirit may enter its shell."

Arianna shivered, recalling how the ghost of Damon had so easily taken control of General Ivo's body, possessing him to do his bidding—and in that case, she was sure the general's spirit, though blackened with hate, had still been in there to put up a fight.

Her body would be even more vulnerable without her soul to protect it; she ran her hands up and down her arms, as if to lock her spirit inside safely forever.

"I understand," said Arianna, nodding. "There's only been one time when this dagger has left my side, and I've never let that happen again."

She remembered it like yesterday, the terrible feeling of losing the dagger to the bottom of her beloved hot springs; before they were family, they were strangers, and Lessa Thur had gained the upper hand when they'd each raised their weapons against one another, fearing the unknown. Fortunately, though, the ghost girl of the Vanishing Tunnels had promptly returned her treasure, fate intertwining their lives forevermore.

"The spirit world has latched onto you in more ways than you know," said Master Tayshin, eyeing her suspiciously as Arianna delved into her memories. "Now, let's see how well *you* take to it."

"What do you—"

Master Tayshin took another big inhale from his pipe, and then he blew out a cloud of smoke that engulfed them both. It smelled of something sweet and sticky, and Arianna choked on it as she inhaled.

Through the fog, she could see his lips moving.

"*Sensorial depriva tempe.*" His voice felt far away as he whispered the spell, its magic all-consuming.

Arianna's mind spun, seeming to sink into itself.

"Remember, don't linger long!" Master Tayshin called out. "It won't do you any good to dwell."

AS THE SMOKE HUNG IN THE AIR, suddenly that's all there was—a watery, gray cloud that became the present. Strangely though, Arianna didn't feel lost nor scared like she had when Death had tried to keep her in the afterlife. She felt completely uninhibited as an inexplicable weight was lifted from her.

It was so much easier to move without the burden of her

heavy body dragging her down, the feeling exhilarating as she resisted the urge to float away into the abyss.

Then the smoke lifted; she could see.

Though she had considered her reflection many times before, struggling with understanding who the real Arianna was, she knew that the girl she looked upon now wasn't just a reflection—it was quite literally *her*.

She finally had the chance to see what others saw when they looked at her.

And though Arianna knew that she suddenly held this power to go anywhere in the world in this astral form, or even worlds beyond, all she could do was gaze upon this sleeping, peaceful version of herself to try to understand her better.

She noticed her dagger, too, still grasped tightly in hand. Just as Master Tayshin had promised, a beacon of brilliant, white light radiated from it to guide her spirit home when she proved ready. And just in case, he sat protectively nearby, smoking his pipe all the while.

Taking this all in, she smiled—or rather, she felt her spirit do something like smile—because even without a sword and without a soul, Arianna Belvedor still looked strong.

UNDONE

A SCREAM IN THE MIDDLE OF THE NIGHT started it all, hurled them back to a state of chaos. Still in her night clothes with her cloak pulled on in haste, Arianna burst into the main garden with Solza and Demetrius right behind her. The lake ran red with blood, and Jeom stood near someone's still body in the grass, the Axe of Crissy in hand.

"Jeom!" she cried, fear overtaking her as she looked on in horror. "What's happened to you…"

Demetrius gasped, covering his mouth with one hand. His other gripped his staff; Arianna was so thankful in this moment that he'd at least thought to collect his weapon.

I should have grabbed my swords.

Tobias was lying on the ground at Jeom's feet, fatally wounded and on his last breath by the looks of it; Jeom had his back to them, slowly pacing by the edge of the water as if deep in thought.

As soon as the way to Tobias was clear, Arianna ran to his aid. She dropped to her knees by his side, calling out for Lessa, hoping she would hear—she had still been fast asleep when they'd followed the sound of the screams.

"It's going to be all right," she said, trembling as she lifted his head into her lap, his hat falling to the side. "Tobias, no."

She couldn't help the whimper that came out of her as she realized how much blood had been spilled. It spread out around them in what seemed like a never-ending pool, his small body feeling cold in her arms. She looked up at Demetrius with pleading eyes, unsure of what to do.

Demetrius couldn't hold back his tears as he observed his dying friend too, someone they'd all grown close to in these past months. He forced himself to address his brother.

"How could you have done this?" he demanded, stepping toward him. Jeom didn't move nor even acknowledge his words. "Look at me!"

He turned around slowly, his head bowed low so that his face was not visible. Still, he said nothing.

Demetrius and Arianna awaited an answer—something clearly wasn't right.

"I said look at me, Jeom!"

At this, he lifted his eyes to his brother; Demetrius was momentarily taken aback.

Arianna understood his confusion, for Jeom's eyes seemed oddly empty, like maybe he could be sleepwalking. He ran toward Demetrius, swinging his axe dangerously close to him.

Arianna was so caught off guard that the only reaction she could muster was her mouth dropping open in surprise, frozen as Demetrius dodged out of harm's way.

"Are you out of your mind?" she yelled from the floor. "Stop this, now!" She looked down to Tobias. "I'll be back in a moment, all right? Lessa will be here to heal you soon. Hang on, Tobias."

He couldn't even find the strength to answer as she gently laid his head back to the ground.

Arianna called again for their healer, for anyone to help. She got to her feet, intending to put an end to this nightmare; without her swords to lean on, she turned to her magic, careful of what came to mind so she didn't fatally hurt Jeom.

"*Levantis bora*," she said, attempting to charm the Axe of Crissy from his hands at a safe distance.

She could see Jeom resisting the magic, struggling to keep a grip on the weapon—the axe began to glow an ominous red, and Arianna was flung off her feet. It was as if her spell had ricocheted off the axe's defensive magic; she found herself right back on the ground next to Tobias.

Jeom aimed his weapon at Arianna now.

Solza didn't hesitate to attack to protect her master. She sprang into the air, paws outstretched and teeth bared, but Jeom was ready for her.

He swung the axe with determination, the air churning menacingly as some type of wind magic formed from the action, stretching out like a wall at his front. Solza whined in pain as she collided with the enchanted barrier, smashing to the ground.

"Solza!" called Arianna. "Stay there, girl. It'll be all right. We can handle him."

Arianna had never seen the Axe of Crissy produce such magic before. It was much more powerful than they'd known...

She wondered if its peculiar magic could somehow be messing with Jeom's mind.

"Have you gone mad? Just put the axe down, Jeom," said Demetrius, glancing back toward Arianna. She signaled that she was all right as they both exchanged looks of pure panic. "Let's talk about this."

Jeom stood in his path, gripping the Axe of Crissy with a ferocity unlike anything he'd ever shown before, his knuckles turning white and his muscles shaking with effort. His stare appeared hazy, as if a cloud of smoke enveloped his eyes, and Arianna thought she'd seen such a look before.

This all felt too familiar—she tried to grasp onto some kind of explanation, one that she was certain her past memories could unlock. The answer was *just* out of reach.

"Demetrius, be careful," she stuttered as General Ivo inexplicably floated to the forefront of her mind. "I… I don't think we're dealing with Jeom anymore."

"What are you talking about?" he whispered, not taking his eyes off his brother. "He won't hurt me. I know he won't."

Jeom still hadn't uttered a word, but in response to Arianna's remark he had returned a sickening smile.

She suddenly knew exactly why General Ivo had popped into her head—a human under the possession of a *ghost* would not be able to speak.

And his deadened gaze was a sure sign that something supernatural had taken control of Jeom's body… just like Damon had done to General Ivo long ago.

But she'd understood too late.

As Demetrius tried to reason with Jeom, the warrior in Arianna snapped into action. She got back to her feet and ran toward them without a second thought.

"No, it's not him," she screamed, waving her arms. "That's *not* your brother, Demetrius. Watch out!"

As her thought formed to words, Jeom was already swinging the axe; Demetrius barely had time to lift his weapon and defend himself, stunned that Jeom would really attack.

Before Arianna could even attempt to call on her magic again to protect him, the axe had cut clean through the wood of Demetrius' staff—and then it cut clean through his leg.

Arianna felt as if her heart had been ripped from her chest, stopping cold in her tracks at witnessing such a horrendous scene. A sharp inhale piercing her lungs.

All she could do was watch.

Demetrius hit the ground hard, his face contorted in pain. It was the first time, she realized, she had heard him scream, a sound that wouldn't be easily forgotten.

It was so full of pain.

He writhed on the floor, hands shaking violently as he squeezed at his thigh to try to find some relief.

Jeom lifted the axe to strike again.

"Jeom, don't! *Please*, you'll kill him," said Arianna, trying desperately to summon her magic.

This time, it didn't come at all, unable to even escape her mind—something, or someone, was intentionally blocking it.

As Jeom advanced, towering over his defenseless brother, Demetrius put his hand up, crying out for him to stop. Arianna thought that surely this would be the last moment of his life.

Jeom raised his weapon high above his head with the intent to kill. He brought the axe down swiftly, leaving no room for even an expression of remorse.

As Arianna waited for the inevitable end, a shield of what could only be powerful magic grew between the two brothers, preventing the fatal blow to Demetrius and knocking Jeom off his feet; he slammed against the tree, and the axe fell away from his hand.

Arianna was astounded. *Does Demetrius foster powers of his own?*

She didn't have a moment to question it, wasting no time to try to subdue Jeom.

She straddled him before he could get back up, grabbing his hands by the wrists to keep him down. He was strong, much stronger than her, but when he tried to fight her off, a silver light began to radiate from her palms.

"What magic is this?" she breathed, feeling it tug from somewhere deep down inside of her—it was unlike what she'd tried to call to before.

Whatever it was, she held on tight, concentrating as best she could to release this untapped power.

Jeom cried out in such a way that Arianna knew her touch agonized him—it was the first sound he'd made since they'd confronted him. As if the real Jeom was trying to break free, his voice filled the Greenhouse, booming off the glass walls.

She had no idea where this magic came from or what it was capable of, just as surprised by it as Jeom seemed to be, but her intuition recognized it as warm and welcome—she trusted it. And right now, it was the only thing that appeared to stand a chance against Jeom and the Axe of Crissy.

In the next moment, just as she had suspected, the ghost of an unknown woman was abruptly forced out from his body. When she was free of him, Jeom passed out.

Arianna stood to confront his possessor.

"I'm sorry! I didn't want to," said the woman, in hysterics. "I couldn't fight his control. Thank you, thank you for releasing me. You're my savior."

The ghost floated toward the top of the Greenhouse, disappearing in a crackle of light before any further explanation could be drawn from her.

Arianna hadn't realized she'd been holding her breath all this time, an instant wave of relief washing over her as the ghost vacated her friend. But it was quickly replaced by dread—the damage had already been done.

The ghost may have passed on, merely a pawn in the King's game of life, but clearly he was still winning.

"This has to be Vladamor's doing. He's here somewhere, hiding," she said to herself.

Arianna kept her attention to the ceiling for just another few seconds, fixated on the enchanted Greenhouse flame; she was terrified to face the horrifying things that would enter her line of sight should she lower her gaze.

Eventually, she forced herself to focus back on her friends, silent tears streaming down her cheeks.

"By gods, what happened here?" shrieked Lessa, finally coming into the gardens with Sano beating her to the horrific scene. "Was that… did I just see a *ghost?*"

Arianna nodded, but now wasn't the time to explain.

"I don't know how, but I think I did some kind of magic to release her from Vladamor's hold, like in the desert," said Arianna. "She hadn't wanted to possess him. It was necromancy, I know it! But I couldn't stop Jeom before…" She choked on her words. "Les, just hurry or we'll lose them both!"

This seemed to snap Lessa into action.

"My leg, my leg," whimpered Demetrius, reaching toward his severed limb in the grass.

It had been completely separated from his body.

Arianna briefly wondered if she hadn't accidentally traveled to the past during her astral journey lesson with Master Tayshin, thrust back into her Warrior's District days, wandering around the Dueling Arena on a particularly nasty training morning before a Free Falls Festival. She'd seen this kind of thing before, was used to it even. But this was *Demetrius*, her gentle, light-hearted friend, not some stranger from the Jar she could bury in her past with all her other traumatizing memories.

It didn't seem real.

"All right, honey, don't panic," said Lessa, dropping to her knees at his side and cradling him in her arms. "Everything is going to be fine."

Arianna went to wait with Tobias, feeling her magic return to her much too late.

"He's losing so much blood," called Lessa, forcing Demetrius to lie still. "Sano, quickly! There isn't much time."

Sano placed his shining paws upon Demetrius' leg above the open wound; his skin immediately began to stitch together.

When Sano's healing magic had run its course, a striking silver swath of skin replaced where Demetrius' knee would normally be—only now, there was nothing below. His wound had healed like a beautiful cap of metal, twisted onto his skin to hold him together.

Sadly, there was no way to really see the beauty in this magic when focused on such sudden and severe loss; Demetrius was overcome with disbelief.

"No, no, no!" he cried, his hands blood-drenched as he felt through the air where his leg used to exist.

He couldn't even bear to look.

"Lessa, *please*, you have to fix it," he begged, his face pale.

Arianna thought he might pass out at any moment.

He clutched at Lessa's robes in desperation, his normally happy, shining eyes now swimming in sorrow.

"You have to fix my leg!" His hand hovered over the bloodied mess of his former limb.

"I… I *can't*," she said, hugging him to her chest. "I'm so sorry, but you would've died. You were losing too much blood. I'm sorry, Demetrius. I wish I could, but I can't do anything about it now."

"No," he shouted. "Get off me. No!" But his grip only tightened, his arms locked around her as she hugged him back as hard as she could, trying to keep her tears inside so he had the room to shed his own.

"Why would he do this to me? He's my… he's my brother. *Why?*"

"Hush now," said Lessa, stroking his hair as she tried to calm him. "It's going to be all right. We'll figure this out."

She glanced in Arianna's direction for an explanation, but there were no words.

"The King," said Tobias, blood sputtering from his lips. "He desires the Axe of Crissy."

"But why go through all this trouble for an axe?" said Arianna, eyebrows knitted in confusion.

Tobias grabbed her hand and squeezed hard.

"Because it's power," he said. "And he's afraid of you." He

locked eyes with her, and she didn't dare blink. "Survive, Arianna, and he'll continue to lose his power. Just… survive."

With that, his body went completely limp and the last of his breath left his lungs.

"No! Hang on, Tobias. Don't leave us," she said, sobbing. "Lessa, he's dying. Have Sano heal him too!"

Lessa gazed to the ceiling, as if the answers might be written there—all the while Demetrius crumbled in her arms and Tobias in Arianna's.

"Sano won't have the strength now. He'll be too drained," she choked out. "Healing magic takes so much energy. If I just had some of my potions."

She looked longingly toward their sleeping quarters.

Arianna took a deep breath, forcing herself to look upon Tobias one last time. "It doesn't matter now," she said, solemnly. "It's too late. He's already gone."

She gently closed his eyes and placed his hat back on his head so that he looked more at peace, like he could be sleeping.

"Rest in paradise, my friend," she said through the tears.

Solza made her way back over now that it was safe, and Arianna clung to her for support. Sano remained close to Lessa.

Seconds later, Master Tayshin and Talis burst out from a side corridor and into the main gardens with the other guardians racing behind them.

"What's going on? We heard shouting," said Master Tayshin, clutching his sword as he took in the horrific scene.

"Oh no… Tobias," murmured Cyn, hand flying over her mouth. She clutched Sergios' arm.

"Not here," said Rowina, going rigid.

Talis kneeled down next to him to check for a pulse, but Arianna shook her head, looking away.

"There was nothing we could do," she muttered, tears again welling. "When we got here, he was already… we couldn't—"

"I understand," he said, forcing her to look at him. "It's not your fault, Arianna. You didn't set this fate upon him."

She felt hands helping her up from the ground—Eli was there, supporting her to stand.

"Are you all right?" he asked, looking her over for injuries.

"Not in the slightest," said Arianna.

The elder guardians began to swarm the main gardens, singing incantations meant to secure their sanctuary from whatever evil was trying to get in and doing what they could for Jeom and Demetrius.

"Master Tayshin," Arianna called across the gardens. "It's Sir Vladamor. I know he's behind this."

He gave a curt nod of understanding.

"Our location has been compromised," he stated, gravely. "Solomon surely found a way to lead the Shadow Resistance here despite our precautions."

"We should all get to the ship," said Margery. "Now's a good time to put it to the test."

Arianna couldn't believe that only yesterday she had confronted the elder guardians about the secret dragon ship on the shores, also confiding in them her idea of returning to the Four Corners. In a moment of solidarity, they'd agreed to consider the proposal and had given her and her friends the courtesy of explaining their intentions behind the creation of the magically endowed vessel—it had begun to feel like everything was headed in the right direction, everyone all on the same page about the future.

Alas, once again, the future had been set on fire with no clear way to see through the smoke.

"Quick, through the tunnels then," said Vance. "Let's go!"

"Eli, lead the way to the beach entrance. I know you know where it is," said Talis. "And someone help the girls with Jeom and Demetrius!"

Lessa and Arianna shared only a glance before shouting in unison, "*Levantis bora!*"

Jeom and Demetrius rose into the air.

"We don't need any help," said Lessa.

"But somebody grab our weapons and our things," added Arianna, concentrating on the magic. "I don't think we'll be coming back for them."

She saw Cyn racing back toward their quarters.

As the Kane brothers, both unconscious, floated eerily above them, Arianna thought they looked like broken versions of the young men she knew to be strong.

The Guardians of Gold had been thrown into a panic, trying to organize themselves quickly for whatever evil surely awaited them outside of these walls. And with Tobias dead and Demetrius mutilated, another guardian safety net had been ripped apart, snatching from them much more than just a luxurious refuge this time—they were no longer welcome in the City of Zambienth, and she wasn't sure if there was anywhere left in the world they could run to before King Devlindor finally got what he wanted.

AFTER HASTILY GATHERING their most precious belongings and preparing for a fight, the occupants of the Greenhouse all rushed outside to the beach using the secret entrance that Arianna had only just learned about.

Keeper Yahindi was there with a crew of city regulators.

Guess the secret's out…

Arianna searched their faces and, to her horror, saw that several of them were not just any regulators—she recognized many from the mind magic memory where they'd witnessed the slaughter of the giants.

Though they were much older now, she was certain that these were the faces of the Shadow Resistance. They'd come to do the

King's bidding with Keeper Yahindi in the lead, but Arianna knew who really pulled the strings.

"Solomon must have tipped her off!" shouted Gabriel, readying a bow and arrow.

"Prepare yourselves," said Iris, gripping a two-headed axe as the other guardians followed her lead. "I've been waiting for this for a long time."

A deafening battle of both magic and metal began mere seconds later, the waves crashing behind them as if a terrible melody to underscore their fight. Now with her swords in her hands, at least Arianna could defend herself.

She cut through hordes of regulators and shadows, trying to carve a safe path for Jeom and Demetrius, who still floated in the air.

The guardian ship seemed so close, yet so far away, as they all battled to reach it. Every time they drew nearer, more regulators would show up, and Shadow Resistance followers crawled down the cliffs in swarms to block their way.

Arianna began to feel her energy wane—she and Lessa didn't have the strength to keep holding the boys up with the levitation spell and battle at the same time.

As if hearing her thoughts, Eli was already racing toward them on the back of his horse. He came to a halt at their front and hopped off.

"Set Demetrius down on his back," he said. "He needs Phantom more than we do right now."

Arianna gave him a nod of appreciation. "It's a good thing Phantom was close by again."

"Somehow he always is," said Eli, giving him a strong pat on the side before throwing himself back into the fight.

The girls gently laid Demetrius down across the horse. Jeom, though, was accidentally dropped on the ground without so much finesse—he jolted awake.

"Protect your brother," said Lessa before rushing forward to battle another regulator. She swung her bow to her back and tackled him to the ground, fighting him there until he fell still.

Arianna ran forward, too, battling a regulator who clearly had no powers to show. And though the woman was strong and swift with her attacks, Arianna was better. Not to mention, she had magic on her side.

She felt the tip of her sword rest at the woman's steel breastplate, but armor wouldn't be enough to stop this weapon or this warrior with magic in her eyes. With the jeweled hilt of her sword gripped firmly in her palm, Arianna remembered some of Solomon's last words to her before he had turned to the dark.

'If you let them, they may teach you something special.'

And in this moment, they truly did.

Magic she had once only been able to conjure with her hands became echoed within her blades—she'd somehow reached a new level as a young sorceress, finally tapped into a power she'd always known was there, waiting to be grasped.

Her sword cut straight through the regulator's steel and into her flesh.

The woman's eyes went wide with confusion as she began to cough up blood, and Arianna had a sick feeling she hadn't even known what magic was; the Shadow Resistance elders here were definitely in the know, but she expected that there must be countless regulators upholding the King's laws who had not even an inkling of the enchanted side of Olleb-Yelfra they fought to suppress, mind magic probably aiding in keeping them ignorant.

Down with the King!

She ripped her arm back, her blade coming with it, and the woman fell dead at her feet. She moved on to the next, no time to stop and lament on who might be innocent or not—they were sorely outnumbered.

Master Tayshin, Talis, Iris, Rowina, Cyn, and Vance were gathered a little farther down the beach, doing their best to defend the guardian ship so they could escape. And Lessa, Gabriel, and Margery sent arrow after arrow to try to keep the battle at bay. Arianna kept Lessa in her sights, fighting alongside Eli, Nico, and Sergios—all trying to reach the ship as well.

As the battle raged on, Arianna felt her magic wane until hardly anything would pull to the surface without her exerting extraordinary energy; she kept Solza close, sensing her avatar was feeling out of sorts as well. Something was weakening her powers again, but at least this time she had her swords.

She tried to concentrate fully on the chaos around her with her magic at odds, but her ears kept ringing with Jeom's frantic voice coming from behind.

"I'm sorry, brother! I didn't mean to," she heard him say to Demetrius as he used his axe to protect him from the onslaught. "Please, *please* forgive me for this. I can never atone."

Arianna glanced over her shoulder and found Demetrius still unconscious, Jeom leading him and Phantom a safe distance away from the battle toward the water.

She wanted so badly to help her boys, but she couldn't focus on them now. Their enemies were closing in—she needed her magic to come.

She looked to her hands. *Why won't it come?*

Arianna felt as if it was clogged at the surface of her mind, being suppressed by something strong, just the same as when she was trying to stop Jeom in the Greenhouse.

"Can you do anything?" she called to Lessa.

"No! Something keeps blocking me." She had to scream over the madness to be heard, peeling an arrow back and letting it fly; their tips were no longer doused in magical flame. "Sano, stay close!"

They both beckoned their avatars to keep near, forced to battle toward the ship the traditional way.

Alas, they were beginning to falter under the magic and combat skill of the Shadow Resistance.

"There's too many of them," called Talis from down the

beach as he swung his sword, seeming to struggle under a younger regulator's strength. "You have to get out of here. The King has brought war!"

"The Shadow Resistance must be jamming our magical connections somehow," said Master Tayshin. "We can't win this way. Everyone, fall back. Ara, take your friends and run!"

"No, we won't leave you," she said, trying to cut her way toward them.

"You have to! You have to survive," shouted Cyn, fighting alongside Vance and Rowina.

Arianna's mouth dropped open as she watched her gentle caretaker kill a regulator on her own, a slender sword in hand. She couldn't help but think that Solomon must've taught her a trick or two just for such occasions.

Gabriel had at some point slipped away in the madness to help Jeom. They had dug out the boat that had first brought them to Zambienth, pushing it back out onto the water with Demetrius and even Phantom loaded safely inside.

"Over here!" they called, waving to the girls. But there was a wall of regulators and Shadow Resistance to knock down, splintering them off. "We can't hold them much longer."

Jeom slammed against another poor soul with the Axe of Crissy as Gabriel defended his other side. And Eli started carving his way through as best he could, trying to clear a path for Lessa and Arianna to reach the water.

"Talis, look out!" she heard Master Tayshin yell from across the battlegrounds.

Without magic to aid him, Talis was reduced to an old man with not nearly as much practical dueling experience as the rest of them; Arianna watched in shock as the keeper's sword pinned him through the middle to the cliff at his back, as if he were nothing but thin air.

Iris slammed against Keeper Yahindi with her axe, fighting her way to him, but it was too late. Talis' fate had been sealed.

Arianna looked back, locking fearful eyes with Jeom.

"Lessa, don't!" he shouted at the top of his lungs.

But there was nothing anyone could do to stop her as she ran back the other way—away from safety.

"Talis!" screamed Lessa, racing toward him.

They had been so close to reaching the water, to having a chance at escaping with Jeom, Demetrius, and Gabriel. But if it had been Solomon, before he'd given up faith, Arianna would've done the same thing.

"I'll go after her," she said, gesturing for Jeom to wait. "If you have to leave without us, go! We'll make it to the ship and find you later." She could feel Eli at her heels, not willing to leave her side as they battled their way toward Talis—Lessa was farther ahead, ruthless to anyone who tried to get in her path.

Master Tayshin stopped her just before she reached her dying master, grasping her by the shoulders.

"There's nothing you can do for him now," he said, practically lifting her off her feet. "You *have* to get out of here."

"I won't! Get off me," said Lessa, whipping an arrow on him so fast that he jumped back.

She shoved past him, running to Talis.

"Master, I won't lose you like this," she said, frantic. "I can help. Sano, hurry!"

Talis let out a loud moan of pain, clutching the sword that still pinned him upright to the wall; Sano placed his paws upon the wound but nothing happened.

"I think we have to get the blade out first," said Lessa.

"Les… you know that won't work," said Arianna, reaching her side. "You said it yourself, Sano's too tired. It took an immense amount of magic to heal Demetrius. And with the block on our magic…" She shook her head, solemnly, her heart breaking as she did.

"But we must help him, Ara," she said as Master Tayshin joined them.

"Talis, old friend," said Master Tayshin, gently grasping his hand. "I'm sorry I was too late."

"You've never had good timing," Talis said, coughing.

"I've failed you again," he said, bowing his head, unable to meet his eyes. "I can't lose another apprentice."

Talis grasped Master Tayshin's hand.

"Look at me," he demanded, seeming to choke on every word. "Master, you gave me magic. You gave me freedom, and you brought hope to my world when there was none." His blue gaze flicked to the girls. "They *will* survive this, and you'll guide them to their freedom too… all of them."

He touched eyes with each of the guardians—all hovering around him now.

Keeper Yahindi took this chance to regroup her warriors.

"Oh, Master Churry, no. Please, don't do this!" cried Lessa, burying her face in his cloak.

Talis smiled down at her, his eyes twinkling. "You're so bright, child. Don't you remember what I told you?"

She shook her head, hardly able to speak.

"You'll always find the answers if only you remember to—"

"Keep faith… even during the darkest of hours," she finished.

Talis tilted her chin up so she had to hold her head high. "Lessa, you have such a light in you that I know you'll stay strong, even long after I'm gone. You've given me so much to live for, truly have made me proud."

He sucked in a deep breath, trying to hide his pain from her. But she could see it in his eyes. They all could.

"In all my dreams, I never thought the little troublemaker I raised into a proper healer would also turn out to be a proper witch and a Guardian of Gold."

"I wouldn't be anything without you, Talis." She sobbed. "*Please*, don't go. Let us help you."

She looked around to the elders, but nobody moved.

"There, there," he said, patting her back. He looked to Arianna and whispered, "You take good care of her, you hear? She can't always do the healing."

"Yes, sir," said Arianna, her voice cracking—then she tried to pull Lessa from him at his signal.

"Master, *please* don't say goodbye like this," she cried.

Arianna looked over her shoulder and saw that the rest of the group had slipped back into fighting furiously in order to protect them while they tried to comfort Talis; Jeom and Gabriel were still protecting Demetrius from the waves and warriors trying to kill them from every angle.

"Lessa, I want you to forget this moment," said Talis, so much sorrow in his expression.

"What do you mean?" she said.

Talis' eyes flicked to Master Tayshin, who was still by their side, guarding them.

"No!" Lessa's shoulders shook as she wept tears onto him still. "No, I can't. Please, don't make me forget. I *won't* forget you."

Master Tayshin looked uncertain. "Talis, I—"

"*Jon,*" said Talis, pleading with him. "She needs to. Do it now. She's not strong enough yet. The mermaids took a toll on her mind, and this pain will distract her." Talis glanced at Arianna. "They can't afford any more distractions. Not now."

"But my magic is blocked," he said, shaking his head.

"You *can* reach it. It's always there for you. No one could ever fully take away someone else's magic," said Talis. "You know that. You just need to concentrate."

"Don't you dare," said Lessa, snapping at Master Tayshin, an arrow pointed at him before Arianna could even blink. "I will *never* forget!"

"Do you want to live?" Talis choked out, drawing her focus back to him. "Because we need you to live. We're so close to the end." Arianna felt Talis' eyes lock on her. "She has to forget, or she won't survive this moment. I know it."

It was then that Arianna understood. She knew what grief could do to a person, and if she had a chance to postpone that pain for Lessa until this fight was far behind them, she would take it. In one swift move, she got the bow away from Lessa and pinned her to the ground, though she struggled against her.

"I will never forgive you for this, Arianna!" she screamed.

"Yes, you will," she replied, softly. "I'm sorry, but I won't lose you again too."

Master Tayshin placed his hands on Lessa's temples and forced her to forget Talis' death, screaming out in concentration to try to overcome whatever suppressive magic kept them from wielding their powers. And as Arianna stood idly by during Talis' last moments of life and Lessa's loss of memory, she saw in the distance the golden glint of Jeom's axe—he, Demetrius, and Gabriel bounced along the waves away from the shores of Zambienth, the regulators storming up the beach behind them.

"May we meet again," she whispered—she and Jeom locked eyes one last time.

"Survive," she saw him mouth back.

A thundering explosion drew her attention next, the night sky coming alive in a burst of fire. She looked up and saw that the regulators had set fire to their only other getaway, the golden dragon vessel.

"The ship," she said, staggered by the force of the fire, the heat choking the air.

"Arianna!" snapped Master Tayshin. "It's done. I'm going to take out the sword now." Talis was on his last breath.

She couldn't bear to watch… but she gave him the respect that he deserved and did anyway.

The sound of metal leaving flesh somehow steadied her spiraling thoughts, focused them. *Kill the King!*

It was a sound that Arianna had never quite grown used to in the districts; it still sent chills up her spine.

When Master Tayshin had fully removed the weapon from

Talis, she knew that his soul had abandoned his battered body. She just hoped with a heavy heart that it had gone somewhere far away and peaceful, where the sounds of battle could not reach.

Arianna turned reluctantly to Lessa to see the outcome of Master Tayshin's magic—her friend met her with a blank stare, the memory of her beloved master's death surely gone, for the moment at least.

But Talis had been right. They didn't have the time for such grief now, not if they wanted to live. It seemed like their whole world was crumbling as life handed them one chaos after another, and tears were not going to get them through it.

Their next actions would be crucial in survival, and there was no more rest ahead of them—King Devlindor had brought his army to their doorstep before the guardians had even the chance to gather their own, so they needed to survive this horrible night and find one fast.

"You were my best apprentice in magic," said Master Tayshin, gently closing Talis' eyes and laying his body to the sand. "Until we meet again, old friend."

His voice cracked on the last word as he stood back up. Then he turned around to face Arianna.

"You must go," he said, his face shadowed with concern.

"Where can—" she stuttered.

"For once in your life, just listen to me, girl!" he shouted. "I've spent these last few months spreading word of you, of our resistance. We all have. The time is now! It's here, and it's all because of you, of *your* faith and your fight." He pointed his sword at her. "And if people will follow your lead, if the Guardians of Gold are to follow you to freedom, then you can't die here! So get somewhere safe, anywhere, and do a better job at this than I did. I'll see you again soon… I hope."

He turned to Eli, placing a hand on his shoulder.

"Look out for them, son. They're the future, and it's in your hands now."

"Yes, Master Tayshin," he said, standing taller. "I won't let you down."

"You stay alive too, Jon," said Arianna, resigned to watch him go, to watch others risk their lives for them to live.

"That's 'Master' to you," he said, narrowing his gaze at her as if in scolding—then he lifted a fist to his chest, affirming his allegiance.

"For now and always," she said, returning the gesture as confidently as she could.

Master Tayshin jumped right back into battle, doing his utmost to ensure the rest of the guardians would live to see tomorrow. But Arianna didn't miss the shimmer of tears glinting in his eyes, one last look saying all the proper goodbyes that she needed.

Never forget.

"Come on, let's go," said Eli, grasping Lessa's hand to help her along; she seemed disoriented. "We have to find another way out of here."

"Solza, Sano, stay close to us," said Arianna, following along the cliff in Eli's footsteps.

"We'll go back through the secret tunnel and find another way out of the city," he said.

"Not so fast," whispered a voice from behind as they came upon the tunnel entrance.

A figure stepped out from the shadows.

"Keeper Yahindi," growled Arianna, moving Lessa out of harm's way.

She looked so intimidating from this close up, sharp features and a sinister smile giving her a dangerous gleam in the night. Arianna couldn't have been more thankful for Lessa's memories not being there to aid her in revenge…

Looking upon the person who had stolen Talis Churry from their world too soon, she could hardly contain herself from doing something rash. *If Lessa remembered, she'd have definitely gotten herself killed.*

"I have orders not to let you leave the premises, Arianna Belvedor," Keeper Yahindi barked. "I *loathe* orders, and you lot will suffer for them."

Lessa leaned heavily on Eli, unable to fight, so Arianna stepped forward, swords at the ready. She wished they could do any sort of magic, but she felt that even Solza was still having some sort of energy blockage.

As Arianna considered her dwindling options, she noticed red silk lining the keeper's ensemble—a Warrior's District native. If they were anything alike, following the rules wasn't very high on Keeper Yahindi's list.

She decided to try to talk her down before getting into a battle she wasn't sure if she could win in this state. The city keeper wouldn't be an easy opponent.

"If you hate following orders so much, then just let us pass," said Arianna.

"And disobey the High King or Head Guard! You mad, are you? He's even got his wolf trying to sniff you out," she said. "I'd rather die first than face their wrath."

So I was right.

"That can be arranged," said Arianna, flying forward on the wings of her blades—all sense was gone as soon as Solomon had come back into the picture.

Negotiating just wasn't the warrior way.

They spun around in battle, Arianna nearly gaining the upper hand. But then Keeper Yahindi showed off her magical prowess and the battle was over.

Arianna was blasted backward into Eli and Lessa, all three tumbling to the ground, helpless, as Solza and Sano stood guard. When she looked up, Keeper Yahindi had raised her weapon against their avatars, no magic to defend them from a blade.

"Stupid cat!" she said, swinging for Solza.

"You won't lay a hand on her," screamed Arianna, trying to shift Solza to safety behind her.

Arianna, her friends, and the two avatars were now all tangled on the ground at the mercy of the city keeper.

Keeper Yahindi smiled, clearly finding this amusing as magic sparked across her fists, her guards flanking her now.

She crouched down in front of Arianna, unable to resist gloating at her position over them; Arianna thought fleetingly that Grinda Risso would've made a fine city keeper.

But just like Grinda had done before she died, Keeper Yahindi let her guard down; Arianna swiftly unsheathed her dagger and stabbed her in the neck, shutting her up for good.

As Keeper Yahindi fell, her guards closing in for the kill, Arianna couldn't have wished harder to be anywhere else in the world.

ASTRAL JOURNEY

FALLING AGAIN WITHOUT END, Arianna wondered if this time she might finally hit rock bottom and die. But when she opened her eyes, she was surrounded by the glint of beautiful jade stones and warm water splashing her face.

"What happened?" said Lessa, rubbing her head and checking that Sano was safe. "I don't—"

"The soul of the star again," said Arianna with certainty. "Syrifina was right."

She looked down to see her necklace glowing brilliantly before returning to normal.

"What about the others? Demetrius, Jeom, Talis?" said Lessa, coming out of her daze.

They heard a groan and turned to find Eli lying on his side. Arianna ran over to check on him, not willing to lie to Lessa's face about Master Churry's devastating end.

"They escaped with the old boat," she said, helping Eli to sit up. "As for us, I couldn't help but wish for a safe place when I saw we were cornered. I suppose that's why the star's magic sent us here."

She gazed around, feeling a wave of relief at the familiar setting—coupled with terror as she thought of what lay just beyond.

"I've always felt safe here."

"And where's 'here,' exactly?" Eli staggered to his feet, taking in the stunning backdrop.

"We're… back in the Four Corners," said Arianna, letting out a big breath. "In an unmarked part of the Vanishing Tunnels." She could hardly believe it herself, yet here they were.

Lessa gasped. "We're back?" she whispered, taking in the hot springs of their past. "Just like we planned?"

"Not exactly," said Arianna, bowing her head. "This wasn't at all like we planned."

She thought of Tobias and Talis, silently praying to all the gods she could think of that nobody else had lost their lives. But now that they were there, she wouldn't waste a second working out what to do next.

"I don't understand," said Eli. "We were just at the… and then…" He shook his head. "Arianna, how? No, *why* are we here?"

"You know why, Eli." She got to her feet, feeling more empowered. "We're here to gather an army."

Whatever had suppressed her magic before had been wiped away, allowing it to flow back to the surface in one big swoop that filled her with courage. She felt it in Solza, too, as if subduing their strengths for so long had actually had the opposite effect, making them all the more powerful.

"What do you expect to do now?" said Lessa, starting to seem herself again—she began checking their supplies, hands shaking with worry. "We can't just waltz back into the districts without a plan."

Arianna thought about this for a moment as Lessa unwrapped

provisions and passed them out.

"Master Tayshin taught me how to astral project just before everything happened," she said. She grabbed for Lessa's hand, fingering the ring made of aura and ora stones that Keeper Kassime had left to her. "I can teach you."

"What? What for?" said Lessa, flustered. "I mean, I know what astral projection *is*, but how on earth would that help anything?" She let out an exasperated sigh. "And how do you expect me to learn it right now?"

"We can control our destinations, go where our desires guide us," said Arianna. "Maybe if we do it now, we can see what we're up against in the districts, see where we can hide and where to avoid. Make a real plan of attack." She looked toward the path to her district. "Who knows what it's like now."

"How do we even—"

"It's easy," said Arianna, pulling Lessa toward the edge of the hot springs. "Master Tayshin used smoke to help me tap into the magic, but he said warm water has a similar effect. We couldn't have asked for a better situation!"

"Have you *lost* your mind?" said Eli, throwing his hands into the air. "I'm not sure now is the time for practicing magic. We need to sort ourselves out first. That back there… we need rest, I think. To get our heads on straight."

He was clearly one thread loose from a mental breakdown.

"There's no more time to rest! Just make sure we don't drown," she shot back.

She threw off her robes and stepped into the water with Lessa following loyally behind.

Their avatars shifted to their water forms to join them in the hot springs, and Arianna felt almost as if she were a child again; it was nostalgic to hear the thunderous waterfall splash down behind her and to see the sparkling firebugs twinkling on top of the jade stones. Unfortunately, though, their circumstances were less than ideal for a trip to the past.

She put her focus on the present.

Clutching her dagger still covered with Keeper Yahindi's blood, Arianna quickly recapped Master Tayshin's teachings to Lessa.

"No time to explain further, Les. Just repeat after me and *don't* take off your ring," she instructed.

"*Sensorial depriva tempe!*"

With the words of the spell, she sensed the stones of aura and ora ignite and felt the world fall away again, along with the weight of her body. But instead of traveling to the districts to scope it out as she had hoped, her eyes settled on unfamiliar territory; Lessa was nowhere to be found.

Master Tayshin warned of this…

Arianna had been a fool to assume she could handle this magic after only a lesson—as the fog of the astral plane cleared to let her see properly, she was certain she'd somehow traveled to the Palace of Saindora.

True to her *actual* greatest desire, she was spying on King Devlindor in his very own throne room in the present day.

Though his skin was pale white underneath all the glittering garments and he boasted a young face for someone so old, all she saw was a dark and dangerous monster. He sat stone still, tapping his fingers along the arm of his throne, and his jaguar companion—one she knew now to be an avatar called Raja—sat obediently by his side.

Arianna also noticed the way his colorfully jeweled crown slanted over his slick, black hair; it clearly didn't fit. And she thought it quite too big a responsibility for him to carry much longer. *I must relieve him of it.*

The King stood, and she watched his every movement—he took off the golden crown and placed it gently on the cushioned seat of the throne, as if he'd felt her threat. Then he glided down the steps with Raja at his feet, walking to the middle of the chamber.

He stopped there, looking toward the door, clearly waiting for something.

Enthralled by the King's presence, Arianna couldn't bring herself to blink—if sight even worked the same way in this form. As she floated above him, seemingly safe to observe, a spy locked away in the mirrors of his ceiling, she felt a shudder of fear rush through her that urged her to run.

His head snapped up—he was staring right at her.

Arianna gasped with shock, knowing that King Devlindor could somehow hear her, *see* her, even in her astral form. She felt her soul prickle as he calculated her, drinking her in like a delicious wine he'd been dying to sip.

Has he been waiting for me? Did he know I was coming?

Arianna had far underestimated the King's wisdom and power compared to her own, but this was more than sobering.

"You ambushed us," she choked out, finding the courage to address him. "Had your Shadow Resistance suppress our magic somehow, didn't you? And Vladamor possess Jeom?"

King Devlindor gave a single nod, a smile shifting across his face—the fact that he had replied at all shook Arianna awake. This was no dream.

This is real, no matter what form my soul takes.

She was so close to the person she'd vowed to kill, yet so far away from her goal as her swords and her body remained underneath the Blancoren Mountains. Truly, Arianna was as distant as she could possibly get from a victory, the King more in control now than ever with the guardians disbanded again.

She wanted to scream out loud, feeling trapped, unable to do anything but speak as the monster of her nightmares taunted her from the safety of his palace.

"I'm coming for you," she said with much more bravery. "We're coming!"

"No," he replied with a slight chuckle, his voice sharp, haunting. "You'll be dragged to my feet in chains like the slave you are,

Twenty-Two." He ran his fingers lazily through his hair, as if this was any other day in the life of a wicked king.

Arianna's attention was drawn to the staff in his hand. The ruby at its center began to glow too bright, making her eyes burn—even still, she couldn't look away, rooted to the spot.

The King's voice echoed all around her then as he spoke the words to a spell she did not know.

Sir Vladamor abruptly appeared, and with him a rolling, black smoke engulfed the chamber; Arianna felt as if she were drowning in it. And as her spirit desperately tried to reconnect to her physical body, she realized that she actually was.

Still unable to move from the mirrored ceiling, which now felt more like a glass cage, she readied herself for pain. In the next moment, the King's avatar ran and leaped into the air, transforming into a giant black hawk that seemed to glide on the clouds of darkness filling the room. Its claws were outstretched and aimed right for Arianna's astral body.

She squeezed her eyes shut.

ARIANNA WOKE BACK IN HER REAL BODY with a shout, splashing in the springs and coughing. Her throat burned terribly as she choked on the water. Or was it from the necromancer's smoky dark magic?

Finding her bearings, Arianna looked around the hot springs; the avatars were nowhere in sight, and Lessa and Eli were in the restraints of Warrior's District regulators.

"Thank the gods you're all right," said Eli through gritted teeth, a knife to his neck.

"They found us," said Lessa. "Don't struggle."

Something in her eyes told Arianna not to disobey.

She registered the swords and arrows a moment later, pointed at them from every angle. Even if they tried using magic to fight back, there was no way to be certain that the regulators wouldn't take one of them out first. They'd gotten the upper hand.

Arianna had been waylaid again in her precious utopia by enemies.

"If you try anything, we'll kill them," said a regulator unknown to her. He seemed like a weak replacement for the ones she'd killed before. "General Bell only requested you."

"I'm not going to struggle," she replied, keeping her hands by her side. "Trust me, he'll be more than pleased with three."

Under the water so no one could see, Arianna secured her dagger in its sheath at her thigh. Then she lifted her arms above her head in surrender, walking out to meet them on the edge of the hot springs.

Although she itched to release her magic, she refrained, not willing to take any more risks today with the lives of her friends.

The waterfall splashed down like always, hiding Solza or Sano; but Arianna had never seen the waters this riled before.

Then again, there had never been two avatars, masters of water, roaming her hot springs.

She looked back and glimpsed the silver belly of Solza in her dolphin form as she sliced through the water. And the bright orange eyes of Sano in his turtle form peered up at her from below.

Arianna couldn't help the smirk that crawled across her lips then at the memory of her first encounter with Lessa; she'd thought herself so silly to believe that there might be monsters lurking in the depths of the hot springs—now, she couldn't believe she had ever thought otherwise.

There are always monsters nearby… at least these ones are on our side.

"Don't get caught," she whispered, knowing Solza and Sano would hear.

The regulators began to drag them toward the tunnels.

"The general has been waiting for you," said a guard as he forced Arianna to her feet and removed her weapons—everything except for her dagger.

"I don't doubt it," said Arianna.

As the regulators forced them down a familiar path where brilliant firebugs still lined the way, she had to glance back to her utopia one last time. But instead of meeting the worried eyes of their avatars as she expected, she found two ghostly faces watching her, bewilderment in their expressions.

Jacob, Damon!

"We need your help," she mouthed as the regulators hauled them away. "Help them."

She shifted her gaze to the water where the eyes of their avatars glittered with fear, confident Jacob and Damon would understand her plea. They consented with a nod.

Arianna was relieved, at least, that somewhere in the Four Corners they had allies… even if they were ghosts.

34

JOURNEY TO THE PAST

THEY WERE DRAGGED THROUGH the firebug-lit tunnel, the acrid smell of rotting wood hitting Arianna in the face like a wall as they came closer to the end. Her skin prickled when the warmth from her overrun utopia vanished, replaced by the biting cold of the wretched Jar. Here, the sun was just setting as the moon fought to take over.

Arianna gaped at it, comprehending just how far they'd traveled with the star's magic; only an hour ago they had been fighting for their lives in Zambienth in the thick of night.

"Welcome back," said the voice of a woman that gave her even more chills than the snow melting on her face.

She located Ophelia, the King's pet seer. Her gray eyes looked back at her—seeing nothing, yet seeing all.

"We've been expecting you," she said with a sickening smile. "Take her to the general!"

Arianna spat at Ophelia's feet, thinking of all the world had lost because of her, just one woman. But she wasn't *just* a woman… she was a Golden Age creature with unfathomable powers of future sight that the King greatly coveted.

Ophelia alone had upturned the plans of young guardians twice over now, spanning two different generations. But Arianna wouldn't consent to a third.

"You wicked *w-w-witch*," she stuttered, unable to help the chatter of her teeth. It was *so* cold, and she and Lessa hadn't been given a chance to dry off before leaving the tunnels.

She pulled her robes around herself to try to lock in some heat.

"I could say the same for you," Ophelia said with a cackle.

She held out her arm for her personal protector to take. He escorted her away, her braids swinging behind her like the hands of a clock, counting down to their sure trial.

Arianna noticed for the first time the thin, black outline of a snake coiled on the nape of her neck; Ophelia was no longer an imprisoned seer but an honored member of the Shadow Resistance.

She wondered how many more with power had bowed down at the King's feet long ago, and stayed there.

Arianna glanced back, finding Eli and Lessa struggling against the hold of the regulators.

Lessa mouthed, "Sano!"

She turned toward the entrance of the tunnels—two pairs of distinct eyes stared back at them, watching them; Solza and Sano were at the ready should they need them, and Arianna was sure they would.

The regulators stopped only to tie the ropes around their wrists tighter, and then together, she, Eli, and Lessa were dragged through the empty streets of the Warrior's District. Arianna felt as if time had reversed altogether, bringing her back to a world that she had once known so well. But walking these paths, two years later and with more experiences to her name than she would've ever dreamed possible, made her feel as if she were still in her ethereal body—floating above it all and seeing everything in a new light.

This place didn't belong to her anymore, and she was so glad for that. The giant buildings that she had always thought made up her district were really only small, dingy, rotting structures that barely stood the test of time when compared to the palace life she'd lived or the sprawling cities she'd seen. And the snow wasn't bright white or new, just gray where the flakes met the ground.

There were no wide, winding paths but rather tiny, narrow lanes that made up the prison, keeping slaves strictly in line and from discovering anything new. And when she passed by the Pit on the way to the Square, it didn't strike fear into her heart—it gave her courage and determination to set those souls free and to take her freedom all over again.

These are the bones of the forgotten children of Olleb-Yelfra, of those sacrificed by the blade of King Devlindor for nothing less than greed. This is why I'm here. I'm no longer a slave. I'm a guardian, a witch, a warrior!

It was in this moment that Arianna let her worries drift away. She was exactly where she needed to be, had wished to be—her mind linked with Solza's then, their avatar magic eager to be released.

She glanced at Lessa, and her eyes were rimmed with silver just the same; they were not slaves any longer but powerful sorceresses shaped by great gifts granted to them by the Olleb herself. Now was the time to put those gifts to the test.

"Solza," said Arianna through their connection. "Get ready to fight. We're not leaving here without our army."

In the distance, she swore she heard the mighty growl of her avatar echoing within the mouth of the Vanishing Tunnels. Whatever happened next would be one for the history books of the Warrior's District.

We must survive.

Coming upon the Square, Arianna realized why the rest of the district was so quiet today. A sea of red robes buzzed anxiously in the stands.

All eyes were on them as excited whispers snaked through the crowd; she felt as if it were the same day she'd invited Grinda Risso to the Warrior's Challenge, so nervous as she'd stood front and center, the entire district waiting on edge for their epic battle.

But today marked another annual Free Falls, and they had arrived just in time to attend. Though, at *this* festival, Arianna wasn't proudly donning robes of red. She was shackled in chains of silver.

As she, Lessa, and Eli were dragged to the center of the Square, Arianna lifted her eyes to find Solomon Bell sitting in the seat once occupied by the late General Ivo, Ophelia sitting to his right. With his black robe sprawled out behind him, he looked just as regal as she last recalled, even more so now seated upon a district general's throne.

This time, though, he didn't smile.

Arianna supposed it was better that way, for Solomon's smile was what she had loved most about him; and she'd die before she let this monstrous version of her master steal that memory, too. Or rather, *he* would die.

"Where do you want them, General Bell?" asked one of the regulators.

"I've saved a special seat for them," said Solomon. "You see, I knew they were coming. I just had the strongest *inkling.*"

He winked to Ophelia, and she returned a knowing smile.

Solomon snapped his fingers and another group of regulators unlocked what looked to be a large, barred cage directly beneath his platform. The regulators dragged them into the cage, latching it tight before Solomon walked down the stairs to meet them.

He stepped up close to the bars so that he could look Arianna squarely in the eyes.

"This cage has been spelled," he said so that only they could hear. "Don't even *think* about doing any magic. That won't work here, and you will certainly regret trying."

His lips curled up into a sneer as he considered them for a long moment; they glared back at him.

Before Arianna could retort, Lessa began to tremble uncontrollably at her side; she curled over and let her stomach go for all to see.

"What's happening?" she stammered, squeezing her head between her hands as if to make a loud noise stop. She let out a howl of pain. "It *hurts*, Ara. Make it stop!"

"What are you doing to her?" screamed Arianna, lunging toward the bars—just a touch to the metal and it burned her hands badly. She had to let go.

Eli went to Lessa's aid, letting her lean on him as she crumpled to the ground, looking to Arianna with such worry.

"Stop this," she pleaded to Solomon through gritted teeth. "Lessa doesn't deserve this, and you know it."

"I'm not doing anything," he said over her screams, eyes on Lessa. "I can gather from this reaction that whatever magic she's had done to her has just come undone. I suppose it was something painful by the looks of it." He shifted his attention back to Arianna, void of any emotion. "Shut her up, will you? I haven't even yet begun to make you all scream."

Arianna turned her back on Solomon so he couldn't see her expression.

"Damn you," she breathed, fists balled at her sides as she observed Lessa.

He didn't have the slightest clue as to what had just happened to her, but Arianna understood perfectly.

"Lessa, I'm *so* sorry," she said, bending down to try to console her. "Please understand."

She didn't even know how to deal with this right now. Emotions and feelings had no place in war, but here they were, attacking them from all sides.

Lessa was just shaking her head, hands still pressed upon her ears. "No!" she said. "No, this isn't true. What's happening? Wake me up, Ara. Wake me up!"

She cried out to her, tears streaming down her cheeks.

Arianna and Eli exchanged a troubled look.

"You have to gain control," said Eli after a moment. "It's your memory coming back. Master Tayshin took it away. Talis... he thought it would be too painful for you—"

"Stop!" she shrieked, glaring up at Arianna with disbelief. "We *have* to go back. We must! We have to help him."

She pounded her fists against Eli's chest as he held her down, trying to calm her.

"Ara, what did we do?" she cried, searching for answers.

"What is she whining about?" snapped Solomon. "Quiet her this instant or you can all die here and now."

"She's heartbroken!" retorted Arianna, unable to hold back. "I know you've sold *your* heart to the shadows, but maybe you'll still care to know that Talis Churry is dead. Or don't you know already?"

She flicked her eyes to Ophelia and then jumped to her feet, swiftly plunging her arm through the bars to grab a fistful of Solomon's robes so that he couldn't back away.

He didn't resist, so Arianna pulled him closer, looking him square in the eyes. "After all, it was basically your hand that ended his life, the life of someone you once called a brother."

Solomon actually had the decency to look momentarily shocked before a regulator ripped her hand from his robes. Arianna yanked it back to the safety of the cage before he thought to use his sword to sever it from her body.

Her mind floated to her other friends.

Demetrius, Jeom, please survive... in case we don't.

"How do you mean?" inquired Solomon, his lips pressed into

a tight line. He cleared his throat. "How did he die?"

"Keeper Yahindi ambushed us and killed him in the process," she said, another pang stabbing her heart as Lessa whimpered again, barely consolable. "He gave his life to protect us, as did Kassime. Well done, *Master*. You've certainly taught us another important lesson."

Without bothering to reply, Solomon scowled and strode back up the stairs to his podium to address the crowd. Still, Arianna didn't miss the shadow that had crossed his face the moment she spoke the truth of Talis' death.

Although she had never had a chance to witness the supposed friendship between the young Keeper Kassime and Solomon Bell, she knew without a doubt that there had been a point in time where he had loved Talis Churry like a brother. And even if he'd abandoned his heart now, she believed there was still a hollow in his chest where the ghost of those memories lingered, waiting for it to return and free him from his spiraling descent into darkness.

"Slaves of Warrior's District," said Solomon, his tone much too somber for what should be an electrifying address. "On this 289th Free Falls Festival, you shall be honored with the ultimate reminder of what you're fighting for!"

His voice resounded throughout the Square, but Arianna saw that all eyes were still on them; she thought Solomon must be gesturing to the cage, drawing attention to it for how they all gawked. The looks differed from one face to the next—contempt, shock, confusion, excitement... *fear*.

"So, what is it that you're fighting for? I want to hear it," said Solomon, drawing them all back in so that the burn of eyes lessened on their prison.

Arianna shuddered as the word 'freedom' echoed all around her like she was trapped in some tortuous nightmare. It was a stark reminder of what she desperately wanted, was so close to reaching, but would never achieve for what felt like an eternity.

To make matters even more bleak, Lessa wouldn't stop crying, and neither Arianna nor Eli could do anything to bring her comfort. The spell meant to shield her from pain had more than backfired at the worst of moments; she seemed to be reliving the memory of Talis' death over and over.

Arianna was thankful for Eli in this moment, thankful that she wasn't going through this alone, because Lessa had completely checked out. She doubted her dear friend even realized where she was right now—and they were in a *whole* lot of trouble.

Alas, she worried for Eli too. He had begun to pace back and forth in the cell with clenched fists; Arianna could only assume that being locked up again was causing him to re-experience unpleasant memories as well.

And while she stressed over their predicament and her friends' sanity, trying to hold it together for all their sakes, the eyes of her former warrior-slave peers found hers again, seeming so confused at her presence.

She gazed back, feeling as if she stared at herself a thousand times over. The gentle flow of the red robes created a picturesque wave like the rolling of lava over the earth or the embers of a dying fire. Then she spotted the soon-to-be warriors, or more likely soon-to-be dead seventeenth years.

Each on the cusp of eighteen, they readied their weapons nervously for their one and only chance at a future. The anxious faces didn't include, of course, the minority of Grinda Rissos who pranced about the arena like they had already been set free.

But none of them mattered in the slightest anymore—Arianna Belvedor was now the main event of today, and everyone knew it.

She was certain that many probably recognized her, maybe had even known her personally from her time growing up there.

Had we trained together once? Been something like friends, perhaps?

She imagined how shocked they must be to see her alive and well, already two full years since stealing her freedom. Now, she was caged by her former private trainer and their current general when before she'd been his star apprentice.

Oh… if Grinda Risso could see me now!

She couldn't resist laughing then, though cynical it was.

But Grinda couldn't take joy in this moment—Red Risso was dead; Arianna had handed her that fate, and anyone who tried to stand in her way now would soon join her and the other countless bodies consumed by Blancoren.

"This cage represents the Jar you're living in," continued Solomon, surely gesturing to Arianna. "Make no mistake, real life is better than this darkness you live. *However*, if you want more than a taste, if you really want to have ownership of your freedom, then you must earn it here and now!"

He paused for effect, his voice dying out in the quiet.

"Until then," he said, "you're nothing more than slaves to this world, no matter how far you dare to run. And no matter how fast you go, we'll always catch you. A slave is *always* a slave until the King or his chosen few say otherwise—"

There was a long pause and again all eyes shifted to hers.

"Isn't that right, Twenty-Two?"

Arianna glanced up through the top of the cage to find Solomon staring down at her, waiting for an answer. There was no top to this prison, so she would've shot a spell right at him if his magic wasn't suppressing her own.

Isn't that right, Twenty-Two?

Arianna couldn't stop his words from ringing in her head, sending her back into the rage of her youth. But he didn't allow her to speak, turning again to the crowd to gloat more about his capture of the elusive escapee; if she didn't get out of this mess, she would stand as a frightful example for every slave thereafter that dared even think to do something like try to escape or break the King's laws.

Arianna gave her attention back to Lessa, taking this brief moment out from under scrutiny to comfort her friend.

"Lessa, please don't cry anymore," she said, softly. "I need you right now. I need you to be strong if we're going to get out of this alive."

"I can't," she said, the words tumbling out. "It all just keeps repeating in my head on a loop. Why... *why* did you let him do that to me?"

"You were inconsolable," she said. "It was Talis who pressured Master Tayshin to take the memory away. Only temporarily. And how could we have argued with his last wish... he just wanted you to be safe, clear-headed in case—"

"In case we ended up in a cage at the Warrior's District Free Falls with Solomon and Ophelia to deal with?" she spat, letting Arianna pull her to her feet. "I'm so *angry* with you, with everyone, I can't even think straight."

Arianna forced a small smile onto her lips. "You can hate me later, but please stand with me now," she said. "I'm sorry, Les, but we can't do this without you. Will you be all right?"

"No," she said, wiping her eyes as something seemed to harden inside her. "I'll never be all right again. We can't die here. I *won't* die here like this. We have too much to do now."

"I couldn't agree more," said Arianna, taking her hand and giving it a squeeze.

She knew that Lessa's time with Syrifina had already hardened a piece of her, and now the loss of Talis would surely solidify it. But in this moment, Arianna couldn't help but think that it probably wasn't a bad thing.

Lessa had been through unthinkable traumas... just like her, both Jeom and Demetrius, and even Eli. They were all bonded by their losses, their weaknesses, and their failures.

But most of all, they were bonded by their love and courage despite everything—that's what counted, and Arianna counted a lot of it now.

"We're not going to die here," she tried to say with confidence. "We just need to wait for the right… moment. We're sorely outnumbered, but there's a way out of this. I *know* it. Just breathe." She took Lessa by the shoulders. "Can I count on you? We'll cry later, yes? Together, I promise."

Lessa nodded, sniffling as she reeled in her emotions and tried to focus.

"I just can't believe he's gone," she whispered, looking at the palm of her hand where the dragon shone.

"It's going to be all right, Lessa," said Arianna. "I swear, we'll do right by your master once we're out of here. We will avenge him and the others lost."

She reached out to Eli too.

"I can't be locked away again," he muttered, shriveling away from her touch.

Arianna could see the hairs standing up on his neck, his eyes wide. She had already tamed one distraught friend, but how to tame another?

This cage had reduced Eli to a scared captive once more, and they all needed to be clear-headed if they were going to get out of this alive.

"Elijah!" said Arianna, snapping her fingers. "Stop pacing and look at me."

He paused with an obedience only gained in captivity, helpless as he met her stare. His eyes looked just as haunted as the day she'd found him buried in the Luose Dungeon.

"Can you trust me?" she asked, holding his gaze.

He nodded, and she held out her hand for him to take.

"I… I do trust you," he said with a sigh, coming back to his senses. "You know I do."

"Good," said Arianna, squeezing his hand.

She stepped forward and hugged him tight, whispering in his ear, "I'm sorry… for everything. I trust you, too. Stay with me now. Don't give up."

Her words seemed to shock Eli back to normal; he returned her embrace, stretching out the moment. Then he took a deep breath and let go.

A part of Arianna wished he hadn't—something about being in his arms just felt so safe.

"All right, let's do this, dammit," he said, holding out his hands for both girls to take. He held his head high. "We need to get the heck out of here."

They all stood side by side now, linked as another Free Falls Festival began, waiting for their numbers to be called. And though the cold pressed upon them like a suffocating blanket, Arianna felt a trickle of warmth return, bound together with friends; she held on to that warmth for dear life.

35

FIRE CATCHES

THE THREE WATCHED this year's Free Falls contestants die, one by one, sometimes mere inches from their cage; Arianna was beginning to feel sick to her stomach. There was nothing she could do to help them. Then, with Solomon's booming voice and the decisive sound of the bell signaling the start of another match, the inevitable had arrived.

"It's time," sang Ophelia, clapping her hands.

Solomon nodded his approval, and two regulators swung open the door to their cage. They pulled Arianna and Lessa out from behind the bars and tossed them into the center of the Square.

Arianna could feel the oppressive magic from the cage starting to wear off—but not soon enough.

Solomon gave a kill order.

"Let's see if you remember anything I taught you," he called down to her, after commanding that the regulators return their weapons. "Remember, only *one* may survive." The bell sounded again. "Begin!"

"No," said Eli, pushing on the barred door to try to keep the regulators from leaving him behind. He let go with a howl, magic he probably didn't even understand burning his hands.

Arianna looked to him and mouthed, "Stay calm."

But that wouldn't be enough to subdue his anger or worry.

She knew he wouldn't take his eyes off them, even if he had to watch them die. Eli would never leave them again unless death snatched him away, and Arianna felt ashamed at herself for taking such a long time to comprehend that.

He had fought his way into their family, and he'd finally earned a place in her heart. She just hoped they could survive this long enough for her to tell him.

"What do we do?" said Lessa, drawing back Arianna's attention as she nocked an arrow. "My magic is still too weak for it to be of any use."

"Mine too," she replied, twisting her swords in her hands.

They both at least *looked* like they were playing at Solomon's game, trying to buy time before he forced their hands; Arianna paced around Lessa, just as she'd start off any normal duel. And Lessa held her aim steady on her.

Arianna was having such trouble concentrating, racking her brain for an out. She tried and failed to drown out the cheering voices urging them to fight and her own subconscious speaking so many doubts. She wasn't sure of anything at this point, least of all what to do next. The only thing she had resolutely decided on was that if one of them were forced to kill the other, Lessa would have to make the strike.

Arianna would never raise a sword to her sister.

After a long time, neither of them had made a move, whispering fruitless ideas of escaping with their lives.

"Enough of this, Bell!" said Ophelia from her perch. "They're stalling."

She signaled something to the regulators on the ground.

They retreated as gates opened up on the far side of the arena—wolves from the attacks on earlier contestants slunk out into the open, gray fur matted with the blood of their last victims.

The girls were relieved to not have to pretend to fight each other anymore, but they weren't out of this mess yet; Arianna recalled the last rabid pack of dogs she'd dealt with in the Vanishing Tunnels with Lessa by her side—the lavahounds.

She reminded herself that at least they'd survived far worse together. *We're stronger than before. We can handle this.*

Although, this didn't feel quite right without Jeom and Demetrius fighting with them.

Arianna and Lessa moved back to back; the wolves surrounded them quickly. Then they pounced, attacking them from all sides to the roaring delight of the crowd.

They tried their best to keep the wolves at bay, but they were relentless; Arianna thought the animals had been starved to the point of madness, nothing to hold them back from trying to get to their next meal. Snarling, the wolves forced them all the way back to the door of the barred cage.

"What are we going to do?" came Eli's panicked voice. "Watch out. On your left!"

"We? You're the safe one right now." Arianna gasped as she ducked, Lessa letting another arrow fly.

"Now's not the time for jokes," he growled.

"I wasn't joking!" said Arianna—she kicked a wolf square in the mouth with the heel of her boot.

"I'm out already," said Lessa. "Used most of them up in Zambienth."

The wolves had them cornered now, their jaws dripping red with blood.

Arianna stepped in front of Lessa as another attack came, swiping her swords as fast as she could. Together, they had taken out several of the beasts, but there were just too many left.

A howl came loud across the night, but it wasn't from any wolf here—everyone turned to locate the culprit.

Arianna and Lessa looked too, finding Solza in her snow leopard form; she was standing next to a giant wolf with bright white fur sparkling all over its body, its eyes a shocking orange. They were positioned at the top of the stands, gazing down over the arena.

"Sano!" cried Lessa with happiness, mouth agape. "You've transformed."

"He's *stunning*," cheered Eli, pumping a fist in the air. "Now, that's what I'm talking about!"

"Incredible," said Arianna, lowering her swords. "It's his earth form. By gods… they look just magnificent together."

Hope enveloped her mind.

Sano howled again toward the moon, a deafening sound, as if marking his territory; the wolves attacking Lessa and Arianna went from snapping their teeth to panting like puppies. They sat on their haunches, instantly obedient to the avatar.

Solza and Sano ran to meet their masters, the crowd crawling over each other to get out of their way and to catch a glimpse of the remarkable creatures. They came to the girls' rescue just in the nick of time, Sano holding pure command over the other wolves—it was evident that the vicious pack recognized Sano to be *their* master, for avatars were masters of all and any beasts, the kings of their kind.

"Damn avatars," hissed Solomon, glaring toward Ophelia. "In the King's name, how did you not foresee this? You're losing your touch, old woman." He stood from his seat, locating his regulators. "Stop this at once!"

At his command, an archer from the stands let an arrow fly; Arianna didn't have the time nor strength left to dodge it.

Solza, on the other hand, was more than ready. She leaped into the air in front of her, as if she meant to sacrifice herself.

Arianna reached toward her in a panic. "Wait—"

As her paws left the earth, an incredible explosion of magic ensnared her. And when the magical dust settled, Solza had transformed into an exquisite black and white owl, too large not to be extraordinary.

In her silver claws, she had caught the arrow with such a speed that if Arianna had blinked, she would've missed the entire thing. Her talons then snapped it right in half, the broken pieces falling to the ground. She soared back to Arianna, perching on her shoulder as if it were all a routine—as if she hadn't just saved her life and made her *third* transformation like Sano had done.

"Solza, such a surprise you are!" sang Arianna, nuzzling her head against her avatar. "I wasn't expecting that, but I'm sure glad you came." She glanced to Sano. "Both of you."

Arianna felt as if Solza were a magical shield sent from the heavens. She locked eyes with Lessa in that moment, sharing the same thought.

Both of their avatars had now mastered their third forms.

Earth. Water. Air. That just left one more to go, the rarest transformation of all—*Fire.*

The crowd cried out in shock as Lessa, Arianna, and the avatars faced them; they were clearly bewildered and terrified at the sight of such astonishing and inexplicable things. The Warrior's District had seen magic this night, and one of the most beautiful, rare kinds at that... the transformation of an avatar to a new stage.

Like the flicker of a flame, there was nothing to hide it, nothing to stop the questions from spreading. And Arianna knew that the King and his necromancer were far away in Saindora; there was no time to erase it from their memories.

She wouldn't let there be time.

Arianna planned to make sure that King Devlindor could never take such a lesson away from them again.

With Solza lending her charms, she felt her magic almost fully renewed now, hot and raging, and she was finally ready to use it.

She cleared her mind, concentrating on the powerful mind magic she had only just started to grasp after countless lessons from the elder guardians; she focused on a spell that could strengthen one's memory, make it more lasting. And true to its nature, this particular spell was known to counter any other mind magic previously endured by the receiver.

She lifted her sword to the sky, feeling the silver flood her eyes as her magic danced at the surface of her tongue.

"*Memorium solio!*"

Her voice came loud with the effort it took to do the enchantment on so many people, even with Solza's support. She felt nearly all the magic race to leave her body to ensure that the Warrior's District would never forget this moment in time—*and* that they would remember all they had forgotten from before. The only way it could be undone was if Solomon wanted to risk turning the Olleb's entire future of warriors into brain-dead mush.

The gathering fell silent, her magic washing over them in one fell swoop. Then the confusion swiftly settled in.

"Give them more!" Eli yelled from behind in support as the warrior-slaves fell into a panic.

Arianna was happy to oblige.

With the memory spell complete, she sheathed her swords and tapped into Solza's newest powers, the wind at her mercy. She felt the ground vibrate beneath her feet; Lessa and Sano had joined her, testing out their new powers over the earth.

Arianna was very aware of the avatar magic channeling through her in this moment, so aware that she waited on edge for the power to overwhelm her completely, as it had done during the desert battle.

But Arianna remained calm, all her practice paying off. Instead of trying to control this beast inside of her, she set it free. And though fully relinquishing control produced immeasurably less power than she'd wielded in that frightening moment against Sir Vladamor, in a way, it felt like more…

This time, she *let* the magic take the lead.

She gazed at Lessa, who returned an encouraging nod, also finding her command over her own avatar gifts. As if they shared a single mind, the girls focused in on the crowd.

Seeing the frightened faces of her warrior peers staring back at them, Arianna remembered her goal.

'Show them what's worth fighting for.'

She clung to the wisdom of Master Lethander, to the words of a ghost who had once been a great leader of a powerful and influential elven tribe.

Show them what's worth fighting for. Then they'll follow.

Arianna let her magic flow freely—beautiful, unconstrained magic that would make a lasting impression on anyone watching this night.

"Enough of this!" shouted Ophelia. She leaned forward from her seat, knowing what would happen before Arianna did—she wondered what the future held. "Kill them. Kill them all, now. For the King!"

"No, don't!" countered Solomon, waving his arms. "They'll be martyrs. We should think this through. You could launch us into another war. Is that what you want? We don't know how many more are on their side. They cannot publicly be slaughtered."

But the archers in the stands were too confused and too scared, so their arrows blotted out the sky and ripped holes through the long-standing flag of the Four Corners.

Lessa's avatar magic ebbed from a bout of fear, and she was clearly too tired to conjure it back. She fell to her knees, hugging Sano around the neck; her eyes raised to the sky, magic still swirling in them, watching the arrows fall.

But Arianna wasn't ready to give up yet, and with Solza's endless energy gift, she didn't have to. Instead, she allowed her avatar's powers to flow through her even more, filling her from the inside out. She glared toward the arrows nearly upon them, and a spell surfaced in her mind.

It was not avatar magic, rather a simple enchantment she had mastered long ago in the company of friends on a stormy night in the Palace of South Luose. She remembered how the rain had frozen beneath the clouds, if only for a moment, and she lingered on the happy memory that accompanied it; Jeom's laughter, Demetrius' contagious smile, and Lessa's joyful eyes, full of hope, as they imagined their future—one full of promise—under a warm and welcome rainfall.

Arianna felt her heart buzz with renewed life as she let that memory fill her, and with it came all the magic she needed to survive. She said that spell now, with the wordless voice of her *mind*.

The rain of arrows instantly froze above them. And they didn't drop to the ground until she was ready to let them go.

There was an intake of breath all around the Square as everything went silent and still. She released the magic, the sound of wood and metal colliding with the ground to create a strange echo across the arena, like the finale of a song.

Before anyone even understood what had happened, Arianna directed two of the arrows toward the highlife platform.

Solomon was fast and dodged the one clearly meant for him by a hair; it landed smack in the middle of the snake's head in the Warrior's Crest on the podium wall.

Ophelia, on the other hand, wasn't quite as lucky.

"Didn't see that one coming, did you?" said Eli, jumping for joy from the confines of the cage, encouraging them on if nothing else.

Solomon got to his feet as Ophelia hunched over in her seat, dead after sure centuries of life.

The crowd hummed with fear, but Arianna didn't feel afraid to turn her back on Solomon's challenge. The stage was finally hers, and she was ready to act; if she didn't speak up now, she may never have another chance to be heard.

She drew in the bulging eyes of the anxious gathering and unsheathed one of her swords, its weight in her hand giving her courage.

"Now, pay close attention," she called, quieting the Square. "Remember all that you've seen here today, and ask yourself why it is that you haven't even a word for what it's named. Lies are all you know, but I have learned the truth. That's why I *took* my freedom from the Four Corners, and you can take yours, too."

She prayed to the gods for them to really hear her, to truly understand.

"The world is about to change, and you're either on the wrong side of history or ours. We offer you a chance to stand with us and truly earn your freedom away from your oppressor, the one responsible for caging you in this Jar. We offer you a choice."

She heard Lessa pulling one of the fallen arrows into place on her bow.

"And in case it's not already perfectly clear," Arianna pointed her sword back toward Solomon—in her line of sight was the arrow that had barely missed him, piercing the head of the golden snake in the crest, "we're slaves to *no one*, and we no longer hail to the King!"

At first there was silence, but then she saw movement and a bush of orange hair near the low wall. She remembered the day not so long ago that she and Liam had sat in that very section, waiting for their turn at freedom.

Noah lives, she thought with a smile.

He was one of the seventeenth years waiting to earn their citizenship this Free Falls. She nodded to him, and he raised his fist to the air.

"Belvedor, Belvedor!" he shouted, urging on his peers so fiercely that Arianna couldn't believe that this passionate young man was her sweet, little Noah.

His words seemed to grow louder and louder as others in the Square took to their feet alongside him. Eventually, the entire arena was roaring out Arianna's name so forcefully she thought her eardrums might shatter.

"Belvedor, Belvedor!" Their swords and weapons shot into the air to make for a staggering demonstration, shining silvers and reds blending together as one under the dark of night; it was as if the warrior-slaves had created a magic all their own.

"*Belvedor*," came a voice from behind.

Arianna felt the momentary glory of the cheering crowd—her fellow warriors finally in the know—disappear in an instant.

Solomon had taken Eli from the cage and now held a sword to his throat.

The cheering of the crowd began to blend in with a howling wind that seemed to burst out of the clouds and over the mountainsides from out of nowhere. With it came the snow, a blizzard brewing quickly as the 289th Free Falls came into its final round; Arianna knew her avatar connection was at play, driven again by her emotions after she'd been so taken off guard.

She could sense it taking over, the magic lifting her off the ground on a cloud of her own making—Solza was still perched on her shoulder, their minds melting together as one.

Could she find her calm before she destroyed everything? Scared away their only shot at building a stronger alliance?

Alas, just as soon as Arianna had her peers in her grasp, everyone began to run for shelter, the distinct red of the Warrior's District robes—the red of what could've been their army—vanishing behind a wall of silvery-white snowflakes.

"I'm sorry," said Eli, shame in his voice as he met her eyes.

"It's not your fault," she whispered—her voice seemed to be the wind and the wind her voice.

She lowered her weapon, trying to focus on her breath, trying to find herself before the magic fully took over. For if she lost it, not only Solomon would die…

Eli, Lessa, and their avatars would surely go with him.

She wasn't sure Eli had even heard her over the now roaring

gusts. She could hear Solomon, though, for he spoke his words quite clearly.

"Are you ready to be the reason another dies?" he said, twisting his blade at the nape of Eli's neck. "If my blade doesn't kill him, your magic surely will."

"Ara, don't listen to him!" Lessa's voice came faint in her ears, easily ignored. "You must kill him!"

Everything had disappeared for her as she stared into Solomon's deep, dark eyes. "You will not harm Eli," she demanded, lowering herself to the ground; the wind encircled her still, as if they were one and the same.

Her hair whipped at her face, the snow pelting everyone furiously—Arianna, Solomon, her friends, and the avatars were soon locked together in a lethal vortex.

"I wouldn't take another step if I were you," shouted Solomon over the howls of the storm. "Release your magic! And if you try *anything* more, he'll be dead before you can speak the spell in your mind."

He tapped his forehead and smiled; even in such a state of power, Arianna was afraid to challenge him, her master—and her first teacher in mind magic.

"What do you want from me?" she said through gritted teeth, trying to concentrate, trying to release her power to let her friends live.

"I don't want anything *from* you," he said, forcing Eli forward with the sword at his back.

Arianna could see how painful it was for him to even stand this near to her. If she didn't let her wind shield down, he'd be torn to pieces.

"I just want you."

In the next blink of an eye, Solomon shoved Eli forward, and Arianna felt her wind magic immediately dissipate—the fear of ripping her friend to shreds had been the key to unlocking her trance.

Startled by the severed connection, Solza flew from her perch on Arianna's shoulder and into the air.

"*Gods*, you're so predictable," said Solomon with a dark laugh.

Eli stumbled into Lessa's arms, and Arianna fell into his place at the point of Solomon's sword; it was her old sword with the bronzed handle, and she could feel his power radiating through to the tip of the blade.

Avatars or not, Solomon Bell was, and always would be, a sort of god when it came to wielding magic and weapon. They were novices in his eyes, and she respected that even now, whether or not she hoped to see him dead.

But, as it stood, Arianna was too impatient to wait centuries for her powers to match up to his or the King's before she faced them in true battle. Sheer will, a little luck, and a lot of practice would just have to be enough.

Win or die!

She didn't struggle against him as the magic fled her eyes, leaving her utterly drained. And yet, the storm raged on.

She knew that no matter if she could get away or not, Solomon's magic was stronger, his skill was better. And someone would die before he finally fell if she challenged him anymore on this night. *Eli? Lessa? Solza? Sano? Me?*

She couldn't bear the thought of who might suffer the sharp end of his sword, especially if she could prevent it.

She saw Lessa help Eli up, then they began to fight the force of the storm, trying to walk back in their direction.

"Don't," she called to them. "He'll kill you."

But her friends didn't listen.

"Let her go, Solomon. I won't let you have her." Lessa's eyes glowed a startling silver again.

"I wasn't asking permission," said Solomon.

"*Solza ven immito.*" Fire grew in the palm of Lessa's hands and she thrust it toward him. "Ara, run!"

Arianna tried to duck from the attack, but Solomon wouldn't let her; he pulled her into his chest and held his sword at their front.

The fireball hit her and Solomon square in the middle, but a shield of his magic protected them from any harm; the fire exploded around them in a forceful, sparkling display. And with only the wave of his hand, he sent Eli and Lessa flying off their feet to land in a heap on the snow.

Sano didn't hesitate to help, lunging for Solomon's throat on behalf of his master. Arianna searched the sky to try to connect with Solza again—she was struggling to fly straight within the storm.

But Solomon was too fast, and she regretted even trying; something like the piercing sound of the bell began echoing endlessly in her ears, and Arianna knew his defensive magic was at work.

"What's going on?" said Eli as Lessa and Arianna screamed out in agony, Solza and Sano screeching as well.

He seemed unaffected by this particular spell, so Arianna assumed it had only been conjured to stop them from connecting to their avatars.

"It's some kind of… mind magic," said Lessa through tears, barely able to form a sentence. "The avatars must be linked."

Sano howled again in terrible agony, his newly gained pack of wolves scattering.

Arianna crumpled to the ground at Solomon's feet, desperate for any relief from this unbearable noise. It seemed to burrow deep into her mind. She found the will to look up to check on Solza, and more horror overcame her still—her avatar was falling from the clouds in a blur like a rock thrown from a cliff.

"Eli, save her!" she screamed through the pain, pointing to the sky.

He didn't fail her, opening his arms to catch Solza in nearly the next moment.

"I've got her," he gasped, holding her close and checking if she was all right.

"Stop, please! I'll go with you. I'll go," said Arianna, feeling as if she might pass out—she wouldn't be able to stop him regardless.

"Ara, what should I do?" said Eli, beginning to panic. "Solza… she's not waking."

His voice seemed so far away.

"Just get somewhere safe," she whispered. "Save yourself."

"Didn't I teach you better?" spat Solomon, yanking her back to her feet and forcing her to face him. "There's no such thing as a safe place in Olleb-Yelfra."

His face looked sunken and his eyes void of the life she'd once admired.

"I suppose I still have a lot to learn then," she said, trying to catch her breath as the excruciating magic finally subsided.

Solomon shook his head.

"I always said your stubbornness would be the death of you. Sadly, there are no more lessons left in your future." He shook his head, such contempt in his expression. "You shouldn't have come back here, Arianna. Now I've no choice but to hand you over to the King."

"Just don't hurt my friends," she growled, catching Lessa's eye in the distance.

"Any harm that they endure is purely your blame to carry for dragging them into your despicable mess." He glanced up to search for them, magic still in his eyes. "Damn, where did they go?"

Arianna smiled to herself, knowing they were all safe.

Only moments ago, when Solomon was focused on her, she had spotted a head of red hair sneaking through the blizzard—Noah had helped Eli, Lessa, and their avatars get away quietly while she distracted the wolf.

The Guardians of Gold will survive… I will survive.

"I guess somewhere safe," said Arianna. "Even in the Four Corners, there is such a thing. Otherwise, I assure you, I wouldn't even be here today."

"It's no matter," he said, trying to hide his annoyance. "King Devlindor only wants you… so you he shall have."

"What he'll have is war!" screamed Arianna, fighting against his hold now that she knew her friends were out of harm's way.

Solomon tightened his grip, eyes boring down on hers.

"You need soldiers for a war," he said with an exasperated sigh. "Look around you. No one is by your side anymore. Your friends have gone, and you're all alone. *Besides*, the true war has already been fought long ago. All you can do now is surrender, and maybe this will end quickly for you."

He gave her a somewhat solemn look. Or was it pity?

"That's the only mercy I can offer now."

"Are you being *merciful?*" She glared up at him, unable to stop the tears welling in her eyes. "Because it feels more like betrayal, Master Bell."

"You'll find that mercy comes in many forms."

He pulled a bag of powder out from his robes and blew the contents into her face.

She struggled against its effects, but it was futile.

"Sweet dreams, Twenty-Two," he whispered. "Maybe you can try again for freedom in your next life."

The blizzard appeared to shift into stars, and the stars seemed to dance all around Arianna's head like a dazzling tunnel. Too bad she couldn't see the South Star anymore, nothing to help guide her out of this mess. Somehow the semblance of freedom she had held tight to over the past two years had slipped right through her fingers.

With one last morsel of fight left in her before she drowned in the oblivion Solomon had cast around her, Arianna felt a fire burning deep in her soul. It burned so strongly that it actually materialized outside of her master's control; she glimpsed the flag of the Four Corners—it turned to ashes by the lick of a bright and hungry red flame.

As she fell to the will of her mind and into the arms of a traitorous friend, she took comfort in the things she *had* succeeded in—her real friends, her family, would survive to see another day, and the Warrior's District knew of magic. And although, for Arianna, the Free Falls Festivals were officially over, she still felt free in her heart, a slave no longer.

Arianna knew who she was, who she was meant to be, and she knew she had, at the very least, set the path for the destruction of a tyranny. That alone was freedom enough for her.

EPILOGUE

THE SEER

"BROTHER, WHATEVER IS THE MATTER with you?" said Princess Elisa, sauntering into the throne room. He was standing in the middle of the chamber, staring up at the mirrored ceiling as if waiting for something.

"This slave…" he said, "she's much more powerful than I had at first assumed. Her magic has grown strong, and Sir Vladamor has brought word that they control avatars." Each word was so forced, heavy with an underlying accusation. "How did we let them get this far?"

He tore his eyes away from the mirrors, settling them on her.

"It's the guardians," she stuttered, shrinking under his probing glare. "They've more knowledge of the Golden Age than we ever suspected. We've sorely underestimated them…" She averted her eyes. "For the second time, it would seem."

Something like a roar came out of the King then. He whipped around to face her, catching her chin in his hand.

"Dearest sister, do tell me something I don't know."

Raja let out a caw, distracting him—she landed on his shoulder in her hawk form, feathers a silky black.

The King let out a disgruntled huff, whispering something to Raja. Then he released Princess Elisa, stomping up to his throne to retrieve his crown; he placed it firmly on his head.

Princess Elisa regained composure, brushing her long, silver hair out of her face and tightening her fingers around the lasso forever draped about her neck.

She cleared her throat.

"If you want to ensure your safety, *mine*, and this kingdom you've built, you need to train your focus not only on Arianna Belvedor."

She tried to speak in a much firmer voice, one more representative of who she actually was.

The King scoffed. "What do you mean? She is the cause of all this chaos. The prophecy must speak of her!"

"Yes, it's quite likely, but the prophecy *could* also speak of more than one person. We don't know for certain, do we?" said the Princess in a gentle voice.

The King folded his arms across his chest like a child but let her continue—she always knew how to calm him, though he frightened her still.

"This slave has gained much power on her journey, yes, but she can't possibly win a fight against you alone. Why, *you're* the mighty High King of Olleb-Yelfra with three centuries to your name."

The King seemed to regain confidence with just her words.

"She'll need all the elements on her side if she has any hope of defeating us. She's surely a novice avatar master compared to your powers, my lord." The Princess tossed her hair back. "I bet I could even take her on alone."

She let out an exasperated sigh.

"Alas, from what Solomon says, unlike you, she is *never*

alone. The guardians cling to her like flies."

The King raised his eyebrow at her, intrigued. "So, what are you saying, then?"

Princess Elisa felt her confidence grow, gaining back some control—she hated when she let him get to her like that, scare her. They were, after all, siblings.

She was the only thing he loved in this world... besides power.

I mustn't keep showing him my fear, or he'll never respect me as equal.

"I'm *saying* that you need to focus on her allies," said the Princess, sternly. She walked up to his throne, chin lifted high, and took his hand in hers. "Focus on eradicating the eldest guardians and the other slaves who have escaped alongside her. For she who stands alone will easily fall."

This thought seemed to placate King Devlindor.

Princess Elisa began to rub his shoulders, as if to will the stress out of him.

"Brother, we need to make sure she's utterly isolated when the time comes for you to meet face-to-face," she implored. "Wouldn't you agree? If Solomon has heeded Ophelia's most recent vision, he'll be delivering her to us soon enough, and we need to be prepared. We don't want any more problems with these pesky guardians than we already have."

"Yes, very well," he replied in a stoic voice, eyes again glued to the glass ceiling. "But we shouldn't take any more chances. Let us consult the other seer. We need her sharp for what comes next if we want to keep the upper hand."

"But... she's just a girl," said the Princess.

She felt the King's muscles tighten; she let go.

"She's young still, but her powers are impressive," he said. "Maybe even more so than Ophelia's at times. And what purpose does she have if not for war tactics?"

The Princess bowed low at his resolution, her navy dress dazzling under the firelight.

"Yes, my King," she said—the word 'war' bounced around in her head.

Has the time truly come for another test of power?

It was almost unthinkable, after all they'd done together to lead the life they led… all the horrors they'd already inflicted on the world for a life of luxury.

She dreaded what lay ahead for them to keep it, should they truly be challenged by this slave.

NOT LONG AFTER THEIR DISCUSSION, King Devlindor and Princess Elisa entered a chamber deep inside the palace. In the center of the room sat a beautiful young woman chained by her ankles—she was the newest seer under the King's control, locked away from the world in the depths of the Saindora Dungeons for only the King's use.

And as with all seers, she had been unseeing since birth.

"Your Majesty," she said in a small voice, getting to her feet, the shackles tinkling against the floor. "To what do I owe this pleasure?"

Her clouded eyes were bloodshot with tears.

"What's wrong with her?" asked the King, waving his hand at her in disgust; he looked back to his sister for an explanation. "We've given her everything."

Princess Elisa walked ahead of him to inquire—the young seer whispered something in her ear.

"She says it's her mother," explained the Princess, gazing back at her brother with apprehension. "She claims Ophelia is dead. My King… her death was by the hand of the slave."

Barely noticeable to the untrained eye, King Devlindor's expression went from cool and collected to shocked, but he composed himself quite quickly.

Still, Princess Elisa had not missed it; she'd had centuries of practice to learn to read him, to protect herself from him.

"Is that so? *Shame.*"

He appeared unperturbed now.

"Ophelia was quite useful. Now South Luose will fall to the other fools on the council. Have Sir Vladamor reinstate a keeper there at once. We must keep things under tight control. These are fragile times."

The Princess bowed. "Certainly," she said. "I will attend to this matter myself."

"My mother's death was because of you!" shouted the young seer.

The Princess nearly jumped out of her skin—it was the first time she'd heard someone raise their voice to her brother in many years.

"It's not some inconvenience to be ignored, you wretched soul."

The Princess shook her head in reflex, warning, but it was a useless effort; the girl could not see.

The King was silent a moment, probably in a bit of shock himself. But then he was angry…

Princess Elisa stood out of his way.

"Your mother was an old hag, far past her expiration date for this world if you ask me," said the King with a bite to his tone. "You're lucky I even let her live as long as she did."

"You're a monster!" she retorted.

"*I'm* the monster?" he said—his laugh was a disturbing sound that echoed off the windowless walls; he'd never learned to do it properly, from a place of joy. "You think you knew her well, do you? That she was coming back for you?"

He snickered, shaking his head.

"And once more we're reminded that a seer's future sight has its flaws." He cocked his head to the side. "I forget myself... what's your name again, child?"

He circled her like the vulture he was.

"My name is Odessa," she said, trying to sound brave.

Alas, she couldn't help the quiver in her voice.

"Well, Odessa," said the King, "the one gift newborns are granted to keep in this world from their parents is their given names, but *your* mother isn't one you'll want to remember any gifts from. This, I assure you."

"What are you speaking of?" she asked, balling her fists at her sides.

Though beautiful she was—as most Golden Age creatures taking human forms proved to be—Princess Elisa considered that Odessa seemed a bit sickly, with a painfully frail frame and ghost-like skin.

Nevertheless, seers were extremely powerful beings by nature; it would seem that King Devlindor hadn't completely squashed the fight in her yet.

"As if you don't already know," he said, eyeing her with something of curiosity, envy even. "However, I'm happy to re-mind you of your history, should it be lost somewhere in your endless mind."

He tapped his temple.

"After giving birth to you right here in this very room, your mother offered you to me for a lifetime of servitude in exchange for her own freedom." He stepped closer to her, gently brushing the hair out of her eyes.

Odessa cringed away from his touch but let him go on—Prin-cess Elisa could tell by her pained expression that the seer did already know the words he spoke, trying fruitlessly to ignore the truth of who she was.

She recognized it because she sometimes wore the same.

"Before you bore those chains, so did she. And much like the rest of the world, you were born quite literally into slavery. Only your freedom can *never* be earned, because your mother sold it to me in a trade for hers. So, until you bear a child of your own as an equal offering and swear your fealty to the Shadow Resistance, you too will be chained to this room forevermore."

He shrugged, mockingly.

"A seer's life is a long one, so I hope you take a fancy to the guards at your door."

Odessa lunged for him, but the King didn't even flinch as he took a step back, her chains keeping her at a distance.

"I'm sorry, did you want to say something else?" he asked, the satisfaction clear in his voice. "By all means... speak up."

With the snap of his fingers, the shackles at her feet unlocked; Odessa was startled by the sudden freedom and backed down immediately, surely knowing better than to challenge her royal captor.

Princess Elisa couldn't even remember the last time she'd acted out in such a way—he almost had the new seer fully in his grip.

"I didn't think so," he said, hands crossed behind his back as he studied her.

He grabbed her by the neck and lifted her up so that her toes barely touched the floor; Odessa scraped at his wrists to try to free herself, but it was no use. He could squeeze the life out of her right there and then if he wished, and no one could stop him.

"Brother! Control yourself," said the Princess without thought. "Why must you be so cruel? We need her alive if we're to survive this. She's the last of her kind now for all we know."

"Quiet your tongue, Elisa!"

He threw Odessa to the pillowed bed behind her, and she didn't dare try to stand again, coughing to regain her breath.

"Are you going to behave now?" he asked, his tone daring her to challenge him again.

The seer nodded, bowing her head as silent tears streamed

down her cheeks.

"Good," he said in a much lighter tone. "As long as you behave, you needn't be chained. This is your home, and I want you to be comfortable." He tickled her chin as if she were a child who had only been chastised. "Now tell me, Odessa, where might I find the slave called Arianna Belvedor?"

Odessa closed her eyes, trying to find her calm. When she opened them, they were shining bright, swirling with magic.

"I see much death," she choked out. "Bodies scattered over black sand. Guardians of Gold and Shadow Resistance alike. It looks like you might need to replace yet another keeper…" She smirked, and the Princess admired her bravery. "In Zambienth."

"Go on," urged the King, clinging to her every word, almost entranced by her cloud-like stare.

"I see waves, a boat. And a blizzard merged with fire."

"But who?" he asked through gritted teeth, trying not to frighten her out of her sight. "The pesky guardians are so hard to pin down, and we've already disbanded most of them, from what my sources say."

"Arianna Belvedor is one of four that make up the prophecy my mother predicted," said Odessa. "So, as I *see* your sister has advised, take out the others." She lifted a single finger. "Then all that will be left is one."

Odessa quieted for a moment, her brow furrowed, as if she were trying to decipher something else in her vision.

"Start with the Kane brothers. They've been separated from their elders, escaped on the water during the ambush in Zambienth but very vulnerable and weak. Kill them, secure the Axe of Crissy, as you've *failed* to do so many times, and the power on your side will most surely be greater. You'd be unstoppable against the rest, including Arianna."

"Ah, that bloody axe," he growled. "Those dwarves were such a nuisance! It should be mine by now." He looked to the ceiling, whispering the words of a spell as the ruby of his staff began to glow bright. "Sir Vladamor, where are you?"

"Yes, my King?" came the necromancer's voice like an echo—then he materialized out from the shadows.

"Find the ones they call the Kane brothers. Find them and kill them," he demanded. "You've failed to retrieve the axe, *again*, and you've failed at killing the Belvedor slave. Do not fail me a third time, or it shall be your last."

"Yes, my liege," he said with a low bow. "I'll not return until I control their souls."

He vanished as quickly as he'd come, a trail of dark shadow in his wake that Princess Elisa tried her utmost best to avoid.

"That will be enough for now," said the King with a satisfied smirk. "We'll return for the next vision once the Kane brothers have been dealt with. Goodbye, for now, Odessa."

Princess Elisa followed her brother obediently toward the door, but she looked back one last time. It was then that she heard Odessa speak within her thoughts.

"*If he goes after the Kane brothers, it will throw him off course. Do not let the King catch Arianna Belvedor. She's the one who will change everything,*" said Odessa. "*It is her destiny, and hers alone.*"

The Princess knew that seers were excellent at mind magic, maybe even the truest masters of the craft out of all the magical beings she'd encountered in her lifetime—even more so than elves. But she had never experienced a seer's magic quite like this before.

Unable to contain her curiosity, a question formed in her mind. "*What happens if he does catch her?*" she asked. "*What happens if she fails?*"

Odessa answered, each word as loud and clear as if they were having a true conversation.

"*Then her army shall never come, and the world will continue to crumble into dust,*" said Odessa, sharply. "*Princess, no matter if the dark or light controls your heart, we cannot let this happen. For if the world ends, it ends for us all… Death does not discriminate against any one soul. That's the beauty of the Golden Rule."*

As Princess Elisa pulled the door shut behind her, Odessa's clouded eyes—filled with so many possible futures—were the last she could see of the young seer before she returned to solitude and darkness. Unable to stop the seer's warning from echoing in her mind, the Princess felt in her soul that an even darker future awaited the world should her all-powerful brother, the High King of Olleb-Yelfra, capture and kill the district slave he had the whole world hunting.

She prayed the King wasn't spying on her thoughts in this moment now, for she couldn't help the treasonous words that slipped into her mind.

Arianna Belvedor, please… just survive.

Dear Guardian

You trekked across a desert, escaped a necromancer, crossed an unforgiving sea, and reunited with the Guardians of Gold... just to end up back in the Four Corners!? What's done is done. But now Solomon has his claws in you.

There's no time to waste—the Four Corners is awake, thanks to your magic, so let everyone know the truth of what's at stake before it's too late!

What part of your journey through the desert surprised you most?

Spread the magic on

amazon goodreads BookBub

I do hope you can reunite with your friends again, guardian. I'd advise you to wish for luck, but alas, you only have one left.

Sincerely,
Ashleigh B.

ACKNOWLEDGMENTS

The first draft of *Belvedor and the Desert of Secrets* was published in 2017, back when I was navigating my late twenties in New York. Prior to moving to the Big Apple, I had lived all around the world—Mexico, South Korea, Europe, a stint in the Middle East, and East Africa; the wanderlust never left my soul, no matter how long I've called New York 'home.'

Desert of Secrets is a journey strongly inspired by those real-life adventures. As we begin to travel further across the Olleb, discovering magic along the way, every starry sky and beautiful beach feels like a memory to me. **So, can I say thank you to our world?** Without real exploration, the Golden Age might have never been born from my imagination.

Lisa, you have my major gratitude for this novel—she's insane for mermaids, so if you're in Syrifina's camp, you have her to thank! She begged for the addition, and what an important one it proved to be. Love you, chica, for that and so much more.

Mom, Dad, and Christina, you're the best fam—I'll always have you to thank for how far I've come. For loving my stories in the first drafts and for supporting my wildest dreams, even when they change from day to day.

To my ruthless (and incredible!) editor, Hannah McCall—thank you for sticking with me through yet another one. You make me dig deeper, and my stories are stronger for it. Three books down and I've learned so much. Without you, every paragraph would start with 'suddenly' and leave nothing as a surprise.

To my spellbinding designers—**Mirella Santana**, you did it again! I wish the Island of Idris was a real place because the cover you designed makes it look like a fantastic getaway. **Jessica Khoury**, if Arianna Belvedor and her friends had such a beautifully detailed map as the one you illustrated, they might never have gotten lost.

Last but not least, to my readers—you've made this writing journey so much fun. The *Belvedor Bookworms* are growing every day, and it's been amazing to connect with you all. Thank you for reading!

Turn the page for

BELVEDOR
BONUS MATERIALS

Behind the Scenes with the Author

Real World Magic

A Belvedor World Breakdown

Invitation to the Belvedor Bookworms

Sneak Peek of Volume IV
Belvedor and the Trail of Fire

BEHIND THE SCENES

Ashleigh Bello answers questions from the Belvedor Bookworms!

What was your favorite part to research for this book?

Definitely learning about deserts! I've spent very little time exploring this type of terrain and would not make a useful guide if I had to cross one on foot, but it was fun to research. Google was my friend for accuracy. I spent a good chunk of time trying to figure out how long someone might be able to survive without water versus food, and how to live through a night-time sandstorm. Word of advice to those preparing for a desert trek: a little magic in your back pocket is never a bad idea.

What kind of reader are you?

When I was young, I was a voracious reader. My interest in books started with children's stories, then quickly grew into a love of all fiction—mainly fantasy, mysteries, and thrillers. I think stories get better the second time around, so I know something is on my 'favorites' list if I read it more than once.

Gone are the days that I have time to devour a book all in one sitting like when I was a child, but I still cherish the moments when I can; I'm convinced this is how great fantasy stories are meant to be read. It's the best way to become fully immersed in the world.

What was your favorite scene to write in this installment?

Wow, that's a difficult one for me to choose. I'm tossing with several, but I think I might have to go with the moment when Eli kisses Arianna in the desert… it was her *first* kiss!

I didn't focus too much on romance throughout this series, because that's not what her quest is about. However, love and romance *are* human experiences, and it was fun to explore that side of Arianna in my writing. I can be a huge sap for romance when it comes down to it.

I mean, who doesn't appreciate a scenic, passionate kiss with a handsome warrior boy once in a while? ♥

What was the creative process like for you when writing about the mermaids? They're not your typical *Ariel*.

I remember calling my best friend, Lisa, and talking to her for a ridiculously long time when the idea for Syrifina Myr's character struck me. She had been impatiently waiting on the addition of mermaids to the series for years; they were always part of my world-building plan, but it wasn't until the making of *Desert of Secrets* that they finally fit in with the narrative—it just felt natural to introduce them along with Idris.

Also, it was so much fun putting my own spin on this traditional fantasy creature. Syrifina was one of my favorite characters to write throughout the series because she's *so* insane, and her backstory was full of drama (scorned woman takes revenge is never dull to pen). I'm glad she ended up being such a significant addition to the storyline. Olleb-Yelfra would be too safe without her.

If you were trapped on the Island of Idris and could wish for one thing, what would it be?

Since there's magic in the world where Idris exists, I'd wish for the ability to turn into a mermaid at will… as long as I don't have to drink blood. I'm so fascinated by the underwater world (I'm actually in the middle of a scuba diving course as I write this). Transforming into a mermaid seems like a quick fix to be able to finally explore the deep blue sea without fear.

But real talk, I'd probably wish for a friend to be lost along with me. I'd go crazy telling stories to myself.

REAL WORLD MAGIC

The adventure of your dreams could be just outside your door.
Take the leap and go explore!

There's so much beautiful nature in *Desert of Secrets* as the world of Olleb-Yelfra unfolds before Arianna's eyes. I was definitely inspired by real places I've traveled to as I imagined her journey in this one.

For example, Arianna and Eli watch a storm rolling toward Zambienth from over the sea—I painted that picture from the beginnings of a memorable storm I experienced in Jamaica (one of the first countries I ever visited abroad), giant purple and gray clouds bowling over the ocean. Also, I think Zambienth itself was born from a combination of Mexico and Kuwait; both countries have places where the sea and sand meet one another, and it's pretty spectacular to witness.

But one of the most direct correlations I recall was writing the description of the Island of Idris from Arianna's viewpoint when they wake at the top of the hill—I was awed by a view just like that once in Guatapé, Colombia.

Photo at the top of
El Peñol—a 700 ft climb!
Guatapé, Colombia (2016).
These views inspired the
Island of Idris.

A BELVEDOR BREAKDOWN

You've nearly made it to the finale now. The Guardians of Gold are scattered across the Olleb at the worst of times and Solomon finally has Arianna in his grasp. Much has transpired since our initial escape from the Jar, so let's take a second to recap.

If you're anything like me and have trouble remembering the names of your co-workers or classmates, let alone the names of fictional characters and made-up magical concepts, then this breakdown is my gift to you.

The final chapters in Arianna's quest for freedom—*Belvedor and the Trail of Fire* and *Belvedor and the Golden Rule*—are bursting with magic, Golden Age visitors, and adventures around Olleb-Yelfra that will have your head spinning. Here's a refresher on some key players and places we've already explored to have you ready for the next Belvedor binge-read, and you can always refer to the world map at the front of this book!

OUR PROTAGONISTS

Arianna Belvedor of Warrior's District
Lessa Thur of Healer's District
Jeom Kane of Creator's District
Demetrius Kane of Agrarian's District

GUARDIAN ELDERS TO NOTE
(SOME GONE AND THOSE STILL WITH US)

Master Jon Tayshin • Caretaker Cyn • Gabriel
Rowina • Sergios • Iris • Margery • Vance
Keeper Helix Kassime aka Ferlon Ragaric (deceased)
Master Talis Churry (deceased) • Tobias (deceased)

ENEMIES AT LARGE

King (Kyrone) Devlindor
Princess (Elisa) Devlindor
Sir Vladamor, necromancer and Head of the King's Guard
Master Solomon Bell, Wolf of the East

PLACES WE'VE TRAVELED ACROSS
THE KINGDOM OF OLLEB-YELFRA

City of the Four Corners (Blancoren Mountains, Jar of Stone)
Vanishing Tunnels · Tombs of Blancoren
City of Undor (what remains)
Village of Draminet · Nicora Forest
City of South Luose · City of North Luose (what remains)
Black Sand Desert · Sea of Saindora
Island of Idris · Empress Isle
City of Zambienth

GUARDIAN SANCTUARIES
South Luose Palace Attic
The Greenhouse (City of Zambienth)

IMPORTANT GOLDEN AGE HISTORY
WE'VE UNCOVERED

Dwarves · King Undoriamus, former ruler of the City of Undor
Elves · Master Lethander, former Lord of the Nicora Elven Tribe
Mermaids · Syrifina Myr (living), Mother of Mermaids and queen
of the Island of Idris and Empress Isle
Seers · Ophelia and Odessa (daughter of Ophelia, living in captivity)
Monarchs · King Damas and Prince Neas (son of King Damas),
former rulers of the thriving Kingdom of Saindora

OTHER GOLDEN AGE INHABITANTS
Giants · Fairies
Sorcerers and Sorceresses

KNOWN AVATARS AND THEIR
TRANSFORMATIONS

Solza, loyal to Arianna
· Snow leopard (earth form) · Dolphin (water form) · Owl (air form)
Sano, loyal to Lessa
· Monkey (air form) · Sea turtle (water form) · Wolf (earth form)
Raja, loyal to King Devlindor
· Jaguar (earth form) · Hawk (air form)

WEAPONS AND TRINKETS OF EPIC PROPORTIONS

Solomon's swords, belonging to Arianna
Axe of Crissy, belonging to Jeom (formerly King Undoriamus')

GUARDIAN RELICS

Dagger Aurora, belonging to Arianna (formerly Solomon's)
Compass, belonging to Demetrius (formerly Tobias')
Ring, belonging to Lessa (formerly Kassime's)

MAGIC AND SPELLS WE'VE CASTED

Onasyuda · a powerful (and rare) revival enchantment
Luzcora · a dangerous, electric surge (used in offense)
Operium undrio · opens any lock not sealed by magic
Helthra saludis emencia · a healing aid spell
Solza ven immito · a fire conjuring spell
Cementas cuerpal · a spell to control a person's ability to move
Levantis bora · a levitation spell
Ni passe · a barrier spell
Sensorial depriva tempe · an enchantment to aid in astral projection
Memorium solio · a spell to enhance a person's memory

DWARF LANGUAGE
(USED IN CONJUNCTION WITH THE AXE OF CRISSY)

Hydfrömeh · to hide
Reveliantom · to reveal
Protelium ahortor · to conjure a shield of protection

That's it, bookworm!

You're good to set off
on your next adventure.
See you on the beaches
of Saindora.

With Gratitude,
Ashleigh B.

Photo: Horseshoe Bay, Bermuda. **July, 2019**

THE BELVEDOR SAGA | VOL 1
BELVEDOR AND THE FOUR CORNERS
ASHLEIGH BELLO

THE BELVEDOR SAGA | VOL 4
BELVEDOR
AND
THE
TRAIL
OF
FIRE
ASHLEIGH
BELLO
Not all that burns is evil.
Not all that burns is good.

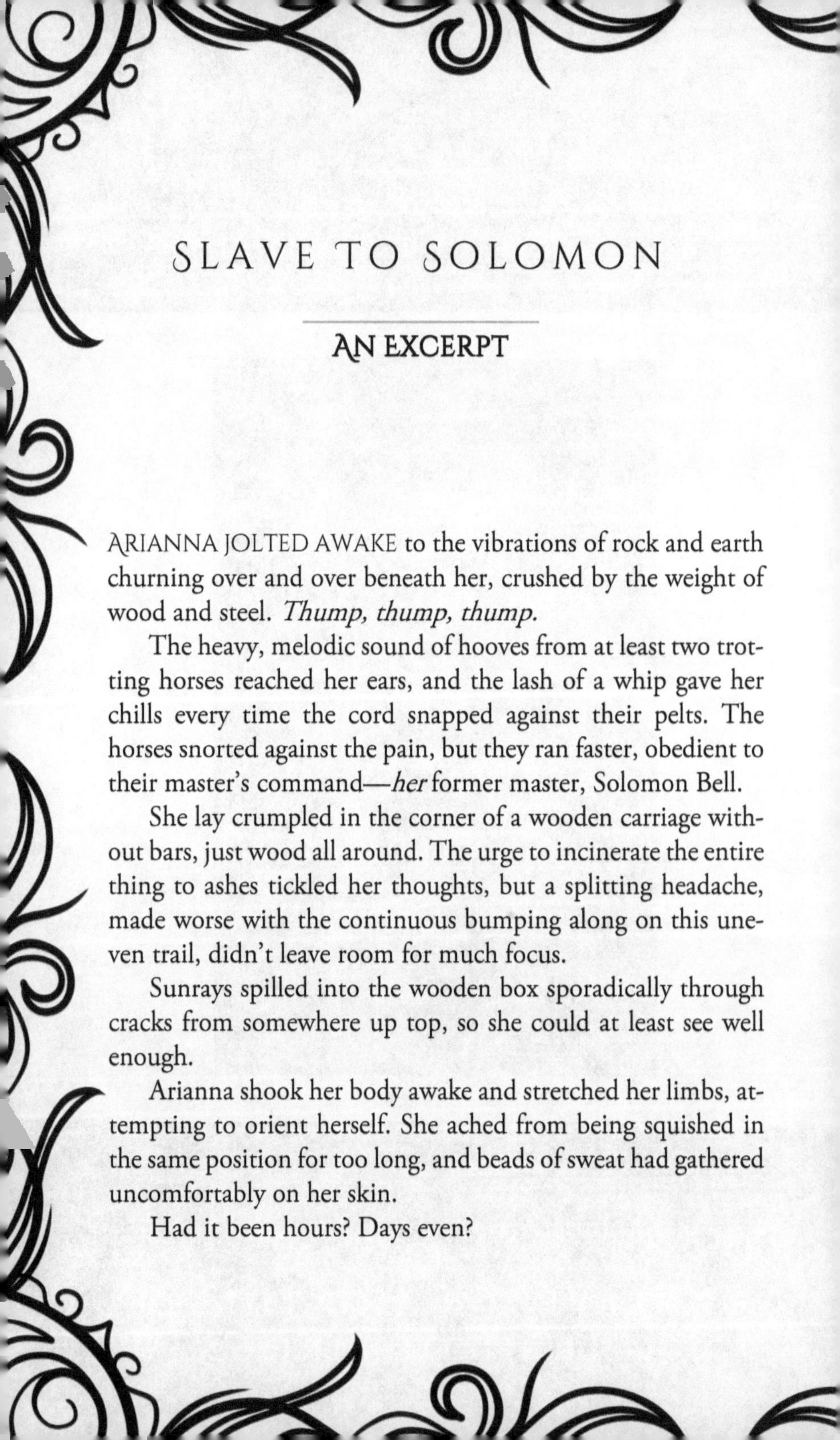

SLAVE TO SOLOMON

AN EXCERPT

ARIANNA JOLTED AWAKE to the vibrations of rock and earth churning over and over beneath her, crushed by the weight of wood and steel. *Thump, thump, thump.*

The heavy, melodic sound of hooves from at least two trotting horses reached her ears, and the lash of a whip gave her chills every time the cord snapped against their pelts. The horses snorted against the pain, but they ran faster, obedient to their master's command—*her* former master, Solomon Bell.

She lay crumpled in the corner of a wooden carriage without bars, just wood all around. The urge to incinerate the entire thing to ashes tickled her thoughts, but a splitting headache, made worse with the continuous bumping along on this uneven trail, didn't leave room for much focus.

Sunrays spilled into the wooden box sporadically through cracks from somewhere up top, so she could at least see well enough.

Arianna shook her body awake and stretched her limbs, attempting to orient herself. She ached from being squished in the same position for too long, and beads of sweat had gathered uncomfortably on her skin.

Had it been hours? Days even?

She had no idea how much time had passed, but even a short while was too long. There was still a lot of work to be done. *Down with the King.*

"Let me out," she murmured, pulling herself up toward the light, pressing her hands against the ceiling to try to peer through the cracks.

Her voice came out scratchy and weak, sounding just the same as her body felt.

She took deep, slow breaths to try to anchor herself to the here and now, dizzied still from the magical beating she'd endured. She pressed a shaking hand against the wall, trying with all her might to make her magic come, to obliterate this cage around her...

It wanted to, but it couldn't yield to her now; that piece of her mind felt locked away, suppressed by an unwelcome force that she was in no state to combat.

When there was no more use trying, her focus drifted over excruciating memories—they came back sharply with each inhale.

Lessa, Eli, Noah. Had the regulators done them in?

Jeom, Demetrius, Gabriel. Did the sea now claim their souls?

Master Tayshin, Cyn... the other guardians who were ambushed in Zambienth. Had the Shadow Resistance finished them off, as they had poor Talis and Tobias?

Arianna's dry eyes began to water slightly, and a choke caught in her throat at the thought of so many potential lost lives, building up on top of the ones that could no longer be saved.

The moments before she had been defeated in the battle of the Four Corners flashed through her mind next.

Solza... Forced to sever ties with her without even a goodbye.

Alive or dead?

Arianna had no idea, but she felt the emptiness without her now.

It was painful, to be cruelly denied the endings of these stories she'd witnessed the start of. Not knowing about any of their fates was maybe even a worse agony than if Arianna was certain of their deaths, for it saved room for hope in a situation that seemed completely void of it.

However, there was one positive thing she did recall from that treacherous night, faint though it was—the golden dragon symbol of the guardians, shining bright through the blizzard. *Conjured by my friends, or by my imagination?*

It was hard for her to believe it had been real. Everything at the end was such a blur, but if there was any hope left at all for her to cling to, it was that dragon.

She sucked a breath in through her teeth at a sudden and unwelcome sensation—it felt as if someone was digging into her mind, spying on her fears.

I know the stink of your mind magic by now, she thought.

"Get out!" screamed Arianna.

She lifted her hands to her head, the wood panels vibrating all around her as some of her power seeped through the blockage.

Alas, it was only a dull shake and had taken every ounce of the energy she had left.

She slid back down to the floor, defeated; Solomon's magic-resistant precautions were infallible.

As she caught her breath, a flap toward the front clicked open. Sun drenched her cage, stinging her eyes.

"Ah!" she cried, shielding her face—she had to blink several times before noticing a barred space on the wall across from her.

"Save your energy," spoke Solomon. "You'll be needing it where we're going."

Just hearing his voice wrap around her made her feel ill. She jumped back to her feet, head brushing the ceiling as she peered through the thick, steel bars so that she might lock eyes with him.

She wanted Solomon to feel her hatred, to see the promises of revenge written there in just one sharp look. With her fingers curled around the bars, she gently pressed her face against them, wishing to push her way through to the other side.

"I hope you rot in whatever darkened afterlife awaits fallen souls like yours," she whispered, wondering if her hand might fit through the small space to snap him dead.

"Tell me, child, what do you consider 'dark' compared to a world like this?" he asked with a sickening formality.

"I don't know," she replied. "But the world would certainly be a better place without monsters like you and the ones you serve."

Solomon spun around to meet her glare.

Arianna couldn't stop her rash confidence fleeing back to fear as she saw the magic flare up in his irises, like two dark cups filling to the brims with silver liquid.

She flinched on instinct, afraid at what might come next; she knew that look, the silvery stare of a master sorcerer with powerful magic just itching to discharge…

She knew because she experienced it the same.

But Solomon was too fast, too strong, too practiced. Arianna had already lost the battle with him, as she had lost every time before; she was in no position to challenge him now.

"It's time for you to go back to sleep," he commanded, the magic on his very breath entangling her like the heavy blanket of her district days.

There was nothing she could do but surrender to his will. In an enveloping wave, her body suddenly felt as heavy as stone.

She slumped back to the floor.

How many times had they done this dance before?

The only thing Arianna knew with any certainty was that this wasn't the first time she'd been drugged with sleeping spells on this wretched journey… she was starting to remember. Each time she woke, she got a little stronger—stayed awake *just* a little longer.

She always tried to fight him, but every inch of her being, both physical and mental, seemed weighted down. Solomon's magic urged her to give in to her dreams and forget this world.

Yet, this time was different than the last; in the moments before her mind succumbed to his magic once more, Arianna had enough wit to grasp an idea that might save her.

"Sleep won't protect you forever," she muttered before her eyes shut tight—though, not before thinking three little words as she felt for her dagger, Aurora, still strapped securely at her thigh.

Solomon had not thought to remove it.

Sensorial depriva tempe.

THE BELVEDOR SAGA

By Ashleigh Bello

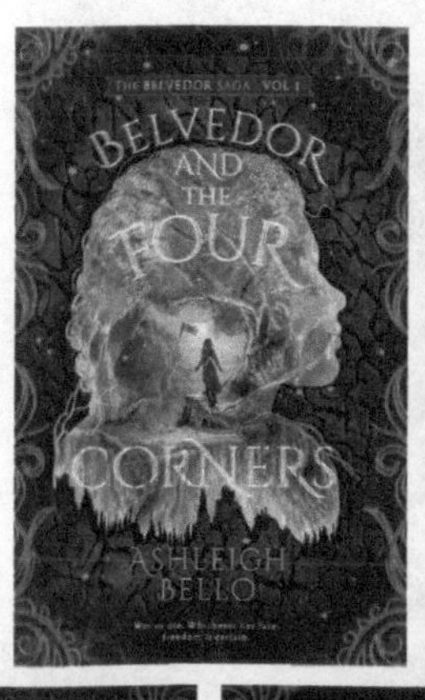

Find the completed series on Amazon.
Follow the Magic!

ASHLEIGH BELLO is the author of *A Myrmaid's Kiss* and the *Belvedor Saga*. She graduated from the University of Missouri-Columbia and currently lives in Brooklyn, New York. She also teaches and practices vinyasa yoga in her community and is the co-founder of Yoga Block Party, a female-owned yoga events and retreats business. She enjoys spending time with friends and family every chance she gets and is always daydreaming about her next novel. Her endless passion for travel and spontaneous adventure continues to be her inspiration for future works in the enchanting world of Olleb-Yelfra and beyond.

Connect with the Author
www.ashleighbello.com
@ashleighbello
#belvedorbooks

Follow her on TikTok!
Scan the QR code to follow her main bookish social account